PARANORMAL TALENT AGENCY

EPISODES 1-3

HEATHER SILVIO

Panther Books

Published in the United States by Panther Books, Las Vegas.

Correspondence to the author may be sent to:
heather@heathersilvio.com

Cover design by Sonia Freitas at Chloe Belle Arts
https://www.ChloeBelleArts.com

ISBN (Print) 978-1-951192-02-0
ISBN (E-book) 978-1-951192-03-7

BOOKS BY HEATHER SILVIO

PARANORMAL TALENT AGENCY

Lights, Camera, Action (Episode One)

Reset to One (Episode Two)

That's a Wrap (Episode Three)

An Unexpected Sequel (Episode Four)

Jumping the Shark (Episode Five)

The Season Finale (Episode Six)

NON-SERIES FICTION

Not Quite Famous: A Romantic Comedy of an Actress
on the Edge

Beyond the Abyss: Tales of the Supernatural

Courting Death

NONFICTION

Special Snowflake Syndrome: The Unrecognized
Personality Disorder Destroying the World

Happiness by the Numbers: 9 Steps to Authentic
Happiness

Stress Disorders: A Healing Path for PTSD

ACKNOWLEDGMENTS

Thank you to everyone who supported this series from its
original inception to completion.

Episode One

Lights, Camera, Action

CHAPTER ONE

"Las Vegas?" I asked the question slowly. This could be an amazing career move, but I loved New York City. I rubbed my hands over the soft leather of the office couch on which I perched at the edge. I was delaying my response. Las Vegas? It was hard to imagine that people actually lived there.

"Catherine. Don't overthink it. What does your gut say? Do you want to establish the West Coast arm of the Peterson Talent Agency in Las Vegas?" Sidney Peterson asked again, green eyes watching me analyze the opportunity in my head. He knew, despite his directive to the contrary, I was absolutely a think-before-I-speak kind of woman.

I stood and walked to the floor-to-ceiling windows of Sidney's office. The spectacular view of the city never failed to mesmerize. My mind whirled with possibilities and my stomach tightened with anxiety. Or maybe exhilaration? If Sidney was right, and he believed he was, this would be an incredible opportunity to get in on the ground floor.

With the proposed increase in tax incentives provided by the state of Nevada, many in the entertainment world believed that significantly more production companies would start filming in the state, and that the existing talent agencies might not quite be ready to handle the influx of larger projects. If PTA opened a branch now, well, we'd be able to sign the most promising acting prospects. And I could live in Sin City, where it was a heck of a lot warmer than in the Big Apple.

"Why me?" I finally asked. "You have more senior agents." Although admittedly, I was repping our biggest client: Gracie Corsini, recently married and newest star of one of the remaining soap operas shooting in NYC, "Heart's Home".

"I do," he agreed, running a hand through his buzz cut brown hair. "However, you're extremely creative. You've demonstrated considerable management skills of the organizational challenges of this business and the sometimes difficult personalities. And you've done so while always remaining calm. I imagine we'll need a lot of all of that in Vegas."

I thought for a few more moments while watching Sidney's body language. He projected the air of calm expectation that I'd say yes. His steepled fingers on his desk and the tightness in his jaw betrayed his doubt. He believed I could do it. I guess he wasn't sure if I believed I could do it. He should have more faith in his instincts.

"I'll do it," I declared and Sidney smiled.

"My realtor, John, has a hold on some office space; I'll want you to check it out and okay it."

"Sure, no problem. Anything else I need to know?"

"I'd like to have you up and running by the end of the month. Can you do that?"

Gulp and a breath. "Absolutely."

"And, John sent me an article; the biggest entertainment story right now is the death of a young twenty-something actress of a heart attack."

"Oh my gosh, that's terrible! Though we clearly need to give them a bigger story to care about."

Sidney laughed. "Yes, we do."

"And we will by the end of the month," I said with a smile.

"You know what caught my eye about the story?"

"Nuh-uh."

"How much she looked like you, with her blond hair and blue eyes."

"Okay, that's creepy, Sidney. Besides, I am not a young twenty-something."

"You could pass for it, though."

"Moving on."

Sidney laughed again. "I trust you, Catherine, and I know you'll make us proud."

Only thirty years old and I was about to head up the West Coast branch of one of the top New York City talent agencies.

Nice.

CHAPTER TWO

A two-room office was all I felt necessary at this point – waiting area and my personal office. Thus, Sidney's realtor John pleasantly surprised me with the tentatively chosen space. Our new office would be in a smaller four-storefront strip mall next door to a larger two-story artists' center. We'd be right in the middle of the action, but by having our own space, we could still have the quiet that came from separation. Once I had signed the rental documentation, I made quick work of interior decoration. A successful trip to RC Willey and they had agreed to deliver my furniture and artwork within three days.

I stood in the waiting room, eyeing the two tan love seats with bright yellow throw pillows. Local artwork on the beige walls gave the space personality. A small desk for my assistant (note to self: hire assistant) sat near the door to my office.

My actual office was the perfect size for me and minimal furniture. Filing cabinet disguised as a tall hutch tucked in one corner. Burnished wood desk stood in front of a decent sized window. Comfortable black faux-leather chairs for me and one guest.

A soft bell drew my attention. I thought I had locked the front door.

"Hello?"

I turned at the unexpected greeting and exited my office. We weren't exactly open yet. I still needed to post some social media ads requesting actor submissions.

"Are you Catherine Rodham?" A woman so average she was instantly forgettable took several hesitant steps into the waiting area.

"Yes," I responded, plastering a smile on my face. "How may I help you?"

"I've forgotten my manners," she answered my question with an apology and extended her hand. "My name is Robin Landon." Her handshake was like gripping a dead fish, cool and slippery. "Of Landon Talent."

Ah, the competition. I peered closer at her mousy brown hair and half-smile as I released her hand. "What can I do for you, Ms. Landon?"

"Please, call me Robin," she insisted. "I wanted to welcome you to Las Vegas."

Hmm, that's not true. "Thank you," I said anyway. I opened my mouth to say more then changed my mind.

"You're wondering how I knew you were here already if you weren't open or advertising yet?" Her eyes twinkled at the question, but there was steel underneath.

"I am curious," I admitted.

"My staff keeps an eye on the business licenses granted to comparable businesses." I nodded and she continued. "How'd you manage to get yours so fast?"

I shrugged. "I didn't submit it, so I couldn't tell you." I smiled broadly. "I'm looking forward to meeting folks in our industry and beyond, now that we're here and about to be up and running."

"Wonderful," she said, with a smile that did not quite reach her eyes. "I'm also here on another matter."

"Oh?"

"Councilwoman Barbara Knollman would like to personally invite you to join the Las Vegas Chamber of Commerce."

My eyebrows rose in surprise. "I'm not familiar with the councilwoman, since I'm new in town. I appreciate the invitation. Please tell her I said thank you."

"You'll join then? We have a meeting in two weeks."

I frowned. "I'll consider it." I'd had every intention of joining, but this was feeling like a command requirement, not a simple invitation. I wasn't going to be pushed around just because I was a newbie.

"Please do. The councilwoman would consider it an insult to ignore her invitation."

I nearly laughed; that had to be a joke. The talent agent sounded like a bad gangster movie. She believed what she said though. I kept my composure and nodded. "I'll take that under advisement."

"See that you do." Robin nodded, face tight. "Thank you for your time." She turned to leave before I could respond.

"Thank you," I told my closing front door. "That was weird."

For most of my adult life, I've had the ability to know if people told the truth or not. Call me a human lie detector. I've always chalked it up to extreme empathy, though an internet search suggested I might actually be an empath. Today it told me there was more to Robin and the councilwoman than was presented.

I made mental notes to remember both Robin Landon of Landon Talent and Councilwoman Barbara Knollman.

CHAPTER THREE

I loved my new condo. Prices in Las Vegas were so much more affordable than in New York City. I knew that of course – I didn't live under a rock – but it's different when you're actually comparing what you can get for your money. After considering the various neighborhoods, I decided I wanted to be in an up-and-coming neighborhood, so I chose Newport Lofts, a condo building near the Arts District, walking distance to art galleries and restaurants. And when the weather cooperated (which was most of the time), I could even walk to work.

My obsession with a local entertainment morning show started my first full day in the city only two weeks ago. I settled back on my maroon couch and clicked on the television. My teenage tabby cat jumped into my lap, purring and kneading my belly. "Hey, Momma," I said and scratched her behind the ears. "You ready to be entertained and informed?" She meowed in response and settled down in my lap.

"Good morning in the Valley! Welcome to *Entertainment Daily*. I'm one of your hosts, Elizabeth Addison." The perky brunette showed chicklet teeth when she smiled and I guessed her age as late twenties or early thirties. Her smile fell and her tone hushed. "According to police, a second actress has been found dead in her home of apparent unknown causes."

I set my cup on the coffee table and leaned forward. This was not good. An image of a cute blond appeared over the newscaster's shoulder. She gestured to the picture. Hadn't Sidney said the first dead actress was a blond too?

"Kelly Stevens was a 25-year-old local actress. Her talent agent reports she was currently filming a television pilot and had no known medical issues that would have contributed to her death. Police say they found no evidence of self-harm or foul play at the scene, nor did they find drug paraphernalia. Toxicology reports have been ordered, however they won't be in for a few weeks. Unofficially the cause of death is being considered medical, possibly a heart attack. Viewers of this show know that this is the second apparently healthy actress in two months to die of a "heart attack" without any history of medical issues. Police decline to confirm the two deaths are related." Despite my newness to Ms. Addison's reporting, even I could tell she did not believe that. A smirk and a twinkle in her eye appeared as she leaned toward the camera. "But, guys, stop with the crazy conspiracy theories on social media." She shook her head. "Magic, witchcraft, voodoo. Y'all are reaching." She winked and then turned to another camera, signaling the end of the story.

The show continued but I muted Ms. Addison's co-host. Two deaths in two months of local actresses. And right when I was launching the new office. Not the best timing. However, thus far, the odd deaths hadn't seemed to impact the interest generated by my social media posts for new clients.

February was an unpleasant weather month everywhere, even Vegas. I learned this shortly after my arrival and was not happy. I sighed as I pulled out of the underground parking lot of the condo building in my bright blue VW bug. At least my NYC winter wardrobe wasn't going to waste. My commute to the office I rented was mere minutes. I parked the VW in a spot in the tenants' lot behind the strip mall and, ducking my head, moved quickly from my car around to the front of the building. You wouldn't think 40s would feel so cold when you're used to 20s and blizzards. It did.

I leaned against my door, took a deep breath, and crossed the waiting area to my office. I stashed my coat on a hanger in the closet tucked into one corner of the room, smoothed my hands down the navy shift I'd chosen for my first day auditioning clients, and sat behind the desk. Not five minutes later, my assistant, Cherie, arrived and we organized for the day. Hours later, I stood to stretch out my sore neck and did some trunk twists to get the blood flowing.

"There are a lot of actors in Las Vegas."

Cherie laughed with the uncertainty of the young and newly hired, unsure of the appropriate response to my comment. I smiled inwardly.

"It's great to have this much talent to choose from," I clarified and she nodded. "How many more do we have today?"

Cherie checked her notes, curly brown hair bouncing as she slightly bobbed her head. "Two more men. Alexander Moore and Michael Onyx."

I did another little stretch and tried not to yawn. While I was thrilled my social media notices pulled in so many actors interested in representation, after a while all the faces started to run together. "Show me what Mr. Moore emailed us." Cherie pressed a few places on the screen before passing me the iPad. Oh wow. Alexander Moore was certainly photogenic, with his black hair just long enough to be sexy, electric green eyes, silky smooth skin, and jealousy-inducing high cheekbones and long eyelashes. I must have made a noise.

"I know, right? He's yummy."

I laughed and Cherie blushed.

"No, you're absolutely right. Let's hope he has some talent to go along with that," I added then changed screens to look at his submitted resume. Lots of local credits, mostly independent and student films. Could go either way, talent-wise. A soft bell informed us that the door to Peterson Talent Agency had been opened. "Please go admit Mr. Moore."

"With pleasure." Cherie left my office and I heard her speaking to someone. The other voice sounded definitely male, and definitely sexy. Cherie reappeared in my office, eyes wide, and she gave a slight tilt to her head before stepping back out of the room to remain in the waiting area during the audition. I had an idea what she meant by the head tilt but still felt unprepared when Alexander Moore entered my office. I stood and walked around my desk to greet him.

"Mr. Moore, I'm Catherine Rodham, talent agent for Peterson Talent Agency."

"Please call me Alex, Ms. Rodham. It's a pleasure to meet you." He gripped my offered hand.

An immediate tingle rushed through my body at his touch and I found myself looking up into his amazing eyes – and that didn't happen much, given that I'm 5'10". I vaguely recalled seeing on his resume that he was 6'3". I blushed like a schoolgirl and pulled my hand free.

What the hell? Why was I having this reaction? I've met plenty of handsome men before. Sheesh. I broke eye contact and returned to my desk, but not before I swore I saw Mr. Moore smirk. Hmm, I guess he's used to this reaction.

I sat at my desk and gestured for him to take a seat opposite, which he did. "Thank you for your interest in our agency," I began, reciting my introductory speech by rote memorization while I continued to check him out, from the black t-shirt form-fitting to his muscular chest, obvious even under the outer blazer, to his jeans which were also, ahem, form-fitting.

I managed not to fan myself.

CHAPTER FOUR

"What do you have for me today?" I asked, blushing again when Alex gave me a knowing look. "What monologue or scene do you have prepared?" I amended my question and he smiled.

Alex retrieved two sheets of paper from his backpack and handed them to me. "This is a scene from that new legal drama on Netflix," he explained. I quickly scanned the pages. Fairly innocuous, some opportunity for him to show fiery lawyer passion.

"Looks good, you can start whenever you're ready."

It became obvious working the scene that Alex's acting skills matched his looks. I found it hard to maintain eye contact; every glance seemed to spark. Ugh, I sounded like a romance novel. Still, there it was.

"Ms. Rodham," he began.

"Please, call me Catherine."

"Catherine," he restarted and my hands began to sweat. I fiddled with a piece of paper on my desk. "I've resisted signing with an agent thus far because in Vegas it hasn't really seemed necessary."

Oh good, business to focus on. "I completely understand. Since you're here, I presume that means you're more open to signing now?"

"Yes, absolutely. Tell me why I should sign with you; what do you have to offer?"

My body! Wait, what? Thank goodness I didn't say that out loud. Instead, I coughed lightly and answered, "At Peterson Talent Agency, we consider ourselves more of a boutique agency, representing only a limited number of actors in a given market."

Was I imagining the sexual desire I saw in his eyes? And was it that obvious in my own? I glanced down to break the tension before continuing. "By limiting our actors, we're able to focus on the careers of the very best in that given market." I glanced back up. "Based on your experience and what you've demonstrated this afternoon, I believe you could be one of those actors. We take a hands-on, personal involvement with all of our actors."

"Hands on? That would be nice."

My body temperature shot up with his comment, but I kept my voice calm. "I know the Vegas market tends toward non-exclusive representation. Given our boutique approach, we require exclusivity."

"I'm all for exclusivity," he said, speaking the truth, albeit a layered truth. I didn't pursue that curiosity. I'm fairly certain my eyes darkened with desire.

"Great!" I responded enthusiastically. I brought it down a couple of notches and slid a form across the table. Alex reached for the paper and his hand rested lightly on mine. Another tingle raced through my body. He squeezed my hand slightly before taking the form to read through. I stared at him, again wondering at my bizarre overreaction.

"I look forward to working closely with you," he said with another knowing look, handing the form back. I consciously avoided touching him again.

"We look forward to working with you, too." I stood and Alex followed. I remained acutely aware of his eyes on me. I opened the office door, then reached my hand out automatically to shake goodbye.

"Thank you for an interesting meeting," Alex said as he took my hand. I was so taken with my physical response to his touch that I did not initially register his unusual choice of parting words.

"You're most welcome," I responded automatically. We stood for a few seconds that way, our hands entwined, eyes locked, until a slight cough from the waiting room broke the spell.

"Catherine?" Cherie asked, clearly not wanting to interrupt whatever was going on.

I released Alex's hand, reluctantly, I'll admit. "Yes?"

"Our final audition of the day just called to cancel. Said something came up."

"Thanks, Cherie. Please show Alex out."

With a final heat-filled glance, Alex turned and followed Cherie to the door. I'll confess that I watched his amazing derriere the entire time.

What was that about? I've never ever had a reaction like that to any man, let alone an actor we've signed. Maybe I've been single too long. I wondered too about the undercurrents of Alex's statements that my ability caught. Typical actor misdirection…or something more?

I called up the information for the cancelled audition. Good looking blond twenty-something actor, toothpaste commercial smile. Resume contained decent credits. I shook my head in regret and typed the letters DNH at the top of his information sheet. Do Not Hire. Canceling within minutes of your audition time, without a real explanation? Never going to be represented by PTA.

If I was honest, Michael Onyx canceling his audition didn't bother me. It gave me more time to prep for the Chamber of Commerce meeting. I had decided not to let Robin Landon's odd demeanor, or the councilwoman's oddly worded request, determine my choice. It made good business sense to go. I checked my watch. The meeting started in an hour; plenty of time to head home to feed Momma and catch her up on my day.

CHAPTER FIVE

The chamber held their meeting in a business center near my condo, which was handy. It was too cold for me to walk. At least it was a short drive. I approached the double doors to the cavernous room. Soaring ceilings, white-linen-draped high-top tables, and tinkling music greeted me. Over one hundred people milled around, like at happy hour. Somehow, I'd expected something more businesslike, dry and boring, frankly.

"Do you need to check in?"

I turned to the young woman in a fitted pinstripe suit seated at a folding table off to the side. "Yes, I guess I do." I gave her my name, she checked in the appropriate spots, and then I was sticking a name tag below my right shoulder. I offered a thank you before entering the room.

Muted conversation abounded. Since everyone I saw carried a cocktail, I scanned the room for a bar. Ah, there it was, on the far wall. I made my way along the perimeter of the room, pleased to see a wide variety of people socializing. I loved the diversity in NYC and would have been disappointed to lose that here. Once I reached the bar, I kept it simple with a glass of white wine and then headed into the crowd.

Thirty minutes of exchanging introductions and elevator pitches of our businesses later, and I drifted toward an unoccupied high-top table to rest. I was pleased that my anxiety had thus far not surfaced.

"Catherine."

A woman approached me, a partial smile on her face. It took me a moment to place her. "Hi, Robin. How are you?"

"Wonderful. So glad you could make it. The councilwoman will be pleased."

She was telling the truth. "That's great." I uttered the words, unsure what else to say.

"I'll let her know you're here."

"Okay," I responded to her back. She had already turned and quickly melted into the crowd. Simply bizarre.

A few more people paused at my table to introduce themselves and then I saw Robin about twenty feet away. Beside her walked a tall brunette, age anywhere from 40-60, in a burgundy dress with matching nails. Even from here they looked like talons. A chill passed through me at the sight of her. I gave a tiny shake of my head. I let

Robin's obsequiousness invade my brain, clearly. I hadn't even met the (probable) councilwoman and already my subconscious was telling me to be careful.

"Ms. Rodham? I'm Councilwoman Barbara Knollman." Her smile revealed a row of small sharp teeth. There was an aggressiveness in her stance. Showing me who's boss?

I accepted her offered handshake and tried to clear my mind of these unhelpful thoughts. I kept my smile while she ground my bones together in her vise-like grip. When the shake lasted longer than was customary, I pulled my hand free. Was that a look of triumph?

"Good evening, Councilwoman," I replied evenly.

"I'm so glad you were able to make it tonight."

She was telling the truth, but it was incomplete. I took it at face value. "It's important to me to be tied to the community, especially the business community."

"Of course, that's what we're here for," she agreed.

Now that was a lie. Why? An awkward moment passed. I felt increasingly uncomfortable the longer I was in her presence and I did not wish to prolong it.

The councilwoman's smile broadened – at my discomfort? – and she leaned in. "What made you decide to come to Vegas?"

I gave her my standard response to the question while I considered her appearance at this closer angle. Her eyes were dark, nearly black. She had pore-less skin, which contributed to my attributing a wide possible age range. Up close, I guessed her in her fifties; maybe had some good work done?

"Hopefully you and Peterson's will stay in the Valley for a long time," the councilwoman concluded our conversation.

"A long time," the talent agent beside her echoed.

They both lied, yet there was a sliver of confusing truth. "I hope so," I responded blandly while my mind raced. The three of us smiled for a half second and then the women left, walking in lock-step toward another table. Stepford assistant, I thought with a laugh about the talent agent. The whole interaction was weird, and I knew something else was going on, but I could identify no objective reason why. Only my instinct about their truthfulness. Or not. I took a deep breath, made another round of the room and then called it a night. I was shocked when a glance at my watch informed me that it was already after nine.

Tension slipped away with every block closer I got to the condo. A meow greeted me when I opened the door. I scooped up my kitty and we bumped heads.

"Hey, Momma." I scratched her behind the ear and set her down. "What an odd night." She circled my legs, rubbing against the bare skin above my shoes.

"I'm getting your food. Don't worry." I spooned some Fancy Feast into her dish and set it on the floor.

She licked my hand to say thank you and chowed down. I laughed.

"Let me tell you about the meeting." I had already told her about the auditions from earlier, so I regaled her with stories about the men and women I met tonight, especially Robin and Barbara.

Momma finished her food and followed me as I moved through the condo to the bedroom. She jumped on the bed and watched me while I wrapped up the stories.

I hung the blue shift back in the closet and walked to the bathroom to brush my teeth and wash my face. I mumbled my words trying to talk around the toothbrush in my mouth. Momma meowed at me.

"Okay, okay," I uttered after spitting out the toothpaste. "Sorry, I know you can't understand me like that."

In bed, I pulled the earth tone comforter up to my chin, crooked my arm for Momma to curl up against me. "Interesting day," I told her and drifted to sleep.

*****

I walked from the doorway to my office desk, an uncomfortable feeling growing within me. Fear. Why? Nobody else was present. Lights shone brightly. I heard faint noises from my neighbors. And yet... Fear. I placed a hand on my desk, steadying myself.

Was it really fear?

Maybe not. More like uneasiness or uncertainty. I sensed I was no longer alone. I spun around, my eyes met his green ones and I took a sharp breath.

"Alex! What are you doing here?"

"Hello, Catherine," he ignored my question. He approached, his long legs making short work of the room. He stopped within arms' reach and made no move to touch me. He simply looked at me.

Unsure what he wanted, and feeling a very different emotion building, I echoed his greeting. "Hello, Alex."

He smiled his sexy smile and, incredibly, leaned in…to smell me. He took a deep breath and then exhaled out, his breath warming the side of my face. I involuntarily closed my eyes to enjoy the warmth and that broke the spell. The uncertainty returned and my eyes snapped back open. I stepped away from him.

Alex looked surprised. He turned up the wattage on his smile and moved toward me again. Our eyes locked, he reached his hand up, fingers lightly grazing my cheek. I tilted my head, wondering. Using both hands, he cradled my face, his eyes searching mine for…something. He moved closer still, yet our bodies did not touch. His hands slid down my neck, continued lower to take my hands in his.

"Until next time, Catherine," he whispered.

"Next time," I agreed.

*****

Abruptly sitting up in bed, I knew I was alone, and not in my office, and had just had one heck of a sensual dream.

"What the—" I began, before stopping. I could still feel the excitement in my body, my desire to have Alex touch me carrying over from the dream.

Momma, who had moved to the foot of the bed, now padded toward me. "Meow?"

I scratched her behind the ears and we bumped foreheads. "I don't know, Momma." As the feelings subsided, and Momma curled back up and began to lightly snore, I chalked it up again to my extended singledom.

I really needed to go on a date.

CHAPTER SIX

Sidney was absolutely right. I had reviewed another dozen production company requests for assistance with casting their projects here in Vegas. Three weeks since we established the West Coast arm of the Peterson Talent Agency and we had more to keep us busy than we ever imagined. Thankfully.

I scrolled through the requests – a major sequel to an insanely popular franchise movie; two episodes of a cable network show; a Chinese movie and an episodic (that was interesting); and several pilots for new shows. Cool. Mostly independents or foreign projects.

Wait, this sounded intriguing – major motion picture looking for a male actor for a month-long shoot. Supporting role. Character description – tall, attractive, and fit. Open to ethnicity and race. Oh, do I have the perfect guy for you.

Picking up my phone (I know, I know, who has a landline in this day and age…), I dialed Alex's number, which I had to look up. No, I did not know it by heart. Yet.

Good grief.

"Catherine, is that you?"

I heard Alex's voice and realized that he had answered while I was talking to myself like a dang schoolgirl. Focusing on his voice, I was all business.

"Yes, Alex, it's Catherine. I was calling to see if you would be available for an audition tomorrow. It's for a supporting role on a major motion picture."

"I'm available. Can you text me the address and any specific character information I'd need for the audition? Are there any sides?"

For those new to the entertainment biz, 'sides' were sections of dialogue sometimes provided by casting directors for actors to memorize in advance of auditions. It helped the casting folks get a better sense of acting ability; instead of assessing someone's ability to cold read (or audition with dialogue they've never seen before). But, I digressed.

"No sides, though they've said to expect that they'll likely do callbacks. Unless someone is perfect for the role, of course. I'll text you the information as soon as we hang up."

"That sounds great. Catherine?"

I had thought I'd escape the call with solely the professional talk. It appeared that was not meant to be. "Yes?" I responded, with only the slightest bit of trepidation.

"How have you been?"

"Uh, good," I stammered.

"That's good," he responded, and I reflexively laughed at the awkwardness.

He laughed in response. "God, that's awkward," he commented, as though reading my mind. Or it was truly that awkward. "I'll let you know how the audition goes. Although I guess they'd tell you," he trailed off.

I laughed again. "Yes, they will, if they like you. If you wanted to call to tell me how you thought it went, that would be okay, too." Did I just tell an actor to call to tell me how an audition went? What was I smoking?

"Okay." His voice sounded huskier, or maybe that was wishful thinking.

"Okay, talk to you soon."

I hung up before I could say or do anything else borderline unprofessional. Seriously. I'd been doing this a long time and met a lot of hot guys. I stared at the black retro-style phone for a moment, picking it up and setting it down several times. I moved it back to the corner of my desk, my mind wandering.

What was up with my response to Alex?

*****

"Um, Catherine?"

I glanced at Cherie, hovering in the doorway to my office. "Yes?" My focus remained on arranging auditions for more roles. It had been a crazy busy day.

"Um, Catherine…Mr. Moore is here. In the waiting room. Right now."

The intensity more than the words caught my ear. I gave her my full undivided attention.

"Who is here, Cherie?"

"Mr. Moore."

She tried to give the side eye to indicate his presence behind her.

Saving her from her facial gymnastics, I responded. "Send him back, thank you." I was impressed with myself that my voice did not change inflection. Though my heart was certainly racing.

I made a mental note of where I was in my pile. Alex replaced Cherie in the doorway. He leaned against the frame, a slight smile on his lips. A green t-shirt stretched tight across his broad shoulders. Low slung jeans fit exactly the way they should. No man needed to look this good. I sighed and sat up straighter.

"Alex. What can I do for you?" I gave him my most professional smile and he entered the room, closing the door behind him. He somehow managed to do that without breaking eye contact and my insides noticed.

"I was in the neighborhood, and thought I'd stop by to tell you how the audition went." He walked over to my desk, taking a seat in the chair opposite.

"Oh. I figured you would call," I responded lamely.

"Now what fun would that be?" He smiled mischievously.

"No fun at all," I found myself flirting back.

"I'm glad you agree."

"How did it go?" I asked him, to get us back on a professional track.

"It was great. They told me unless someone came in after me that blew them away, I'd be cast. And, since I was toward the end of the audition time, I doubt anybody did." He smiled with that sexy yet aggravating self-confidence. "Have they called you yet?" he asked with an innocent look.

"You already know they called me, don't you?"

My blatantly calling him out surprised him, but he recovered so quickly, I wasn't sure I didn't imagine it. "I do."

"How do you know they already called?"

"I have my ways." A deflecting answer, though true. He shrugged, signaling this part of the conversation was over. Fine, let him have his little display of power.

I smiled sweetly. "Then, I guess our conversation is concluded. They'll call me with details for the first day of filming. Thanks for stopping by." Heart still racing, I pointedly looked down at the paperwork I had been shuffling when he arrived. Two can play this juvenile game.

To my surprise, Alex chuckled softly. "I guess so. Until next time, Catherine." I heard his chair move when he stood. I snuck a peek to watch him walk to the door, admiring the shape of his rear again. At the doorway, he stopped and turned, catching my lustful staring.

His smile broadened. He said nothing about my faux pas. "It was lovely as always to see you, Catherine."

My face flushed with embarrassment. "You, too, Alex. Have a wonderful evening. We'll be in touch soon with the production details."

"I hope so."

CHAPTER SEVEN

And so, it was less than a week later that I found myself on set, watching the crew set up for the first scene of the Las Vegas shoot. Why do people like to shoot in Vegas? The Strip, of course, and this production was no different. We were outside the Bellagio to film sequences with the famous synchronized fountains as the backdrop.

Lights were currently going up all around a coned off section of the sidewalk. A couple of security guards stood at each end, directing curious tourists to go around. A middle-aged man with a slight paunch and a clipboard hurried past me.

"Excuse me?"

"Yes?" His eyes remained on the clipboard, though he had quit moving forward.

"I'm looking for Mia Fynn. The producer."

Now he looked up and squinted.

"She's expecting me," I amended. "Catherine Rodham, talent agent with Peterson Talent."

He seemed to vacillate for a moment and then with an almost imperceptible shrug, gestured toward the fountain railing. "She's over there. Long green hair. You can't miss her." He hurried away and I scanned the group closest to the railing. Sure enough, he was right. You couldn't miss Mia. Long green hair pulled into a high ponytail accented her amazing cheekbones. Based on those around her, she was average height or shorter, and very thin, wearing a long-sleeve t-shirt and jeans. I strode over to join the knot of production staff.

"Excuse me, Mia Fynn?"

The brightest green eyes I'd ever seen met mine with a questioning look.

"I'm Catherine Rodham. You'd said I could pop by."

"Give me one minute."

"Of course."

I stood and watched her address a few more prep issues and then she turned to face me full on.

"Welcome to the set."

"Thanks for letting me crash. Since my office is the baby in town, I want to meet more people in person. Put faces to names."

"Always a good idea in this business," she agreed. "I like to be on set for at least the first day of shooting, to see where the money has been going." She grinned. "Let me introduce you around." We spent the next ten minutes talking to various small groups of people. Mia, true to her word, must have introduced me to every person on the set. We approached a group of actors and my breath caught. This did not go unnoticed by Mia. She glanced at me and then back at the group, nodding knowingly.

"You're Alexander Moore's agent, correct?"

I was glad it was nighttime. Maybe she wouldn't see my neck flush.

Mia laughed, the sound like delicate wind chimes, and put a hand on my shoulder. "He's a looker, that one."

"Mmm-hm."

We had reached the group. In addition to Alex, there were two women and one other man. They were all good-looking actors, around my age I speculated, and dressed to the nines. Apart from Alex, one of the young women was adorable – straight out of the 1920s with a blond bob, fair skin, dark red lipstick, and even wearing a flapper dress. I shook everyone's hands, noticing that while Alex's was warm, the flapper woman's was cool.

Alex's eyes found mine and everything retreated. We were the only two in the universe. I distantly heard Mia tell me to visit for however long I wanted, and the actors to be ready in five. Then she and the group scattered.

"It's good to see you," Alex's voice washed over me.

"You too. You look wonderful."

He truly did, in a dark brown pin-stripe suit and white shirt, open at the collar.

"What are you doing on set? I didn't think agents usually came out."

"They normally don't. I'm trying to meet as many people as possible."

"Makes sense."

A conversational lull left us standing alone in the crowd, me shifting my weight back and forth.

"Do I make you nervous?"

I stopped moving and gaped at him. "Why would you ask that?"

"I don't know. You seem nervous around me."

I waved off the comment. "I'm probably just cold and still trying to adjust to my surroundings."

He lifted an eyebrow but didn't comment on the absurdity of my explanation. I silently thanked him.

A production assistant saved me by yelling instructions.

"Break a leg filming," I offered for a goodbye.

Alex gave me a mock salute and turned away. I watched the final preparation for the first scene of the night, again pondering my insane reaction to this man.

"Lights, camera, action!" A smattering of laughter indicated everyone knew this wasn't usually said. Mia grinned at the director and I smiled. The production was underway. I shook my head and called it a night.

CHAPTER EIGHT

Sitting on my balcony, sipping the most delicious of café mochas, I almost missed the newscaster's melodious voice telling Las Vegas that the next story would be about the latest salacious murder in Sin City. The words filtered through my brain, the coffee nearly came out my nose, and I lost interest in the mountain view I'd been enjoying.

I tripped over the door frame entering my condo but made it to the couch in time to clearly hear Elizabeth Addison sadly inform viewers that a third actress had been found dead of unidentified causes. I clutched my coffee mug so hard I thought it would break.

"Viewers may remember that this makes the third unexplained death in as many months in the entertainment industry here in Las Vegas."

I stopped listening. A series of photographs were shown of three beautiful young blond women; I barely paid attention to them either – my eyes were glued to the words at the bottom of the screen:

Big Budget Bombshell – Major Star's Film Delayed by Murder.

I sent people to that set. Panic rose. They started filming last week. I didn't recognize the poor young woman who had died, thankfully, though who knew what this would do to the production timeline. Wow, that sounded harsh and indifferent, even in my head. I gave myself a physical and mental shake.

"Time to focus," I announced to Momma. "If only I knew what I should do first." She unhelpfully meowed.

The universe responded and my cellphone rang.

"Catherine Rodham speaking," I answered when my caller ID did not show a number I recognized.

"Catherine Rodham of Peterson Talent Agency?"

"Yes?"

"This is homicide detective Jacob Dawson, investigating a death on the set of *John Doe*."

"Homicide?" I squeaked out the question. "The news said it was an unexplained death."

"Yes, ma'am, at this time the death is considered unexplained."

I gripped the phone tighter. "How can I help you?"

"We are trying to confirm who was authorized to be

on the set in the past week and we understand your agency sent several actors. Is that true?"

"Yes, we sent six. I can provide you their names and contact information when I go into the office later."

"Call the number on your caller ID and ask for me directly. Thank you for your cooperation."

"You're welcome." I disconnected the call, feeling weird about the formality connected with death.

Momma meowed.

"I'm going to talk to my six actors myself to find out if they know anything," I responded. She meowed again. First, I wanted to check in with Mia.

"Hey Mia, it's Catherine Rodham."

"Hi, Catherine. What can I do for you?"

I heard the strain in her voice. "I understand the production has been halted for the moment." I left the *why* unspoken, since of course she knew. "Do you need a break? Maybe get a cup of coffee," I improvised.

She let out a deep sigh. "That would be fabulous."

CHAPTER NINE

Makers & Finders Coffee was a locally-owned coffee shop walking distance from the condo. I already knew they had an awesome Mexican spice latte that I adored. Mia arrived about ten minutes after me, her green hair again in a ponytail, lines of tension around her eyes. She waved and joined me at the table. A waiter came by to take her order. Based on her quick response, she was also familiar with the coffee shop.

Mia breathed in deeply, eyes closed, before focusing on me. Her amazing eyes sparkled, though the worry was obvious. "Thank you so much for the invitation. I needed this."

"You're welcome. I can only imagine."

"I love producing films, and I understand sometimes things happen, but sheesh. An apparent serial killer hit my set," she muttered.

My eyes widened. She spoke the truth. "The press is saying they're still just unexplained."

Mia chewed on her lower lip. "You know that would be a mighty big coincidence."

"True. And I spoke to a detective on the case," I spoke softer, glancing around. Nobody was paying us any mind.

"How did that go?"

Her curiosity was normal, but I sensed something under the surface. I watched her carefully as I answered, explaining it was a simple conversation and he would be interviewing my actors. She deflated somewhat with my not-too-exciting answer. I wondered what she was expecting. I turned the conversation. "What about you?"

"What about me?"

Deflection. Interesting. "What do you think about the murders? You really think it's a serial killer."

Mia regarded me for a moment before answering. "Yes, I do."

"Do you have an idea who it is?" I didn't believe she did, though she was clearly hiding something.

"No, I do not," she answered slowly, breaking eye contact.

That was a complete lie. My heart sank at the thought she might be involved somehow. I doubted she was the killer, but she knew something. "Have you spoken to the police yet?"

She shook her head. "My people have. I haven't yet. I was barely on set after the first night making sure everything started smoothly. I'm a producer, not a director," she added with a hesitant smile.

"I plan on speaking with my actors who were on set. I'll be sure to let the detective know if I learn anything."

"Playing junior detective?" There was no malice in her voice, only tiredness.

"Something like that," I agreed with a chuckle. "I'm sure everything will work out," I assured her, though I had no basis for my confidence. She undoubtedly knew that, but reached out to squeeze my hand.

"Thank you. The director was told we'd probably be clear to start by the end of this week."

"That's wonderful."

"Hopefully it's smooth sailing from here on out."

"Hopefully," I agreed. After a few more minutes of idle chitchat, we ended the coffee. I left with a sense that something important was unsaid. Or something I missed, perhaps, but no idea what.

*****

"Thank you for coming in," I ushered out actor number five robotically. So far, nobody saw or heard anything even remotely suspicious. I informed them they would be contacted by Detective Dawson and if they told him what they told me, it'd probably be perfunctory.

Despite the coffee with Mia earlier, I was tired.

Only one actor left to see. I didn't need to look at my sheet. I knew who it was by the flush creeping up my neck.

"Alexander Moore is here," Cherie announced five minutes later.

I had sufficiently calmed my hormones down in those few minutes so that I greeted Alex like an agent should.

"Alex, thank you for coming in on such short notice." I indicated he could sit in the chair across from the desk.

"You said that it was connected to a death?"

"Did you see the news this morning?"

Alex shook his head.

"An actress who had been on the set of *John Doe* was found dead." I managed to say this with almost zero tremor in my voice. Or so I thought.

Alex immediately rose from the chair and came around the desk. Startled, I rose to match. We stood close enough that I could smell his aftershave (which was quite nice). He put his hand gently on my shoulder.

"Are you okay? Did you know her?"

I was taken aback from his unexpected display, so different from the borderline cocky flirtation he normally demonstrated.

"I'm okay," I finally uttered. "No, I didn't know her," I further assured him, surprised still by the genuine reflection of concern in his eyes. I placed my own hand over his hand on my shoulder and smiled warmly. "Thank you for asking."

We stood like this for a long moment. Were we basking in the warmth? I don't know, but I realized, for that moment, I wasn't thinking salacious thoughts about him. And then I was. I took a half-step back and indicated he could retake his seat. He mirrored my smile before doing so.

"Do you mind if I ask you a few questions?"

"Am I a suspect?" He laughed to be sure I knew he was joking and I chuckled in response.

"Should you be?"

"Absolutely not."

I waited for my intuition to tell me if he was being truthful; yes, but incomplete. I frowned.

His face became serious. "What happened?"

"The police don't know. They confirmed that the young woman died an 'unexplained death'," I said, finger quoting the key piece of information. "I called some of my fellow talent agents and learned her name was Cindy Matthews." I watched his face for signs of recognition with the name. "Did you know her? Speak to her on set?"

"I don't recognize the name; I might have spoken to her without knowing it. What did she look like?"

"She was Caucasian, early- to mid-twenties, long blond hair and blue eyes."

Alex shook his head. "I don't think I even remember seeing her. Was she there at the same time I was?"

"I have no idea," I admitted. "Did you see or hear anything outside of the ordinary?"

"No. I wish I could be more help. Do the police have any idea at all how she died?"

"They told me no, but that doesn't mean they didn't hold something back."

"True." He frowned. "Do you know when the movie is going to restart?"

"I received word the delay will only be a few days since the death didn't occur on the set. I believe you'll go back by Friday."

Alex smiled widely and my heart gave a little flutter. "That sounds great. I look forward to resuming."

I stood suddenly, startling us both. "I'll let you get back to your evening. Thank you again for coming in, Alex." I walked around the table to properly escort him out.

Except Alex didn't make a move toward the door and I nearly walked into him standing next to the chair.

"Excuse me?" I asked in confusion.

A look of uncertainty alighted on Alex's face and he leaned in to hug me. I responded, holding tighter than I expected to, resting my head on his shoulder.

"I'm glad you're okay and that, sad as it is anyway, you didn't know the woman," he whispered into my ear.

"Thank you," was all I could respond. I wasn't sure why I couldn't fully get a read on this guy, but he seemed sincere.

We separated less awkwardly, two people supporting each other.

"I'll see you later, Catherine."

"I look forward to it, Alex." This time I gave the saucy smile and flirtatious inflection. His grin widened and then, like a flash, he was out of the office.

Who'd have thought a sweet guy was underneath that posturing exterior?

CHAPTER TEN

I stared at my reflection, admiring the view. I'm not really that vain. I actually tried to clean up for this. After three blessedly murder-free weeks, production wrapped on *John Doe*. And, as is customary in the entertainment world, they were holding a wrap party. As in 'that's a wrap' and we're celebrating the successful completion of shooting. I was invited by one of the actresses from the Agency who had appeared in the film and by Mia. I hadn't been to a wrap party since New York City. I got dolled up.

Taking advantage of my height, I chose a floor-length body-skimming red satin dress with a plunging neckline and backline. Normally, I don't show so much skin, but what the heck, it was a Vegas party! I decided to leave my blond hair long and loose; I hoped I presented a great combination of fancy and casual. If I didn't, that was okay too. I liked it.

My cellphone alerted me that my Lyft driver was one minute away from the building. I rode the elevator to the ground floor and walked out of the building at the exact moment the Honda coupe indicated on the phone arrived. Perfect timing.

The car pulled up to one of the most exclusive restaurants in the city. One that would normally be a crazy financial extravagance. After waiting for a month to get a reservation, of course. I reminded myself that being even loosely connected to Hollywood had its privileges and walked into the lavishly decorated place.

Gorgeous arrangements of flowers adorned every table. Roses, lilies, and orchids, surrounded by delicate baby's breath. Rhythmic music, Latin-flavored, played lightly in the background. Intimate lighting cradled the people in the room. Oh, the beautiful people. They were out in spades. Everything from floor length gowns like mine to barely there mini-dresses, kitten heels to six-inch stilettos, and tousled messy hair to savagely upswept do's. There was an open bar and it seemed everyone had a drink in their hand. Not to be left out, I headed that way.

"I'll take a whiskey sour," I requested of the bartender, the stereotype of a good-looking young male service worker. He smiled broadly and made the drink.

As he handed me the glass, I noticed his eyes shift to over my shoulder, so I was unsurprised when I sensed someone's presence behind me.

"Hello, Catherine. I didn't know you were coming to this shindig."

I turned at the velvety sound. "Hi, Alex. Jessica invited me." I somehow managed to keep my jaw from dropping. Alex had also apparently chosen to go all out for the party, dressed in an actual tuxedo. There were no words to describe how amazing he looked. I had resisted the urge to contact him while he finished filming, desperate to keep our relationship professional. Now I wanted to throw that right out the window.

I must not have hidden my response, because Alex gave me a Cheshire cat grin. I took pleasure in watching his eyes darken with desire, his gaze traveling down my dress and back up to my face.

"You look stunning."

"Thank you, Alex. You look pretty good yourself."

We smiled at each other for a moment of silence. At the second it seemed about to turn awkward, he found his voice.

"I'd do the chivalrous thing and offer to get you a drink, but you look like you're doing okay."

Noticing his empty hands, I flipped the script. "Would you like me to get you a drink?"

Alex laughed. "Sure, I'll take a gin and tonic."

I turned my head to address the bartender, who nodded that he heard. Once Alex had his drink in hand, we walked together to an oversized television showing a slideshow of still photographs taken during filming. Alex identified people I didn't know and regaled me with a few stories from the set. As he wrapped one up, a hand touched my shoulder.

"Ms. Rodham?"

"Yes?" I turned toward the voice. A petite brunette with luminous dark skin and eyes smiled hesitantly.

"Jessica, how many times have I told you that you can call me Catherine?"

"Yes, ma'am."

I smiled inwardly. You could take the woman out of the South but you couldn't take the South out of the woman. "Thank you again for making me your plus one."

"I had such a good time on set. It seemed only right to thank you for helping me get my first real role."

Out of the corner of my eye, I saw someone wave at Alex. He gave a slight wave back.

"Excuse me, ladies." And then he was gone.

I only half-listened while Jessica talked about being on set, my attention on Alex. He began having an animated conversation with an absolutely gorgeous woman in one of the micro-dresses and stilettos I had noted earlier. They seemed very friendly. I wondered at the jealous tinge to my thoughts and gave myself a mental shake.

More and more people arrived and much mingling took place. Occasionally, I saw Alex but we didn't speak again that night. A few times I noticed he had an odd expression on his face, like he smelled something he was trying to identify. What that could be, I had no idea.

As the evening wore on, and more alcohol was imbibed, the party became louder and raucous. I'll admit I had three or four whiskey sours. I can really hold my alcohol; I was only a bit tipsy. I groaned when Robin Landon headed my way. She looked blandly nice.

"Hello, Catherine. Are you enjoying the party?"

"Of course. Are you?"

Such scintillating conversation. I glanced around, looking for an out, before focusing on the woman in front of me. No reason to be rude.

"I am, thank you."

Interesting. She lied about having fun. "Thank you for introducing me to the councilwoman the other week."

"You're welcome. We missed you at last night's meeting."

Another interesting answer. Lie mingled with truth. "You and the councilwoman?"

"Yes."

"The two of you seem close," I said, curious about her reaction.

Robin blushed. "Not really."

Absolute bald-faced lie. "Really? That's not how it seemed at all. She seemed to rely on you." That wasn't true, but I had a hunch.

Robin beamed. "You think?"

"Definitely."

"I try to be there for whatever she needs."

Truth. Not a romance, though, and from what I'd sensed of the councilwoman, a one-sided relationship, whether business or friendship.

"I'm sure she appreciates that." I doubted my words but wanted to be kind.

A male hand tapped me on the shoulder.

"May I have this dance?"

"Excuse me," I said to Robin, who merely shrugged and turned away.

I danced with several men and although it was fun, more than a couple of times I saw Alex dancing with the hottie in the short dress.

And then, I looked around and didn't see either of them. I walked the perimeter of the room and, I can't believe it, even checked the restroom, looking for the woman. Neither were to be found. The party was winding down anyway (it was 3 in the morning, after all).

Not only was I jealous that Alex might have gone home with the woman, I was angry that he didn't ask me to dance. Ugh. Maybe the alcohol was having more of an impact than I thought. It was definitely time to leave.

CHAPTER ELEVEN

I woke up the next "morning" in time for the midday news. After making myself a café mocha, I curled my legs under me to sit on the couch. Momma jumped up beside me. I turned on the television and was surprised to see Elizabeth Addison; I didn't realize she did the actual news in addition to her morning show. She had the perfect newscaster expression of sad and caring while she announced the latest breaking news.

"An actress was found dead this morning in her Summerlin apartment. This marks the fourth unexplained death of an actress in four months in the Valley. Karen Weston was last seen at a party following the conclusion of filming for *John Doe*, leading some to wonder if the production was cursed."

A picture of the dead actress was displayed on the screen. I actually spit my coffee out, something I thought only happened in the movies. An outrageously attractive blond-haired, blue-eyed twenty-something smiled engagingly from what was clearly her professional headshot. I immediately recognized her. The woman Alex had spent much of the night with.

Could he be a killer?

Images of Alex and Karen whirled in my head. I tried to decide what to do. Should I call Alex to ask him about her? Should I call the police to tell them what I saw? In my heart, I didn't believe he was a killer. Technically, the police weren't calling any of these deaths homicide, I didn't think. Though how they were explaining four deaths in four months of young attractive actresses, I had no idea.

My phone ringing saved me from having to make a decision. "Catherine Rodham speaking."

"Ms. Rodham, this is Detective Jacob Dawson. We spoke before."

As if I could forget. "Yes, Detective. How may I help you?" My stomach had already begun churning, while I imagined where this was going.

"I understand you were at the party last night for *John Doe?*" He asked this as a slight question, though it seemed obvious to me he already knew the answer.

"Yes, I was."

"Would you be available later this afternoon to answer some questions?"

"Um, sure. Do I need to come downtown?"

"I'll come to you."

Awesome. "Of course. Do you need my address?"

"I have it, thank you."

Ugh, I was slow sometimes. "Okay, well, what time?"

"3 p.m."

"See you then," I said, more cheerfully than the circumstances lent themselves.

"Thank you, ma'am." The call ended.

I set my phone on the coffee table and shakily stood. Momma meowed from the couch. I scratched her behind the ears before I walked over to the sliding glass door that led to my balcony. I leaned my forehead against the glass. This did not bode well.

*****

The hours passed in a blur. I became increasingly anxious as 3 p.m. drew nearer. When there came a knock at my door, I about jumped out of my skin. My tabby freaked from my nervous response and ran for the bedroom. I'd probably find Momma under the bed later.

I opened the door and appraised the gentleman standing before me. He defied my internal representation of him from when we spoke before. He was tall, with a lithe swimmer's build and close-cut blond hair. I realized I was stalling when he spoke.

"Ms. Rodham? I'm Detective Jacob Dawson. We spoke on the phone earlier."

"Yes, of course. I'm sorry," I stammered, before standing to the side to allow him room to pass. "Please come in."

"Thank you, ma'am." He entered and walked toward the dining room I had arranged in the middle third of my studio condo. He looked at the table though did not move to sit.

"Pardon my manners, please be seated."

As we both sat, he smiled unexpectedly, blue eyes kind. "You don't have to be nervous. You're not a suspect."

I knew he was telling the truth. Still, the comment threw me for a second. "Wait. A suspect. I never thought I was a suspect."

His smile dimmed. "Oh, usually people worry they're a suspect when a homicide detective comes by."

I hesitated, uncertain, before finally blurting out. "If someone at the party last night is dangerous…that's what worries me. That I might know him."

"Him?"

"Aren't men statistically more likely to do harm?"

"That's true." I could read his disbelief in my explanation.

I smiled and tried to look helpful. "How can I help, Detective?"

The questions began innocuously enough; general timeline type questions to establish when I arrived, when

I left, that sort of thing. Then we got to the meat of the matter.

"Did you know Karen Weston, the actress who died?"

"I did not." I answered succinctly before asking, "Was she murdered?"

"That's unclear at this time."

"Huh? There are four dead actresses, right? All young and healthy? All blond and blue-eyed? You guys have nothing?" I heard the hysterical note creeping into my voice.

"Ms. Rodham, this is an ongoing investigation." He paused before continuing. "The news reports actually have it right so far. All four women seem to have had a heart attack. Yes," he added as I started to interject, "that's statistically unlikely, so we're looking at other explanations. Comprehensive drug testing came back on the first two victims and they were clean. The others have been requested." The detective looked vaguely surprised to have told me this much. I wanted to reassure him this happened all the time; I have one of those faces. People liked to confide in me. Or maybe it was part of my poorly understood empath abilities.

"No evidence of poison," I said slowly. "That seemed like the most logical explanation."

Detective Dawson unexpectedly laughed. "Do you watch a lot of crime television shows?"

I blushed slightly. "A few."

"Keep in mind, some poisons clear the system faster than others, so it's possibly something like that."

"Which brings me back to my fear that someone at the party is a killer."

His eyes narrowed. "You said that before. Is there someone you have in mind?"

When I didn't immediately answer, he leaned forward in the chair. "If you know anything, please share it. Help us catch whoever is doing this."

I closed my eyes briefly. "I had never seen Karen before last night, but I definitely noticed her."

"How come?"

"She was dressed rather … provocatively. Designed to draw attention."

"And did it?"

"It seemed to."

"Anybody in particular?"

I hesitated again. If Alex was innocent, this would be a minor inconvenience. If not, if my gut was wrong and he was a killer, this might save a life.

"One of the actors from my agency seemed to spend a lot of time with her," I finally stated.

"Alexander Moore?"

"Yes," I answered, surprised.

"Thank you for confirming what we'd already been told by others at the party."

"Okay. Isn't poison the choice of female killers?"

The detective smiled again. "Yes, that's true. However, remember that we haven't confirmed poison – and we're just gathering information."

That was not an entirely truthful statement; Alex must be a person of interest. My chest tightened.

"Did you see anybody else or anything that stood out as suspicious?"

Like when Alex sniffed the air repeatedly, I immediately recalled but chose not to share. I didn't understand what it meant, if anything, and I had already made up my mind to track down Alex. For the detective, I simply shook my head.

"Well, since you've seen a few detective shows you know the drill," Detective Dawson said with a playful smile. He reached into his pocket and removed a business card. "If you think of anything else that might be helpful, please give me a call. My cell is on there; you don't have to call the station."

"Of course."

He stood and I followed. At the door, he turned to me. "Please be careful, ma'am, until this is solved."

"I will, thank you," I responded, rattled slightly.

He smiled a final time and left.

I needed to talk to Alex to find out what happened. I wondered if I needed to wait for the detective to talk to him first. Unable to decide at that moment, I chose to go to the office and answer emails until I could make a decision. I'm a pretty good judge of character and I didn't believe Alex was a killer. And a serial killer at that. Four dead women in four months. It didn't seem possible.

*****

When I arrived at the office, the decision was made. Alex was sitting on the ground, slumped against the door, with his head in his hands.

CHAPTER TWELVE

"Alex!" I hurried to him. He looked up with such hope in his eyes when he saw me that I melted a little. He stood so that we met at the door.

"Catherine, I didn't do anything, I swear."

As before, that rang true but incomplete. I had never gotten such mixed impressions from someone before, and I didn't like it or understand it. "Hang on a minute; let's go inside," I stopped him from speaking further and inserted my key into the lock. He stood there, the anxiety rolling off of him, igniting my own.

We silently passed through the waiting area to my office. He collapsed in the chair, eyes wide, silently begging me to believe him. And I did. Mostly.

"What happened?" I asked instead.

"Has a Detective Dawson spoken to you yet? If he hasn't, he certainly will soon, I'm sure. He spoke to me this morning at the station. I'm apparently a suspect. What should I do?"

I didn't respond immediately, because I realized that the detective had already spoken to Alex before coming by my condo. Questioned and released. Sneaky.

"Catherine?"

I refocused on the distraught man before me. "Tell me what he asked you."

"He asked me all about last night, including whether or not I had spent time with Karen. The actress who died," he added, not realizing I already knew.

"What did you tell him?"

"The truth, of course. I danced and talked with her off and on throughout the night."

"What happened when you left with her?"

Now it was Alex's turn to stay silent. "What makes you think I left with her? Did you tell the detective that?" He managed to look both wounded and angry.

"No, I didn't. He didn't ask."

Alex appeared relieved. He grinned suddenly. "Did you really think I left with her?"

I shrugged and averted my gaze. "Both of you vanished at the same time."

"Did we now? And how do you know that?" He leaned back in the seat, hands interlocked behind his head. He smiled broadly, worries of a murder suspect forgotten, at least temporarily.

"I noticed you talking with her. Then you were both gone," I finished, rather lamely to my own ears.

"Were you tracking me?" He seemed interested rather than irritated.

"Yes, yes I was," I astonished myself by admitting.

"I'm glad."

"You are? I thought you were interested in Karen."

"Karen? She was sweet and liked to dance. That was all." He paused before continuing. "I wasn't sure you'd ever act on your attraction for me. Because of our work relationship."

"My attraction?" I asked the question, though we both knew the answer.

"Yes. The one that is definitely reciprocated by me," he replied flirtatiously and I smiled back, feeling a flush of heat in response.

"Wait. Let's stay focused. What happened to Karen?"

He paused a beat too long before answering. "I don't know. I didn't leave with her. Although I left after her."

Again, that incomplete truth. "How do you know that?"

"I looked for her before I left and didn't see her."

"Why were you looking for her?" Did you want to leave with her? This was the unspoken question.

"No," he answered my unasked question. He didn't elaborate, but I knew it was the truth.

"Then why?"

"I was worried."

"About what?"

Another too long hesitation. "I'm not sure. Something seemed off that night."

That was more lie than truth; what was going on? "Is that why you kept sniffing the air? Or at least that's what it looked like to me."

He seemed almost impressed with my question. "Yes, I was. There was a smell that seemed off. Wrong."

That was almost a complete truth. Now we were getting somewhere. "What? Like pot? You know that's legal here now."

He chuckled with me, the smile not quite reaching his eyes this time. "I can't really explain it."

Mostly lie. Damn it. "Can't? Or won't?"

"A little of both."

"Will you tell me one day?"

"Yes. Not today."

"Not today," I repeated. That was the truth. "I guess that's okay."

"You believe me that I'm innocent? That I didn't hurt Karen or the other women?"

"Yes, I do." He didn't respond. "Are you surprised?"

"A little, if I'm honest. You don't really know me."

"That's true," I acknowledged. I wasn't ready to explain my human lie detecting ability to him. "But, I'm a good judge of character and I don't believe you're a killer."

"Thank you, Catherine."

"You're welcome."

He grinned. "Will you go out with me?"

"Yes."

"Just like that."

"Just like that."

"What about the professional relationship thing?"

"We'll work that out as we go."

"That sounds wonderful." He walked around the desk and stood over me. I remained sitting. He put his hands on the arms of the chair and leaned in close. "Are you sure?"

"Why wouldn't I be?" My breathing quickened at his nearness, even though we weren't touching.

"There are things," he swallowed audibly, "about me that you might not like." He pushed back and turned away.

"So solemn," I teased and when he turned, I was shocked to see real pain in his eyes. I stood next to him, our heat comingling. "I know you have your secrets. Let's take it one day at a time. Okay?"

"Okay." He smiled shyly. "Meet you tomorrow at eight? If Thai is good, I'll text you a place I like."

I reached a hand up to touch his cheek. He took that hand in his own, held it in place. We'd work everything out moving forward. I trusted my instincts. They'd never let me down before – I pushed down the awful memory of the one time I ignored them.

"I'll see you tomorrow night."

CHAPTER THIRTEEN

The next morning, I clicked on the television to watch *Entertainment Daily*. I was already excited about my date that evening. Elizabeth Addison's smiling face filled the screen. Except she was silent. Oops, I forgot to unmute the television. I hit the button. A solemn expression replaced her smile. And then I gasped. Alex's headshot appeared in the corner, where the dead women's images had been before.

My heartbeat throbbed throughout my body. I sank into the couch. He couldn't be hurt.

It was much worse.

"Alexander Moore, a local actor, was questioned yesterday as a person of interest in the deaths of four actresses over the past four months. He was released and not charged. The police remain tight-lipped over why they questioned him."

The screen switched to a video clip of the newscaster shoving her mic into Alex's face outside a restaurant. She asked him why he was questioned by police. He stared directly into the camera before speaking. His short answer was lost in the wind buffeting the mic, but his face was tight in obvious irritation. He held up a hand to indicate he was finished and turned away from her. She started to follow, then stopped. The video was replaced on screen by an unsmiling Elizabeth.

"Mr. Moore had no comment when we tried asking for his side of the story. We'll bring you more of this developing story later during the news broadcasts." I hit mute when the show went to commercial.

His side of the story? I thought I already knew it. Did I? I debated whether or not to call Alex, and finally settled on texting.

Are you okay?

Yes. Why?

Did you see Entertainment Daily this morning?

No, but that reporter questioned me last night.

I know, I saw.

How bad was it?

She insinuated. Had no evidence.

She wouldn't. I didn't do anything. You having second thoughts about our date?

Nope. I'll see you tonight.

Looking forward to it.

*****

Was I crazy to trust my instinct that Alex hadn't hurt those women? The question kept running through my mind while I dressed for our date. Of course, I lied when he asked if I was having second thoughts. I'd be crazy not to. I wondered if I was making a mistake, trusting my instincts.

I focused on deciding what to wear. I chose a cute little purple cocktail dress with ballet flats. I didn't want to look like I was trying too hard, but I wanted to look like I had tried. I sighed when the question returned yet again.

Was I crazy to trust my instinct that Alex hadn't hurt those women? I didn't think so; of course, every woman hoodwinked by a serial killer thought the same thing.

"Momma?" I sat on the edge of my bed, listening to her claws as she ran across the concrete floor to the doorway of my bedroom.

"Meow?"

"Am I crazy—?" I stopped myself.

Momma crossed the room and hopped up on the bed, careful not to rub against me and get cat hair on my dress.

"Am I crazy to trust my instinct that Alex hadn't hurt those women?" I gave voice to the question on repeat in my mind.

"Meow!"

I laughed. "That was pretty forceful, Momma."

Softer meow.

"Okay, okay. I'll trust myself. Thanks, Momma." I scratched the back of her ears and she purred before flopping on her side, exposing her soft belly. I gave her a quick belly rub and a kiss on the forehead.

"Gotta go, Momma. Love you."

She stretched and meowed. I laughed again before I moved to my front door.

Was I crazy to trust my instinct that Alex hadn't hurt those women? The question returned again as I took the elevator down to the parking level under the lobby.

Was I crazy to trust my instinct that Alex hadn't hurt those women? And the question again as I drove my car out of the parking garage and onto the street.

Was I crazy to trust my instinct that Alex hadn't hurt those women? And one more time for good measure as I pulled into the parking lot of the restaurant.

Then a variation.

Why was I going out with him at all if I had doubt? Did I really have doubts or did I watch too much true crime television? Honestly, I had no idea. I made the decision to trust him and explore our mutual attraction. I'd make sure I met him in public places the first few dates. Listen to me. Already assuming additional dates.

Alex stood waiting for me outside the restaurant. I exited the car, smiling at his chivalry. He must be waiting to hold the door open for me. Then I noticed he wasn't alone. He stood close to a smaller, thinner, younger man with blond hair. The younger man looked familiar, but I couldn't place him. I squinted, trying to see him clearer or jump start my memory. It didn't work, though even from this distance, I could see both men were angry.

Alex and the other man leaned in and exchanged words. I wished I could hear what they were saying. I looked down while I closed my door, to make sure it completely shut. When I looked up, Alex had placed his right hand on the other man's left shoulder. I watched, unmoving. Alex leaned in further toward the man. Neither spoke. Confusion filled me. What was I seeing?

As I continued to watch, hand on top of my car, the other man exhaled a white mist that Alex then inhaled. What the—? I looked around to see if anyone else had witnessed what I had. We three were alone in this part of the parking lot. The transmission, if that's what it could be called, lasted mere seconds. Alex said something. The man nodded, turned, and left without another word or additional interaction with Alex.

I stood on wobbly knees, mesmerized by what I had seen. Alex sensed someone watching him and glanced around. His gaze landed on me. His eyes widened – to match mine, in fact.

Unnerved by what I'd seen and unwilling to listen to any more likely lies (how could he possibly explain this?),

I yanked open my car door and got in. Through the glass, I saw him running toward the car and heard him calling my name. I resolutely looked away and started the car. I glanced in the rearview mirror to make sure I wouldn't run him, or anyone else, over. I backed out and sped away. I met his eyes as I drove past him.

He appeared devastated. I kept driving and didn't stop until I was safely back in the underground parking garage at my condo building.

CHAPTER FOURTEEN

A new question was stuck on repeat in my mind – how could I have been so wrong?

Momma greeted me at the door and followed me into the kitchen. I gave her some canned food, still focused on that question stuck on repeat.

"How could I have been so wrong?"

Momma paused in eating to meow at me.

"I know, I know. I can't help it. I have to trust myself. But, what if I was wrong this time?"

Stop! I commanded myself silently. My phone rang and when I glanced down, I was unsurprised to see it was Alex. He had called twice during my short drive from the restaurant to the condo. I let the call go to voicemail again. He did not leave a message.

I headed for the bedroom, kicking off my shoes as I entered. I sat on the bed and tried to play devil's advocate in my head. I couldn't explain what I had seen BUT that didn't mean Alex was a killer. And since I hadn't given him a chance to explain, was I maybe being unfair? He had, after all, acknowledged earlier that he wasn't telling me everything. And hadn't my instinct been to trust him?

No! The other, colder side of my brain insisted what I saw had to be related to the unexplained deaths. Maybe whatever I saw breathe between the two men was some kind of toxin that caused heart attacks. Maybe that's what killed the four women?

I glanced down when Alex called again, wondering if I should either answer it or turn it off, ultimately deciding to do neither. I watched it go to voicemail again. No message.

What could the explanation be for what I had seen? From the safety of my condo, curiosity was getting the better of me. If I accepted my instinct that Alex was not a killer and something else was going on in the parking lot, then I really wanted to know what that was. I already doubted my theory that it was a toxin because the mist had moved from the other man to Alex. It would be hard to kill someone with a toxin in reverse. Plus, honestly, even with all the true crime I watched, I had never seen a toxin that worked like that.

There had to be another explanation.

A soft knock on my door. I almost missed it. Tentative?

Peering through the peephole, my jaw dropped open.

"Alex?" How did he get past security downstairs?

"Yes, Catherine. May I come in?' The closed door muffled his voice.

I stared in disbelief. My logical brain shrieked at me while I undid the lock and opened the door to allow him access. Momma took off from the kitchen, probably heading for underneath my bed.

He walked in, tentative, like his knocks. He closed the door behind him, but stood right inside, uncertain.

"How did you know where I live?"

His gaze dropped. "I tracked you."

"What? Like with an app, Google, something like that? Or did you follow me?"

"Um, no."

"That's it. No?"

"I don't know what to say," he admitted.

"The full truth would be nice," I responded with a sigh.

"Why don't you tell me what you saw first?"

"Don't think I'm missing your evasiveness." I stared hard at him, then relented. "Fine."

"Thank you."

He sounded so damn sincere. "When I arrived, I saw you arguing with that other man…" I prompted him with a pause.

"Michael Onyx."

I cocked my head at the name; it seemed familiar, like the man himself, though I still couldn't place it. I sighed. Alex did not jump in with more information. Okay. "I glanced away for a second and when I looked back..." This time I paused because fear flared at the memory. Alex closed his eyes, almost like he knew what was coming would physically hurt. "I saw a white mist move from the man to you; then the argument stopped and he walked away, like on autopilot. That's all."

Alex gave a half-smile. "Not exactly all. That's when you ran away from me."

"Drove away, to be exact," I responded with a half-smile of my own. And then part of the answer hit me like a ton of bricks, as they say. "I know why he looked familiar!"

"You know Michael?"

I heard the concern in his voice. "He was scheduled to audition the day I met you. Immediately after you, in fact, the last audition of the day. He canceled while we were wrapping up." I scrunched up my face, thinking.

Alex had gone white. "I know why he canceled."

"You do?"

"He must have seen me go in and didn't want to risk crossing paths."

"Why not? Who is Michael Onyx?"

"He's like me."

"Like you, how?"

"Maybe it would help if we backed up a bit and I gave you more of an overview of the supernatural world in town?"

"Supernatural world?" I repeated.

"Oh yeah."

"What do you mean by supernatural?" My brain tried to process what he was telling me.

"Beings who are not human or—"

"Are different?"

His lips quirked at my question but I didn't elaborate. Would I fall in that category? "Like we see in the movies, on television, and read about in books?" I asked instead. I focused on asking questions to quell my racing heart. This couldn't be real. Could it?

"Las Vegas is practically a beacon for many supernatural beings—" he started.

"Many?" I interrupted. "How many different types of beings are there?"

Alex shrugged. "Not really sure. Besides your classic creatures, like vampires and werewolves, we have less well-known ones like," he hesitated, "naiads."

That's not what he wanted to say. "Okay, vampires and werewolves I get. What is a naiad?"

"Naiads are female spirits who preside over various forms of water. Sometimes they're called nixie."

"Seems like a desert would not be the ideal location for such a creature," I analyzed.

Alex laughed at my comment. "That's very logical of you, Catherine."

"Logic trumps anxiety," I retorted.

His face crumpled before recovering. "Think of all the fake bodies of water that have been created in Sin City," he reminded me.

"True."

"All of these creatures are drawn here. Some in part because of the nightlife. You could see why a vampire might like it, right?" I nodded. "Others are drawn because of our anything goes attitude. What happens in Vegas stays in Vegas? Unfortunately, because people still fear the unknown, they are definitely NOT out in society."

Despite my anxiety and disbelief, I found I was enjoying this (possible) education about my adopted city. "That all makes perfect sense. How fascinating."

"To answer your question, though, I have no idea how many different types of beings are here. I don't know how many they number in total either."

"They could be anywhere?" A chill raced down my spine.

"Yes, but for the most part, they aren't dangerous. They want to live their lives in peace."

"For the most part…"

"Obviously, like in purely human society, you have individuals who cause harm. It's the same in the supernatural world."

"Like Michael Onyx, that man you were arguing with?"

"Exactly like Michael Onyx."

"Who is he, Alex?"

Alex didn't speak and his face froze. "A better question to start with is, what is he? What am I?"

"Actors?" I tried for facetious, didn't pull it off.

Alex's mouth turned down.

"What are you?" I whispered this, before adding haltingly, "Are you human or supernatural?" I couldn't believe I was even asking that question.

Eyes and face expressive and open, trying to convey trust, Alex reached a hand out toward me, then dropped it at his side. Resolute. Expecting a specific reaction, I guessed.

"Not entirely either," he finally said. "I'm a half-incubus."

I laughed. Even though my instinct told me he was truthful, I couldn't help it. "A half-what?"

"Half-incubus," Alex repeated.

"What on earth is that? I've never heard of it." I was genuinely curious – either Alex really was only half-human or he was seriously delusional. My internal lie detector told me he clearly believed what he was saying.

"Have you heard of a succubus?"

"I recognize the name. I couldn't tell you what it is," I admitted.

"A succubus is a female—" He paused, frowned. "What?"

He closed his eyes. "A female demon," he said through gritted teeth.

"You're a demon!" I'll admit I may have slightly shrieked this.

"A succubus is a female demon that can seduce men."

"And?" Please don't say what I think you're about to say.

"An incubus is essentially a male succubus."

Dammit. "You are a demon," I whispered, turning and fleeing further into my condo.

Alex followed. "Please, Catherine, hear me out. It's not what you think."

I had reached my dining room table and sat in a chair. Supernatural beings. I leaned forward to put my head between my legs. Vampires, werewolves, naiads. I took deep breaths and willed myself not to pass out. An incubus, a demon. I felt a panic attack coming on, something that hadn't happened in a decade.

CHAPTER FIFTEEN

Alex pulled a chair close to me and sat. He was careful not to touch me, I noticed. "Catherine? Are you okay?"

I sat up so abruptly, our heads nearly collided. "Am I okay? Am I okay?" My voice rose a notch with each question. I stopped and regained control of myself. "Continue."

"Yes, an incubus is a demon. I am a half-incubus. My mother was a human seduced by an incubus. Normally children don't result from these unions, but," he shrugged, "I'm here."

"Yes, you are."

This time Alex remained silent.

"You seduce women?"

"Um, I can actually seduce women or men; it's not necessarily a sexual thing."

I smirked when a blush spread across his face.

"Wait. How does that work? Have you seduced me? Is that why I find you so attractive?" I stared at him incredulously.

He grinned wickedly at those questions. "Not at all, Catherine. I swear to you that I have not seduced you – at least not in that way. Though I'd still like to explore—"

That was not fully true and a knot formed in my stomach. "Not yet," I stopped him and he obliged. "How does it work?"

"The seduction, simply by proximity. Pheromones, I suppose."

I nodded. That seemed reasonable. You know, given the topic.

"To make irresistible suggestions to other people, I inhale a tiny amount of the other person's soul."

"That's the white mist I saw?"

"Yes."

"Wait. You inhale part of their soul?"

"Yes."

I felt the blood draining from my face. He inhaled their souls. "It is you, killing the women!"

"Rumors of the deadliness of my abilities have been greatly exaggerated," he quipped.

"How can you joke about this?"

Immediately contrite, he explained. "I rarely use my abilities, and when I do, it's only the smallest amount of soul necessary to achieve the desired results."

"You sound so clinical."

"Sorry."

I waved off the apology. "You said you rarely use your abilities. When do you?"

"Mostly if I need to calm someone down."

"Like Michael Onyx outside the restaurant."

"Yes."

"You've never used them to harm anyone?"

"If you're asking if I've ever killed anyone, I can't say that." I inhaled sharply and he hurried to continue. "I didn't always know how to use my abilities safely. But, I have never taken deliberate advantage of anyone. And I didn't kill those four women."

I noticed his careful word choice. I still found myself sympathizing. What he said was true; and how would I handle it if I learned I could suck souls and control people? I'd struggled with feeling like a freak when I found out I could tell if someone was being truthful.

"It seems that sucking out someone's soul would be bad even if you didn't kill them. Does it," I struggled for the right word, "grow back or regenerate?"

Alex chuckled. "Yes, it replenishes. Think of it like the liver," he explained. "You can lose some—"

"Like from drinking alcohol?"

"I was thinking more like from trauma, but probably," he answered with a smile. "The development of new cells will continue; the soul is somewhat like that."

I hesitated, considering the logic in the analogy. "Okay," I finally said.

"Okay?"

"I believe you."

His jaw dropped. "Really? All of it?"

"Yep."

"You accepted that quicker than I thought you would."

"You're not the only one who's different," I said with a shrug. He started to respond and I cut him off, my turn to deflect. "When I was 18, I adopted a cat who was the reincarnation of my mother," I explained. As if on cue, a small meow came from under my bed.

"Of course, you did," he responded without missing a beat.

"I'll tell you that story another time. For now, let's stick with you," I brought us back to the subject at hand. "Are there many of you? Incubuses? Incubi? How would you say it?" Even while I uttered the inane questions, part of me knew I was stalling. This wasn't lost on Alex.

"It's okay, Catherine. Despite adopting your mother as a cat," he paused with a slight shake of his head, "I know this is a lot to take in."

I nodded in agreement. "Yeah, it kind of is."

"Michael is another incubus in town. I believe he's the one responsible for the deaths of those actresses. You were absolutely right, Catherine. If an incubus sucks out too much of someone's soul, they die. The death typically resembles a heart attack. Like with the women. That's what Michael and I were arguing about when you saw us. I withdrew a bit of his soul to calm him down—"

"You can use your ability on another incubus?"

"Yes. We prefer not to."

"It's like a code of honor?"

He grinned. "Something like that. Anyway, I was planning to ask additional questions, and then I saw you." He smiled warmly. Our eyes met and I felt a flush of attraction. "A beautiful distraction, but a distraction nonetheless." His smile fell. "I was terrified of what you had seen and would think."

"Oh, Alex." I couldn't help myself. I reached out to take his hands in my own. We sat silently for a few moments, me trying to offer some degree of comfort, knowing I couldn't until the real murderer was caught. I knew I mustn't forget that the police still thought Alex was the killer.

Alex broke contact, removing his hands and averting his gaze. "I wasn't able to get the full information." Back to business. "I can't tell if he has less control of his abilities, or less desire to control them."

I shuddered. "He's either inept or a serial killer. I don't like those choices."

"Neither do I."

"What are we going to do?"

"We?"

"Yes, Alex. We. I'm in this with you all the way."

He smiled so happily that, sappy as it sounded, I felt bathed in sunlight. "You are absolutely amazing, Catherine."

I blushed furiously, heat radiating through my neck and face. I tried to change the subject back to problem-solving. "What are we going to do?"

"I'm not sure," he admitted. "Any ideas?"

"Not right now. Let's think about it, maybe meet tomorrow morning at my office to discuss options?"

"That sounds perfect."

Our plan for the moment decided, we found that now we were sitting inches apart, staring at each other, attraction still chugging along, and completely uncertain what to do. I stood and he followed suit. "Okay."

"Okay."

"I'll see you in the morning?"

"Absolutely."

I walked toward the door, Alex following. Although he glanced away, he wasn't fast enough for me to miss the look of disappointment on his face.

"Scheming starts tomorrow?"

"Tomorrow for sure," Alex agreed. He smiled sexily and then sashayed toward the elevator. I laughed at the display, closed the door, and headed to the bathroom for a cold shower.

CHAPTER SIXTEEN

Sifting through snail mail and email in my office, waiting for Alex, I wanted to crawl out of my skin. There had to be something I could do to help. I identified two options: prove Alex's innocence to the detective or prove that someone else was guilty. I made a mental note to review timelines and Alex's alibis for the nights the four women died (well, three, since I mostly already knew where Alex was when number four died).

What could Alex and I do to prove Michael was the murderer? If he really was. I'd need to talk more with Alex about why he believed Michael was the killer. Surely, it's more than he's also an incubus. We never really got to that last night.

Last night. I flushed slightly thinking about being so close to Alex, longing to touch him, kiss him. Sigh. I needed to focus.

And then I saw it. A gift from the email gods:

> From: Mia Fynn, Producer
>
> Subject: Calling all creatives
>
> Don't miss the masquerade ball this Saturday beginning at 8 p.m. and lasting until…the final person goes home. Whether you're in front of the camera or guiding from behind it, this masked ball is the place to see and be seen Saturday night in Las Vegas. At a location to be texted the afternoon of the ball to everyone who RSVPs…don't miss what is sure to be the event of the season.

Mia's name and description were all I needed to see. One, it's a masked ball. Hello? How fabulous is that? And two, more importantly, since the party would be a meet-and-greet for actors, writers, crew members, and producers in town, odds were good that Michael Onyx, possible murdering incubus and actor, would be there.

A knock on the open door to my office shocked me out of my excited thoughts.

"Sorry to startle you," Alex began. "Your front door was unlocked and when you didn't respond to my knocking, I let myself in."

I berated myself for not locking the front door — someone more nefarious certainly could have taken advantage. Then I noticed Alex's arms laden with food and drink. He saw me notice and smiled.

"I brought coffee and bagels."

"My hero."

We grinned at each other for a moment before Alex made the move fully into the office. He set the bounty on my desk and pulled a chair closer before sitting directly across from me.

"I hope you're hungry."

"Absolutely." We began to unwrap our bagels. When I suddenly set mine down and gasped, Alex jumped to his feet.

"What's wrong?"

"I got distracted by the breakfast." He sat back down and watched me. "I have an idea."

"Great, let's hear it."

"I'm going to forward you an email invitation for a masquerade ball this Saturday."

"That sounds like fun."

"Yes, though that's not why I think we should go."

"It's not?"

"Nope." I shook my head. "It's a meet-and-greet for cast, crew, production staff." I paused expectantly.

"I think I know where you're going with this."

"Yep. Michael Onyx. Since he has allegedly killed four actresses, and he's an actor, he's in the industry. This might be the perfect way to flush him out."

"Flush him out?"

"Yes. Although, I never did hear why you think he's the killer."

"Besides the fact that an incubus kills in exactly the way these women seem to be dying?"

"Besides that. Because if that's the criteria, you would also be a suspect."

"Ouch. Touché. Honestly, it's a mix of my gut instinct and some off-color remarks he's made about women."

"Off-color?"

Alex actually blushed. "I'd rather not repeat them."

"I'm a big girl," I reminded him, "but that's okay. I won't embarrass you."

"Thanks. What's your plan?"

"We use the ball, so I can draw him out," I began and Alex shook his head. "Hear me out," I hurried to add.

"Fine, but I can already tell I'm not going to like a plan that involves using you as bait. That's it, right?" His eyes darkened with a mix of anger and fear.

I faltered slightly. "Well, yes. I think it's a good one, though. And you'll be right there the whole time. I mean, we'll have to arrive separately," I amended. "But still."

"If something goes wrong?"

"Either way, we have our proof."

CHAPTER SEVENTEEN

Saturday night arrived and my heart jackhammered in my chest as I got ready for the masquerade. Ugh, if this kept up, I'd die of a heart attack before Michael could try to kill me. I widened my eyes in the mirror and applied my eyeliner and mascara. No reason to be worried. It'll be in a public place. We'll get Michael to express interest, I'll draw him away somewhere private, and then I'll use my feminine wiles to elicit his confession. I stopped laughing before I poked myself in the eyeball with the mascara wand. The plan would work. I had no doubt.

Although disappointed we wouldn't be going to the ball together, Alex had agreed with my logic that Michael would be unlikely to respond to me if I arrived with another male. Of course, to be convincing that it wasn't a setup, I'd have to flirt with several men. Including Alex. I was definitely looking forward to that.

I stood before the full-length mirror hanging on my closet door, surveying the damage (of the good kind). Halter neckline, bodice emphasizing my narrow waist, and material length longer in the back than in the front to showcase my legs. One of the benefits of being relatively tall. I couldn't remember the name of the material. It was soft and flowing, a mix of beautiful deep blues, greens, and purples. I felt like a goddess, which was funny, given that I intended to flirt with demons. My mask was a beaded and feather confection that perfectly matched the dress. I was ready.

True to the email, I had received the address for the ball by text; I was mildly surprised it was a private address at one of the mansions in Queensridge, not a hotel or ballroom. Although, some of those places were gigantic. I figured they could handle the numbers. The drive was uneventful. I gave my name to the security guard at the gate and he handed me a printout of instructions on how to reach the home. Then the barrier gate lifted to allow me access to where the other half lived.

I drove along the tree-lined main road, watching for my first turn. Soon, I found myself in front of a massive two-story white stucco mansion with actual underground parking. That's pretty legit, I had to admit, while I followed another car into the garage. As always, since I lived in a studio-sized condo, I wondered about paying for utilities and who exactly cleaned the monstrosity. Of course, presumably, if the owner wasn't in hock up to his or her eyeballs, the owner had the means to pay for such pedestrian concerns. I chuckled and exited my vehicle. Time to focus.

Entering the home, it was clear it had likely been remodeled yet still held vestiges of its earlier incarnation. There was marble everywhere – I mean EVERYWHERE – from the floors themselves to the floor-to-ceiling columns placed strategically on the sides of the foyer. Huge picture windows ran the entire length of the back half of the house, allowing unobstructed views of the backyard resort-quality pool area. Hard to see what else the views were of since it was nighttime. Probably something equally stunning. I tried not to sound like a realtor in my head. I couldn't seem to help myself in noticing updated door hardware, lighting fixtures, and an absolutely marvelous modern kitchen, all gleaming metal and clean lines. Gotta love an open floor plan.

I smiled when I saw Mia approaching. "Please tell me you don't live here all by your lonesome," I teased. The producer was a vision from one of her movies, her long green hair perfectly curled, glitter eye makeup peeking from behind an elaborate sea green feathered mask, and an aquamarine sequined ball gown that showed off every perfect curve. She looked like a dang mermaid.

"Goodness no," she answered with her tinkling laugh. "It's a friend's place; he's in Europe on a project.

He's letting me host the party here because he's awesome."

"It's amazing, but huge."

"Absolutely. Way too big for me."

"Me too." I decided to take a risk. "Do you know Michael Onyx?"

Something unreadable flashed in her eyes before she answered. "Why?"

Hmm, not really an answer. Interesting. "He had submitted a headshot and resume when I first opened my office. He canceled last minute with no explanation and no request to reschedule. That seems odd for a professional actor." I shrugged my shoulder with feigned nonchalance.

Her eyes pierced me. "True."

Neither of us spoke for a moment, and I couldn't understand what made the conversation awkward. What did Mia know about Michael?

She sighed. "He's newer in town and I would be willing to bet his listed credits are exaggerations or outright fabrications," she allowed.

I knew Mia genuinely believed that, but there was more. "Good to know," I responded, thinking of how to word my next question. "Is there anything else about him that I should know?"

Mia opened and closed her mouth once, before smiling broadly. "Nope. That's all that's relevant I think."

That was a blatant lie; I remembered her reactions during our coffee and hoped again that she wasn't involved in whatever Michael might be. "Okay, thanks for letting me know about the credits, at least."

"Anytime. Welcome, and have fun!"

I watched her glide away and shook my head. There was something about her – I couldn't put my finger on it.

I sensed him behind me before he spoke. He really needed to stop sneaking up on me.

"Hello, Catherine."

I turned and he took my breath away. "Hi, Alex."

"You look gorgeous." His eyes beamed behind the black and gold mask.

"You look pretty awesome in that tux."

He held out his hand. "We should dance so we can continue to talk without raising suspicions."

I accepted his hand, a tingle running through me while he led me to the dance floor. It was a classic waltz, which amazingly enough, we both knew how to do.

"Raising suspicions? Does that mean you've seen him?" I chose not to use Michael's name, in case we were overheard by someone not friendly. Alex took the hint.

"Yes, he's definitely here. I lost him once I saw you," he admitted, a hungry look in his eyes.

My gaze faltered; the intensity of his feeling evoked a mirrored response in me. Alex pulled me closer.

"Careful."

He released slightly. "Why?"

"Don't want to mislead him," I reminded Alex.

He smiled ruefully. "Okay, if you insist."

"I do."

We enjoyed dancing in each other's arms for the remainder of the song and released with regret when the song finished.

I danced with man after man, always keeping an eye out for our suspect, but only seeing him out of the corner of my eye, or only at the start of a song, when it would be awkward to break away from another dancer.

Then I saw my opening. As one song ended, I spotted Michael getting a drink at the bar. His flat black mask was perched on top of his head. I excused myself from my dance partner and made my way over.

"What are you drinking?" I winced at the come-on nature of my question. Michael turned and smiled. I understood how he was so successful with women. Whereas Alex was a hunk of smoldering man, Michael had that alluring blush of youth, blond-haired, blue-eyed, strong jaw, and perfect white teeth. He filled out his black long-sleeved shirt and dress pants nicely. No wonder he was finding success as an actor, too, the agent side of me commented. If he wasn't a killer who had stood me up for his audition, I would probably have signed him.

Michael's perfect smile dropped completely. "I know what you're trying to do. And it won't work."

CHAPTER EIGHTEEN

My insides liquefied and I found myself dumbstruck. He was on to us! Before I could say anything, his smile returned, if possible even bigger than before.

"I already have an agent, so I won't be signing your exclusivity contract," he said with a wag of his finger and a laugh. I weakly echoed his laughter.

"You're on to me," I agreed with an even weaker smile. Michael didn't notice, or if he did, ascribed it to other causes.

"And I really must apologize."

"Apologize?"

"For my last-minute cancellation of the audition."

"I forgot all about that," I lied.

"I'd like to apologize and explain anyway."

I lifted my mask to the top of my head and sipped my drink noncommittally.

"I'll be honest. I had thought I wanted to sign. Ultimately I wasn't ready to go exclusive."

Interestingly, that was mostly true. I guess he really wanted to be an actor. I wondered again if we had the right man…er, incubus.

"I'm still not," he continued. "That doesn't mean we can't share a drink and a dance."

I half-heartedly laughed again and turned to the bartender. "I'll take a whiskey sour." The bartender nodded and began mixing the whiskey, lemon juice, and sugar. I refocused on Michael. "I'm Catherine, or did you remember that?"

"Nice to meet you, Catherine. I'm Michael; of course, you already knew that." His shrewd look had me trying to decide if he really thought I still wanted to woo him to my agency or not. Seemed a little narcissistic, but hey, he was an actor. It wasn't unheard of.

"You'd been pointed out to me," I admitted, my attempt to both be honest and stroke his ego.

His smile widened. "I hope you only heard good things," he said with a wink. Uncertain how to interpret that, I did the girly thing and giggled.

"Wouldn't you like to know." I was proud of that response because it wasn't a lie, and hopefully was mildly flirtatious. It seemed to work. Michael focused more on me.

"Would you like to dance?"

"I thought you'd never ask."

We replaced our masks over our faces to maintain the theme of the evening and he extended his hand. We hit the dance floor, making idle chit-chat about the entertainment industry in Las Vegas. When the song ended, Michael bowed dramatically.

"Thank you, miss. That was lovely." And then with another wink, he walked away.

Well, shoot, I didn't pique his interest. Flooded with disappointment, I made my way back to the bar. How on earth was I supposed to elicit his confession with my feminine wiles, if my feminine wiles weren't doing it for him?

A light hand on my shoulder startled me and I turned with fists clenched.

Robin Landon laughed nasally and took a step back. "Sorry, Catherine. I didn't mean to scare you," she assured me. Her yellow mask made her skin look sallow.

"I guess I was wrapped up in my thoughts."

Her eyes widened. "That must have been some deep thinking. What could be so captivating at a social event? Perhaps the good-looking young man you were just dancing with."

I tilted my head, considering her comments. Coincidence? "Oh, Michael? Do you know him?"

My question seemed to throw her and she stared at me a moment too long. "Sure. He's an actor in town."

She shrugged. "I represent him. As do other agents, no doubt." Her lips thinned in a forced smile. "I believe you know you're the only *boutique* agency in town." Her lips puckered in distaste, like she'd sucked on a lemon.

Hmm, interesting that the agencies were threatened by my approach. I silently chided myself for getting distracted by business. Robin told the truth about representing Michael; however, like so many others this evening, her comment was incomplete.

I spread my arms wide. "Our approach works in New York and so far, it's been working here."

"How is your agency handling one of your top actors being investigated for murder?"

My jaw dropped at the question. I snapped it shut and shook my head. "I'm sure I have no idea what you're talking about."

Robin chuckled. "Please, Catherine. Everybody in town saw Elizabeth Addison's report that Alexander Moore is a suspect."

"That is inaccurate," I disagreed. "He was a person of interest—"

"Everyone knows that means suspect," she interrupted.

"Interviewed and released," I continued as though she had not spoken. "Not a suspect."

CHAPTER NINETEEN

"Are you ladies enjoying the party?" A musical voice cut the tension.

"Yes, Mia," I answered, silently thanking her for the interruption.

"Of course," Robin answered perfunctorily.

"I'm so glad to hear that," Mia said, clapping her hands. Her voice washed over me and I found the tension from the conversation melting away. Mia placed her hands on my and Robin's shoulders, gently squeezed, and then moved on to another small group of partiers.

Robin opened her mouth to speak, but her eyes focused on something over my shoulder. Or some*body*. I turned to look and was shocked to see Councilwoman Barbara Knollman staring daggers in our direction. I presumed the daggers were for me. I smiled widely in her general direction and Robin stepped away.

I watched the councilwoman close the distance between us. She wasn't wearing a mask. She did at least dress up, though it was more mother-of-the-bride than night-out-in-Vegas.

"Ms. Rodham, how lovely to see you."

I didn't need my empath abilities to know that was a lie. I smiled anyway. "Councilwoman, I'm surprised to see you at an industry event," I redirected the conversation.

"Why wouldn't I be?" she countered. "All business in the Valley is the council's business."

She definitely believed that, and undertones to the sentence suggested a meaning I was missing. "That makes sense," I agreed with her. "What can I do for you?"

"Do? Why nothing, of course. I'm simply stopping by to say hello."

What an odd thing to lie about. What the heck; I'm going for it. "That's a lie," I said in a lowered voice.

Her cheeks flushed at my comment and her lips smiled tight across her sharp teeth. "Why would I lie? What other reason would I have for coming over here?"

Her questions were so reasonable. And still. "That's what I'd like to know," I challenged her.

"I can't give you an answer I don't have," she said, still smiling, though the words were clipped.

I couldn't get a read on her; her comment was… empty. She waited for my next salvo. I had nothing. This whole thing was weird, but I was getting nothing specific.

"My mistake, then."

"Apology accepted."

The councilwoman reached out her hand and I took it, for appearances if nothing else. A shock of cold flooded through me at her touch. She smirked at my reaction. "Until next time, Ms. Rodham."

"Definitely, Councilwoman."

I watched her walk away, head held high, greeting others when she passed them, a stereotypical politician. I knew that was a façade. Hiding what?

Right now, it didn't matter, I reminded myself. Focus. I frantically tried to think of a way to lure Michael. As the night wore on, it became apparent that the incubus wasn't going to take my bait. Dang, and I looked so good tonight. In frustration, I headed back to the bar.

This evening was NOT going as planned.

"I'll take a vodka gimlet." The familiar-looking blond standing at the bar next to me stared beneath her pink feathered mask. Not challenging, but questioning. I stared back before catching myself. "Forgive me for staring," I apologized. "Were you on the set of *John Doe*?"

The blond smiled, her dark red lips parting slightly, and nodded yes, sending her 1920s ringlets bouncing. "I was. Were you?"

"Only the first day." I extended a hand, which she took, her cool fingers wrapping around mine. "Catherine Rodham, talent agent with Peterson Talent."

"Evelyn Jones, actress. You can call me Evie."

"It's nice to meet you again, Evie."

"You, too, Catherine." She stared at me, appraising. "I saw you speaking with Robin and Barbara."

Alarm bells began ringing. "Yes, are you friends with them?"

Her nose wrinkled. "Not exactly. I'm familiar with them." A delicate shoulder lifted in a shrug. "I was represented by Robin in the past."

"Was?"

"Turned out we weren't a good fit. What were you talking to them about?" Evie shut down her side of the conversation fast.

"Not much," I evaded, before reconsidering. "I was asking them about Michael Onyx."

"Why?"

Now it was my turn to shrug. "Professional curiosity."

She stared at me. "I saw you dancing with him."

"You did?"

"I did."

"Hmm."

Her eyes bored into me. "What do you know?"

CHAPTER TWENTY

"Know? About what?" Confusion washed over me. I felt like there was a whole layer of conversation I was missing. Just like with the councilwoman.

Warmth filled me and I knew Alex was near.

"Hi, Evie," his voice came over my shoulder. I watched her eyes find him and then a curtain fell. She gave me a lovely, if fake, smile, and wished me well. She walked away from us, her short pink flapper dress swishing with her sashaying hips. I turned to Alex.

"What was that about?"

"What are you talking about?"

"Don't sidestep my question. I saw her look at you and then decide to leave."

"She must sense the sexual tension between us." He smiled his wolfish smile and all thoughts fled my brain. Dang it. He leaned in. "Where did he go?"

Although distracted by his breath against my ear, I followed the conversation change. "I don't know. Do you think he left?"

"It would appear so."

I looked at Alex in despair. "Now what?"

"Just because the plan went bust doesn't mean we can't enjoy the rest of the evening," he purred.

"Now that sounds like an excellent Plan B," I concurred. "Before we do, did you see the two women I was talking to before?" He shook his head. "Robin Landon, another talent agent, and Barbara Knollman, city councilwoman. Do you know either of them?"

"Only by name. I don't think I've spoken to them."

"You never auditioned for Robin?"

"Nope. I got plenty of work through a couple of other agents. Before I signed with you, of course," he said, his eyes crinkling at the sides when he smiled.

"Of course," I agreed, matching his smile.

"Why?"

"I'm not sure. There's something off with both of them. I can't put my finger on it."

"Did you try smelling them?"

I laughed aloud and then covered my mouth with my hands. "Careful. We don't want to draw attention."

"Sorry about that." He clearly wasn't sorry. I shook my head and led him back to the spacious living room-turned-dance floor.

Alex and I danced several more times, both of us surreptitiously keeping an eye out in case we were wrong about Michael having left. Neither one of us saw him again at the party.

Dancing with Alex and learning about his life before Vegas (originally from Florida, wanted to be a beach bum before finding himself in Vegas) captivated me. Staring into each other's eyes, feeling his strong arms around my waist, and the heat of his breath as he whispered into my ears. The plan may have been a bust, but yeah, we definitely made the best of it.

At the end of the night, we walked together to the underground parking. I saw the worry in his eyes.

"Be careful."

"I will."

"Call me when you get home. So I know you're safe. I know you can take care of yourself, but still."

"I will. I appreciate the concern." I smiled warmly at him, the concern he expressed demonstrating that our attraction was more than physical.

*****

The drive to the condo was blissfully uneventful. Once upstairs, I kicked off my heels and promptly removed my phone from my purse.

Autodialed Alex.

"You made it home?" More question than statement.

"Yep. I had fun tonight." I hoped he heard my smile.

"I'm glad. I did too," he responded, and I was certain I could hear a smile in his voice.

A knock on my door startled me. I walked toward it, turning on the kitchen light as I passed. "I see you tracked me again," I told Alex flirtatiously and then disconnected the call, though a part of my brain registered that he was saying something.

Opening the door, I saw I was right. An incubus had followed me home.

The wrong one.

CHAPTER TWENTY-ONE

My heart racing, I instinctively backed up. He stood in the bright light provided by the hallway fixtures. I remained in the dim light filtering from the kitchen and plastered a fake smile on my face. I hoped Michael wouldn't realize I was frightened out of my wits. Apparently, I'm a better actress than I would have guessed.

Michael took my retreat as an invitation and stepped into my condo. I viewed my space through his eyes: he quickly appraised the small office space, the dining area with table and four chairs, the kitchen area along the wall opposite floor-to-ceiling windows providing a view of the mountains. His gaze sighted my couch and he headed straight for it. Momma hissed at the incubus from under the dining table when he walked past her.

"Come on in," I belatedly invited him, following with no small amount of both confusion and fear.

Michael stopped at the backside of the couch and placed his hands on top. He inhaled and turned with a smile. I stood opposite him with the dining table between us. Momma fled the room, heading toward the bed. I'd probably find her underneath when this was all over. I realized I still clutched my phone and wondered if I could be fast enough to call 9-1-1. I set it down to free up my hands. For what, I wasn't sure. I'd see where this went.

"I hope you don't mind my showing up like this," he said with what I imagined he thought was a disarming smile.

Time to disabuse him of that notion. "Actually, it's more than a little creepy. We shared one dance, you vanished, and then, poof, you're here. In my home," I added pointedly.

His face hardened and anger sparked in his eyes. With concerted effort, his face smoothed out like the emotion had never been there. "I apologize. Perhaps I misunderstood at the party." Now with a wounded puppy dog look, trying to ingratiate himself with me, I found myself watching him from an almost clinical perspective.

He was so calculating. If I didn't know what I knew, I might fall for it. A truly scary thought.

When I didn't respond, he continued. "I thought you were interested in me; I didn't want to make a production of it at the party since it was a business event."

"How do you know where I live?"

He paused before shrugging. "Google."

I knew flat out that was a lie. Not just because I could sense it, but because I had hidden all of my online personal information. I decided not to further antagonize him. Really, I just wanted him out of my home. This was not part of the plan.

Michael took several calculatingly uncertain steps toward me, still playing the part. The dining table remained between us and he began to walk around it, talking the entire time.

"You looked so beautiful tonight. I wanted to sweep you off your feet. Since I couldn't do that at the party, I decided the next best thing would be to surprise you at your home so we could continue the party privately." He stopped a foot from me and smiled. I saw the predator beneath the façade.

Frozen, I did not back away when he reached out a hand to touch my face. With the skin to skin contact, I felt a rush of sudden heat, not unlike when Alex touched me. Now confusion surged stronger than my fear. Was Michael exerting his incubus control to make me feel this way? If so, did that mean Alex lied to me about my reaction to him? Did he use his abilities on me, even though he swore he didn't? Or did this mean I found both men attractive?

Michael leaned in for a kiss and this time I did respond. By stepping back. I simultaneously noticed white mist leaving my mouth and an angry, surprised expression on Michael's face. Clearly, he had not expected this. Though the mist did answer at least one of my questions.

Michael was trying to suck out a part of my soul.

I noticed I wasn't as angry as that thought seemed like it should make me. In fact, I felt funny. I smoked pot once and it was kind of like this; funny, yet pleasant. I smiled goofily at Michael. He smiled back, oozing self-confidence now, and moved closer to me again. He ran his fingers along my cheek and jawline, his eyes locked on mine. He stepped closer, our heat mingling. He leaned in once more for a kiss and just before his lips touched mine, a loud banging sound erupted.

I barely noticed, but Michael turned his head, breaking contact with me to look toward my door. Anger emanated from him. It didn't pierce the pleasant fog surrounding me. I heard words from the other side of the door that I did not understand. Michael obviously did. Confusion, anger, and worry flashed across his face. He released me and turned fully toward the door, hands fisted at his sides.

I shook my head to clear the cobwebs. Enough self-awareness returned that I acted on impulse.

"Michael!"

Hearing his name, he turned back toward me. I grabbed him by the shoulders and kneed him in the groin.

He cradled himself and fell to his knees in pain. The door to my condo broke open. I stared in shock at the splintered wood surrounding one beautiful, dangerously angry and scared incubus.

Alex's look of worry vanished when he saw Michael curled on the floor in the fetal position, still holding himself. Alex smirked, "I guess I don't need to come to the rescue."

CHAPTER TWENTY-TWO

"Alex!" I threw myself into his arms. He held me close and I felt our heartbeats, at first rapid from the excitement, then slowing as we calmed. His arms circling me provided a cocoon of safety. I closed my eyes and inhaled his clean, intoxicating scent. That reminded me.

"Can I ask you something?" I mumbled this into his shoulder.

"Of course. What is it?"

"When Michael touched me, I felt a similar reaction to when you touch me." Alex stiffened, and not in a good way, so I hurried to continue. "Why is that, if you weren't using your incubus powers on me?"

"They're not powers, just abilities," he corrected, though I heard the smile in his voice. He released me, keeping his hands on my shoulders and holding me at arms' length. "Listen to me very closely Catherine. Every incubus possesses the ability to simulate physical, um, bodily attraction," he appeared slightly uncomfortable, "and what that means is that what an incubus can create would mimic what really happens when someone is truly attracted." His eyes searched mine to determine if I had understood.

"What you're saying is that Michael was able to create a fake version of what you naturally create." Now I blushed furiously.

Alex smiled happily. "Yes, that's exactly it. It was the same because between us it's real."

"It is?" Part of me hated that I sounded so sappy. Another part of me was thrilled my feelings were reciprocated.

An unwelcome voice from the floor interrupted. "Oh, please, are you buying any of that?" Alex and I watched in horror as Michael slowly rose to face us. The mask was gone and for the first time, I could truly see the demon lurking below the human exterior. Michael laughed at Alex. "Tell the woman the truth. You know you drew her in." He winked at me. "He isn't *that* attractive. Didn't some of it feel wrong?"

And so help me, I felt a stab of doubt. Michael smiled smugly and Alex rapidly shifted his gaze from Michael to me and back again, clearly wanting to address me directly, but without taking his eyes off the killer.

"Catherine, you don't believe him, do you?"

"Is he lying?"

"Yes."

A sob caught in my throat. "You're lying," I told him softly. "When we first met, of course I could appreciate that you were attractive. However, I was drawn to you in a way that didn't feel natural. I couldn't understand it. Now I'm beginning to."

"That's not how it is," Alex responded. Our eyes met briefly and my heart contracted at the pain I saw. I looked back at Michael.

Michael continued to smirk at our exchange. I wanted to smack the expression right off his face, but he was controlled at the moment, and I needed this resolved with Alex now.

"Do you deny that you … amplified … my natural reaction to you at the audition?"

Alex paused for too long and I had my answer. "That's not the whole story though," he insisted.

A single tear tracked down my cheek. "Why?"

I sensed more than saw his shrug. "It was an audition; I wanted to make sure you agreed to represent me. It wasn't personal."

I spun on him. "It wasn't personal? You manipulated my response to you. For a job." Disgust filled me. Motion caught my eye and I glared at Michael, who leaned back against the dining room table, lifting his hands in surrender. "You stay put. It's not your turn yet." I looked back at Alex. "Anything else?" I knew there was more. Would he be honest?

"What do you mean?"

I closed my eyes for a moment. "That's not an answer. When we first met, did you use your abilities in any other ways?" I could not be more explicit than that and his sharp intake of breath confirmed what I suspected. "Please do me the courtesy of the entire truth."

His shoulders slumped. "I entered your dream. Only once," he hurried to add.

"That's rich," Michael crowed, slapping his hand against his thigh. "Look who's high and mighty now."

I took a step toward Michael and pointed at him. "Shut up. Regardless of anything Alex did or did not do, YOU are a serial killer. So shut up." My finger shook. Not with fear. With rage. Adrenaline from the night's events, including these nasty revelations, coursed through me. Michael gave a mock salute and continued to casually lean against the table.

My eyes met Alex's and I saw sorrow reflected there. "Why?" The word barely an audible whisper.

"It was an accident. I didn't consciously do it."

That was true, but... "What else?"

"Once I was in your dream, curiosity got the better of me and I didn't immediately leave. You didn't respond the way I expected."

"I didn't just swoon over you."

He flushed. "You were clearly interested, but. No, you didn't." He paused. "What are you?"

That tripped me up. "What am I? I don't understand the question."

"Your response to me, how you always know whether I'm telling the truth. I know you're different, but you seem human."

I barked an unhappy laugh. "I am human."

Alex and Michael waited for me to continue.

"But, I am different." I hesitated. "I don't know what or how exactly. An empath seems to be the closest fit." I shrugged. Understanding dawned in the men's eyes. "I can feel what others around me are feeling and I can tell if they're being truthful or deceptive."

"Not all the time, though?"

"No, Alex, not all the time. I'm like a living, breathing lie detector, though with the same flaws. If someone truly believes what they're saying, I'll read it as true. Even if it's a lie. Also, sometimes psychopaths can mask whatever it is my brain reads and feed me what they want. And, sometimes it's blank. I haven't figured out yet what that is; maybe some people can block themselves entirely. I don't know."

Michael slow clapped. Alex and I stared at him. "That's pretty good. I knew Alex was on to me. I didn't know you were going to be bait. Excellent job."

"Why did you do it?"

Michael took my conversational redirect in stride. He shrugged. "My first one was an accident." He tilted his head in Alex's direction. "Just like him *accidentally* entering your dream."

Alex scowled. "It *was* an accident. And I made sure it never happened again."

My heart swelled at the truth in his statements. He never meant to enter my mind that first time and he never did it again. That meant our feelings were real. My body flooded with warmth at the thought and I grinned at Alex. "I know." I turned back to Michael. I needed to know the whole story. "And then?"

He shrugged again. "It's such an interesting phenomenon," he waxed philosophical. "There I was, this beautiful dead girl at my feet. And, what can I say, I found that I liked it. So I kept doing it."

I gaped at his nonchalance and he laughed.

"Don't look like that, little empath. We're at the top of the food chain. When I accepted that, and truly accepted who I am and what I liked... well, it was easy after that. I moved from city to city." He frowned. "Until now. You two screwed up my system." He stepped forward hands fisted at his sides.

"Don't move, Michael," Alex commanded him. "You know I can't let you leave here."

Michael laughed. "Are you going to call the police?"

"No, I'm going to call—" Alex glanced quickly at me "—someone better equipped to take care of you."

"No, you're not." Michael looked at me, imploring me. "Are you really going to let him kill me?"

Kill him? I looked at Alex in confusion – we needed to call the police – and that was the opening Michael wanted. Without waiting for a response to his question, Michael attacked Alex, launching himself, hoping the element of surprise would be sufficient.

It wasn't. Alex rebuffed the attack, then struck with an uppercut that rocked Michael backward. The incubus fell, his head cracking on the dining room table.

Alex grabbed Michael by the neck in a grip so tight that I could see white knuckles on Alex and an increasingly red face on Michael.

Alex leaned in and breathed deeply. Michael tried to shake his head, to break eye contact, to disrupt the flow. A white mist left Michael's mouth and entered Alex's.

He's breathing in his soul. The panicky thought whirled in my mind.

Michael's face paled. Alex had said he could call someone in the paranormal world to handle this, not kill the other incubus.

"Alex! No!" I grabbed his head and turned him toward me. He released Michael, who fell to the floor, gasping. Alex stared at me, comprehension dawning.

"I almost—"

"But, you didn't."

"Thank you," he whispered and leaned toward me.

Michael staggered to his feet, touched his fingers to the back of his head. They came away bloody. "You tried to kill me." The outrage in his little boy's voice saddened me. Had he always been like this?

Michael jerked forward, his eyes rolled into the back of his head, and he fell to the ground.

Alex and I stared in shock at the unconscious demon on my concrete floor.

"What the heck?"

The incubus began vibrating.

"What's happening?" I dropped to Michael's side.

"I think he's having a seizure," Alex answered and dropped to Michael's other side.

"Do we need to get something for him to bite down on?" I swung my head around, trying to identify what might work in my condo.

"I don't think it'll be necessary."

I sat back on my heels, stunned. Michael's shuddering decreased until stopping completely.

"Is that normal?"

Alex's wide eyes met my own. "I have no idea."

Our stares returned to Michael.

The murdering incubus was dead.

I had a dead demon in my condo.

Now what?

CHAPTER TWENTY-THREE

"Such a shame he couldn't disintegrate like a vampire does when he dies," I quipped. Yes, I made jokes when I was nervous. And right then, my nerves were beyond frayed. I stared in both consternation and horror at the dead body of the incubus. "That is what happens when vampires die, right?" I turned to Alex for confirmation. He tried unsuccessfully to hide a smile.

"Yes, it is. Am I going to be your living, breathing Google for monsters?"

"Probably. Wait, is that offensive?"

"Not in the least, Catherine. I'm not a delicate flower."

I laughed, pleased to note it was only slightly hysterical, and then sobered quickly. "We'd better call the police."

"That seems the practical thing to do."

"Or do we need to call the other…group…you mentioned?"

"That's not necessary now," he answered without explanation.

I guess we'd deal with that later. I focused on the issue of the dead body. "How are we going to explain this? Even though he's the killer, there's still only circumstantial evidence that he is. And our word. Against the dead guy on the floor. Do you see where I'm going?"

Momma slunk out of the bedroom and approached the dead incubus. She sniffed at him, hissed and took a swipe at his head. Satisfied the beast was dead, she meowed up at the two of us and then padded softly back into the bedroom. I assumed I'd find her later, either under the bedspread or under the bed itself. Alex and I faced each other.

"Don't worry about it," he assured me.

I hesitated.

"I promise it'll be okay, Catherine."

"Okay. I trust you." I grabbed my phone off the dining room table and unlocked it to call 9-1-1. Alex put his hand on mine.

"Do you?"

"Do I what?"

"Do you trust me?"

"Yes." With the threat of Michael gone, I found my concern about Alex returning. "I'm angry that you lied to me. My instincts tell me what you said earlier tonight was the truth. That you…amplified…a little at the audition and then accidentally entered my dream that night. And you haven't done either since. I know that. But…"

He smiled. "Trust your instincts."

My return smile was a ghost of his. "I don't know whether to believe my feelings."

"You can. I promise that after that first day—"

"I know." And I did. Completely. I smiled then.

He frowned.

"Why are you frowning?"

"Why didn't you tell me the truth about *your* abilities?"

I dug my foot into the floor, looked anywhere except at him, while I gathered my thoughts. "It's something I'm still coming to grips with."

"Have you always been an empath?"

Tears flowed from my eyes at his simple question and he reached for me before pulling back. "I'm sorry. What did I say?"

I shook my head, waited for the tears to pause. I had to spit the words out. "After my mother came back into our lives, my father and I shared her."

"Like shared custody?"

A small smile flitted on my lips. "Something like that. I had recently graduated high school. The next few years were bliss. There had been such a hole in our lives after my mother died, that getting her back, even in such a peculiar way, made us whole again. On the night of my 21st birthday, while out celebrating with friends, I started having these weird impressions when I talked with people. I chalked it up to mild inebriation. It didn't stop. If anything, it became stronger. Everything people said triggered a truth or deception response in my brain. I tried to ignore it, but it was tough. I thought I was going crazy. Then one day, while visiting my father, he had a coughing fit. I asked him if he was okay. When he said yes, it pinged as a lie. I dismissed it. Six months later he was dead. Lung cancer."

I tensed when Alex wrapped his arms around me, and then I relaxed. He rested his chin on the top of my head. "I'm so sorry," he murmured.

"Thank you. I never challenged him. Maybe if I had, he would still be alive." My voice cracked on the last word.

Alex pulled back, used the pad of his thumb to wipe the tears from my cheek. "Catherine, you are not responsible for your father's death. If he lied to you, he knew what was going on. What could you have done to make things different?"

Tears fell faster and my voice dropped. "I don't know what treatment he was getting, if any. Maybe he thought with my mother back, I'd be okay. He never recovered from her death, even when she returned."

"Oh, honey, this is not your fault. Do you think your father would want you living like this?"

I shook my head. "No. He wouldn't." I inhaled deeply and let out a trembling breath. "And that's why I've tried to pay attention to my gift. Not dismiss it. But I did anyway." This last said harshly as I ripped myself from his arms and turned to look out the windows on the city below. "I knew you were hiding something and rather than push it, I ignored it. And you used me."

Alex put his hands on my shoulders from behind. I stiffened and he released me, though didn't move away. "I know."

I closed my eyes, let the hurt wash over me.

"If I could go back and change it, I would. I don't know what compelled me to even try. I haven't gone into someone's dreams since the beginning, even accidentally. I…" he stopped.

I glanced over my shoulder at his head hung in shame. The rest of my body turned and I faced him. "Look at me." The expression of hope in his eyes floored me. "Do you genuinely want a relationship with me?"

"Yes."

The truth of his simple answer filled me with such lightness. A smile burst onto my face and I threw my arms around him. He responded eagerly.

"We'll figure this out as we go," he promised me and I knew he was telling the truth.

And then I remembered the dead body. With a sigh, I disengaged and pointed at Michael.

"Oh yeah," Alex muttered. "I forgot about him."

I giggled and then bit my lower lip. "Actually, I have another question."

He watched me warily. "Yes?"

"Earlier, I could have sworn I saw the demon beneath his human mask. Was that my overactive imagination?"

Alex's eyes widened at my observation. "You saw that?"

"It was real?"

He shook his head ruefully. "Yes, unfortunately. Humanoid demons are interesting. They have human form but the demon soul can sometimes become visible."

I felt the blood rush from my head. "Do you—?"

Alex laughed loudly. "Thank goodness, no. With a half-incubus, my demon essence is just that. Essence. It does not have a physical manifestation at all. At all," he repeated for emphasis.

I sighed in relief. "Okay good. Wanted to make sure you weren't gonna grow devil horns at some point."

Alex caressed my cheek. "No, I'm not." He glanced at Michael's inert body. "Guess it's time to call 9-1-1."

CHAPTER TWENTY-FOUR

"9-1-1, what's your emergency?" the professional, dispassionate voice asked on the other end.

"I've been attacked in my home by a man. And I think he's dead," I said, unsure how I should disclose what happened.

The dispatcher's voice sharpened. "Ma'am, are you hurt?"

"No."

The dispatcher's voice faded to the background, though I continued to answer her by rote: Did the man have a weapon? Did I know the man? Was anybody else in the home?

"The police are on their way, ma'am. Please stay on the line with me until they arrive, just in case."

I noticed belatedly that while I had been talking, Alex had opened the door to my condo.

"Las Vegas Metro."

Before they could utter another word, I was at the door. "Please come in. He's…over there." I gestured generally toward the couch, though given the size of my condo, they saw Michael after taking three steps through the door. One officer made a beeline for the body. The other stopped at my side, though kept an eye on his partner.

I watched the first officer check Michael's pulse, turn to look at his partner, and give a small shake of his head. Confirming the death. Well, not officially until the medical examiner's arrival, I supposed, yet enough confirmation that they didn't have to worry about him being a threat. The first officer called some information in; based on my vast array of knowledge (from crime shows, of course), I assumed he was making sure the Medical Examiner and the Crime Scene Investigators were coming. I almost called out to have him contact Detective Jacob Dawson, lead investigator on the Actress Murders, then decided he'd figure that out for himself. Of course, it was well after midnight. Maybe the detective wouldn't be on call?

I focused on the officer before me. About my age, with that former military look I could usually pick out of a crowd, and was very no-nonsense while he asked his questions. I explained what had happened, including that I had been on the phone with Alex when Michael showed up, which was how Alex knew I might be in danger. The officer stopped me.

"What made you suspect the deceased was the Actress Murderer?"

I glanced at Alex, which the officer did not miss. I shrugged and Alex jumped in, walking close enough to the officer that I had a feeling I knew what was coming.

Making intense eye contact, Alex breathed deeply while explaining. "I knew Michael. I knew he had met at least two of the victims. I asked him about it one day. I thought his answers didn't make a lot of sense."

My eyes grew big as I watched white mist leave the officer's mouth during exhalations. His eyes softened and he nodded. "That makes sense. I'll pass that along to the detective; he may want to ask you additional questions."

Alex took a step backward. "Of course, Officer. Whatever I can do to help."

I smothered a laugh when the officer, still looking a little confused, turned and walked over to his partner.

More commotion at my doorway drew our attention. I recognized Detective Dawson and surmised the others entering were medical and crime scene people. Two of the EMTs approached me and Alex.

We allowed them to look us over, but balked when they insisted we needed to go to the hospital.

"Ma'am, we'd like to make sure he didn't hurt you."

"I appreciate that, but do I look hurt?"

I smiled winningly and happily, to show, 'See, I'm not just good, I'm great.' It didn't work, though the young man did offer a small smile in return.

I couldn't believe I was about to do it. I looked over at Alex and gestured for a little assistance. A little incubus assistance. Alex shook his head slightly at my audacious turn and complied.

He stepped in close to the young EMT, who startled but did not give ground. Alex leaned in like maybe he was someone who didn't recognize personal space. He smiled his beautiful smile (even the EMT responded slightly to it) and spoke. "We really appreciate everything you've done for us. You can clearly see we're both perfectly fine. We'll wait to speak with the detective when he's ready and be done with this whole thing. You understand, right?"

Dazed, the EMT nodded. "I completely understand. I'll make a note that there were no physical injuries requiring treatment or further examination. I'm glad you're both okay." He and his colleague jotted down a few notes before heading over to speak with the detective, who was wrapping up a conversation with the original responding officers and the medical examiner.

I felt guilty when Detective Dawson approached and I saw the suspicious look on his face.

"Can either of you explain this without sounding like you're making the entire thing up?"

CHAPTER TWENTY-FIVE

Alex and I remained quiet. Detective Dawson sighed. "From what I've gathered, Michael Onyx attacked you in your home," he started with a nod at me. "You arrived to assist," he turned his attention to Alex. "And somewhere in there, Mr. Onyx wound up dead from head trauma."

"That's correct, Detective," I finally spoke up. What happened was self-defense. There was no reason not to be up front about it. "He attacked me, Alex's arrival distracted him, and I kneed him in the balls. Once he sufficiently recovered," I shrugged, "he admitted he was the Actress Murderer, and Alex punched him in the face when he tried to attack us again. He hit his head, falling, had a seizure, and died." My voice caught on that last word. Michael was a killer, but still. I had never seen someone die in person before.

Alex murmured his agreement to my account.

"About that," Dawson responded. "You say he confessed to killing the women. Even though no concrete evidence has been supplied to suggest that today…or previously." He stared long enough for me to feel uncomfortable.

"But pretty decent circumstantial evidence," I countered. "All the women had similar appearances and Michael was present at all the scenes."

The detective sighed again. "That's true," he agreed, though continued to stare at us.

As if sensing it was time again for his magic, Alex stepped closer to the detective, who put a hand out immediately. "Please stay back, Mr. Moore."

Alex looked nonplussed by this statement but complied.

I wondered how he would work his incubus influence without the necessary distance. Suddenly, Alex began having a coughing fit. He rudely did not cover his mouth as he directed the forced air at the detective. Dawson turned and reflexively exhaled.

Ah, that's how.

Detective Dawson made a face in apparent disgust. When Alex inhaled the white mist, though, Dawson's expression took on an open visage. I didn't think I'd ever get tired of seeing Alex work his magic.

Now when Alex leaned in closer, the detective did not hold up a hand or say anything. "You already had

Michael Onyx on your radar. Other witnesses reported they saw him speaking with several of the victims in the days leading up to their deaths. You believe he poisoned them with chemicals that simply aren't remaining in the system long enough to be identified by the lab. We are innocent bystanders. Do you understand?"

"Yes."

"I think it's time for your team to go. Okay?"

"Okay."

I watched in awe. The detective spoke to his team members, everyone gathered up their belongings, and they left. They actually left.

"Won't they realize later that what they're thinking doesn't make any sense?" I asked once they were gone.

"Not exactly."

"What does that mean? Do your suggestions eventually fade?"

"They do, just not completely. It's hard to explain. They may recognize that something seems off or maybe doesn't add up, but they'll remain convinced they have their guy. What usually happens is they'll change the way they look at other information so that it fits the suggestions I gave them. Plus our story is the truth."

"What usually happens? Hmm, how often do you use your ability?" I was teasing him now, and he knew it.

"Much more since I've met you," he admitted, walking over to me.

"You're in my personal space," I told him, holding a hand up like the detective had.

Alex wrapped my hand in his. "I hope to be in even more of it soon," he said, his voice a husky growl.

"I think that can happen," I responded, pulling my hand from his and wrapping both arms around him. Our bodies fully touching felt electric.

Our lips met, lightly at first, then with deepening desire and intensity. A first kiss that met all the promises hinted at before.

I pulled back, knowing passion mirrored in our eyes. "Stay with me, my incubus," I whispered.

"Always."

EPILOGUE

The phone rang, jarring me. I might have to reconsider having a landline in the office. I had only slept a few hours the night of the ball or even Sunday night. I yawned. Cherie had taken a personal day, so I was answering my own phone.

"Hello?" I pulled my gaze from the laptop and gave the caller my undivided attention.

"Good morning, Catherine."

It took me a second to place the voice. "Good morning, Robin," I replied perfunctorily. I softened my tone; I wished I understood my instant dislike for the talent agent. "How are you this morning?"

"I'm well. Happy this nastiness with Michael Onyx was wrapped up."

"Indeed."

"I heard that he was killed in your condo."

I remained quiet.

"By Alexander Moore, one of your clients."

I sighed. She called to gossip. Lovely. Well, none of that was a secret. It had probably been all over the early morning news. Not that I had watched, of course; I was trying to get some sleep, albeit restless, unfortunately. I refocused on the call. "That is correct," I gave a neutral response.

"Interesting that Mr. Moore was in your condo in the middle of the night."

I gaped at the phone. What are we, in middle school? "Did you need something?"

"I'm calling to say I'm glad you're okay," she said insincerely. "The councilwoman will be on *Entertainment Daily* this morning talking about the story."

"Why?" It popped out of my mouth before I could stop myself.

Robin sharply inhaled. "Why wouldn't she? She's very involved in the community."

Now I rolled my eyes at the offense she took. Good grief, was she the councilwoman's lackey? "Of course, she is. I'll be sure to watch. Was there anything else?"

At least she didn't miss the tone. "No. I'll see you at the next chamber meeting."

"Have a good day." I hung the phone up in relief. She was so odd – and I still couldn't really explain why. I typed on the laptop keyboard, calling up the television show's website. They didn't stream the show live, but the videos were loaded almost immediately after.

My cellphone pinged arrival of a text and I smiled when I saw it.

Good morning sunshine.

Good morning Alex.

Did you get any sleep?

A little. Btw, Robin the talent agent called. She said to watch Entertainment Daily this morning. Councilwoman will be on.

The one that you were asking about?

Yep.

I'll watch.

It's on a time delay for me; I'm watching on the computer.

I'll text you if anything interesting happens, in case you want to skip it.

Lol. Dinner tonight?

Pick you up at 7.

I sent a few smiling emojis, minimized the show's page, and focused back on the documents I had been working on. About fifteen minutes later, my cellphone pinged another incoming text.

Definitely should watch the show…

Anything I should know…

Just watch. Curious about your take on it.

Now my curiosity was piqued. I barely maintained attention on my documents until the show finished and its website reflected the video upload.

Finally. I clicked start and maximized the screen. Elizabeth Addison's smiling face appeared. After welcoming viewers, her smile dropped. "In a stunning conclusion to the Actress Murders, the serial-murder-at-large has been stopped. Councilwoman Barbara Knollman, a grand supporter of the film production community in the Valley, is here with us this morning to discuss what happened. Welcome, Councilwoman Knollman." She turned and the image switched to the camera on the councilwoman. Barbara lifted her head, her brown hair shiny under the lights, and smiled her creepy smile. I imagined she meant for it to be ingratiating.

"Thank you for having me, Elizabeth."

The camera pulled back for a two-shot of the women, seated next to each other on two matching blue cloth chairs, as though meeting for tea in someone's living room. The councilwoman, in a severe charcoal pantsuit, paled in comparison to the newscaster-attractiveness of Elizabeth in a hot pink fitted dress. And yet, there was something that compelled the eye. Perhaps this was why she kept being reelected.

Elizabeth provided a quick summary of the case for any of her viewers who'd spent the last months living under a rock and then opened the floor for the councilwoman. "Can you tell us what happened?"

"Of course." Barbara stared directly into the camera, normally a no-no; however she clearly wanted everyone's attention. It certainly worked on me. I stared at her obsidian eyes. "Two nights ago, following a masquerade ball hosted by a Las Vegas/Los Angeles-based production company—" Interesting that she didn't mention Mia by name. "—at the home of talent agent Catherine Rodham, local actor Michael Onyx was killed in self-defense by another local actor, Alexander Moore."

Buzzing filled my head. I considered her words. None of that was a lie and probably was mentioned in the newscasts this morning. But. I refocused on her continuing to talk. I already missed some.

"The police are confident that they have their man, so to speak, and that the city can sleep safe again tonight. Michael Onyx was an animal. A danger to civilized society. And we must be ever-vigilant to stop such threats from infiltrating our city."

When the camera switched back to Elizabeth, she smoothed out her expression; not so fast that viewers missed her looking askance at the councilwoman. "That seems an... unnecessarily strong sentiment," she said with a tight smile.

The camera returned to Barbara, her smile showing those small, sharp teeth that unnerved me. She shook her head slowly. "Oh, Elizabeth, it's not. We're at war."

My jaw dropped open – along with Elizabeth's, though she recovered faster. "Thank you, Councilwoman. It's been interesting."

"Thank you, Elizabeth. Always a pleasure."

The video ended and I stopped it before the webpage could auto-play the next in the series. I sat back in my chair. Holy cow. I grabbed my cellphone.

What did she mean? We're at war?

I have no idea.

Could she know about…?

Possible.

What will you do?

It'll be discussed in the appropriate circles and dealt with as necessary.

Okay then. That was quite a statement with no real information. Lol

Better this way.

I have no doubt.

See you tonight.

Again, we exchanged smiling emojis and then I got back to work, troubled by what I had seen, unsure of what it meant, and knowing I was entirely out of my depth anyway. Better for Alex and the supernatural world to address it.

*****

"I heard you have a greater level of understanding of my needs." She crossed her legs, blue and white polka dot stockings peeking out below her mid-calf blue silk dress.

Normally that could be a cheesy sexual come-on, but since this was the fourth vampire sitting across from me in my office in less than a week, I understood exactly what she meant. Plus, we had met previously, and I knew she wasn't propositioning me.

"I do, indeed, Evie," I assured her. I loved how she still looked straight out of the 1920s with her blond bob and blue eyes, dark red lipstick contrasting with her creamy pale skin. I guessed that was her thing.

I took her through my standard spiel and paperwork. "I think that about wraps it up," I concluded.

"One final thing."

Uh-oh.

"Thank you."

That caught me off guard. "For doing my job?"

"For being here. For being understanding and sympathetic to us. Not everyone is, or would be."

"I appreciate that."

"If you haven't already, you can definitely expect more of our kind, as word continues to spread about you, and the Peterson Talent Agency."

"I hope so. These are exciting times." In so many different ways, I was finding out.

Evie stood and I did the same. She walked to the door, turned to give me a high-wattage smile, and walked out the door.

Welcome to the Paranormal Talent Agency!

Episode Two

Reset to One

CHAPTER ONE

Today was my 29th birthday. Again. That's the joke, right? At some point in the latter 20th century, women decided to stay 29. So, they celebrated turning 29 every year, and their friends laughed and everyone had a good time. Forever 29. Except that I really would be forever 29. After all, I was a vampire.

And where was I on my 92nd 29th birthday? At an acting workshop organized by my new agent, Catherine Rodham, of the Peterson Talent Agency, or as individuals of my persuasion had been calling it, the Paranormal Talent Agency. Aren't we clever? In all seriousness, though, she's pretty cool – open to the other-than-human set, dating a half-incubus, and earlier this year, even helping to catch a serial killer!

On this beautiful summer evening in Las Vegas, six of us sat on uncomfortable metal folding chairs in a circle, staring at each other. Sizing each other up. Checking our internal files to see if we'd met before at an audition or on set. Catherine had done a great job mixing the group: three men and three women, race and ethnicity across the spectrum, ages from twenty-something to fifty-something, and several different species. They said don't judge a book by its cover, but after over one hundred years on the planet, I had pretty good "species" radar. Three humans, pixie, werewolf, and me. As my gaze followed the circle, I caught my breath when it landed on one of the humans. Well, now, who did we have here?

I watched his luscious full lips while he said his name. "Hi, everybody. I'm Ryan Walter." I drank in his lithe frame in the seat, glimpsed muscles at the edges of his running shorts and marathon-finisher t-shirt. An athlete. Yum.

"I recently relocated here from Los Angeles. Smaller market, I know, but I can't afford food and rent in LA." Everyone around the circle chuckled in agreement and his smile revealed perfect white teeth. I noticed, however, the smile seemed forced.

"I also work as a paralegal. It's fun and pays the bills." For an actor, he didn't hide his distress very well. But, it wasn't my concern. The auburn glint in his hair mesmerized me. Was that dyed or natural?

"I'm happy to be here." I doubted this, but nobody challenged the comment. He finished and the next person in the circle began speaking. I was definitely not listening. I noticed that Ryan's hazel green eyes, with just a fleck of gold, seemed anxious.

Our eyes met (now didn't that sound cliched) and he checked me out the way I had checked him out. I tried to see myself through his eyes. I was turned in the 1920s but gave up my preferred style for years. One of the benefits of Vegas, however, was that, much like New York City, anything went, so my eccentric style was nothing more than that. Eccentric. Short, 1920s curly blond bob over blue eyes, very pale skin, and dark red lipstick. I looked like someone called for a stereotypical 1920s flapper from Central Casting, in all honesty. At least I wore jeans with my Gatsby-inspired green tank shirt and black ankle boots. I smiled widely at Ryan, who responded by looking at the ground. Hmm, that didn't usually happen.

I realized it was time for my introduction.

"Hi, I'm Evelyn Jones. Everyone calls me Evie." Jones, of course, was my latest fake name. "I moved to Vegas from New York to get away from the cold." Everybody chuckled and nobody caught that I didn't include a time frame.

"I've been acting in independent projects for years." Decades really, but who was counting? "I'm looking forward to working with all of you." Despite my flippant attitude generally, I really was looking forward to working with them. I loved acting.

With introductions completed, the instructor, Anthony Gullo, explained the workshop plan. Without intending to, my gaze returned to Ryan, who kept checking his watch. I frowned. If he had somewhere else to be, why didn't he just go?

Anthony asked Ryan a question. His head snapped up and he looked confused. "I'm sorry, I missed that."

"Is everything okay? I notice you keep checking your watch." Kudos to Anthony for calling Ryan out.

Ryan reddened in embarrassment. "I'm sorry. I'm distracted. Personal issue."

"Anything we can do to help?" the pixie asked and her offer seemed genuine. I looked around at the others, who were nodding.

Although it seemed to me that his statement suggested he didn't want to talk about whatever was bothering him, he opened up after that single question. I felt for the guy, I really did, but honestly, was this the time and place for his therapy?

Ryan spoke haltingly. "My best friend, Jim, was arrested. For murder." Several small gasps were heard. "I know he didn't do it and I don't know what to do." His gaze moved around the circle, as though looking for an answer. Silence greeted him. Until he reached me.

I shrugged. "Not to be mean, but how do you know he didn't do it?"

"Excuse me?"

"How do you know he didn't do it?" I repeated.

He frowned. "Of course, he didn't do it."

"I understand you believe that," I tried again. "But how do you know that?"

Anthony jumped in. I suspected he regretted opening this can of worms. "Maybe we'll shelve this conversation until the break? Ryan, if you need to leave to help your friend, we'd understand."

Ryan shook his head. "I'd rather stay. There's nothing I can do until he's released on bail. Which should be sometime tonight." He checked his watch again. "I could use the distraction. Thanks."

We resumed the workshop, which went well. We all had new scenes that we worked. As we were wrapping up, I noticed in my peripheral vision Ryan was approaching. Uh-oh. I hoped I didn't upset him earlier. I sometimes had that effect on people, even when I wasn't trying.

"Evie, right?"

"Yep. Ryan?" Like we didn't both know each other's names. Such a convoluted dance humans did.

"Yes." He hesitated. "I wanted to ask you what you meant by your comments earlier."

"I didn't mean anything by them." I could see the pain on his face and I didn't want to add to it. "I was just playing devil's advocate."

"Devil's advocate? This is my friend's life." He lowered his voice. "Sorry."

"No need to apologize. I can imagine how hard this is." Certainly, in my 100+ years, I've had friends jailed. Of course, they were guilty.

"Thank you." He stopped but didn't leave. He shifted from foot to foot.

"Was there something else?"

Our eyes met again, and damned if I didn't feel something. If only he wasn't so caught up in his friend's drama. He could be fun. Oh well. His phone beeped.

"It's Jim." The color drained from his face. His reaction perplexed me. He believed Jim was innocent. Wouldn't he be happy Jim got bailed out? Although, it equally baffled me that he couldn't entertain the possibility his friend was a killer. This fascinated me.

"I need to order a Lyft," he muttered to himself and turned away, fiddling with his phone.

"Do you need a ride to pick him up?" Both of us looked shocked by my offer.

"I do. Are you sure?"

"Definitely. Let me make up for what I said." That wasn't really why I offered, I realized. I wanted to know more. I wanted to understand how he could be so sure of someone else's behavior.

His dazzling smile returned. "Thank you. I appreciate it." We exited the building together.

"Hmm," I started, as we stood next to my dark green Fiat convertible. "How tall is your friend?"

Ryan laughed, a deep unexpected rumbling that caused me to laugh in response. "He's average, I suppose. He'll fit fine."

We drove in companionable silence to the detention center to retrieve Jim. The red brick building looked like a prison and I shuddered when we entered the parking lot.

"Do you know where we need to go to get him?"

"He said he'd be waiting out front."

Big brown letters across a tan semi-circle announced we had reached our destination. Sure enough, a guy stood in front, off to the side, scuffing the toe of his shoe on the ground. He looked like a stereotypical surfer, with his bleached blond hair and lean, wiry appearance. I couldn't see his eyes from the car. My guess was blue.

"That's Jim," Ryan confirmed my unspoken assumption and I directed the car to the curb. I watched out the window while Ryan embraced his friend. They talked for a second before Jim followed Ryan to the car.

I twisted in my seat to say hello to Jim, now ensconced in the back seat, chuckling internally because I was right. His eyes were blue. Then I felt bad for my internal chuckle. Poor man. His eyes had that lost look. His face somehow already seemed wan, like he'd been in jail for months, not just long enough to be bailed out. He managed a slight smile.

"Nice to meet you, Evie. Thanks for the ride."

"No problem. Where to now?"

Silence greeted my question. I'd have thought Jim wanted to go home, given the late hour, but since nobody said anything, I went with my gut. "You guys up for a late-night snack?"

Jim looked so grateful for the suggestion that I actually felt guilty for a nanosecond, given my ulterior motive. For some reason, it bothered me that Jim was hoodwinking his friend. I was determined to show Ryan he was wrong and that I was right. People couldn't be trusted. It didn't matter how close they were to us.

Ryan suggested a Denny's midway between here and Jim's home in Southern Highlands and I started in that direction.

"How are you doing?" Ryan tried for nonchalance, like we hadn't just picked Jim up at the jail.

The silence stretched for a few blocks and I wondered if Jim was going to answer. And then he did.

"I'm not sure," he admitted. "I feel like I'm underwater. Ever since I was arrested. My lawyer hadn't been certain I'd get bail. Even without a criminal record. Because I was arrested for a felony." Jim fell silent.

Nobody said anything the rest of the way to the diner. I had so many questions, my mouth wanted to blurt them out. I refrained, figuring that maybe food would loosen Jim's tongue. After all, how could I find the holes in his story if I didn't know his story?

CHAPTER TWO

Ryan and Jim must have been trying to communicate telepathically, based on the meaningful glances they kept sharing. I, on the other hand, not possessing such skills, was bored. We'd been sitting in the diner booth for pushing fifteen minutes with no chatter. Nada. Zip. The cheerful waitress brought us waters and took our orders, egg biscuits and French fries for the guys, and nothing for me. They didn't know I couldn't eat regular food, so I said I wasn't hungry.

"I…"

Yes! Jim was starting to speak.

"I didn't kill Monica." He looked exhausted, like uttering that phrase sapped all of his strength.

"Of course, you didn't," Ryan immediately agreed. I naturally had no idea who Monica was, but Ryan seemed to.

"My wife." Jim directed this at me, as if he read my mind, though likely I had a quizzical look on my face.

"I don't know what happened," he admitted, dropping his gaze to his lap, hands locked in nervous fidgeting.

"What do you know?" I asked the question gently. I felt bad for him; he seemed genuinely saddened and scared. Still, I was on a mission.

"What happened?" Ryan added this question. Silence followed. Jim appeared to be considering what to say in response.

The waitress returned with their food, sparing Jim from having to respond. She placed the dishes, told the men to enjoy, and departed. Jim sighed deeply.

"We had gone to the theater, the one in Chinatown," he explained. "It was a longer show, so it was already after 10 when we left. Nothing seemed wrong when we got home. No lights were on in the house. No strange vehicles were parked nearby. I pulled into the garage and closed the door. All like I normally did. We entered the house from the garage and that's when we noticed something off."

"Off? What do you mean?"

"As weird as this is, Ryan, there was a smell."

"A smell?"

"Yeah. It smelled woody."

"Like the woods?"

"Not exactly. Just woody," he said, face pinched. He closed his eyes briefly. "I joked with Monica about her sneaking a guy into the house and she laughed. We assumed." He stopped. "I don't know what we assumed, to be honest. It simply never occurred to us that someone could be in the house. Like I said, no lights were on, no cars were outside, we didn't hear any sounds." I wondered if Jim was trying to convince himself almost as much as he was trying to convince us.

"We were laughing, joking about the show. I locked the door behind us and we went to the kitchen, turning lights on and off while we made our way there. Monica tossed her purse onto the counter and I grabbed a bottle of red wine to pour a couple of glasses." His recitation had the familiar feel of a story oft repeated; how many times had he already told it to the police?

Jim stopped again, the silence stretching so long that I was unsure if he would start again without a prompt. His eyes closed. Ryan and I exchanged glances. We remained quiet. Jim ate a French fry, took a sip of water. He was clearly delaying.

"You know what our kitchen looks like?" This was directed at Ryan, who nodded. "I was at the counter near the side window, pouring the glasses, when Monica screamed. I dropped the glass, it shattered. As I was turning around, I sensed movement by my head, I was overwhelmed by that woody smell. And then nothing."

He sipped more water, the glass shaking in his hand.

I tried to pay attention to Jim's physical changes, looking for the tell to suggest which parts he was lying about...or maybe just omitting. Except I found myself distracted by Ryan. His beautiful hazel eyes, so expressive, clouded over. I saw the pain in them, not only for his friend, but for his friend's wife, the murder victim.

"Nothing?" Ryan asked this quietly.

"Based on when we got home, I was unconscious for an hour. I woke up with a throbbing headache, a huge lump on the side of my head, and my wife," he stopped short. His voice hitched and tears filled his eyes. "My wife was dead beside me. Every time I close my eyes, I see her lifeless ones. And there was so much blood." Tears slid down his face, slowly at first, and then a torrent. He lowered his head to his hands, tented on the table. Was he trying to hide from us? Was it grief? Or guilt?

Ryan and I waited for him to compose himself. Jim lifted his head, eyes reddened. "I checked for a pulse and breathing, of course. It was too late. I called the police." His voice cleared, became sharp.

"I was holding her when they arrived. They arrested me for her murder. Do you want to know why?" We nodded, not daring to speak. "Because there were two bloody objects in the kitchen. That small vase on the ledge between the kitchen and the living room." This was directed at Ryan, who nodded his familiarity with the vase. "And a small frying pan. Their theory is that we got into an argument, grabbed the nearest objects, and hit each other. Because I'm stronger, I did more damage. According to my lawyer, they consider it a heat-of-the-moment killing, which is why I was charged with second degree murder."

"What about intent? What could you have been arguing about that would lead to this?" I was curious about both his answer and the police logic.

"I have no idea. My lawyer thinks they've jumped the gun. And since we weren't arguing, I don't know what they plan to say."

"Who do you think did it then?"

"I have absolutely no idea, Ryan!" Jim shouted. "The only thing out of the ordinary was the smell. And I don't know what significance that has. If any."

While Jim's distress was real enough according to his accelerated heartbeat and breathing, he had nothing. Only an alleged woody scent to suggest the presence of anybody else. It seemed as likely that Jim was the killer as it was some unknown person in the house. Not robbing it, apparently. And without a getaway car. Too many details didn't make sense in his story. My poker face must have been slipping because both Ryan and Jim were staring at me. Ryan looked angry and Jim worried.

"I know you just met me, Evie, but I swear I'm innocent," Jim insisted.

I shrugged and Ryan's eyes narrowed.

"Of course, you are, Jim. Let's get you home." Ryan threw more than enough money on the table to cover their bill, and stood. Jim and I scrambled to join him.

An uncomfortable silence filled the car while I drove Jim home. Once we arrived, he did not invite us in. He hesitated before opening the front door. We stayed in the driveway until the porch light went off. Jim had not looked back. Ryan twisted in his seat to face me.

"What is wrong with you?" He wasn't yelling but was clearly angry.

"What?" I asked innocently, though I knew what upset him.

"He lost his wife."

"He might have killed his wife."

"Are you always this thoughtless? Or heartless?"

That hurt. "Neither," I insisted. "I'm pragmatic."

"Are you kidding me?"

"No." I kept my voice steady though his irritation was starting to get to me.

"How could you tell a grieving man he killed his wife?"

"Wait a minute. I said no such thing," I argued.

"You may as well, the way you were looking at him." Ryan faced forward, staring out the front window, hands gripping his thighs, as though trying to literally get a grip on his emotions.

"I'm sorry if I upset either of you," I finally allowed. Ryan said nothing. "I have an idea."

"What?"

"If you're so certain he's innocent, prove it."

Ryan faced me again. "What are you talking about?"

"Put your money where your mouth is. Prove that Jim is innocent." Or that he was guilty, which was what I fully expected.

"You're crazy. You think he did it."

"Then prove me wrong, too."

"Why would you want to help?"

"I believe in the truth."

Ryan's body relaxed, a smile playing on his lips. I felt that unfamiliar flutter in my belly again. Maybe I had mixed motives after all.

"How would we prove Jim innocent?"

I smiled widely. "I don't know. But, they do it on TV all the time." I dropped the smile. "It's worth trying, right?"

He shook his head but the smile told me I had won him over. "Okay, let's do it. Where do we start?"

I had no idea.

CHAPTER THREE

Ryan and I mulled over possible next steps while I drove. We arrived at his one-story three-bedroom stucco home in Henderson. Cute, but looked like at least half of all the homes in Vegas. I vastly preferred my condo. I pulled into the driveway, cut the engine, and faced Ryan before he exited the vehicle.

"I really am sorry about your friend. I wasn't trying to be mean. In my experience, people always let you down, and are never what they seem." I shrugged, dropped my gaze.

Ryan sighed and I lifted my gaze back to his. "Thank you for saying so. I'm sorry that's been your experience." His unasked question of my history hung in the silence. I ignored it.

"A tale for another time." I laughed softly.

"Do you want to come in?"

His question startled me and I hesitated to respond.

"So we can continue to brainstorm," he added as if to show no illicit intentions. Heat rushed to my face at the thought of illicit intentions. My face always showed my feelings; one of the things I had hoped would be alleviated when I became a vampire. Turned out, drinking blood meant you had the same reactions you did as a human. Sigh. Oh well.

Ryan's eyes dilated and I realized I must have sighed aloud. He tentatively reached out a hand to my cheek. A thrill raced through me. His fingers gently stroked my face. I reached up, wrapped my own fingers around his, removed his touch. Now wasn't the time. He may not realize that, but I did. His expression registered surprise.

He smiled an adorably lopsided grin. "I really would like to brainstorm."

My impish smile mirrored his. "Sounds good."

We exited the convertible and he led me to his front door. Once inside, after hitting the light switch, I scanned the immediate area. Shabby chic, I thought they called the mismatched furniture and likely thrift store finds.

"It's a rental," he explained and I chuckled.

"It's cute."

"You're generous."

We both laughed and he indicated I could lead the way into the living room. I sat on the overstuffed blue corduroy couch while he headed toward the kitchen.

"This is really comfortable," I exclaimed in surprise.

"I know, right?" he agreed from the kitchen. "Do you want anything?"

"No, thank you. I'm good," I declined. I heard noises in the kitchen.

He joined me in the living room with a glass of water, sitting opposite me in a matching overstuffed chair. He wasn't smiling now.

"I don't know what to do."

"I do," I responded triumphantly. "I had an epiphany."

"Okay, spill it."

"Let's retrace Jim's steps."

Confusion showed on Ryan's face. "Retrace his steps?"

"Taking his story at face value," I paused, holding up a hand to stop Ryan from defending his friend again. "Taking his story at face value," I repeated, "nothing seemed out of the ordinary on his block, in his home, or after the attack. I agree on this point with the police. To me, it doesn't seem like a robbery gone wrong. It seems personal. And I don't mean Jim did it." Although, I kind of did. "I mean that maybe someone they encountered that day was involved. Either because they saw something or they're actually involved in the murder."

Ryan mulled this over. "Okay, that makes sense. If we retrace his steps, we should start at the theater?"

"Yes. That's the most logical place to go. My thinking is we talk to the folks at the theater who were working that night. Depending on what we get from them, we take a look at the patrons who pre-purchased tickets, since their names would be on their orders. We see if any of them have a connection to Jim or Monica."

Ryan frowned. "I don't think we'll be able to get a list of the patrons from the theater."

"You leave that to me. I may have an in for that."

Ryan and I smiled at each other, co-conspirators on the path of good. Or something like that. He looked at his watch and made a face. "It's after midnight and I have to work tomorrow."

"No worries. I'll let you go to bed." I had an involuntary flash of being in bed with Ryan that stopped me cold. Or warm, I supposed.

"What just went through your mind?"

"Why?" I answered a question with a question, delaying a response.

"I don't know. You suddenly looked like the cat that ate the canary, to use a familiar expression."

I laughed. "That's not too far off the mark," I acknowledged without explanation. He shook his head at me but smiled. I pulled out my phone. "What's your number? I'll text you mine. Go to bed. Go to work. I'll let you know when we're ready to go to the theater tomorrow night."

His phone beeped, he confirmed receipt of my text, and then we reached the front door. He paused with his hand on the knob. "Thank you. I'm not really sure why you're helping me when I know you think Jim is guilty, but I appreciate it." He opened the door.

I stared out into the Las Vegas night before meeting his eyes with a soft smile. "I believe in the truth," was still the most honest response I could give.

CHAPTER FOUR

Around the block from Ryan's home, I pulled over to the side of the road.

Are you awake?

Within seconds, Catherine sent a reply.

Yes. Need to come over?

Yep. Be there in 20.

See you soon.

One benefit of acting was that many projects shoot at night – certainly a bonus for a vampire. It was also helpful because you had a decent chance of others still being available after midnight. Of course, it further helped that this was Las Vegas.

I loved my condo building. It was in the middle of the closest thing to downtown that Vegas had off the Strip. It sat between the Arts District and Fremont Street. All the fun artsy stuff. Plus, we had gated underground parking and 24-hour security in the lobby. I parked my convertible in its underground home and headed to the twentieth floor. I bypassed my own condo and knocked on Catherine's door. Yep. We lived down the hall from each other. I had no idea when I signed with her agency, but it's been handy being neighbors. Plus, I liked her. She'd become a good friend.

The tall willowy blond opened the door, smiled sleepily at me, and held the door open for me to enter.

"You look tired. You sure you're up for company?"

"I was getting into bed," she admitted with a yawn. "Since it's after midnight, I figured it must be important. Plus, I already poured myself wine." She closed the door behind me and I followed her to the living "room". She had essentially the mirror image of my condo – decent studio with sections for a front office, dining area, living area, kitchen along the side wall, and bedroom. She even took the wall option to create a separate bedroom, on my suggestion. Floor-to-ceiling windows encircled half the space.

We faced each other on the couch.

"Okay, I'm sufficiently intrigued. What's going on?"

I summarized meeting Ryan at the workshop and volunteering to help him prove Jim's innocence.

Catherine raised her eyebrow. "This doesn't sound like you." A statement, not a question.

"I know."

"Is it because he's hot?"

Our eyes met and we busted out laughing. She knew me so well. "Believe it or not, that's not why. Though he definitely is. And it certainly doesn't hurt." I paused. "I feel like he's deluding himself. His friend probably is guilty. He just can't see it."

"How are you so sure he's guilty?"

"His story doesn't add up. An unknown, unseen assailant in a locked, dark house kills his wife and attacks him? Please. It's like a bad movie-of-the-week."

"Or *The Fugitive*."

"I doubt this is like *The Fugitive*."

"Doth the lady protest too much?"

"Not at all."

"Hey, whatever your motivation, if it helps uncover the truth, you know I fully support that."

"I know, that's why I'm here." I smiled mischievously and Catherine grinned.

"How can I help?"

"You're on the board of the Las Vegas Independent Theatre still, right?"

She nodded.

"The last place Jim and his wife went before the attack was a show there. Ryan and I plan to go tomorrow to talk to anybody who was present that night that we can. Obviously, in terms of folks in the audience, we don't think they'd just hand that info over if we asked."

"Very true," Catherine agreed. She frowned in thought.

"I can definitely get you a list of the season ticket holders who came that night. Plus, the list of advance online ticket purchases. I should also be able to get point-of-sale credit card purchases. Really, I think I can get everybody except people who paid cash. For those, your only hope is that they came with someone who's on one of the three lists of people," she concluded.

"You'd get all that for me?"

"I'll have it for you by the time you're ready to go out tomorrow night. Um, I mean, tonight," she corrected, and we both chuckled.

"Thank you so much!" I hugged her.

"Careful, don't make me spill my wine," she cautioned me.

"Never," I responded with mock solemnity.

"I'll email you the lists. You'll have them when you get up."

"Thank you again. Seriously. This is above and beyond. I really appreciate it."

Catherine looked at me in wonder. "Of course. And you're sure this has nothing to do with Ryan's hotness?"

I smiled widely and she raised an eyebrow again. "Careful," I warned her, "or your face may stick like that."

"Nice side step."

I lifted my hands in surrender. "I want to show him the truth."

"You want to show him something," she teased suggestively.

"On that note, I think I'll take my leave."

Catherine laughed and followed me to the door.

I hugged her again goodbye and she closed the door behind me. I tried, and failed, not to think of Ryan's hazel eyes and how I felt when he looked at me. I let myself into my own condo.

Locking the door behind me, I tried, and again failed, not to imagine touching his smooth skin and how warm he'd likely feel. I bypassed most of my space, decorated with colorful furniture, artwork, and knick-knacks picked up in the past hundred years.

Removing my clothing in the bedroom, I tried, and failed a third time, not to fantasize Ryan helping me with this task.

Ok, my goodness, stop. You're not a teenager. He's just a good-looking man. You've seen plenty of those in several lifetimes. I shook my head, put on utilitarian men's pajamas, and headed back out to the living space. It was still early. I had a few hours before sun up.

Along the bank of windows opposite the bedroom, my quite technologically advanced sound system (yes, that was a joke) resided against a section of concrete wall. I carefully flipped through my collection of vinyl records, looking for the right one. Ah, perfect. I placed Billie Holiday's *Lady in Satin* on the turntable, lined the needle up at the beginning, and listened to the music flow.

Before I knew it, light shone from the sun peeking over the distant mountains. Time to go to bed and recharge. The fun would begin tonight.

CHAPTER FIVE

After nearly a century as a vampire, my body sensed when the sun was setting and I was fully recharged. I woke rested and raring to go, something I had struggled with as a human. I missed dreaming, to be honest, but when you weren't really sleeping, you couldn't really dream. Though I did need to recharge. I didn't know. I couldn't really explain it. It wasn't an exact science.

The outfit I chose for tonight was another mix of 1920s and present day. Jeans for daily wear were hands down my favorite fashion invention and I wore them most days. Today, I chose a jeweled headband holding my platinum curls in the classic 20s 'do and topped the outfit with a solid turquoise peasant top.

Warmth flooded me from the red liquid I grabbed out of the fridge on my way to the office area. Yes, I drank blood. No, I didn't kill people for it. Turned out a vampire didn't need fresh blood. I mean, it tasted better, sure. But, strictly speaking, it just had to be human. After this long on the planet, plugged in to the right sources, I got it delivered. What could I say? I knew a guy.

In a few seconds, the laptop was up and I was checking email. Catherine's popped out at number one. *Here are the lists we talked about.* She attached three documents to the email. I opened each and sent them to the printer. While the machine spat the documents out, I sent a quick text to Ryan, ignoring the surge within me, an almost electrical current that I recognized as lust. Certainly not my heart fluttering, since I didn't have a heartbeat. Definitely real interest, though, and it had been a while, to say the least. This knocked me sideways for a second. I sat with the feeling, wondering at it, almost like a child. How strange. I was excited to spend time with this human – and my goal was to show him his friend was a killer. Hmm. That did not bode well, I supposed.

I refocused on my phone and texted Ryan.

Are you still free tonight for the theater?

Yep.

Bring your laptop…

Will do.

Pick you up in 20?

See you then.

A glance out the window confirmed the sun had not quite set and I grimaced. I grabbed the papers off the printer, my purse off the hook by the door, and headed downstairs to the parking garage. Once in the convertible, I headed to pick up Ryan.

The few remaining rays of the waning daylight stung when they reached me through the front windshield. Contrary to popular belief, vampires could be exposed to sunlight. It hurt. It also drained. But it didn't kill. Unless it was extended, I supposed. I had no real idea. I certainly wasn't going to test that theory – and I didn't know anybody else who was either. I sighed. And unfortunately, unless I wanted to get pulled over every time I hit the road, I couldn't darken the front windshield as much as the other windows.

Thankfully, the sun had almost set by the time I reached Ryan's house. I parallel parked at the curb and walked with almost no pain up to his front door to ring the bell. I smiled when he opened the door and he reflected that back. We held this tableau a hair longer than was comfortable and then we both broke the gaze. Good grief, we were like teenagers.

"Are you ready?"

"Yes, I am," he responded to my back. I was already heading to the car. Once seated, I handed him the lists I received from Catherine.

"She was able to get everything we asked for," I explained excitedly. "We can show the names to Jim, see if he recognizes anybody. We can run the names down ourselves, see if someone has a connection to Jim that he may not be aware of. But first…" I paused.

"It's off to the theater," he finished my statement with an accented dramatic flourish. Actors. We couldn't help ourselves.

We smiled again at each other. I tore my eyes from his lips and faced the road. Get a grip, girl.

CHAPTER SIX

"Hey, Evie," the woman behind the ticket counter called out after we opened the door to the theater.

"Hi, Gail," I responded. Ryan and I approached the desk. "This is Ryan. I don't know if you've met."

"No," Ryan confirmed. "It's nice to meet you, Gail."

"Likewise." Gail looked at me. "What can I do for you guys? Tickets for the weekend?"

"Maybe after. Has Catherine talked to you?"

"No, should she have?"

"Ryan and I are investigating the murder of Monica Freeman."

Gail's eyes widened and she lowered her voice. "Wasn't her husband arrested for that?"

Ryan bristled beside me and I touched his hand to both comfort and silence him. It worked. "Well, we're trying to find out if the right person was arrested."

"Catherine can't stay out of the crime fighting business, can she?" Gail laughed. She was correct, of course; Catherine fell in love with this stuff after her own experiences earlier this year.

I smiled. "No, she can't. She's helping us out. She said we could talk to anybody who was here that night."

"I was here that night," Gail quickly clarified, then frowned. "Although I don't know what I can contribute." Her face brightened. "On the other hand, I can say for certain that Jim and Monica looked very much in love."

"What makes you say that?"

"You know. They kept touching each other. Not in a creepy inappropriate way," she explained with an eye roll. "Just, you know, holding hands, pecks on the lips, that kind of stuff. I was working the ticket counter, like now, so I saw when they arrived, when they got snacks at intermission, and when they left at the end of the night."

"I'm impressed you noticed and remembered all of that," I commented, though secretly I didn't see how she could have. There would have been about one hundred or so people here that night and, frankly, Jim wasn't that memorable. I mean, he's surfer-boy cute, but still.

"Normally I wouldn't have," Gail acknowledged. "They didn't have tickets for the performance, though, and when they came up here to buy them, they were so cute and flirty that I paid attention to them after that. I like happy couples."

Okay, that made sense. I pondered for a moment. "Let's take a different tack. Did anything stand out that night? Anything at all, positive or negative?"

Gail bit her lip while she thought. Ryan and I waited. Tension radiated off his body. He was really putting a lot of stock in this. I felt a smidge of guilt over my ulterior motive and then dismissed it. Either Jim would turn out to be guilty or not. Gail released her lip and smiled uncertainly.

"I'm not sure if it's important. Several people left the theater during intermission. Not just stepped out to smoke, actually left."

This caught my attention. "Why did that stand out? I've seen people leave at intermission before. The show isn't for them."

Gail nodded. "Absolutely. It stood out for two reasons. One, because when a couple of them left, I could really smell the cologne on one of them. It smelled like I was suddenly in a meadow." She chuckled at the memory. "Way overpowering."

"Could the smell also be described as woody?" Ryan asked this with such intensity that Gail's smile faltered in confusion.

"Um, I guess so," she allowed.

Ryan turned to me triumphantly. "There you go."

"Simmer down, big boy," I cautioned him. "It's just a lead."

"No," he argued, "it supports Jim's story."

I could see Gail was lost by this conversation and I also realized I wasn't interested in starting rumors, so I turned to her, effectively cutting off Ryan's train of thought.

"As Ryan says, that's helpful. You said there were two reasons the people leaving at intermission stood out," I prompted.

The redirect worked and Gail focused on me. "Yes! There was this guy. He was dressed like he was going to Broadway. Full tuxedo, the whole nine yards. He looked fabulous."

I frowned and Gail stopped. "No, sorry, it's nothing, please continue." The description reminded me of my ex-husband and I very much wanted to forget him. I pushed the memory away.

"Anyway, he looked great. And irritated. He practically stalked out of here."

"Was he with anyone in particular?"

"Despite the outfit, I somehow missed his arrival. I don't know if he came with someone or not. He seemed to leave alone. Although maybe that was why he looked irritated," she laughed. "Maybe his date didn't go well."

Ah, bad dates. Gail and I shared a girls' moment.

"Could you tell who was the source of the woody smell?"

Gail appeared confused by Ryan's question.

"He's back on the smell you noticed. The meadow, or woody, smell. Could you tell who was wearing the cologne?" I clarified.

"No," she said with a shake of her head. "Sorry, I couldn't." She paused. "Although, I can narrow it down. I smelled it at the beginning of intermission and then it faded."

"Maybe that means it was one of the people who left early?" I finished the thought for her.

"Yes!"

"That's very helpful, thank you, Gail."

We said our goodbyes and continued the tour of questions. Unfortunately, we learned nothing new.

The woman manning the concession area didn't remember Jim and Monica, didn't notice a smell because she had a cold that night, though she did remember a tall, good-looking man in a tuxedo.

Since a pick-up rehearsal was in full swing, the actors from that night were in the theater. Unfortunately, they were even less help. That night had been opening weekend, so they were focused on the show, and they remembered nothing out of the ordinary.

Ryan and I headed back to the car to regroup.

"Now we have a few things to look for when we cull through the lists Catherine gave us," I said.

"And we have confirmation of the woody smell."

"Yes, we do," I agreed.

"What do you think we should do next?"

I was flattered that Ryan thought I knew what I was doing. I had been flying by the seat of my pants the entire time. But, I did have an idea. "I have two thoughts. First, I'll forward you the lists for you to forward to Jim."

"He can read through them and tell us if he recognizes anybody."

"Yep. Though it'll be important for him not to dismiss anyone as a possible suspect; if he recognizes a name, he needs to tell us. Otherwise, we could completely miss something," I warned.

"Makes sense. And second?"

"Time for some internet sleuthing. We split the names up and google all of them. See if anybody pops up as memorable or remarkable in any way. Once we've narrowed the list to those folks, plus anybody who doesn't have an internet footprint—"

"People like that exist?" Ryan quipped.

I laughed and continued. "Then we go visit those people."

Ryan nodded. "Let's go find a murderer."

Or prove they already found him.

CHAPTER SEVEN

Ryan and I approached my condo door. My nerves fluttered. Why on earth was I anxious? It wasn't like I hadn't brought a man home before. Or several dozen — hey, I'd been single for many decades. Still.

I unlocked the door and my hand hesitated before I pushed it open to grant Ryan entry first. I followed behind, focused on the lock, and not on his butt in his jeans. Argh. What was wrong with me?

The man was fine, for sure.

He politely paused inside the door until I flipped the lock and could lead the way.

"Welcome to my humble abode," I announced with a sweep of my arm. I saw his eyes rove as we walked all the way into the condo. I pointed out the various created sections of the condo and his eyes followed my finger.

"Nice place. That view is spectacular."

"Thanks. It's the main reason I bought it," I acknowledged. "Plus, the neighbors are great. It's a colorful building. And, Catherine lives down the hall."

"Catherine Rodham? Our agent?"

"Yep," I nodded, then frowned slightly. "Though, I don't know if that's common knowledge, so don't tell anyone."

"My lips are sealed," he assured me and we shared a smile.

O-kay, time to focus.

"I thought we could work at the table," I explained, gesturing to the rustic wooden dining table. Ryan nodded and began setting up his laptop, while I grabbed mine off my desk to join him. We sat across from each other.

"I'll send the lists to Jim right now." He typed slowly and methodically. He would never win a typing contest.

"Sounds good, let me know the instant he responds back."

"Will do."

"In the meantime, let's divvy up the names we have and start plugging them into Google."

"Sounds good to me. I can start with the season-ticket holders," Ryan offered.

"And I'll start with the credit card pre-sales."

We smiled at each other before focusing on our screens. His long legs managed to bump my average ones enough that part of me wondered if he was doing it on purpose. Could he be playing footsies? Surely not. Probably just a coincidence. Probably.

About forty-five minutes later, I stood to stretch. Internet searching was not that exciting. And so far, we'd come up with bupkis. Nada.

Ryan's eyes lit up. "Email from Jim."

I walked behind him to read over his shoulder. He smelled good, fresh. Ryan opened the email and we scanned Jim's response. Ryan's shoulders slumped. I returned to my seat.

"He only recognizes a few and doesn't think any of them could be involved."

"We'll run them down anyway," I assured him and he half-smiled.

"Thanks."

Ryan and I quickly concurred with Jim's opinion and eliminated the people he knew as suspects. Mainly because we could not for the life of us come up with any motive. That was how we were eliminating almost everybody at this point.

For the season-ticket holders, most of them were older and retired. Why would they want to see Monica dead? For the advanced credit-card sales, that demographic skewed younger, but still we struggled to identify a connection to Jim, let alone a motive. It wasn't until we were reviewing the final list of names, the walk-up day-of credit card sales, that I saw a name that left me nauseous. Not sure how that could happen to a vampire. Curdled the blood still coursing from my pre-dinner drink?

I didn't think the man had a connection to Jim and Monica. He definitely had a connection to me.

"See someone interesting?" Ryan asked this casually but I breathed in sharply. That got his attention. "What is it? Something promising?"

I heard the lift in his voice and I hated to disappoint him. I shook my head and watched his optimism deflate.

"Just a name I hadn't expected to see."

Now he was clearly curious.

I opened my mouth to explain and nothing came out. I was rarely speechless.

"Is everything okay?"

"Why wouldn't it be?" My flippant response seemed mean given the genuine concern I heard in his voice. I didn't know if I could talk about it.

"Ex-boyfriend?"

He offered this as a joke to lighten the mood but he was too close to a bullseye. And he could see that.

"Hey, no worries. You don't have to talk about it." He held up his hands like stop signs. "Unless you want to."

"Um, not ex-boyfriend," I started. "Ex-husband." The phrase squeaked out.

Ryan's eyebrows shot skyward. "Ex-husband? Oh."

"I haven't seen him in … years." I paused. "He doesn't live in Vegas. I don't know why he would have been at the show the night of Monica's murder." He couldn't possibly be involved, could he?

Ryan's eyes narrowed, so my horrible poker face let something slip. "Could he be involved? Is that at all a possibility?" His white knuckles betrayed his tension.

Seeing him grip the side of the dining room table, I realized I had to be at least a little bit forthcoming.

I closed my eyes and gave my head a small positive shake. "Yeah, it's possible. He's not the—" I stopped, unsure what to say. "Yeah, it's possible," I repeated.

"He's our only lead," Ryan said softly. "We need to talk to him."

"I'll find him. I'll talk to him," I responded firmly. "You can chase down these last couple of names we can't account for."

Ryan's expression objected to the arrangement, but he remained quiet.

I checked my watch. "It's just after 11 p.m. Do you have to work tomorrow?"

"Yes," Ryan sighed. "I can try to leave early to work on these five names. What about you?"

"I'll track down my ex and talk to him. We'll touch base once we have the information. Probably tomorrow after work."

Ryan's lips tightened. "I guess that'll have to do."

I smiled hesitantly. "It'll be okay. We'll have a better idea of our next steps tomorrow."

"I hope so. Let me know if you need me." I bit my lower lip and he blushed. "Um, need me to help you handle your ex."

"Oh, him, I'll be fine," I said, unconvincingly.

"Are you sure? If there's a chance he's involved, could he be dangerous? Are you sure you don't want me to come along?"

"Slow down, hero," I said with a grin. "I appreciate the concern. It'll be fine. If I need anything, I'll absolutely reach out," I assured him. This seemed to mollify him at least a little bit.

"Okay. You have my number," he reminded me.

"I know." I reached across the table to rest my hand on his arm. He took my hand in his. We held hands for a long moment. I enjoyed his warmth and the increase in his heart rate. Our eyes met over the table, both of us questioning what we were doing. I released his hand and stood. "I'll walk you out."

He jumped up, knocking the chair against the table. "I guess that's my cue," he responded with a wink.

"That's not what I meant!"

"I know. However, you're right, I do need to get going. Don't you have to work tomorrow?"

I'd been waiting for this question. After decades of investing, I didn't have to work. I was an actress because it was fun, not because I needed the money. However, I wasn't going to say anything to Ryan about that.

"Nope," I said with a quick shake of my head. "Just waiting to hear from Catherine about my next audition." I saw his curiosity about my ability to afford this condo and, well, life, without a regular gig. Vegas had a low cost of living, but it wasn't free. He said nothing though and we walked to the door. I opened it and he hesitated.

"Thanks again for helping me with this," he said softly.

"Of course. Like I said before, I believe in truth." Even painful truth. Although the more time I spent with Ryan, the more I hoped I might be wrong. Imagining how crushed he would be to get confirmation that Jim was actually the killer pained me.

On the other hand, maybe he needed to learn that lesson. You couldn't trust people. My ex-husband being in town was yet more proof of that.

"Goodnight Ryan." I wondered for a moment if he was going to kiss me, the energy between us pulsed so strong. His eyes dilated and we stared a moment. I broke eye contact first.

"Goodnight, Evie. I'll talk to you tomorrow." He leaned in for a hug – man, he felt good – and then he was gone, taking his heat with him. I watched him walk to the elevator for a moment, enjoying the view. He turned to offer a half-wave, caught the line of my gaze and wolfishly grinned. My face flushed, and I laughed before closing the door. I could hear him chuckling. The elevator doors pinged.

If I had a heartbeat, it'd be racing, I'm sure.

I leaned against the door, breathing deeply. Strictly speaking, I didn't need to breathe. I could force air in and out my lungs, though, and some habits were ingrained. Even after all these years, I found deep breathing calming, even if biologically it did nothing for me.

Shaking off the impact of Ryan and his departure, I strode to my bedroom. Time to change clothing.

If Derek was in town, he'd be hitting the nightclubs.

CHAPTER EIGHT

After flaming out at the typical nightclubs, I struck pay dirt. I stood at the bar, vibrating to the pulsing music, scanning the dancefloor through the fake fog and laser lights. Other vampires surrounded me. I drank an AB-negative cocktail – it was expensive because it was the rarest but, man, did it taste sweet.

And then I spotted him. Derek stood out wherever he went. The tallest man in the room, with a very flamboyant style. He was holding court with a bevy of beauties, also not uncommon for him. Since he hadn't seen me yet, I took a moment to consider him.

Derek Smith. Yes, that was his real last name. He kept it all these years because it was so ordinary. At 6'5" tall, with black hair, eyes so brown they appeared black, and alabaster skin, wearing black leather pants that showed every contour and a white button-down shirt with the first three buttons undone, he looked like a rock star. I watched him with a mixture of appreciation for his frozen-in-time good looks and revulsion for his complete amorality. Not that the vamps around him cared.

Eventually, he registered that someone outside that cooing group of, well, groupies, was aware of him. He looked around with a seductive smile, trying to identify if the person watching was more important or better looking than the women around him. I observed the change in his expression when our eyes met.

Good grief, he looked happy to see me. Really? After everything?

Derek made a beeline for me, to the consternation of the women, who immediately started casing for a replacement.

"Why are you in town?" was my caustic greeting. I had zero interest in being nice to this narcissist.

"To see you, of course," he responded in a low voice, likely intended to go with the seductive look. As if any of that worked on me.

I rolled my eyes and his smile dropped a bit. "Not likely," I retorted. "Why are you really in town?"

He moved closer and I caught a whiff of something. And then it was absorbed by the multitude of other smells in the nightclub.

"No, really, I am," he insisted, reaching a hand out to touch my cheek. He frowned when I jerked away from his touch. "Now, now, is that any way to greet your husband?"

"Ex," I hissed. "Don't touch me. I'll ask one more time. Why are you really here?"

Derek took a step back and held his arms open wide. "I really am here to win you back. I've missed you. The other reason I'm here is to film a movie."

"Film a movie? Since when are you in the movie business?"

He winked. "I was bored. I got involved with some guys. I'm financing their movie."

"You're a producer?" I asked this with a hint of irritation. He was poaching in my territory now.

"Yep," he answered with a grin. "It's fun. I provide the money, so I'm in charge. And I'm surrounded by beautiful actresses."

I rolled my eyes again, which was not lost on him.

"Hey, until I get you back, a vampire's got to have a little fun."

I mirthlessly laughed. "You do you. But, since apparently decades of experience have yet to sink in. There is zero chance you will ever get me back. Zero," I added for emphasis, since he apparently could add delusional to his list of zany attributes.

He looked wounded. "I've changed, Evie. I finally see what I've done wrong. And I want to do better. For you. For us."

He sounded so earnest. Someone without my years of experience likely would fall for it.

"Stop, Derek. You're embarrassing yourself."

Derek's eyes narrowed. I knew that would strike a chord and I was right.

"Don't be like that." He smoothed out his face. "I'm just being friendly."

"Sure. Whatever," I responded flippantly. I didn't know if he was here to produce a movie or to get me back, or some other reason he had not disclosed. Since he seemed to have been at the theater the night Jim and Monica were attacked, I needed to focus on my purpose in seeking him out to begin with – it certainly wasn't to verbally spar with him until I wanted to vomit.

"Fine," I said with a nicer tone. "What have you been doing since you've been in town?"

He appeared surprised by my conciliatory tone but went with it. I supposed because it fit in with his unshakable belief that he was irresistible. "A little of this and a little of that."

"That sounds fun," was my sarcastic response. "Any new clubs, shows, anything like that?"

My sly attempt to ask about the theater worked and he blathered on about the things he had been doing. I was only half-listening, waiting for something useful in the litany of descriptions of females he'd been with. And then he said what I'd been waiting for.

"And I went to this show at the Las Vegas Independent Theatre."

"Oh, what show did you see?"

He frowned. "I don't remember the name. It wasn't very memorable." He laughed.

"You watched an entire show yet can't remember the name of it." I tried for a teasing tone because his response could be critical.

"Not an entire show," he corrected me. "I left at intermission. Because it was so bad," he clarified.

"I gathered that, Captain Obvious." He frowned, so I hurriedly continued. "You know, I had friends who went to see that show."

"Oh yeah." It was clear he didn't care.

"Maybe you saw them? Either that night or later on the news. Jim and Monica. They were attacked that night in their home."

"Wow, that's terrible. I don't remember meeting anybody with those names."

Most humans would not have noticed the subtle change on Derek's face, it came and went so quickly. Except, I wasn't a human. And, I had history with the man. He knew something, I was sure of it.

"You didn't see anything about it on the news?" I pushed a little.

"No, I didn't. I don't watch the news." His answer was curt and his look more glacial and less seductive now.

I definitely hit a nerve. He smiled suddenly. "I have to go," he said, gesturing vaguely behind him. "I'll be in touch. I told you why I'm really here. This isn't over."

No, it most definitely was not, I silently told his back while he walked away from me. Not by a long shot. And not just because he clearly knew something. Also because I got another whiff of the *something* from earlier. A woody scent. Like Jim smelled the night of the murder.

CHAPTER NINE

Are you awake?

I sent the text to Catherine, chuckling a little. This was getting to be a habit. But, I needed her help again. Besides, it was only just after midnight. I was sure she was awake.

Yep. Come on over.

Smiling, I exited my convertible and headed for the parking garage elevator. In mere minutes, I stood in front of Catherine's door, knocking.

She answered with a smile. "This is getting to be a habit," she joked.

"Did you read my mind?"

Shaking her head with a laugh, she held the door open for me to enter. I walked straight for the couch. I stared at the Las Vegas skyline for a beat while Catherine sat next to me, tucking her legs under her.

"What can I do to help?"

"First, thank you again for getting me the lists of the patrons for the theater."

She waved this off. "Of course. You know, anything I can do to help." She stared at me pointedly.

"Second," I continued with a laugh, "Ryan and I eliminated almost everybody on the lists. He has five names we couldn't truly account for, so he's going to knock those out after work tomorrow. I mean, later today. That still doesn't account for any cash buyers," I said with a single-shoulder shrug, "but there's nothing we can do about them anyway. Plus," I said slowly, "we have a new lead."

Catherine heard the change in my voice. "Who? Is it someone we know?"

"Someone I knew," I answered, unable to disguise the bitterness. Catherine knew I was a vampire. She didn't know my story. That wasn't about to change tonight.

"Who?" she asked again, worried now.

I sighed dramatically, deliberately, trying to ease the tension. "My ex-husband."

"Your ex-husband? I didn't know you had been married."

"It was a long time ago. A long, long, *long* time ago," I added for emphasis.

"Oh, I get it. He's a vampire?"

"Yep."

"How can I help then?"

I silently thanked her for not asking additional questions. "His name is Derek Smith. And, yes, before you ask, that was his human name too. Smith makes a good alias, but some people really did – do – have that as their name." I smiled and she laughed. "He says he's here to produce a movie. Some kind of paranormal thing about vampires." Her eyes widened and she jumped up, startling me.

"I got an email about something like that," she called over her shoulder while she headed for her desk. I turned in my seat to watch her flip open the laptop and start tapping. "Yes, here it is. The working title is *Vampire Nights*. That's creative," she said as an aside. "Anyway, they're seeking actor submissions. Oh, now I get it." She realized why I was there. "You want me to submit you for an audition?"

"Me and Ryan," I amended. "I'm certain I'll get an audition, but I'd like to try to get Ryan on set."

"How are you so certain you'll get the audition?" she asked, lasering in on me when she returned to the couch.

I avoided eye contact. "Derek says he isn't here only for the movie."

"And?"

I sighed. "He says he's here to win me back." I snorted and Catherine laughed.

"Is that a possibility?"

My jaw dropped at the question. "Ugh, not at all. Derek and I have a—" I paused. "Complicated history," I finished. "There is no chance I'd take him back."

"Then you must want on the set for another reason?"

"I tracked Derek to an underground paranormal nightclub earlier tonight. That's when he told me about the movie and wanting to win me back. But, there was more," I said excitedly. "One, I've known him too long. I know he was hiding something. Two, he smelled woody. Exactly like Jim said his house smelled."

"Do you think Derek is the killer?" Catherine appeared confused and I couldn't blame her.

"Honestly, I don't know what to think. Derek has no motive that I can guess, at this point anyway. Jim still looks like the most likely suspect. On the other hand, Derek is hiding something and smelled like Jim described. On the other, other hand," I said with a smile, "playing devil's advocate. If Jim smelled the scent at the theater and not really in the house, that would be a good non-clue to provide to try to throw people off the, um, scent, so to speak."

Catherine chuckled at my statement but nodded. "Yeah, any of that could be the case. I can see why you want to be on set."

"Time to put my detective skills to work," I said, rubbing my hands together like an excited child.

"You have detective skills?" Catherine asked this and I threw a pillow at her. I rose to leave before she could kick me out, and we both paused when a tentative knock sounded at her door.

"Robin, what can I do for you?" Catherine asked the woman standing on the other side of her open door. She pitched her voice pleasant but not exactly welcoming. I stood a few steps behind her and wondered about Robin's presence.

I knew about Catherine's encounters during the serial murders last spring with Robin Landon – and the woman who pulled her marionette strings, Councilwoman Barbara Knollman.

"I'm glad I caught you both here," the slight woman began, and I laughed. She frowned at me.

"You showed up unannounced in the middle of the night – in a building with 24-hour security – without knowing we were here? Please," Catherine snorted derisively.

Robin ignored our rudeness and continued speaking, voice smooth. "A certain interested party is aware that the two of you are investigating the Monica Freeman murder—"

"We know you work for the Councilwoman," Catherine mumbled and I didn't have to see her face to know she did a hard eye roll. I'd had enough of this cloak and dagger nonsense.

"You mean the demon," I corrected Catherine and her mouth dropped open. Robin looked nonplussed. "Oh yeah, I guess you didn't know," I added with a wide smile. I stepped in front of Catherine. "And, our girl here is officially a minion."

Robin bristled at the word, eyes glittering angrily. "That's offensive."

"I'm not too politically correct about demons," I retorted. I could hear Catherine spluttering to herself behind me about demons. I turned and placed my hand on her arm and made eye contact.

"I'm a vampire and you're dating a half-incubus; can you really be so surprised that the head of the city council is a demon with minions?"

Catherine shrugged a shoulder. "When you put it that way..." She and I turned to face Robin. "What does the Councilwoman want?" Catherine asked.

"She has a vested interest in your investigation."

My eyes narrowed. "Why?"

"I'm not at liberty to say."

I laughed. "Probably because you don't actually know," I responded, meaner than normal. I'd never liked the minion. I sighed. "Apologies for my rudeness," I backtracked. "Do you have a specific question for me or Catherine?"

Catherine's mouth dropped open again at my conciliatory tone and offer to answer questions. She hadn't learned yet; Barbara Knollman was easier to handle if you let her have the small things.

"We know Catherine gave you theater patron lists. We also know that you and Derek were seen out together tonight. What is his involvement in the murder?"

I inwardly cringed. Of course, this was really about Derek. "We don't know yet," I answered honestly. "What does Barbara want with him?"

"I'll let the councilwoman know," Robin responded to my statement and ignored my question; she inclined her head slightly and then turned silently to head toward the elevator.

"What was that about?" Catherine asked once the elevator door closed and Robin began her downward descent.

"I don't know, but we need to have a talk with security about letting just anybody up here without calling first."

Catherine's barked laugh held a note of hysteria in it. I closed her door and placed a hand on her shoulder.

"Everything okay?"

She opened and closed her mouth a couple of times, processing. "You're correct I'm aware of the supernatural underworld, including vampires and incubi," she enunciated slowly. "But, demons with actual minions?"

The high pitch of her voice asking that question worried me and I hugged her.

"Catherine? An incubus is a demon, remember? Like Alex, your half-incubus boyfriend?"

She nodded. "Can you explain the demon and minion thing again?"

"I don't know much, except that the councilwoman showed up a couple of decades ago. She quickly ascended to running things, on the council and in the paranormal world." I waved a hand dismissively. "I don't think she's high in the demon hierarchy—"

"Demon hierarchy?"

"Um, yeah, I think that's what it's called. Vampires don't really get involved in the political stuff. Well, the heads of vampire families do," I corrected myself. "That's not me." I smiled.

"What about Robin?"

"She does the councilwoman's bidding. Which you already knew. I don't know her story."

Catherine nodded and took a ragged breath. "Okay."

I hugged her again. "I wish I knew their interest in the murder and my ex-husband."

CHAPTER TEN

I checked my phone after I completed recharging the next evening. A flurry of texts awaited. Most were from Catherine and Ryan. I ignored the lift I felt seeing Ryan's name. Get it together. This wasn't a romantic comedy.

I was pleased to see Catherine had confirmed the auditions. Oh shoot, they were tonight. I texted her back, thanking her again, and assuring her that I'd be there.

Ryan sent several texts.

12:30 p.m. *Catherine says I have an audition tonight. Did you get one too?*

1:30 p.m. *I just noticed that the producer's name is Derek. Is that your ex?*

3:30 p.m. *Is everything okay? Did anything happen last night?*

4:30 p.m. *The audition is tonight at 7p. If you weren't invited, maybe you can still crash it. Text or call me…*

It was 5:19 p.m. now. I felt bad Ryan had been worried, and maybe a little happy he'd been thinking of me. I texted him back immediately.

Hey Ryan! Sorry for the delay in responding. Got in late and slept most of the day :) Yes, Catherine sent me the same text. And, yes, that's my ex. I'll explain when I pick you up in an hour. I assume you'd like a ride to the audition?

Ryan must have had his phone right next to him. I received a response before I could even place the cellphone back on the side table. I was still in bed and needed to get up to prepare for the audition.

So glad to hear from you. Yes, would love a ride to the audition. Def curious to know how your ex is involved…

I deliberately ignored the unasked question in the text since I already told Ryan he'd hear all about it in the car.

Sounds good. See you soon!

Ryan responded with a thumbs-up emoji and now I knew I could set the phone down to get ready. Choosing what outfit to wear was a bit of a dilemma. I was confident Derek would cast me regardless, if he was telling the truth that his agenda was to win me back, though I shuddered at that. I didn't want to mislead him in any way, shape, or form by dressing sexy. But I couldn't really wear a burlap sack to an audition.

I sighed and chose to go with my standard audition outfit: dark blue jeans, green t-strap heels, pale green crepe de chine embroidered short-sleeve blouse over a spaghetti strap camisole, with a matching cloche hat. Although consisting of replicas, this outfit, except the jeans, was so reminiscent of my 1920s clothing that I always felt the most comfortable in it. Hence why I wore it to auditions. Even if I didn't need the money, every actress wanted to be cast.

I carefully applied my natural makeup and dark red lipstick. Contrary to popular belief, most women in the 1920s did not do their makeup crazy heavy like in the movies. Other than the red lips, we kept it pretty light and basic.

I texted Ryan to let him know I was on my way. A short time later, I pulled into his driveway. I started to exit the vehicle when his front door opened. I pulled my door closed and watched him walk toward me. Man, he looked good. He'd opted for a blue short-sleeve knit top and dark blue jeans with, I think, brown boots. He looked good enough to eat. Well, not like that. I didn't drink fresh human blood, remember?

Ryan's pupils dilated when he entered the car and I knew it was a case of mutual admiration. The sexual tension in the car rolled around the enclosed space, nearly overwhelming; he coughed. Nervously. I heard his heartbeat accelerating.

I smiled. He smiled back. And just like that, the tension dissipated. For the time being at least.

"I'm glad you got the audition too," Ryan started off, then made a face. "Although, I'm guessing you were a slam dunk for it, right?"

"Yeah."

"Are you responsible for my audition too?"

"Yes and no," I answered truthfully. "I asked Catherine to submit you for it, yes. Though, she likely would have anyway. And neither of us had any control over whether or not Derek would select you to audition."

"Wouldn't he have a casting director to do that?"

I nodded. "Oh sure, but I have no doubt that he's the one calling the shots. He's a bit of a control freak." This was a massive understatement.

"Hmm. Okay," Ryan responded, looking like he wanted to ask a follow up question. Interestingly, he chose not to. "I'm glad we both get to go. Tell me why it's so important that we do. Is it related to Jim and Monica?"

"It seems to be," I hedged.

"What happened last night?" His face pinched like he was choking on a sour lemon when he asked this and I laughed.

"I'm sorry to laugh, but you should see yourself. Trust me, I did not enjoy talking to Derek. I finally tracked him down and we had a mercifully brief conversation. He explained that he's in town doing this movie. I could tell he was hiding something."

"How?"

"It's just something you learn after knowing somebody for so long," I answered with a non-answer. "The reason I think he may know something was his smell. He smelled woody."

"Exactly like Jim described." Ryan thought for a moment. "Do you think he could be the killer?"

"Honestly, I don't know. I have no idea what his motive would be." I chose not to share the alternative theory that Jim smelled the scent at the theater and was using it for misdirection. I was fairly confident that Ryan would not be receptive to this theory. "The only way to find out more is to be around him; the movie set is the easiest way to do that naturally."

"I agree. Good thinking."

"Let's head on over then." I headed toward the strip mall location of the audition. "One more thing," I said with as offhand a tone as I could muster. "When we get there, you should go in ahead of me and we should act like we don't know each other."

"Why?"

"If we're going to be poking around on set, we need to make sure that we both get cast and it's best that he not know we're together." I had a feeling this partial answer would not be satisfactory.

"And, I ask again, why?" He sounded genuinely perplexed.

"We don't want him to know we're investigating him," I answered, and it sounded lame even to my own ears.

"That doesn't make any sense," Ryan argued. "People in this town know and talk to each other at auditions and on set all the time. There would be no reason for him to suspect that we're investigating him."

A quick glance in his direction showed me his eyes had narrowed.

"What aren't you telling me?"

Asked a direct question, I refused to lie. I sighed instead. "When I talked with Derek yesterday, he said he had an ulterior motive for getting involved with this movie." I paused and Ryan waited for me to continue.

"And?" He prompted me with the question after a long silence.

I rolled my eyes. "Ugh, he says he wants to win me back." I heard Ryan's heartbeat accelerate and knew he did not like this news.

"Really," was all he said.

"He has no chance," I assured Ryan, though was unsure why I cared so much. Yes, we obviously were attracted to each other. But, we were focused on clearing Jim's name. Well, Ryan was. The jury was still out on that for me.

"He doesn't?"

"Not. At. All."

Ryan laughed, low and sexy. "Good."

I saw the two-story building ahead and used that as the perfect distraction to the tension.

"We're here," I announced cheerily. I pulled into a parking spot and killed the engine. I turned to face Ryan, who had done the same. "You go in first. I'll wait five minutes. Then I'll go in."

"And you're sure this is necessary?"

"Trust me. It's much easier this way. If Derek thinks we're together, you'll never get cast. I can promise you that."

Ryan shook his head. "Okay. I'll see you inside."

He exited the vehicle and I watched his backside while he entered the ground floor storefront. Dang, the man looked good coming and going.

CHAPTER ELEVEN

Exactly five minutes later, I swung open my car door and prepared to snoop, I mean, audition. Once inside the building, I saw a young woman behind a desk and a few people sitting on chairs around the room. I avoided looking at Ryan. Everyone held audition sides, preparing.

"Hi, you're here to audition," the cheerful woman behind the desk stated. I idly wondered if she was a production assistant or casting assistant.

"Yes," I confirmed.

"Please sign in and take the appropriate sides for the character you'd like to audition for," she instructed, indicating a clipboard and two rows of single sheets of paper.

I signed-in on the appropriate line, noting Ryan's was the only one above me. That was bad. If there was a side with a couple, we might end up auditioning together.

Derek wasn't stupid. His animal instincts were strong; he'd notice the sexual tension. I quickly reviewed the available sides and saw that, unfortunately, there was only one character I was right for. The romantic lead. I sighed and snatched the side off the table.

I sat on a hard, plastic chair, reading over the selected scene's dialogue. A young man came through a door next to the reception desk. He checked the clipboard and called out the name before Ryan's. I gave Derek credit; at least the audition was running smoothly. It was such a crap shoot in this town, pun intended. Some auditions, you were in and out within thirty minutes. Others, the ones we described as *cattle calls* in the industry, could result in hours of waiting. Those sucked.

The owner of the name followed the young man and five minutes later returned. Checking the clipboard, the young man called out Ryan's name and he disappeared behind the door. Five minutes later, they both came out. Except that, instead of leaving, Ryan retook his seat. Shoot. Sometimes I hated when I was right.

The young man, who smelled like a vampire, I realized, called my name. He introduced himself as Orlando. I smiled broadly, confirmed my identity, and followed him through the door. We walked down a short hallway to a larger room. There was an X on the floor, a camera on a tripod five feet in front of it, and four people sitting in a ragged half-circle behind the camera.

"Evelyn Jones," the young vampire announced and then faded into the background.

This obviously wasn't my first time at an audition. I handed my headshot and resume to the person holding her hand out, and walked over to the big X. I was curious to see how Derek handled this. He sat closest to the camera, watched me through dark eyes.

"Hi, Evie," Derek called out. "So glad you could make it to the audition."

I smiled my biggest, fakest, actress smile at him. "Of course. Glad to be here, Derek."

"Show us what you got," he encouraged, "though I know you got it." He winked lecherously at me and I was pleased I refrained from gagging in response. The others in the room, not understanding the undercurrent, chuckled like the sycophants they likely were. Newbie vampires. Ugh.

I performed the side as requested. The woman sitting beside Derek gave a redirect. I performed the side again. Everyone smiled.

"Thanks for coming in, Evie. If you'll wait out front, we'll have you read with one or two of the other actors," Derek said.

"Of course, thank you." Then I was back in the waiting room. The occupants had dwindled to me, Ryan, and another couple. My guess was I'd read with each of the men. And I was right. Soon, only Ryan and I remained in the waiting area. We'd done a good job ignoring each other, but I was a little anxious about how reading with him would go.

Orlando entered the room. "Evelyn and Ryan? We're ready for you."

Ryan and I looked at each other, smiled at the vampire, and followed him back through the door. Here went nothing. Or everything.

The female vampire I previously handed my headshot to indicated where Ryan and I should stand. "From the top," Derek intoned dramatically, and we began.

I stared into Ryan's eyes, embodying the words I was reading. So did he. His voice was husky, his eyes dilated as we read. I mirrored his physicality. He was good. We went through the entire scene. I'll admit it helped doing a romantic scene when you were already attracted to someone. We finished and remained staring at each other, for a beat too long apparently. Someone coughed.

We tore our eyes from each other and looked out at the half circle. I noticed with mild alarm that Derek now wore a half-frown. The female vampire, however, was smiling.

"That was fantastic," she crowed.

"Yes," Derek slowly agreed. "That was quite good." His eyes narrowed. "Have the two of you worked together before?"

"No," we responded in unison, and I inwardly sighed. The answer was true, but who spoke at the same time? Couples did, that's who.

The expression on Derek's face hardened at our response and I realized I needed to do something now or the plan would be over before it started.

"No," I repeated, "but it'll be nice working with *you*." I hated the saccharine tone in my voice and sensed Ryan tensing beside me. However, the ploy worked. Derek focused fully on me, a seductive smile curving upward.

"Yes, yes, it will," he agreed. I channeled every ounce of my inner actress to maintain my mildly flirtatious expression and attitude.

"When will we get the good news we've been cast?"

"We?"

I heard the alpha male in Derek's voice. Dang it, he was so sensitive. "Oh, come on, Derek," I said breezily. "My reading with—" I paused and looked questioningly at Ryan.

"Ryan," he supplied, suppressing a small smile.

"My reading with Ryan was better than with the other guy. Unless you plan on callbacks because you saw someone fantastic earlier this evening, it has to be us."

Derek laughed. "My little minx."

I cringed internally at the word, but outwardly did the cutesy eyes downcast thing that certain men seemed to respond to.

"We'll review all the tape and let agents know by the end of the week," he answered my earlier question.

We made eye contact again and I fought down the revulsion to continue the charade. Miraculously, it worked. "That's wonderful," I purred. The female vampire rolled her eyes and I wondered how often scenes like this played out between Derek and actresses. Despite his expressed intent to win me back, I suspected this happened all the time.

The female vampire stood, smiled broadly at Ryan. Her smile dimmed slightly when directed at me. "Thank you both for coming in. We'll let you know."

Ryan and I echoed her thanks and then began to leave.

"Evie, can you stay a minute?"

I immediately stopped. Ryan wisely chose to keep going, like he didn't hear Derek's question. I could tell by Ryan's physical reaction that he did, and he wasn't happy. I'd deal with that later. I turned to Derek.

"Of course."

The other vampires scattered, presumably to give Derek and me privacy. Ugh. He approached and I plastered my big fake grin on again.

"That was fun," I told him. That part was true; I enjoyed reading with Ryan.

Derek touched my cheek and I was impressed I didn't flinch away. "You're so beautiful."

"Thank you," I responded, though my words sounded stiff to my own ears and I was unsurprised to see his smile dip.

"I told you why I'm in town. Yet you still auditioned. And you're here today pretending to flirt. Why are you really here?"

Uh-oh. A direct question. I needed an answer that wasn't a lie. An omission, by the way, was not a lie. "I really want to do the film," I answered, and I was somewhat surprised to realize that was true. The script sounded fun and even though I wasn't sure how Derek became a part of it, the production company was legit, according to Catherine.

Derek stared at me, as though trying to read my mind. He smiled. "I believe you. And you were flirting just so you could get cast?"

"Yes," I admitted, feeling sleazy, hearing it said aloud.

Derek laughed uproariously. "There was no need. Once I knew you were auditioning, I planned to cast you in the lead. You didn't have to flirt." He took my hand. "Though I enjoyed that you did. How far do you want to go with it?" His voice lowered and his eyes were liquid desire. Oh no, no, no.

I snatched my hand away. "Not that far," I retorted and his expression hardened again. The vampire really didn't like not getting his way. Sheesh. I smiled to soften the blow. I didn't want to screw this up in the home stretch. "Let's take this one day at a time."

Derek returned my smile, reached out to caress my cheek again. "Okay. I can understand why you'd be hesitant. We'll take it one day at a time."

His quick acquiescence surprised me before I realized he knew it was the smart play. "I'll see you on set, then," I stated, effectively ending the conversation.

He knew what I did, shook his head slightly. "See you then."

He walked away. I stood there for a long moment, trying to unfeel the touch of his fingers on my face. He hadn't touched me like that in decades. I hadn't missed it.

I spun on my heels and headed outside for the expected showdown with Ryan.

CHAPTER TWELVE

Ryan materialized out of the dark the instant I left the building. Before he could open his mouth, I quietly directed him otherwise.

"The car, first. We don't want anyone here to see us together, remember?"

He followed the instruction and quickly put about ten feet of distance between us. We met again at the car, opened the doors, took our seats, and slammed the doors shut, all in about ten seconds. Ryan remained quiet until we pulled out of the parking lot.

I sensed the tension rolling off of him and waited for the challenge. In three, two, one…

"What was that about back there?" Ryan asked, trying and failing to keep the question light.

"What do you mean?" I questioned back, even though I knew exactly what he meant.

"You know what I'm asking. What was up with the flirting? I thought you didn't like your ex."

"Oh, come on, Ryan," I responded, exasperated. "You're a smart man. You have to know why I was flirting with Derek."

Silence greeted my statement. I waited him out. The silence stretched through one traffic light and then a second. I still waited him out.

"Okay," he said.

"Okay?"

"You're right. I did know why you were flirting with him. To make sure you were cast."

"We," I corrected.

"What?"

"To make sure *we* were cast."

Ryan smiled. "Right. To make sure we were cast."

"Derek suspected we knew each other. I mean, he flat out asked us if we'd worked together before. That would have been a dangerous road to go down."

"That's true. I guess I'm still not clear why that would have been such a big deal. If we had worked together before."

I hesitated to answer. I heard irritation in his voice again and I was unsure if I should address it; Ryan surely felt the sexual tension between us. Right?

"It's not like we're a couple or anything," Ryan continued when I didn't respond.

I didn't like his statement, so for misdirection, I agreed with him.

"That's certainly true," I said with a forced chuckle. "But, I know my ex. He's a classic alpha male."

Ryan laughed. "I got that impression." His expression sobered. "Still."

"Still, what?"

"I don't know," he admitted. He paused to collect his thoughts. "It still felt like you were playing both sides," he finally allowed.

That shocked me. "What? What does that even mean?"

"That maybe you're using our mission as an excuse to explore the possibility of getting back together with your ex."

My jaw dropped open and I risked a glance at him. I noted the clenched jaw and rigid posture. "Are you kidding?"

"Do I look like I'm kidding?"

"No, you don't. And I have no idea why you're overreacting like this." I was facing forward again and I heard the rustle of his clothing when he shifted in the seat to look at me.

"You think I'm overreacting?"

He asked this with a genuine question in his voice. I looked at him and nodded. "Yes, I do. What I don't understand is why."

Silence again. I assumed Ryan was deciding how, or whether, he wanted to answer what I was asking. I had taken the highway exit to his neighborhood when he sighed deeply.

"Did I tell you I was married too?" He said this almost sheepishly because he already knew the answer. "I didn't," he answered himself.

Somehow, I was not surprised. "And?"

"We married young. We were married for five years. I don't think either one of us knew how to be married."

"It's a learning curve for everyone, I think."

"I honestly thought love would be enough. If she was ever really in love with me." He paused. "I didn't know it until the last year that she cheated on me almost every chance she got. I don't know how I missed it."

"Trust me, cheaters know how to cover their tracks," I assured him.

Out of the corner of my eye, I saw Ryan's head turn toward me again. His expression was almost accusatory.

"I never cheated on my husband," I defensively responded to his look.

Ryan sighed again. "Sorry, I'm projecting."

"Projecting?" That was a therapy word if I'd ever heard one.

"I was in therapy for the last six months of my marriage," he said as if reading my mind.

"Ah," was all I could think of to say.

"My best friend saw her out with her latest boyfriend and he finally told me," he continued. "I didn't believe him. I said some horrible things. Lost the friendship," Ryan said, muted anguish audible in his voice.

"I'm sorry."

"When I first questioned Maureen, she called my friend a liar and denied it."

"Of course."

"But, when I provided the details of what my friend had seen, she spilled it all. That's when I learned the current one was only the latest of a string of men. She had been cheating since we returned from our honeymoon," Ryan stated in a flat voice.

"Wow." I was clearly a brilliant conversationalist, but I honestly didn't know what to say.

"After six months of therapy – alone, since she told me she cheated because she should never have gotten married in the first place – I finally filed for divorce. That was five years ago. I haven't dated anybody seriously since then. I guess you could say I have trust issues," he finished with a shake of his head.

"Now I understand." And I truly did. He clearly didn't want to acknowledge any attraction between us, but he knew it was there, so when I flirted with Derek, his subconscious really did interpret that as *playing both sides* like he accused.

"I'm glad. What about you?"

Oh dang. Here came the expectation of reciprocity. I considered and discarded the option of telling him my ex-husband was also my sire and then wiping his mind of the conversation when we got to his house. "Derek and I were married for a short time. It didn't work out and I haven't seen him in a while." Like decades.

A total pregnant pause followed my statement while Ryan waited for me to elaborate. Luckily, I was saved from having to give an even less helpful explanation.

"We've arrived at your home," I announced unnecessarily when I pulled into his driveway. "Door to door service."

Ryan stared at me for a beat before opening his car door. His disappointment in my failure to be equally forthcoming was etched across his face. "I'll see you on set."

"Looking forward to it," I responded with a smile he did not return.

He exited the car, then leaned back in. "Oh, by the way, none of the names on that list panned out. Derek remains our only suspect in Monica's murder." He closed the door.

"And Jim," I told the empty car while I watched Ryan walk to his door. He let himself in without a backward glance.

CHAPTER THIRTEEN

Having hit a roadblock investigating Monica's murder, the next few days passed in a blur with no real contact with Ryan. I knew I found him attractive. I was shocked by how much I missed him. Our limited contact consisted of: me checking in with him after Catherine informed me we had been cast, me asking him if he wanted to rehearse the scenes for the weekend, and his curt responses to my texts. I could read between the lines. He was clearly still upset I hadn't told him anything about my marriage. At least I'd finally see him tonight, since it would be our first day on the set of *Vampire Nights*. He didn't ask for a ride, and I didn't offer, but he couldn't avoid me on set.

All thoughts of Ryan and solving Monica's murder fled on set. I arrived at the house being used for the opening scenes and immediately saw that something was wrong. The degree of excitement and activity was way lower than normal for a first day of shooting. Nothing looked set up yet – no lights, sound equipment, nothing. I placed my bag on the floor of a dining room off the front door and approached Orlando, the young male vampire from the audition, my kitten heels clicking on the laminate floor.

"What's going on?"

He looked at me for a moment, as though distracted from deep thoughts and was now trying to place me. "Oh, Evelyn! Good to see you," he gushed, though even this was forced, off somehow.

"What's going on?" I asked again.

He stared at me. It was obvious he didn't want to answer my question. I could almost see his brain thinking. He sighed.

"Several of our crew members aren't here," he replied vaguely.

"Do they have an estimated arrival time?" I asked this to determine if the shoot would be cancelled, but also to get at what the vampire clearly didn't want to tell me.

He leaned in closer. "Promise not to tell anyone?"

What were we, in high school? I played along. I leaned in too. "I promise."

"Derek isn't here either. A body has been found," he finished dramatically.

If I had a beating heart, it would have stopped. "A body? Whose? Where?"

"I don't know," he answered with a shake of his head. "It wasn't somebody connected directly to the shoot, but our director, camera guy, and hair and makeup chick, all called in this morning. Apparently, they normally work together, and all three know the woman who was killed."

This caught my attention. "Woman?"

"Yes, she was beaten to death. Bludgeoned, really," he said with a level of glee that reminded me how inhumane some non-humans truly could be.

"Why isn't Derek here? How is he connected?" I tried to ask this offhandedly, but I was keenly aware that Derek was the only suspect in Monica's murder besides Jim. Could he be connected to this murder too? That would be quite the coincidence.

"I don't know. All I know is that he got a phone call an hour ago, made a few more phone calls, and then took off after telling me what I just told you."

I didn't know what to make of this information. I clearly needed to find out more.

"Has Ryan arrived yet?" I asked, and Orlando didn't follow my train of thought.

"Um, yeah, he's over talking to wardrobe." He waved his hand to indicate somewhere toward the back of the house.

"Thanks," I told him and headed that way. I stopped short in the doorway of a back room.

Ryan's auburn hair glowed from the floor lamp behind him. Like fire. Oh, good grief, there I went again, thinking like a romance novel. But, man, he looked good, in a simple pair of jeans and a green t-shirt showcasing his fit body. Our eyes met and for just a moment, he seemed glad to see me, and then a wall crashed down behind his eyes.

Pretending obliviousness, I approached Ryan and the costumer, a short round older male with an easy smile. He gave me the up and down, not lasciviously, but with an eye for wardrobe. He nodded his head in approval at my blond bob, yellow pedal-pusher pants, and daisy accented blouse.

"Hi, I'm Jackson. You must be Evelyn and you are absolutely radiant. Like a ray of sunshine," he greeted me, extending his hand. He had a strong grip.

"Thank you so much and nice to meet you, Jackson. Please, call me Evie," I responded. "Hi, Ryan."

"Hi, Evie."

Jackson's head swiveled between me and Ryan; he sensed the tension, I assumed. I jumped right in. "Do you guys know if the shoot is still happening?"

Ryan frowned. "Why wouldn't it? We were only told there'd be a couple of hours delay. Something about an equipment issue."

"Oh, I must have misunderstood," I backtracked with a short bark of a laugh. "Don't let me interrupt."

I tuned the men out and they continued their conversation. My mind raced. How could I find out more information about this murder? It wasn't someone on this set, but someone with a strong connection to the crew. I wondered if Catherine would know.

"Excuse me, gentlemen, I need to make a call," I interrupted with the quick explanation before I walked to the other side of the room. Ryan's expression suggested he really wanted to ask me what was going on. I ignored it.

At the other wall, my back to the men, I called Catherine. "Do you have a minute?"

She heard the tone in my voice. "What's the matter?"

"Do you know who was killed last night? Or this morning, I suppose," I corrected myself.

"I haven't heard anything," she answered, which was a disappointment. I filled her in on what Orlando the friendly vampire assistant told me, and she said she'd do some digging and call me back as soon as possible. After disconnecting the call, I turned to find myself face to face with Ryan. I must have really been absorbed in my call to miss his approach.

"What murder?" he asked without preamble, his eyes guarded but not unfriendly.

"I don't know yet. Someone with a connection to the set."

"Where's Derek?"

I knew what he was thinking, but I needed to slow him down. "He's gone to check on the crew members connected to the person who was killed. At least that's what I was told," I amended.

"That's an amazing coincidence. Derek being connected to two murders." I heard the accusation in Ryan's tone.

"I agree," I responded slowly, "which is why I called Catherine. To try to gather additional intel."

Ryan smiled at my use of the word intel. Unexpectedly, he reached out to twirl one of my blond curls. "I've missed you."

Hello, left field! "I've missed you too."

"I'm sorry about the other night."

"Me too. I know you want to know more."

"I do. But, I don't want to push you." His hand caressed my cheek and I leaned into it.

We gazed goofily at each other for a moment and then my phone vibrated, breaking the connection. My cheek felt cold when he removed his hand.

"It's Catherine," I told him, receiving the call. He stepped away to provide privacy.

"I have info," she said gleefully. "Although maybe I shouldn't sound so happy. A woman is dead."

"Don't worry about it. What did you find out?"

"The woman who was killed was Sophie Chase, a cinematographer. Beaten to death in her home last night.

No forced entry, though the front door was unlocked. So, she either knew her attacker or at least didn't feel threatened by him or her."

"Probably right, Sherlock," I agreed with a small smile.

I heard Catherine smile through the phone. "She wasn't going to work on *Vampire Nights* because she had another gig lined up in LA, but she was tight with much of your crew. Which is why half of them aren't on set this evening."

"Human or Other?"

"Human, I believe."

"Who found her?"

"A neighbor walking his dog saw her front door open and investigated. Found the body in the front hallway, reportedly covered in blood."

This part of the story bothered Catherine. Even I blanched at the notion of someone being beaten to death. Vampires might have killed for blood in the past. At least the human was bewitched first.

"Any suspects?"

"Ryan's not gonna like this," Catherine warned.

I closed my eyes, foreseeing the answer to my next question. "Why?"

"You can't tell him."

"I won't," though it pained me to make that promise.

"Jim Freeman."

I gasped and compulsively looked at Ryan, who returned my look quizzically. I turned away and lowered my voice. "Any other suspects?"

"Nope. My source in the LVMPD says an arrest is imminent."

"He's already on bail," I exclaimed and felt Ryan boring a hole in the back of my head. He had to have heard that. I resolutely did not turn to face him.

"I know. He'll never get bail for this second charge. He's in jail until the trial – or alternate evidence is found."

"Don't remind me."

CHAPTER FOURTEEN

"Catherine confirmed another body has been found and is being investigated as a homicide," I informed Ryan after ending the call.

"And you suspect Jim?"

"He's a likely suspect."

Ryan took the news better than expected. Just a simple question. "What do we do now?"

"I'm guessing filming isn't happening tonight," I explained. "Time for a field trip."

After informing Orlando that we'd be leaving – and he didn't look too surprised – Ryan silently followed me back to my car.

"Where are we going?"

We were zipping along the 215 heading from Summerlin toward Henderson when he asked. I was frankly surprised he waited that long.

"We are heading for the crime scene."

Ryan laughed. "Of course, we are. Are they going to let us in?"

"Leave that to me," I said cryptically with a quick glance at his face. He smiled.

I parked across the street from the house. There was no way we'd miss it since it had yellow crime scene tape across the door. I was preparing to work my vampire voodoo on any officers standing watch, but nobody was there. I felt some disappointment. That must mean they already finished gathering their evidence.

Ryan exited the car with me and followed me to the front door. It was dark. I hoped no spying eyes had seen us. I carefully removed the yellow tape from one side of the door frame. It dangled from the other side, and I found the image forlorn and disturbing. I refocused my attention and tried the door. Naturally, it was locked.

"Now what? Are you going to knock it down?" Ryan said this with a laugh, though I noticed he kept glancing behind us and at the neighbors' houses.

I was in a quandary. I didn't have magical lock picking skills. I did have the strength to simply break the lock. I didn't particularly want to demonstrate this in front of Ryan. Gaining access to the house would not be worth the questions it would bring.

"Time for Plan B," I announced, and strode through the grass. Ryan, startled by my move, hurried to catch up.

We reached the neighbor's house and I knocked on the door before Ryan could ask what I was doing.

An older man holding a leash answered the door and I was confident I guessed correctly.

"Good evening, sir. I'm friends with Sophie Chase from next door and I was wondering if you could answer a few questions."

The man squinted at me. "Are you a reporter?"

"No, sir. A friend. I'm trying to find out what happened." I opened my eyes wide and faked like I was struggling not to cry. I felt like a heel, but it worked.

"I'm Joshua," he said, extending his hand for a handshake. "I'm the one that found her." His face clouded at the memory, less than 24 hours old.

"I can't imagine how hard that must have been," I commiserated.

"She was so young. So friendly. She always had a nice word for Baxter." He held up the leash. "My Basset Hound rescue. I was about to take him for a walk."

"We don't want to hold you up. Do you mind if we walk with you?"

"I don't see why not."

Ryan and I waited at the door while Joshua moved into the house and returned with Baxter on a leash. Joshua locked the door and then the four of us started walking down the street. I could tell Joshua was a bit hesitant yet wanted to help Sophie's friend.

"Would you mind telling us what you told the police officer?"

"I don't see what it can hurt," he agreed. "Baxter and I were returning from our walk late last night. We normally go around this time, but I had been delayed at work, so it was closer to 11 p.m., maybe even closer to midnight. I don't remember exactly."

"That's okay," I assured him.

"I didn't notice anything when I left the house, but when I was returning, I saw that the door was open."

"If I may interrupt, did you not notice anything when you left because everything looked normal, or because you didn't look in that direction?" This distinction was important because it could establish a timeline for events.

"The cops asked the same question and I honestly don't know. I wasn't really paying close attention. I would never have thought it would matter, you know?" He sounded so sad not being certain that I felt bad asking him to relive it.

"That's okay, Joshua. Every little bit helps," I soothed him.

"I approached the open door – and I saw it from the street because light was coming out the door, which doesn't happen if the door is closed," he added. Ryan and I nodded understanding. "I knocked on the door and called out Sophie's name. I didn't receive a reply. I've lived next door to her for years and I've never known her to leave her door open. I had a bad feeling, so I decided to enter."

"Did you consider calling the police?" Ryan asked.

"No," Joshua admitted. "Even though I had a bad feeling, I had nothing really to base it on. And I know how busy Metro is. I figured, this was that one-off where she thought she closed it but she didn't." He shrugged. "When I walked in, she was right there."

I heard him swallow and his heartbeat increased. "She was on the floor. There was blood everywhere. Under her, on her, on the walls. I went to her, to check for a pulse, you know? There wasn't one. She was dead."

We walked several steps in silence before I spoke. "This may be an odd question. Do you remember if her skin felt warm or cold?"

"That's not odd, the police asked the same thing," Joshua responded. "Her neck felt cool. That was part of how I knew she was dead, even as I was checking for breathing and a pulse."

He shuddered, and I touched his hand for support. He looked at me gratefully.

"I have another odd question," Ryan interjected. Joshua looked at him. "What did it smell like?"

"Funny you should ask that. In addition to the smell of the—" he paused, "blood, there was another smell. It smelled like the outdoors."

"What do you mean?" Ryan followed up and I knew the path he was charging down.

"I distinctly remember after calling 9-1-1 and waiting for the police to arrive that I thought I smelled the outdoors. I wondered if Sophie had gotten a new scented candle. She loved those things."

"Could the smell be described as woody?"

"Yeah, I suppose so," Joshua allowed with a slow nod of his head.

I saw the triumphant look on Ryan's face and knew exactly what he was thinking. I focused on Joshua. "Is there anything else you saw, heard…or smelled," I added, "that you think could be useful?"

Joshua thought for a moment. "No, that's everything. That's what I told the police. Well, except for that bit about the smell," he contradicted himself. "They didn't ask."

"That's okay," Ryan assured him. "You can always call them tomorrow to let them know if you think it might be important."

Joshua looked at us for guidance. "Do you think it's important?"

"I'd call," Ryan told him decidedly. "Let the police decide if it's important or not." Joshua nodded.

By now, we had walked the loop of his neighborhood and were approaching my car and Joshua's house. I indicated the Fiat.

"This is us," I explained. "We'll let you get back to your evening." I took one of Joshua's hands in both of mine. "Thank you so much for talking with us."

"You're welcome," he responded. "I'm sorry for your loss."

"Thank you," Ryan and I said in unison. Joshua smiled. Ryan and I exchanged wry glances.

We remained standing next to my car watching Joshua lead Baxter home. Once the older man was safely inside, we entered the vehicle.

"That tells us everything we need to know."

"It does?" I responded cautiously. I had more information than he did.

"Well, yes. Didn't you hear what Joshua said? He smelled that woody smell. The same as Jim reported."

"And from this, you've concluded that Derek is the killer?" I asked the question to buy time. I wouldn't lie to Ryan, but I promised Catherine I wouldn't tell him Jim's arrest was imminent. Heck, it might have even happened.

Ryan gave me a look. "Um, yes. Haven't you?" His eyes narrowed. "Or do you agree with Catherine that Jim is the killer?"

"Wait a minute, Catherine never said that she thinks Jim is the killer," I disagreed.

"I heard you tell her, 'he's already on bail', during your conversation," he countered. "Are you telling me you weren't talking about Jim?"

That I could answer. "You are correct that we were talking about Jim."

Ryan didn't like this non-answer. "But you don't think Derek could be the killer. Is it because of your history with him?"

"Watch your tone," I responded without thinking and felt Ryan's physical reaction to my harsh words. I looked over at him and tried a half-smile. "I agree with you that it is troubling hearing about a woody smell at both murders. But, it doesn't mean it's the *same* woody smell."

Ryan actually rolled his eyes. "Please. Are you kidding? What are the odds that there'd be an unusual woody smell at both murders?"

"I agree it's interesting," I placated. "I'm not saying Derek isn't the killer. I'm not saying he isn't capable of it. I'm just not seeing a motive." I shrugged.

"What is Jim's motive? At least for this murder, since the police already assumed a motive for Monica's murder." The bitterness in his voice was unmistakable.

"I don't know," I admitted.

"Then why would Catherine say Jim is a suspect?"

I didn't answer.

"What else did she tell you?"

I ignored the suspicion in his voice.

He stared out the window, his jaw clenched. Tension rolled off him.

"I know he's your friend," I tried to amend. "I'm not saying he's the killer. I'm trying to maintain an open mind."

Ryan's posture softened. "I know. Thank you. I appreciate that," he acknowledged. "This is so hard. I've known Jim a long time and I know he's not the killer."

Before I could decide how to respond, Ryan's phone rang. "It's Jim!"

Ryan answered, and I heard Jim already talking to someone in the background. My heart sank. I knew what was coming. "Jim? Jim, are you talking to me?"

"Ryan, can you hear me? I've been arrested again."

CHAPTER FIFTEEN

Not eavesdropping was impossible in a car, so I started driving away, making a show of staring straight ahead while Ryan spoke with Jim. Of course, I heard every word on both sides.

"Did you say you've been arrested?"

"Yes."

"Why did you call me? Don't you need your one call for your attorney?"

"Apparently, that's just in the movies. I already spoke to my lawyer and she's told me I won't get bail this time."

"What? Why not?"

"Because I'm already on bail. I'm going to jail."

"Do you know why they arrested you?"

"I haven't been questioned yet. According to my lawyer, the police think I was having an affair with the victim."

"That's crazy. You would never cheat on Monica."

"I know. I don't even know the poor woman who was killed," Jim said, voice hitching on the last word. "I mean, I'd seen her before, but I didn't know her."

Ryan's heart rate jumped, signaling this statement caught him off-guard like it did me.

"You'd seen her? Where?"

"I was introduced to her at the theater. Oh my god," he exhaled loudly. "It was that night. I was introduced to her the night of Monica's mu- death. Do you think that means anything?"

"I don't know," Ryan responded. My mind was racing. It couldn't be unrelated. I didn't believe in coincidences. Certainly not ones looming large like that. Jim, Monica, Sophie, and Derek were all there that night. What did it mean?

"I can't believe they think I killed her," Jim continued, unable to sustain his brief excitement.

"What evidence do they have?"

"I have no idea. Lawyer didn't say."

"Is there anything I can do to help?" Ryan asked.

"Find out who really did it," he answered softly.

"We're working on that."

"You and Evie?"

"Yes," he confirmed. I glanced in his direction in time to see the disappointed look on his face and knew that we were likely going to have a confrontation.

"God, I hope you come up with something," Jim finished, his despair wrenching my gut.

Maybe he wasn't guilty? If he was, he was one heck of an actor. Could it really be Derek? I refocused on the conversation in time to hear them ending the call. I chanced a quick look at Ryan again, saw that look of disappointment, and returned to watching the road. I almost wished he'd be angry.

"You knew." A statement, not a question.

"I did."

"You knew he was going to be arrested and you didn't tell me."

I reached my hand toward his, and replaced it on the steering wheel before giving him the opportunity to withdraw. I glanced back and forth between him and the road while we talked.

"I didn't want to put you in an awkward position."

"Why would it?"

"If you knew he was going to be arrested, wouldn't you want to warn him?"

No response.

"I'm sorry it worked out like this. I try to respect and help my friends when I can, just like you're trying to do."

He stared at me a beat.

"I promised Catherine I wouldn't tell you."

"Catherine knew too." Again, a statement not a question.

"She told me in the earlier phone call," I admitted.

Ryan faced forward and closed his eyes. I heard him trying to manage his heartbeat, trying to maintain control.

"Ryan, please understand."

"Understand what? That you're willing to throw my friend under the bus for your ex."

I recoiled as if slapped. "That's not what's going on. You know that. We just talked about it," I said, a touch of exasperation in my voice. It did not go unnoticed.

"Gee, is my being upset bothering you?"

"There's no need for sarcasm," I retorted. "We both want the same thing. The real killer found."

"And you believe it's Jim."

"I believe it's a possibility, yes," I answered. "We're talking in circles here, which is entirely unproductive. Do you still want my help?"

A long silence followed.

I waited for him to decide. The wait was excruciating.

"Yes," he finally answered quietly. "I do." He gave me his adorable lopsided grin.

My relief was palpable. I ignored the feeling and what it might mean. We didn't have time for that. We were trying to catch a killer.

"We were just given a big piece of information," I said, clapping my hands, which seemed only slightly out of place, given the circumstances.

*****

"There's no way I'm letting you put yourself in harm's way."

I arched an eyebrow. "You're not letting me?"

"You know what I mean."

I smiled because, of course, I knew what he meant. It was fun to watch him squirm. We sat on his living room couch, discussing my idea. Which he clearly didn't like.

"At least let me come with you," he insisted.

"No," I answered and watched his jaw tighten.

"Why not?"

"If Derek sees you, then he'll know something's up," I explained again.

"Not if I stay out of sight," he countered.

I sighed. "We're going in circles. We need to either confirm or eliminate Derek as a suspect and the best way to do that is for me to play on his intention to win me back by," I involuntarily shuddered here, "flirting with him to get him to talk. It's a classic."

This time it was Ryan who arched an eyebrow. "Exactly."

"I don't want you to see that."

We stared at each other. His heartbeat increased and his eyes dilated. Now wasn't the time to deal with our mutual attraction. I broke eye contact as he spoke.

"I wouldn't want to see that either, but..."

"We need our best shot at getting him to confess."

"And that's why I want to be there. If he confesses to murder, you could be in harm's way."

There was no way for me to explain that Derek couldn't hurt me – not that he wouldn't, I silently agreed with Ryan – but as a vampire, he had to have permission from our vampire Family to do so. And he didn't have that. I didn't think he did anyway.

"He's not going to hurt me," was all I said.

"I don't understand how you can be so sure," Ryan argued stubbornly.

"I just am. More importantly," I stressed, "if he sees you, all bets are off. You know that."

"Okay, okay. I hear the exasperation in your voice," he acknowledged with a smile. "I'll let you do it your way. I mean, let's do it your way," he corrected himself and we both laughed, though I was mildly surprised he was finally giving in. Alpha men rarely did so. It was a good thing. The real reason I didn't want him there was that I didn't want him to find out Derek and I were vampires. I wasn't ready to have the conversation yet, if I ever was.

"I have one condition."

"Oh really?"

Ryan cupped my chin for a moment with gentle fingers, brushing his thumb along my jaw. "Yes. I want full contact info for Derek, just in case. If you don't check in at a designated time, I want to be able to either contact you myself or provide the information to the authorities." His jugular vein throbbed in his neck and I knew how worried he was for me. I placed one hand on his knee, heard his heartbeat accelerate further in reaction.

"Okay," I agreed. "That sounds reasonable."

Ryan placed his hand over mine. "I wouldn't want anything to happen to you."

"I wouldn't want anything to happen to me, either," I quipped. Ryan squeezed my hand slightly and released.

"What next?"

"Let me text Derek." I scrolled through my contacts until I found him.

I assume filming is going to resume? I'd like to discuss my character. Are you free tonight?

Ryan and I watched my phone, waiting for the response, which seemed to take forever, but really was probably less than a minute.

Great! Meet at my hotel?

Ryan frowned and I shook my head at him. "Wait."

Hotel lounge? Or bar?

LOL, sure.

"Such a punk."

"I don't disagree," I responded.

Where?

Ryan and I waited again and Chandelier Bar popped up. Ryan nodded that he saw.

Got it. See you at midnight?

Yep.

"There. We're set," I needlessly stated. I forwarded Derek's number to Ryan. He nodded when the text arrived.

"Promise you'll call as soon as you're finished?"

"I promise."

"If I don't hear from you by one, I'm calling. And if I can't reach you, I'm calling the authorities," he warned. I was touched by his needless concern.

"I'll be fine. Maybe give me until 1:30. In case it takes longer."

His eyes darkened and I didn't need vampire senses to know what he was imagining.

"I'm not going to sleep with him," I assured him, making a face of disgust.

"Things don't always go the way we plan," he responded.

My eyes widened in surprise. "Do you think I'd sleep with him?"

He didn't answer and my heart sank.

I placed a hand under his chin, lifted his eyes toward mine. "It'll never happen," I assured him.

I was acutely aware of the increase in his physical response to me.

Ryan leaned forward as if to kiss me, and then he pulled back. "Good."

CHAPTER SIXTEEN

Although I grumbled at having to pay for parking on The Strip (really, Las Vegas?), I was glad that Derek at least had the sense to stay at the Cosmopolitan, where the first floor of the Chandelier lounge had the best chocolate martinis ever. Not that I drank them, of course, but they smelled heavenly.

The mass of humanity swarming around me as I approached bombarded me with their physical reactions to the scene. When I was a younger vampire, this would have overwhelmed me; luckily, over time, I'd learned the ability to block or at least filter out some of that noise. The hundreds of beaded chandelier strings around the lounge sparkled and reflected the light – almost everywhere. I zeroed in on a dead spot near the bar. Derek. He absorbed the light and energy around him like a, well, vampire. I shook my head at my own silliness.

He sensed me when I ascended the few lighted steps and turned left to the nearest circular couch. He was seated alone, his energy keeping the humans away. Even while I watched, a drunk couple approached, started to enter the enclosed area, and abruptly veered off. I chuckled. It was a good location, facing the bar, our backs to the room. We'd pitch our voices below human perception and use Derek's glamour to mask sounds, but it was still best to take precautions. Some people had been known to read lips and I had a vampire friend called out that way once. Awkward.

Derek was as spectacular as ever, his tall frame folded into the seat, one foot resting on the knee of his other leg. Tonight, he wore all black: tight black jeans, gleaming black leather boots, fitted black button-down shirt with the first three buttons again undone. Had this become his signature style? His dark eyes followed me while I walked toward him and entered the seating area. His skin practically glowed in the mood lighting. He smirked when I carefully sat several feet from him. He smelled like the woods.

"Good evening, Evie. You look like candy," he said, his eyes sliding up and down my figure. "Good enough to eat." I was glad I didn't bother to change into something more seductive from my daisy blouse and yellow pants I wore to set earlier in the evening. I squirmed under his gaze and needlessly adjusted my beret. His smile widened.

Thank goodness, he'd mistaken my reaction as a positive, when really, I wanted to hurl.

"Hi, Derek," I responded, trying a smile, hoping it wasn't as fake as it felt. "You look…nice." I faltered. I noticed that he ordered a chocolate martini for me to pretend to drink and I picked it up, inhaling deeply. I set the drink back on the table and raised my eyes to his.

We stared at each other, neither able to read the other. Derek slowly smiled. "You called this meeting," he reminded me.

"Right," I agreed. "I wanted to discuss filming. I assume the shoot is still happening."

"Yes."

"Do you have any idea when that might be?"

"No."

"Any changes to the cast and crew?"

"No."

Ugh, this was going nowhere fast. His monosyllabic answers allowed for zero chance at expansion. I frowned.

"Isn't this what you wanted?"

"I don't follow."

"You just frowned. But, isn't this what you wanted? To talk about filming," he elaborated.

"I – well, yes."

"No, it isn't."

"It isn't?"

"No."

"Now I'm confused," I admitted, not following his train of thought.

Derek scooted closer. I stiffened. He laughed low and sexy. "You know that's not why you wanted to meet."

"It's not?"

"No."

"Then why did I want to meet?" He surely didn't know I suspected him of murder.

"I saw your reaction when I told you I wanted you back."

My revulsion? I stayed silent.

"You want me back, too," he explained.

Ah, narcissism. There you were. I shook my head in a non-response.

"It's okay. I know this was unexpected."

"Yes?" I asked this, unsure what response he expected.

Derek reached for my hand and I allowed him to hold it. He stroked my palm. One hundred years ago, this might have worked. Tonight, not so much. At least I had my opening.

"I don't know what I want," I admitted, honestly. Not him, of course. But, Ryan? That was another story.

"We can take it slow," he whispered, sidling even closer so that I could feel the chill coming off him. He placed his other hand on my knee, rubbing lightly. I forced myself not to withdraw and smiled instead. "I've changed, Evie. I can be the man you need me to be. The man you fell in love with. The man I was before you married me. In the beginning."

"Reset to one?" I asked sadly, as if that were even possible after everything we'd been through.

Derek laughed at my movie production humor. "Exactly. Reset to one – go back to the beginning."

"I'm worried about everything going on," I said, to try for a redirect. His hands stopped their movement but remained in position.

"What are you worried about, kitten?"

That I reacted to. He hadn't called me by his nickname for me in decades. I smiled quickly to cover my discomfort and glanced away. A tall guy walking past our couch glanced briefly at me. Something about him seemed familiar. Who could tell with his backwards baseball cap and sunglasses? Inside. How pretentious. I refocused on Derek.

"I'm worried about the murders."

Derek's fingers tightened on my knee before releasing. I saw the tension in his face but his response was light.

"Murders? What are you talking about?"

I pulled away completely from him with the question, aghast, and only partly pretending. "What do you mean, what murders am I talking about?"

Derek shrugged. "I know a friend of the crew was killed. Was there another murder?"

I eyed him carefully. This could be a moment of truth. "Monica? Monica Freeman? We talked about her murder," I reminded him pointedly.

"Oh, that," he replied with a dismissive wave. "Wasn't her husband arrested for that?"

"Yes."

"And wasn't he implicated in the other murder?"

"Yes."

"Then why would you be worried? They have the killer in custody."

"If he's the killer."

Derek eyed me for a beat. "What makes you think he's not the killer?"

I picked up the chocolate martini again to think for a second before responding. "I think it's a little too convenient," I answered slowly.

"Maybe that's just because he's guilty," Derek countered with a shrug.

I lifted the drink to my nose again and inhaled. Dang, that was good. I set it down and stared at my ex-husband. Here we go.

"Witnesses at the scenes of both murders reported smelling a woody scent." Derek started at this comment but said nothing. "And Jim isn't the only person with connections to both victims."

CHAPTER SEVENTEEN

"Jim? I didn't realize you knew the accused or the victims." Derek's eyes glittered.

"I don't. Not really."

"Then why do you care?"

"I just do," I said, not wanting to elaborate.

Derek's eyes hardened. "It's that other guy."

My eyes widened, theatrically I imagined. "Whatever do you mean?"

"Cut the nonsense, Evie," he snorted. "I knew there was something going on between you and that actor," he spat out the last word.

"This has nothing to do with Ryan," I argued.

"Ryan? I thought you said at the audition that you just met him." He glared at me.

"What are you accusing me of? I think you're deflecting."

"From what?"

"I saw your reaction when I mentioned the scent the witnesses reported. A scent described very much like what you smell like tonight."

Derek shifted slightly, his only indication that I hit a nerve. "Lots of cologne and aftershave smell like the woods. It's manly," he explained.

"I'm not an idiot. I'm aware of that. I just find it highly coincidental."

"Why do you care?" He asked again, this time lifting both hands at me in a clear gesture of irritation.

I glanced around to see if anybody was paying attention to his raised voice, before remembering the glamour. I noticed the pretentious guy from earlier sitting at the bar. His sunglasses reflected in the mirror.

"I care because I like humanity and I don't want to see an innocent man go to prison."

"You think I'm the killer? Because of some odor?"

"Yes, I do." This might not be 100% true, but I was leaning more and more in that direction.

Derek broke eye contact and sighed heavily. "Dang, Evie, a guy can't catch a break."

"What do you mean?"

"I did it. You're right. I killed both of the women." He watched me carefully to gauge my reaction.

"I don't know what to say." This was the truth. I was stunned. I waited for him to elaborate.

"The whole thing was a mistake."

"A mistake?"

He shook his head.

"How do you mistakenly kill not one, but two, people?"

Derek had the good grace to at least glance away, seemingly embarrassed.

Although, since I knew he didn't care one whit about humanity, there must be another reason. I decided to wait him out. I picked up my chocolate martini and pretended to sip it, inhaling the amazing aroma.

A sigh captured my attention.

I peered over the top of the drink at my ex-husband.

"It was just a job," he finally stated.

"A job? What kind of job requires you to—" I stopped with the sudden realization. "Oh."

Derek nodded. "I'm a Cleaner."

He said nothing more. He didn't need to. Like organized crime, vampire families had Cleaners who took care of issues before they became bigger issues.

"You were sent to Vegas to clean someone?" I asked the question slowly, trying to wrap my mind around the fact that Derek was a Cleaner. When did that happen?

As if hearing my unasked question, Derek elaborated. "A few decades ago, I was bored and looking for something new to do. I put out feelers, wanting to do more for the Family, and this was what popped up."

My mouth fell open. "You've been killing humans for decades?" I genuinely didn't know what else to say.

Derek rolled his eyes. "You always have cared too much for the vermin. Do you even like being a vampire?"

I balled my fists, wanting nothing more than to knock that smug look off his face. He grinned, seeing my reaction, and knowing I wouldn't draw that kind of attention to us. And, dammit, he was right. I released my fists and rested my hands lightly on my knees, thinking.

"The first woman was an accident," he continued as if telling a fun fact. "I was given information that the target would be at the theater that night. It was last minute information and it was wrong." He shrugged, clearly not caring that he killed the wrong person.

"Monica was a case of mistaken identity?"

"Yes, Evie, good grief, are you being deliberately slow?"

"No. I'm not being deliberately slow," I responded between clenched teeth. "I'm trying to understand what a colossal moron you are." That hit home and anger radiated off of Derek in response.

"So, after you messed up…" I prompted.

He might have wanted to respond to my insult. Instead he chose to continue the story.

"I framed the husband. When that didn't seem to be sufficient, I killed that other woman to cement the frame job."

I tilted my head, wondering how I ever could have loved the man before me, even before he was a vampire. This had to have been there all along. I glared at him. "You ruined three lives and – oh my goodness – there's still a woman out there in danger!" The realization slammed into me like the proverbial ton of bricks. "You can't kill anybody else," I warned.

Derek laughed. "I'm not going to," he assured me.

This stopped me cold. "You're not? What about the original contract?"

He glanced away again. "Yeah, so it turned out she was never in Las Vegas at all. She was in Las Cruces. New Mexico," he elaborated. "Before you worry about trying to warn her, she apparently got wind of the hit, and has gone underground, so for now, the contract has been pulled." He smiled widely. "See. It's all finished." He moved in closer and placed his hand on my knee again. "We can forget all about this unpleasantness and focus on the movie. And us."

Before I could respond, I sensed motion as someone approached. Derek and I both turned towards the person, frowning because no human should be comfortable in our energy dead zone.

Oh no. Up close, I realized that I recognized the pretentious guy in the backwards ball cap and sunglasses.

Ryan. He whipped the sunglasses off of his face. Boy did he look pissed!

Derek chuckled and didn't move. I stood immediately, put my hands on Ryan's chest. He jerked away like he'd been burned. My hands fell to my sides. I didn't know what to do.

"How could you?" Ryan hissed this at me.

Wait? Me? "What did I do?" I asked in confusion.

"You blamed Jim for the murders. You tried to convince me he could be a killer. And the entire time you were protecting your ex-husband. Who you're clearly fonder of than you let on," Ryan finished with a snarl.

How was I going to fix this? Before I could respond, Ryan continued, turning on Derek.

"You. You killed my friend Monica and some other innocent woman, then framed Jim for both."

"Thanks for the recap, sport," Derek said indolently.

Ryan raised his hand to punch Derek and time slowed then stopped. I stared at Ryan frozen in time.

CHAPTER EIGHTEEN

I turned to Derek.

"What are you doing?"

"I'm not about to let that idiot hit me," he explained and stood. "I'm leaving. You can sort this crazy out." Derek rolled his eyes again – had he always been this juvenile, I absently wondered.

"You can't just leave," I countered. "It'll look like you vanished."

"So?"

"We already don't know what Ryan somehow overheard. Which he shouldn't have been able to."

"Who cares?" Derek set his drink down on the table. "I'm leaving," he repeated.

"No."

"No?" An eyebrow lifted at my tone. "Who's going to stop me? You?" He laughed.

"No," I snapped at him. "You're going to choose to stay." I smiled. His own smile faltered.

"Why would I do that?"

"So we can find out what he knows and handle this."

Derek stared hard at me for a moment and then fake sighed. "Fine."

"Return time to its normal speed. Please," I added sweetly.

Derek stepped slightly to the side as time returned to normal. Ryan's punch missed Derek's face completely. Ryan appeared confused both by the fact that he missed and that somehow Derek was now standing.

Ryan's gaze swung between me and Derek, his frown deepening. "What—" he started to say and then stopped.

"Ryan, it's not what you think."

"You weren't flirting with your ex-husband, the killer?"

"This is why I didn't want you to come, remember?" I reminded him in a low voice.

"So I wouldn't see you flirting," he sputtered. "With a killer!"

"Shh," I responded, emphasizing with my hands that we needed him to be quiet.

Ryan opened his mouth to continue, and then didn't. The disappointment on his face wounded me.

"I told you that I might have to," I paused, "flirt with my ex."

"This whole thing was a setup," Derek jumped in, incredulous. I was unclear if he was shocked I didn't want to get back with him or that I would, in his eyes, stoop so low as to set him up.

"Yes, murderer," Ryan growled.

Derek's eyes narrowed to murderous slits. "Shut up, human."

"Oh," as if suddenly remembering, "that's the other thing. You're both clearly delusional. Vampires!" Ryan barked out a laugh.

I looked around, worried someone would hear him, and that reminded me. "How could you hear us?"

Ryan looked at me like I'd grown a second head. "Why does that matter?"

I hesitated. Might as well go all in. "As a human, you should not have been able to hear us talking, if we didn't want you to. We definitely didn't want anybody to."

Ryan unexpectedly looked thoughtful. "Actually, I didn't hear you," he began.

"How did you know what we were saying?"

"I read your lips."

My eyes moved to the mirror over the bar. "In the bar mirror? You read our lips in the mirror?" In spite of myself, I was impressed. Even though a friend got busted in a similar way, it honestly never occurred to me that anybody could read our lips in a mirror. Wouldn't it be backward?

I realized belatedly that Ryan and Derek were staring at me while my mind wandered. "Sorry."

"It doesn't matter. I'm going to the police."

"Who will believe you?" Derek challenged.

"Not that the two of you have delusions of being vampires," Ryan clarified. "It's quite simple. I'll point the police toward you, Derek, by mentioning an overheard conversation, woody smells at both crime scenes, and Evie as a corroborating witness."

His shoulders sagged, maybe not as confident and pleased as the words implied.

I reached out again, placing my hand on his arm. He didn't pull away this time, just gazed at me sadly.

"Please don't," I begged.

"Why not?" he asked hollowly. "It's the truth."

"Yes, it is," I agreed. "But…it puts everybody in danger," I finished vaguely.

"Danger?"

With a sigh, I explained. "If you say anything, it will put you in danger. It will also threaten us with exposure."

"Exposure as what? Crazy people?"

I flinched at his words and his self-satisfied expression dropped a notch.

"We're not crazy. I'm trying to protect us. All of us," I hastened to add.

"No, you're not," he disagreed. "You're threatening me." His small voice broke my heart. I hadn't yet figured out if he and I might have a chance at something, but I felt it being snatched away.

"I'm not." I squeezed Ryan's arms gently and he broke eye contact.

"I am." Derek chose that moment to add his two cents. He smiled wolfishly at Ryan, who pulled completely away from me.

"Derek, good luck with that. Evie," his voice hiccupped. "Good luck with everything."

Ryan and I stared at each other; if I could cry, I think I would have. Derek stewed beside me. With a final half-shrug, Ryan walked away. Away from me. Away from us. Or at least the chance of us.

Derek broke my train of thoughts. "I'm going to kill him. You know that."

"That isn't necessary," I insisted.

"Yes, it is. Plus, I plan to enjoy it." Derek allowed his fangs to descend slightly to emphasize his point. I wanted to throttle him.

"What about a mind wipe?" I offered this alternative frantically. I needed to convince Derek before he left, or Ryan was a dead man.

"No."

"Just no? Why not?"

"How can you love a human who is endangering us?" Derek sounded exasperated but my mind buzzed.

"Love? Who said anything about love?"

"Love, like, lust, whatever. You know what I mean."

"I don't want any more innocents hurt," I maintained. Derek saw through me.

"He's a threat. He knows about us, thus he's endangering us," he repeated slowly like I was a child.

Now I was pissed. "He's not the one endangering us. You are!"

Surprised, Derek laughed. "What are you talking about?"

"Are you kidding? It's bad enough you apparently kill humans regularly. This time, you've killed the wrong people. You don't think that endangers us? Hello?"

Derek didn't miss the sniping tone of my statement and actually looked abashed. "We've buried…mistakes… before," he offered.

I stepped closer to him and stood on my tiptoes to bring my face as close as possible. He looked decidedly uncomfortable.

"This is finished. We are finished. There is no us. I will never take you back, under any circumstances. And if anything happens to Ryan, I'll go to the Family and tell them all about your…mistake," I hissed out the last word, spun on my heels before he could respond, and strode from him, down the short stairs, and through the casino. The noise of people laughing, machines clanging, and music playing swirled around me and in my head while I walked. What did I do now?

CHAPTER NINETEEN

The dark house mocked my intent. Yes, it was 3 in the morning, but since it hadn't been that long since Ryan stormed from the casino floor, I doubted he was actually asleep. I knocked again, deliberately not banging. One, because he had neighbors. And, two, because I didn't want to spook him.

I sighed. He thought I was delusional. He was never going to answer the door. I pulled my phone from my purse to text him. A long shot that he'd respond. I figured it was worth the effort.

Ryan. You know I'm at the door. Please open up.

Nothing. I waited, not patiently. Still nothing.

Ryan. Please let me explain. It's not what you think.

Well, in all honesty, it at least somewhat was, I supposed. I confirmed my ex-husband was a killer. No response from Ryan. Okay, time to pull out all the stops.

Ryan. I'll start knocking on your neighbors' doors and tell them all that I'm worried about you if you don't open the door.

I silently counted to thirty, unsure if I even meant my threat. Probably not. I'd probably just go away—

The door opened and Ryan stood in the opening. His hooded hazel eyes betrayed no sense of his emotions. I tried for a smile. It faltered on my lips. *A mind wipe would be so easy* flashed quickly and I banished the thought immediately. I realized that was my suggestion earlier to Derek, but that was born of desperation. Away from Derek, I was convinced that I could explain this rationally to Ryan. He would understand.

We stared at each other. My eyes drank in his mussed auburn hair, cut short yet still long enough to run my fingers through. A forest green t-shirt stretched across his broad shoulders, inviting my eyes to travel the length of him. He didn't miss this and, despite himself, I was guessing, his eyes darkened with desire.

Abruptly, he turned, breaking eye contact, and retreated into the interior of his house. I took the door left open as an invitation and followed. His comfortable blue corduroy couch threatened to swallow even his tall frame. I perched on the edge, next to him but not touching. He leaned forward, head in his hands.

"Ryan," I ventured, just as he spoke.

"Evie."

"You go first."

"No, you," he insisted.

"Okay." Now I was silent, formulating what I wanted to say in such a way that I didn't sound even more bat-shit crazy than he already thought I was.

"I'm sorry." I paused, knowing this was completely inadequate, and yet, unsure exactly what I was apologizing *for.*

Ryan must have sensed this because he lifted his head, eyes narrowed. "How could you?"

"How could I what?"

"I'm such a fool." He looked away.

Tentatively, I placed a hand on his knee. He jerked away from me like I did earlier this evening with Derek. Rejection hurt. I placed my hands in my lap, silently imploring him to look at me again. Amazingly he did. The hurt there was like a knife to my heart.

"You used me."

"What are you talking about?"

Ryan stood and paced the small room. "I should have known something was up when you were so quick to blame Jim."

"The police arrested him," I pointed out.

He stopped moving. "I knew he was innocent. You insisted he was guilty."

Anger rose in me. "Wait a minute. I never insisted he was guilty."

"You sure seemed certain of yourself."

"People are usually who they appear to be," I snapped.

"Yes. They. Are."

We glared at each other for a few long seconds before speaking. "I admit I was wrong," I allowed. "But why are you so mad at me?" I was genuinely perplexed by the strength of his reaction, and my own anger drained away.

His heartbeat increased. "Why? You don't understand why?"

"No," I whispered. "Please, tell me."

At my whisper, his expression softened. "You were working both sides, making me believe that you and I…" The naked fear in his eyes at this unfinished statement startled me and I looked away. "That you were interested in finding out the truth," he adjusted his comment.

"I was. I am," I insisted, standing to approach him. His expression hardened again and I stopped short of reaching out. "I wasn't working both sides. I don't even like my ex-husband," I finished, the revulsion so strong in my voice that I couldn't believe Ryan didn't hear it.

Ryan closed his eyes and breathed deeply. "I don't know." His eyes reopened and I saw sadness there. "It's too convenient. You point the finger at Jim. Derek just happens to come to town. We go to his audition to gather information. Then, you insist you need to cozy up to him to get the truth."

Anger flared bright and painful again. "I did not *insist* I needed to cozy up to him. I told you that was the best way of getting the information from him. And it was. It *worked*. We got his confession. And, dammit, you agreed to the plan."

Ryan fidgeted, maybe unsure what to do with my comments. "I did. Because I didn't understand what was really at play."

"What are you talking about?" I was embarrassed to realize I yelled this and stopped to focus my thoughts before speaking again. "There was nothing else at play besides finding out what really happened to Monica and Sophie. That was all."

"Let's say for argument's sake that I believe you."

Hope filled me and I searched his face for understanding.

"What about the other nonsense?"

I opened my mouth and nothing came out. You would think after nearly 100 years, I would be more adept at handling humans when they found out I was a vampire. Of course, I was usually much better at hiding it.

"Nothing to say," he taunted.

"I don't know what to say," I admitted and his smirk disappeared, his shoulders slumping.

"Do you really believe that you're vampires? Why would you make something like that up? The only reason I can think of is to try to freak me out, to keep me from going to the police about your ex-husband. And that brings me back to why I would believe you were working both sides, and really don't want to turn him in." Ryan said this in a rush, and my mouth fell open in shock. No wonder he was mad at me.

I opened and closed my mouth several times, trying to find the right words to explain. To make him believe. He crossed his arms over his chest, putting his wall even higher. Nevertheless, I reached out again and placed my fingertips on his forearm. He didn't pull away, but the muscle underneath tightened in response.

"Ryan. It genuinely is not like that. You are correct that I don't want you to go to the police." I articulated, choosing my words oh so carefully. His lips thinned with his displeasure at my words.

"Not for the reason that you think." I closed my eyes briefly and then stared directly into his. "You must hear me. I know it sounds crazy. I wouldn't believe it if I wasn't one. Derek and I *are* vampires."

He turned away with an eye roll and shake of his head, knocking my hands off. I reached back out, stopped a hair's breadth from his shoulder before dropping my hand back to my side. "If you go to the police, I don't know what he might do. It's better if you let my people handle it."

Ryan laughed then. I heard the undercurrent of anger and hysteria, knew this was not a happy laugh. He faced me again. "Your people?" he asked, quirking an eyebrow. "You should leave." He sounded so resigned that I wanted to engulf him in a hug, comfort him while he tried to process this information turning his world upside down.

I didn't. I knew it was unwanted. "Okay," was all I said.

"I don't think it's a good idea for you to reach out to me again."

I nodded, in understanding if not agreement. "Goodbye, Ryan," I whispered as I turned from him. I trudged to the front door. Hoping he'd call out. Knowing he wouldn't. Resisting my own urge to turn to look at him one last time.

Exiting the house, I pulled the door closed behind me. I walked to my car, sat inside, turned the key. I drove without awareness back to my condo. My deadened heart felt even more hollow.

CHAPTER TWENTY

"Evelyn?"

"Good grief, Robin! You surely know it's not a good idea to sneak up on a vampire, right?" I asked the talent agent who materialized out of a dark corner of the parking garage when I exited my car.

"You were seen again with Derek at the Cosmopolitan and the councilwoman would like an update on his role," Robin Landon spoke like I'd said nothing.

Swallowing my irritation, I stared at the insipid face of the minion. "Do you guys have nothing better to do than track our movements?"

Robin did not respond; she simply waited.

I sighed. Might as well get it over with. "Yes, Derek and I met at the Cosmopolitan. Did you know they have amazing chocolate martinis at the Chandelier Bar?"

Her eyebrows furrowed in confusion. "You don't drink."

"No, I don't." I left her actual question unanswered.

"And?"

"Oh, fine. I imagine somebody else could provide the information too," I finally allowed. "Derek killed Monica Freeman on accident – mistaken identity – and then killed Sophie Chase in an ill-thought-out plan to hide the first murder."

Robin's eyebrows furrowed again.

"You're not immortal. Keep doing that and you'll get wrinkles," I offered.

"That's it?"

"Man, you're no fun," I told the woman. "There was an actual hit ordered, but that person has gone underground."

Robin sighed. Out of irritation or in response to my information, I couldn't tell. "Anything else?"

"Nope," I responded cheerfully. "And, please pass along a message to your boss. The next time the councilwoman has a question for me, she can ask me herself. I'm not interested in continuing to parlay with lackeys," I stated pointedly. I strode away from Robin but didn't miss her ears redden at the insult.

Probably not a good idea to push the demon. Whatever.

*****

When I awoke from my slumber the next evening as the sun was setting, a glance at my phone informed me that the past day was quite exciting. Notifications of a series of increasingly frantic texts from Catherine filled my phone's screen.

I know you're sleeping. Call me when you get up.

The you-know-what is about to hit the fan; call me.

The sun is setting; are you up yet?? Call me!!

Evie! I have news about Ryan and your ex.

That last text, in particular, worried me. I had already been uncertain about whether or not Derek would stay away from Ryan. I mean, Derek clearly understood my threat to report him to the Family if he harmed Ryan. But this was Derek. His ability to think ahead was directly proportional to his ego's belief that he could get away with anything.

With a groan of frustration, I called Catherine. She answered on the first ring.

"Evie, thank goodness you called!"

"What's going on with Ryan and Derek?"

"Did you know Ryan reported Derek to the police? Said he's the killer?"

I was silent for a beat while I processed the information. I had truly hoped Ryan would not do this. Of course, I never pushed the issue last night.

"You knew!" Catherine answered her own question.

"I had hoped he wouldn't," I explained, my mind racing.

"What does this mean? Did you guys find proof that Derek did it? What will happen next? I mean, they can't really incarcerate a vampire. Right?"

I chuckled at Catherine's rapid-fire questions in conversation with herself. "Take a breath, Catherine."

A giggle came across the line in response. "Sorry. You know how excitable I am."

"No different than me," I assured her with a commiserating eye roll. I quickly brought Catherine up to speed with the events of last night.

Between me and Derek. Between me, Derek, and Ryan. And, finally, between me and Ryan. Oh, yeah, and between me and Robin in the parking garage.

"Wow, you had a busy night," she said, in the ultimate understatement.

"How do you know Ryan reported Derek for the murders?"

"Oh, right. After the second murder involved the entertainment industry, I asked a friend with Metro to keep me updated. My source called this afternoon to give me a heads up that an actor had come in and pointed the finger at a producer in town doing a movie. Even before he gave me the names, I figured it was Ryan and Derek."

"Clearly," I agreed. "Did your source say anything else?"

"Oh yeah. They're looking to bring Derek in as a *person of interest* in the murders."

"We both know what that means."

"They think he's their best suspect. Confidentially, my source said they never really thought Jim was the killer, especially when the second one seemed so flimsy."

"Why did they arrest him then?"

"District attorney who has sights on the mayor's office. Maybe even the governor."

"Does the politicking ever end?"

"I don't even need to answer that."

"No, you don't." I paused to think. "As far as you know, though, Metro hasn't arrested Derek yet?"

"I haven't gotten another call, no."

"Ryan really should have let me handle this," I groused. "Now the idiot has gone and put himself directly in Derek's crosshairs."

"You're pretty sure he'll kill him?"

"For implicating him in murder? Absolutely. I was fairly confident I convinced Derek not to harm Ryan, and to let me handle it. But, now? I'd say all bets are off at this point. My only hope is that I have time since Derek just woke up too."

"Then I'd better let you go. Save the man in distress."

I heard the smile in her voice, knew she was joking to lighten the mood.

"Thanks. Call me if you hear anything else."

"Of course. Good luck."

We disconnected and I sat for a moment in bed clutching my phone. Hoping against hope, I called Ryan.

"You have reached the voicemail of Ryan Walter. Sorry I missed your call. Please leave a message and I'll get back to you as soon as possible."

I ended the call and stared blankly ahead.

If you're not dead already.

CHAPTER TWENTY-ONE

Uh-oh. I parked my car behind Derek's black Porsche 911 and flew up the walkway to Ryan's house. My heightened hearing already knew they were fighting. They were also still talking, so that was a good sign. Mostly.

I barged in the front door. Both men's heads swiveled to me, registered who I was, and then swung back toward each other. They were clearly invested in this fight. Derek stood stock still about half a foot from Ryan, who had grabbed ahold of Derek's shoulders. Interestingly, Derek didn't appear to be physically fighting back. This was good, since with his vampire strength, Ryan didn't stand a chance. But, it was disconcerting. The smirk on his face though was exactly what I expected.

"Why are you even here? I didn't invite you in," Ryan taunted. I rolled my eyes at the attempted vampire insult. Even though Ryan didn't believe we were really vampires, he apparently knew the mythology. Although it wasn't true. We could go anywhere we wanted. Humans didn't have to invite us in.

"A little birdy told me that you went to the police," Derek slowly spoke. His eyes flicked to me and then back. "I thought we had an understanding."

"An understanding? You're a killer! I made it very clear I would go to the police." He abruptly released Derek, who smoothed down his rumpled shirt.

Derek turned to me then. "Actually, I thought *you* said this was handled."

I shrugged. "What can I say? I learned about it at the same time you did."

Derek and I simultaneously turned to face Ryan, who wore such an expression of disgust that I wanted to cry.

Ryan and I made eye contact and I saw sadness warring with the disgust, and this heartened me. Maybe we could still fix us. This. I mean, this.

"Gentlemen," I urged them calmly. "Let's talk this through. There has to be a satisfactory solution."

Derek snorted. Really. "Kitten, you know the only solution is this human's death."

Ryan and I talked over each other.

"Dang it, Derek, don't call me kitten!"

"Did you just threaten me?"

Ryan took a step toward Derek, who flexed his muscles. Vampires took peacocking to new heights.

I stepped between the two men. "Seriously, nobody has to die." I shot daggers at Derek. "There is a solution."

Derek remained silent. Ryan grudgingly asked, "What is the solution?"

"Ryan, you and I want Jim out of jail, right?" He nodded.

"Derek, you and I want to keep vampire society out of the spotlight, right?" A very pregnant pause before he nodded.

"Then the answer is to give the police an iron-clad killer," I finished triumphantly.

Ryan sneered. "Your answer is to frame someone else? We have the killer right here. He admitted it." This last said almost desperately, trying to convince me.

Derek shook his head dismissively. "Nice try, Evie. No. The answer is to kill this human."

I turned to face the true threat and squared off with Derek. We were both vampires; he knew besting me was not a forgone conclusion, like it would be with Ryan. "You'll have to go through me first." My voice was deadly quiet. Ryan's breathing and heart rate quickened.

"No, Evie." Ryan sounded worried and that made me happy, for some odd reason.

With the element of surprise, and seeing my split-second distraction, Derek struck. He pushed me sideways, where I fell rather unceremoniously to the carpet. Boring brown, but rather plush, I thought distractedly.

By the time I rose to my feet, Derek had grabbed Ryan around the throat and begun squeezing. Ryan fought the best he could. He was zero match for the killer vampire. Ryan kicked his legs out, aiming for Derek's crotch. Hit, Derek winced. That was it.

Ryan's hands grasped at Derek's, trying unsuccessfully to wrench them free from his neck. Ryan was turning an unhealthy shade of purple. I jumped into the fray with a sigh.

Derek released Ryan's neck after I kicked his knees out from under him from behind. Ryan coughed violently, filling his lungs with air, and I was pleased to see his face was pinking back up nicely. Derek had already recovered from my hit and grabbed me in a bear hug, his mouth an inch from my ear.

Despite the action, he remained bloodless and cold, cool air from his words tingling my earlobe.

"I don't want to hurt you, too."

"You won't get the chance," I whispered as I launched us, still in an embrace, back toward the living room wall. The plaster cracked where we hit and Derek's grip on me loosened.

I threw him to the side, where he crashed through a small wooden end table, splintered pieces surrounding him on the ground.

Derek shook his head at me, but when he rose, he headed for Ryan, shouting, "Let's end this!"

I grabbed one of the larger broken pieces of the end table and shot toward Derek. I connected with Derek at the same time he connected with Ryan.

A jab to the jaw and Ryan slumped to the floor.

Derek didn't go in for the kill, however. He turned to me, eyes widened in shock, the tip of the makeshift wooden stake pointing through his chest at me, accusing. "You…killed…me," he uttered.

Derek disintegrated. I watched his body slowly turn to ash that fell to the carpet before blinking entirely out of existence. Like he had never existed at all.

Ryan moaned while he slowly regained consciousness. We sat on the carpet, me cradling his head in my arms, wishing I could cry. Like a human. Conflicting thoughts zigzagged back and forth in my mind, fighting with each other for dominance.

I killed my sire.

He tried to kill Ryan.

I killed my sire.

He killed many humans.

I killed my sire.

Ryan's eyes opened, stilling the circular thoughts in my head. His strong heartbeat assured me he would be okay. Derek's punch might have knocked him unconscious, but nothing appeared broken. Ryan smiled briefly before frowning. Remembering. He struggled to sit up. To get away from me. We both scrambled to our feet. Ryan's gaze moved wildly around the room, looking for Derek.

"He's gone," I explained.

"You let him leave," he responded incredulously.

"No." I hesitated.

"Then where is he?"

I winced at his anger. "He's gone. Really gone."

Ryan shook his head, not understanding.

"I…staked him."

Ryan snorted. "Please, tell me the truth."

The hurt I saw before returned to his eyes. I sighed. "It is the truth." I sat on the plush couch, running my hands over the soft ridges of the corduroy.

"Still with the vampire nonsense."

"It's not nonsense." I made eye contact, begging him to believe me. I didn't want to have to provide him with a visual. But, I would.

He broke eye contact first. "If you aren't going to tell me the truth, I think you should leave."

I stood and approached him. His heartbeat increased. "Look at me," I commanded. He struggled but ultimately obeyed, his eyes wild. I didn't like using this ability. Except I needed him to understand. My fangs descended and I bared them at Ryan, who blanched.

"Ohmigod," he whispered. "That can't be."

"It is," I assured him.

"Vampires don't exist."

"Yes, we do."

"No, you don't."

"Yes, we do," I repeated. I couldn't help but smile at the childlike turn of the conversation. I reached out and he flinched away. My smile dropped. I returned to sitting on the couch. To my surprise, he moved to sit beside me on the couch.

"Yes, you do," he said in wonder.

"Yes, we do." I put my hand on his knee and this time he didn't move away.

"Where is Derek?" he asked again.

"He's gone. I staked him. I killed him." This last statement escaped my mouth before I could stop myself. I felt Ryan's eyes on me in response. I turned my head to meet his gaze.

"It's like the movies? Poof?"

I smiled sadly and nodded. "Yeah. Poof."

"He was a bad person…vampire. Murderer." His eyes clouded. "Are you?"

"A vampire? Yes," I said, wondering about a concussion.

"A murderer," he clarified.

"No," I answered emphatically. My eyes widened. "Yes. Today."

"That was self-defense," Ryan argued.

I tilted my head, considering. "Yes."

"How do you live?"

I knew what he was asking. "Bottle service," I explained with a wry smile.

He arched an eyebrow. "Have you always…survived…like that?"

"No, in the past, we had acolytes."

"Acolytes?"

"Humans who willingly provided what we needed." I winced at the sudden increase in his heartbeat. "They never died by my hand. Or anyone I knew," I hastened to add.

Ryan nodded. "You feel bad about killing Derek?"

I nodded.

"Why?"

"He wasn't just my husband. He was my sire."

Ryan's eyes reflected confusion.

"He made me. He turned me."

Ryan heard the anger in my voice. "You didn't want him to?"

And there it was. My opening to finally tell him my story. "You accused me of trying to prove Jim guilty because I knew Derek was guilty and I was protecting him." Ryan opened his mouth and I put up a hand to stop him. "Please, let me get this out." He nodded.

"You were partly right. I did want to prove Jim was guilty. And it was because of Derek." Ryan's expression hardened. "Not in the way you think." I took a deep breath, saw Ryan's quizzical expression, and laughed.

"No, I don't have to breathe. After 29 years as a human and 92 as a vampire trying to blend in with humans, it's habit. And, yes, I'm 121 years old." Ryan looked stunned, so I just continued.

"I wanted to prove Jim guilty because I have…trust issues," I started with a shrug. "In my experience, people are not trust-worthy, so when someone appears to have done something bad, well, usually they have."

Ryan interrupted. "Hey, I'm divorced because of a cheating spouse. I understand trust issues."

I managed a small smile. "True." I looked away, gathering my thoughts. I had never told anyone this story. Other vampires knew, of course, but not from me. And no human had ever been told. "It's more than that.

"Derek and I were in love and to be married. In the weeks leading up to the wedding, he did not appear well. He began to look tired, coughing more and more. Dying, it turned out. The week before our wedding, he coughed into a handkerchief and I saw the blood before he could hide it. He finally admitted to me that he had consumption, what today we would call tuberculosis.

"If you know your history at all, typically once you showed these symptoms, it was a death sentence. We both knew this. Derek insisted we should still get married. Even though I would likely be a widow shortly thereafter, he wanted to make sure I was taken care of, and he was very well-off." I paused; Ryan looked shocked.

"The day of the wedding arrived. On what should have been the happiest day of my life, I was devastated. I knew it was a sham, though I couldn't deny Derek's logic. His parents had died of influenza in 1918, and he had no other family to whom to bequeath the money. Women were still second-class citizens. I knew he was right that his money would help me. And I knew he was suggesting it out of love. Still. I was in such emotional pain that day.

"Given everything, we had decided on a small wedding, at my parents' home. They had no idea how sick he was and I didn't have the heart to tell them. That afternoon, though, when I saw Derek standing near the preacher, he was different. He looked even paler than he had, yet somehow healthier. I couldn't explain it. I walked down the aisle, feeling my trepidation increase with each step and not knowing why.

"When he took my hand, his fingers were very cool. He had been running fevers off and on since the worsening of the symptoms. I didn't know what to make of the change. I wondered if this was some final step. That his death was closer than we had thought."

"We went through the motions of the ceremony. I stumbled through the reception; just a few neighbors we could feign celebrating with. And then it was my wedding night." I looked away from Ryan. "I was a virgin. I didn't know what to expect." I stared at my interlocked fingers moving restlessly in my lap, lost in the memory.

CHAPTER TWENTY-TWO

I lay on the bed, half under the wool comforter. I rub the goose bumps rising where my mildly risqué white nightgown bared my shoulders and décolletage. Derek appears in the doorway, a predatory smile on his lips. Wait. That can't be right. I abruptly sit up, wrap my arms protectively across my chest. I suddenly don't want him to see me and I don't know why. He practically skips to the bed, jumping in next to me. He takes me in his cool arms.

"Don't be alarmed," he whispers in my ear. "Everything is okay now."

I pull away. He doesn't feel right. This doesn't feel right. "What's going on? How do you have so much energy?" All at once I feel hopeful. "Did Dr. Raymond have medicine for you?"

Derek laughs harshly. "Dr. Raymond was useless. Medicine was useless. I found another solution." He looks at me so eagerly, I let my guard down.

"How are you better?"

Fangs descend from his gums.

He cuts off my scream by roughly putting his hand over my mouth. He leans in closer to do so. "Shh, shh, it's okay," he murmurs into my ear, though his hand does not move off of my mouth. I try to push him away, expecting him to be the feeble, sick man he was only a day ago. It's like pushing against a rock. I push harder and he laughs. "Kitten, it's fine. Please stop struggling. I'm better now. Cured." I cease struggling, manage to move my head slightly under his hand so that we are eye to eye again. "Are you going to scream?" I shake my head and he removes his hand. I intake a long, shuddering breath, staring at the still descended fangs. He reaches up to fondle one of them, a gesture almost obscene. I look away and he laughs again.

"You'll get used to them," he assures me.

"I don't understand," I whisper. I don't know what else to say to my husband of five hours.

He unexpectedly leaps out of the bed and spreads his arms wide. "I'm a vampire. I'll never get sick. I'll never die. I'm immortal." He jumps back in bed before I can respond. "I want you to stay with me forever."

Understanding dawns and I gasp. "You want me to be a vampire too?"

Hurt flits across his face. "Don't you want to be with me?"

I hesitate. I married him because I loved him. Maybe this wouldn't be so bad? "What is it like being a vampire?" I ask, tentatively reaching out to run my fingers over his pale, cool skin, and the oh-so-sharp fangs. His smile widens.

"It's wonderful. I have amazing hearing. I can smell everything. I'm incredibly strong." He wraps his arms around me and lifts me clear off the bed for a moment before setting me back down. That one moment is exhilarating – and I wonder. He must see that look in my eyes, because he leans in, earnest now. "We can be together forever."

"But…you can't go outside during the daylight, right? And nobody can know? And, don't you have to eat humans to survive?" I rapid fire ask these questions and he laughs again, gently chucking me under my chin.

"Oh, kitten, it's not quite like that. No, we mostly can't go outside during the day. And, no, your family can't know. But, vampires have evolved. We have human feeders. They don't die," he hurries to assure me, after seeing my horrified expression.

Part of me yearns to be with my love. And there's something enticing about living forever, I recognize. Never getting sick. Never dying.

But. Never basking in the sun. Watching my family and friends die and never know the truth. Derek's gaze hardens as he reads my doubts in my expression.

He smiles seductively, though the word predator flashes in my mind again. "Lay with me first and then make your decision," he suggests.

I am uncertain. But he's my husband; maybe this will make more sense. After. I nod. He leans down to whisper in my ear.

"There's one thing I need to finish," he says, so low I almost don't hear him. His fangs descend and bite into the tender flesh of *my neck. I feel a pinch. As he drinks my lifeforce, I lay unmoving on the bed, my eyes closing. I watch now from above the bed. Waiting.*

He notices my eyes remain closed. He shakes me gently and I still don't move. I realize without emotion, from above the bed, that I am likely dying. He's too new at this, doesn't know how to take without killing. He has killed me on my wedding night. I realize this, yet it does not bother me. The scene becomes fuzzy, so I am only vaguely aware of him shaking me harder, calling my name. A slight smile forms on his lips. He tears his own wrist and holds it to my mouth.

The blood drips down my chin onto my pale skin, but enough enters my mouth. I taste the copper flavor and feel the warmth. My own blood reviving me? I begin to suckle, like a child with her mother, and when the scene regains its focus, I realize that's not entirely inaccurate. He killed me; and now I am reborn.

I stopped talking and looked at Ryan. His eyes glistened with unshed tears. He took my hands in his. "He turned you. Against your will," he said the unsayable.

I leapt to my feet and strode away from him, to the wall against which I earlier had collided with my now-dead sire. I placed my hands on the plaster, replaying that scene in my mind, trying to chase away the long ago one.

Ryan walked behind me. "It wasn't your fault. You didn't do anything wrong. You didn't choose this."

I spun around, eyes glittering in rage. He withdrew in surprise. "You think I don't know that? Of course, I know that! I've been living this undead life for nearly one hundred years."

"I'm sorry. I don't know the right thing to say."

My anger extinguished with his words and I sighed. "They don't make Hallmark cards for this sort of thing."

He gave me a half-smile in return. "Why do you feel guilty for killing him?" he asked, the smile faltering.

"Vampires don't kill their sires," I answered simply. "It doesn't matter how or why you were turned. It isn't done."

"What happens next then?"

"I don't know. I'll go to the Family and explain the entire situation." I shrugged. "On the bright side, there's no reason to call the police again. After I explain to the Family what happened, they'll likely pull their strings to get Jim released."

"On the bright side," Ryan echoed. "Thank you for that."

"I haven't done anything yet," I warned.

"But you think they'll take care of it." He sounded so hopeful and trusting.

I smiled. "Yeah, I think they will."

We stared at each other for a moment and I sensed a change in the room. Ryan broke eye contact and I knew what he was going to say before he even opened his mouth. I let him say it anyway.

"Thank you for telling me your story," he began.

I waited.

"It's all too much," he admitted. "I will forever be grateful if you can get Jim released. But…" He trailed off.

"Maybe it wouldn't have happened if my crazy ex-husband hadn't come to Vegas? And maybe my being a vampire is too much for you to accept?"

"Something like that," he conceded. Sadness, desire, and understanding played out across his face.

"It's okay," I told him. I turned to leave. "I understand. Be well."

"You too."

He remained silent, didn't call out to me when I opened his front door, walked through, and closed it. I heard his heartbeat and breathing from inside the house, could tell he was hurting.

Back to the real world. I started my car and drove away from him and everything we'd been through.

CHAPTER TWENTY-THREE

At the stoplight for South Casino Boulevard, I risked the wrath of law enforcement and grabbed my cellphone from the side pocket of my car door.

Code Black

No response arrived following my text. I continued driving to my condo and within minutes I was parked and heading up in the elevator.

A man and a woman stood at attention outside my door when I arrived. They had no heartbeats and were not even pretending to breathe. Maybe it was not a myth that we could turn into bats and fly, I kind of wanted to say to them. Instead, I merely nodded as I approached.

No words were spoken while they followed behind me into the condo. I headed for my dining room table. "Thank you," I offered over my shoulder when one of them closed my front door.

"Tell us what happened," the female vampire commanded once we were seated around my table.

"No preamble?" I joked. It was clear they would not provide their names. I ran my fingers over the wood table, wondering at my nervousness. Why? I didn't do anything wrong. I called them after all. I focused on the woman before me. Surprisingly appeared middle age – we usually got turned younger – with her black hair pulled into a severe bun. Her mouth was pressed into a thin line. Fit the image of a Fixer, I imagined. She did not respond and I told her what happened, starting from the very beginning.

The male vampire lifted a single eyebrow when I shared the part of the story where I staked Derek, but that was the only response or reaction I'd received so far. He vaguely looked like a skinhead, unfortunately, with his bald head and tattoos. The sharp blue suit took the edge off the look.

I gazed down at his reaction, so minimal it spoke volumes, but didn't hesitate in continuing the narrative. When I finished with walking out of Ryan's house, the male and female shared an indecipherable look.

"We'll handle it," the female stated with finality and rose from her seat. The male and I quickly followed suit.

"Ryan will be okay, right?" I hesitated to ask this since the Family made the decision, but I'd finally put my finger on why I was nervous.

"You aren't going to clean him, are you?" There. I put it out there for all to see.

The two exchanged another glance. "We're Fixers, not Cleaners," the male answered. "The human will be fine."

The intensity of the relief I felt only mildly surprised me. "Thank you."

"This will be over within 24 hours," the female explained while she walked toward my door.

"That quickly?" I was genuinely shocked by that turnaround.

The male smiled, tipped an imaginary hat, and nodded at me. "That's our job." I smiled in return. We'd reached the door; the female opened it and they exited. I closed the door behind them and leaned against it. Now what did I do?

Before I could even consider the question, I heard a rapid succession of light taps on the door. Catherine's breathing and heartbeat sounded loud, and my smile returned.

I opened the door, caught her hand still raised and about to knock again. She was breathless but smiled.

"I thought they'd never leave."

I laughed and pushed the door open the rest of the way.

"Can I get you anything?" I offered when we passed the kitchen. Part of me wanted to grab a glass of blood, except, much like alcohol with humans, it could be a distraction. Catherine declined my offer of food or drink and we collapsed onto my couch.

"Are you okay?"

"I'm fine," I assured her. She cocked her head in response, so I didn't think she fully believed me.

"What happened?"

Thus, I found myself explaining for the second time in two hours the events of the past night. At least I didn't have to start at the beginning with her.

"Wait," she interrupted when I got to the part where the Fixers beat me to my own home. "How did they get here so quickly? What is Code Black?"

"I'm honestly not sure how they got here so fast," I admitted. "We *can* move faster than humans, but it's not like we can fly or shape shift into bats or anything. I don't think," I added with a laugh. After we finished chuckling, I explained the Family code system.

"Code Black is for non-emergencies that still have an important time element. Like in this case, with Jim in jail for something a vampire did. Code Blue is for any kind of medical issue. Turning someone you hadn't intended to, garlic poisoning, that sort of thing."

"Garlic can poison you?" Catherine asked, clearly fascinated by this glimpse into vampire life and lore.

I shook my head ruefully. "Unfortunately. It smells phenomenal, but if it touches us, or worse, if we ingest it, we become incapacitated pretty quickly. And in large enough amounts, it can be fatal."

That sobered us both, so I moved on. "Code Red is a true emergency. Anything that needs to be handled right then, typically when a vampire is in danger or the Family is in danger of being immediately exposed."

"You sent a Code Black. They were still here before you."

"Must have been in the neighborhood."

Catherine's cellphone trilled an incoming call in time to her laughter at my little joke.

"This late?" I whispered, glancing pointedly at the clock on my wall. She lifted a single shoulder and accepted the call.

"Hello?"

"Catherine, so glad I caught you," a soft voice greeted Catherine, who rolled her eyes.

"Hello, Barbara, what can I do for you this early?"

A short chuckle came across the line. "Don't pretend you were sleeping," she chastised lightly. "I know you're chatting with Evelyn Jones."

Two sets of eyebrows shot up at this statement. I glanced around, briefly wondering if my condo was bugged, before figuring she just as easily could have tracked Catherine here.

Catherine's face was stretched tight and she barely managed to control her anger.

"Why are you tracking my movements?"

"No need to be upset. The last time Robin spoke with Evelyn, the vampire made it clear that she wouldn't speak to my associate – my lackey – anymore. I'm simply honoring her wishes."

Catherine stuck her tongue out at me and mouthed thank you before returning to the call. "Then why are you calling me?"

"The reason I'm calling you both is to congratulate you on solving the murders. As a city councilwoman, I believe it's important to give credit where credit is due."

I snorted and Catherine clapped her hand over her mouth to silence her giggles. I snatched the phone from her hand. "Do you really expect us to believe that's why you're calling, Madam Councilwoman?"

If she caught the sarcasm in my use of her honorarium, she did not let on. "I did have some follow up questions, Evelyn."

Of course she did.

CHAPTER TWENTY-FOUR

"What can I answer for you?"

Catherine chuckled at my saccharine tone and I shrugged. They say you catch more flies with sugar than vinegar.

"Did you ever find out who the original being targeted for the hit by the Family was?"

I cocked my head, curious about the question and her use of the word *being*. I suspected she knew much more than she let on.

"No. Why do you ask?"

"For the safety of the city."

"That's a convenient non-answer."

I swore I heard an almost imperceptible sigh on the councilwoman's end of the call. "Let's just say I'd rather that individual remained breathing."

The call ended.

I chuckled. "She obviously knows who the target was and wanted confirmation. I wonder what this was really all about."

"I have absolutely no idea," Catherine stated, adding, "She's been fixated on me since I arrived in town."

"That's weird. I wonder how that plays into this individual who's been targeted for a hit. You have no idea why the demon is interested in you?"

"I really don't." She sighed. "We can figure it out later. Back to our conversation that was so rudely interrupted. Fixers are different from Cleaners, which is what Derek was?"

"Yep," I answered, feeling a bit like I was conducting Vampires 101 at the local community college. "Cleaners take care of problems by making people and, rarely, other vampires disappear. Fixers do exactly that – fix anything caused by a vampire or human that doesn't need cleaning but puts the Family at risk of exposure."

"I don't understand. Ryan knowing that you exist puts the Family at risk. Why not leave Jim in jail and kill Ryan?" She looked chagrined when I winced at her question. "Don't get me wrong. I'm glad they aren't handling it that way. Still…" she trailed off. "Vampires are portrayed as vicious blood-suckers for a reason. Present company excluded, of course."

"Of course," I agreed with an eye roll. "Believe it or not, we try to find solutions that result in the fewest number of innocent folks negatively impacted, whether human, vampire, or other. It's also the most pragmatic approach. To not draw unwanted attention from humanity."

"Okay, that makes sense, I suppose. I'm thankful to you for your part, so PTA can get back to business."

"What do you mean?"

"Well, with dead bodies and killer vampires running around, everything's been on hold while it got sorted out."

"The movie's going forward? Even without Derek?"

"Yes! A new producer has come on board. And, don't worry, she's keeping all of the casting the same, so you and Ryan are still co-stars." Catherine must have seen something in my expression because she reached out to put her hand on my arm. "How are you and Ryan?"

"There is no me and Ryan," I answered, failing to keep the sadness from my voice.

"Why not?"

I looked at her incredulously. "You heard what happened at his house!"

"Well, sure," she agreed. "But that's only a blip."

I laughed mirthlessly. "I don't think Ryan considers it only a blip."

"What do you want?"

This question stumped me. I liked Ryan's personality. We had oodles of physical attraction. But...

"Evie, I could practically hear your entire internal conversation just now."

I smiled sheepishly at Catherine. "There are so many moving parts to this," I finally stated.

"So what? Give it some time," she instructed. When I didn't respond, she continued. "I ran away when I found out Alex was an incubus. I needed time to process."

I nodded at her statement, something like hope flaring bright in me. What had I gotten myself into? I liked this man. I shook my head to clear the cobwebs and glanced out my floor-to-ceiling windows at the sun noticeable over the horizon.

"Time for you to go to bed," Catherine advised.

"Indeed." We stood and I walked her to the door. I opened it, leaning against it in a deceptively casual posture. She noticed and paused in the doorway.

"Give him time. You might be surprised."

After a quick hug, she continued down the hall to her condo. "Good luck" floated past the door as I closed and locked it.

With a final glance out my windows, I entered my bedroom, pulled the door firmly closed, and fell into bed, fully clothed, exhausted from the day I'd had.

CHAPTER TWENTY-FIVE

I hopped out of bed as the last rays of the sun vanished with its setting. I snagged a bottle of my favorite O+ blood from the refrigerator, warmed it slightly in the microwave, and downed it in one long gulp. I tossed the bottle in the recycling bin and hopped on my couch. I turned the local news on.

As I had hoped, it was the top story. And apparently had been all day. Elizabeth Addison, an entertainment reporter who sometimes also appeared on the regular news, was interviewing a woman with short curly brown hair and brown eyes, rocking an amazing power suit.

Elizabeth held the microphone to the woman's face, her perfectly coifed brown hair not moving when she nodded at the woman's words.

"Jim has maintained his innocence from the beginning. I'm just glad that this came out before a true miscarriage of justice occurred." I recognized the name at the bottom of the screen. Gina Johnson. Jim's lawyer. Her brown eyes narrowed, but she smiled widely, the gap between her front teeth drawing my eye. "The Las Vegas Metro Police Department has apologized to my client, and they expect to release Jim before the end of the evening." Uh huh. That look coupled with that sentence? I smelled a lawsuit.

The screen changed to show a smoldering vehicle, make and model uncertain. A bubbly Asian stood across the street from it. She indicated the wreck behind her. "According to police, the charred remains found in this vehicle belong to the actual killer of Monica Freeman and Sophie Chase. The department spokesperson declined to provide additional information, other than to state that the unnamed deceased individual in the car is without a doubt the murderer."

I clicked the television off with a sigh of relief. Thank goodness. No more dead bodies. No more worry. Jim could get on with his life. Such as it was, I realized, since his vindication wouldn't bring his wife back to life. I frowned and considered what I had just seen. The Fixers kept their word. They definitely stuck with the old adage – stretch the truth as little as possible. Aside from the actual identity of the crispy critter in the car (probably an unidentified body from the morgue, if I had to guess), an innocent man was freed and the guilty party was gone. If

I also had to guess, the police would never correctly identify the body or release additional information, and in the age of the 24-hour news cycle, I was certain a celebrity or politician would do something to draw attention. And life would go on.

A knock on the door startled me out of my reverie. My jaw dropped when I saw Ryan on the other side through the peephole. Tuning into him, I heard the nervousness in his body language, shifting from foot to foot.

"Hi," I greeted him when I opened the door.

"Hi," he responded.

We stared at each other. My eyes couldn't help but roam over the lithe muscles straining under the black t-shirt molded to his torso. His eyes sparked in response.

"Can I come in?"

"You want to come in?"

Scintillating conversation aside, his presence at my condo floored me. I moved to the side of my doorway so that he could enter.

"Can I get you anything?" I asked out of habit and he chuckled.

"I'm okay, thanks."

Yes, you are, I thought to myself as I watched him walk toward the couch. The man filled out a pair of jeans like nobody's business. I inwardly rolled my eyes and smacked myself. Stop it.

We sat on the couch, mere inches apart. It could have been miles. I bit my lower lip. His eyes zeroed in on the movement and became pools of desire.

Geez, I sounded like a romance novel. But, really, they did.

I cleared my throat. "How's it going?"

Ryan belly laughed. "Sorry. I'm not laughing at you."

"You're not?"

His face fell. "I'm not."

"I'm kidding," I assured him.

"I know. It's not that." He stared out the window. "I love that you have a view of the Fremont area on one side and the Strip on the other."

I cocked my head at the non-sequitur.

He looked directly at me. "Thank you."

I heard the sincerity in his voice, but there was an undercurrent of something else. "I let the Family know and they took care of it." I shrugged. "We always fix our messes."

Ryan looked abashed unexpectedly. "Still."

"You're welcome," I responded simply.

"I didn't know if you'd see me," he said quietly.

My lack of response created an awkward moment. The seconds stretched by.

"Say something. Please."

"I don't know what to say. I didn't think I'd see you again." Though I certainly had hoped, I didn't add aloud.

"I didn't think I'd see you again, either. But I wanted to say thank you."

"Okay."

"I hurt you."

"Yes."

"I was so focused on Jim that –" He shook his head. "That's no excuse. I messed up. I'm sorry."

"I forgive you."

We stared at each other. My arms ached to hold him. My lips—

Ryan pulled me into his arms and our lips met. Soft at first, giving way to deeper desire. We melted into each other, the blood coursing through his veins warming me through my clothing. I clutched him closer and he moaned in response. Our lips separated but we stayed in each other's arms. I rested my head on his shoulder, allowing his heartbeat to surround me. This felt so right.

"I guess that answers that," he murmured into my hair. I felt the rumble through his chest when he spoke.

"Answers what?"

"How you feel about me?"

I nestled in even closer. "I didn't think that was ever in doubt." He tensed and I pulled away.

Not touching now, we gazed at each other, such conflicting emotions. "When I heard Jim was going to be released tonight, the first person I wanted to call was you." He half-smiled. "I picked up the phone so many times, even scrolled to your number. I never pushed Call. I tried texting. I never pushed Send."

"Yet, you're here now?" I was almost afraid to ask, to shatter the moment that was building.

"I waited for the sun to start going down since I figured you would be sleeping." He grinned in response to my giggle. "Then I grabbed a Lyft over. I wanted to see. To see you. To see if…"

"I'm glad you did. But."

The light in his eyes dimmed. "But what?"

"I don't know if this is the right thing to do," I admitted helplessly.

Needing to move, I stood and walked to the sliding glass door. I opened it a hair to feel the wind on my face. Ryan moved behind me, snaked his arms around my waist, and rested his head against mine.

"We can work on our trust issues together."

I rotated in his arms so that we were pressed together. His reaction mirrored my own. I kissed him lightly on the lips.

"Yes, we can," I agreed and he smiled. "That doesn't solve the bigger problem."

"That you're a vampire," he said flatly.

"Yes. I'm an undead immortal being. And you're a living mortal."

I closed my eyes against even the thought. "I don't know how we can do it. Me watching you grow old and dying. You becoming bitter when I stay forever young and beautiful."

He smiled at my attempted humor.

"Why do we have to decide my entire life and your entire afterlife right now?"

"Live more in the moment?"

"Yeah."

"Vampires don't really do that well. We're usually in it for the long game; since we have all the time in the world. Typically," I added, as an image of Derek with the stake in his chest flashed in my mind.

"Don't think about that," Ryan responded, and I almost wondered if he heard my thought.

"So, you're suggesting we don't focus on the happily-ever-after?"

"Nope. How about, happily-for-a-human-lifespan," he offered.

I laughed. "Ugh, no. I like your other idea better. Living in the moment. Happily-one-day-at-a-time."

"Happily-one-day-at-a-time," he agreed. "And if one day, we decide to have that bigger talk, we will," he promised.

"We will," I echoed.

Our lips met in a replay of our tender kiss from before. I relished the feel of his lips on mine, his arms holding me against him, our legs intertwined. We separated and he smirked.

"Besides, Catherine told me the movie's a go again with a new producer. You'll see me every night for three weeks anyway."

"I guess I'll see you on set!"

EPILOGUE

"I'm so glad you could meet me for drinks," the green-haired, green-eyed being sitting across from me said with a wide smile.

We were at a paranormal café, *Soprannaturale*, Italian for supernatural. The owner was a werepanther from Italy. Tucked behind some nondescript storefronts on Main Street, it was unlikely an unsuspecting human would stumble upon it.

"Thank you for inviting me, Ms. Fynn," I responded with my own smile.

"Please call me Mia."

"Thank you, Mia."

"I wanted to meet with the leads of *Vampire Nights* before filming recommences, since I'm coming in late."

"You're a step up from our last producer," I quipped, though felt a stab of pain at the thought of

Derek. I didn't regret killing him exactly, but still. He had been my husband and sire.

Mia must have seen something on my face because she reached over to take my hand in hers. "I know I'm not a vampire, but as a fellow being different from most, I can sympathize with what you're going through."

"Thank you for that," I told her sincerely. "I'm looking forward to no more unexpected deaths and smooth sailing for the entertainment industry in Las Vegas and for Catherine's company, the Paranormal Talent Agency. That's not too much to ask, right?"

Episode Three

That's a Wrap

CHAPTER ONE

One thing I adored after 200 years on the planet was the ever-evolving technology. It still seemed almost like magic to sit in my home office watching someone online, and I happened to know that magic was real. Right now, the lead actor in my movie was starting a Facebook Live video.

"Hi, everybody, I'm Chad Anthony – though hopefully most of you already know that." He laughed, his boyish good looks meshing well with his charming demeanor. He ran his hand through his wavy black hair, the only indication to me that he might be nervous.

We wrapped filming of my latest movie last week and this was the first bit of post-production online marketing. Chad was great. Cute young man. I suspected this would be his breakout role – and I'd been around a long time!

While I'd been admiring his good looks (occupational hazard as a movie producer), he'd continued to talk to his online audience. The likes and the comments floating by on the screen thrilled me.

Chad frowned, and that drew my attention.

"I swear I just heard something." He turned in his chair to check behind him, then back to the laptop camera with a shrug. "Must be the wind knocking a tree branch into a window," he said with a half-smile.

But, now I was frowning. Yes, the weather could differ drastically across the Valley; however the air in my part of Vegas remained dead calm. Could it really be that windy near him? I leaned closer to the screen where Chad had continued to discuss the recently concluded film.

He stopped, his brown eyes narrowing as he turned again to look behind him. "I swear I heard someone. What the heck?"

A mix of comments appeared below the video. People worried for his safety, making fun of Chad for being so jumpy, or flat out accusing him of making this up to increase likes and the likelihood of going viral. Suddenly, loud popping noises came from my laptop. They didn't sound like gunshots, so I quickly dismissed the comments on the video warning Chad that he was about to get shot. Though they did sound familiar. Almost like firecrackers. I couldn't quite put my finger on what the sound reminded me of.

Chad faced the screen, his olive skin paling. "Do you guys hear that? What is it?"

The comments came fast and furious now.

"Get out of the house now!!! This is how someone in LA died!!!"

Wait? What? I tried to grab the user name of the person who typed the comment, but it was already gone, scrolled up and away.

The firecracker noises were louder now and more people were commenting that Chad should call the police, that it couldn't be normal. The young man, on the other hand, seemed frozen in his chair, wide eyes staring at the computer screen. I didn't know if he was reading any of the scrolling comments. I wondered if he saw the one about Los Angeles.

I perched on the edge of my seat, cellphone ready, preparing to call Chad, when the noise abruptly ceased. In the silence, Chad's face relaxed for a mere second before his eyes bugged out and an unseen force pulled him backward from the chair.

My jaw fell open. I stared at the room now visible behind where Chad had been sitting. The comments below the video became frantic. I pressed his number on my phone. I didn't hear it ringing on his end (he listened to me and turned the ringer off, I guessed). When his voicemail engaged, I closed my eyes and took a deep breath. This couldn't be good.

"Hi, you have reached Chad Johnson. If you are interested in auditioning or hiring me for a gig, please call my agent, Catherine Rodham, at Peterson Talent Agency, 702-555-6735. If you need to reach me, you know what to do after the beep."

I stayed silent for a moment, speechless in the face of what I felt fairly confident was going to turn out to be a very bad thing. "Chad, are you okay? It's Mia Fynn, your producer, in case you don't recognize my voice. Or missed my name on the caller ID," I added with a mirthless laugh, babbling. "What did I just see? Call me when you get this. I'm calling the police and will meet them at your place."

While leaving the message, I realized I should have called the police first. I did so now.

"9-1-1, what's your emergency?"

I gave the CliffsNotes version to the dispatcher of what I had seen and she logged the information into her system. I heard a sharp intake of breath before she unexpectedly stated I was the fifth call in the past few minutes to report concern for the young man.

"Did anyone give you his address?"

The dispatcher said yes but asked me for it anyway. I provided the address and told her I'd meet the police officers at the location. She started to tell me that was not a good idea. I thanked her for the commentary and pressed End on my cell.

CHAPTER TWO

Ten minutes later, I pulled up to Chad's apartment complex off West Spring Mountain Road and parked my ruby red Mazda Miata behind a black and white SUV, lights still strobing. I counted at least a half-dozen vehicles as I approached a uniformed officer on the path to Chad's apartment.

"Sorry, no one is allowed through," the officer intoned when I tried to step past him on the concrete walkway.

I peered around him, eager to catch a glimpse of someone I might know. I'd lived in Vegas a long time, maybe I'd get lucky. There!

"Catherine!" I called out to the willowy blond standing next to an attractive man in jeans. She glanced in my direction, half-heartedly waved, and I could tell by her expression I was right to expect a bad outcome.

The officer blocking my way frowned slightly. "Please stay where you are."

Catherine appeared engaged in a deep conversation with the man in jeans, so I realized I would have to handle this on my own. I hated doing it, but desperate times, and all that.

I put on my widest smile. "Officer, I really need to get to my friend." I watched as his frown faltered and his eyes took on the expected glaze.

"I have my orders," he said in a monotone, and I nodded sympathetically.

"Of course, you do. But, it's okay. Isn't it." This last I stated rather than asked.

Slack-jawed, the officer stepped to the side, allowing me passage. I hurried along before the enchantment broke, and joined Catherine and the man, who I realized was law enforcement, judging from the shiny detective's badge clipped to his jeans. My eyes wandered lower and I snapped my gaze up. Good grief.

Catherine enveloped me in a hug, easy since she was several inches taller than me, even without her heels. "He's dead, Mia. He's dead." Her voice cracked and I tightened my embrace.

I felt eyes on me as I released Catherine.

"And who might you be?"

I turned to the voice and watched, bemused, as the detective looked back and forth between me and the officer who abandoned his orders by letting me through. The detective's eyebrow lifted slightly.

"Don't be mad at the officer. I simply explained that I needed to get through," I answered the unasked question.

"Why did you need to get through? Who are you?" he repeated as he took in my appearance.

Inwardly I sighed. Although I was about 200 years old (after a while, who really cared to keep track?) my appearance suggested early-thirties, probably about the same as the detective. I didn't have your typical appearance; my high cheekbones could cut glass and my electric green eyes have been known to stop conversations.

Plus, there was my hair. I watched his eyes move over the emerald green waves that flowed to my waist. I checked him out as well before answering his questions. He looked like a world-weary Captain America, frankly. Blue eyes. Close cut blond hair. A cute crooked nose, probably from being broken at least once. Nice body, maybe a surfer, now or in the past. And, as we silently assessed each other, I felt an itch to touch his lips, his arms, his—what??

"I'm Mia Fynn," I answered with a glance at Catherine, to break the contact with the detective.

"You knew the victim," he responded, his eyes softening when he saw mine pool with unshed tears.

"I produced the movie he was promoting."

"This is Detective Jacob Dawson," Catherine introduced the surfer cop. "He's been assigned to investigate Chad's death."

I closed my eyes and took a deep breath. "What happened?"

"That's what I'm going to find out, Ms. Fynn."

"Please, call me Mia," I said, extending my hand. He automatically reached to grip mine in response, though his attention was elsewhere. Until our skin touched. I pulled my hand abruptly from his as our eyes met.

"Static electricity," I offered with a bark of laughter.

"Uh huh," he responded, his pupils dilating.

Catherine seemed unaware of the sexual tension between me and Jacob. I seized the opportunity to address her. "I take it you saw the Facebook Live."

She nodded. "I was describing it to Jacob when you walked up."

"You saw it too, Ms—Mia."

Tears threatened again. Catherine and I walked the detective through exactly what we both watched. Jacob frowned when we got to the part about Chad being pulled backward by an unseen force.

"An invisible killer?"

"We didn't see anybody," I answered and Catherine agreed. "What did you find in his apartment?" I gestured toward the two-story stucco building behind us.

Jacob stared at me for a long minute. "Why not? It'll be all over the news by tonight, I'm sure." He paused again, gathering his thoughts. "We found the victim – Chad – deceased upon our arrival. We had to break into the apartment."

"Everything was locked? No forced entry?"

Again, Jacob stared at me for a moment. This time Catherine didn't miss the tension, but it was not sexual, it was distrust.

"Mia and I really like those forensics shows," she inserted with a forced laugh.

"No. No forced entry. There was one door in and out. Locked. Windows were closed and locked. From the inside."

I heard the frustration in his voice. I placed a hand on his arm and he startled from the snap of electricity. "Sorry," I said and crossed my arms over my chest.

"Nothing appeared disturbed in the apartment. His computer had gone into sleep mode, but when our tech guy woke it up, or whatever, it was still on Facebook."

"How did he die?" I didn't really want to know, but…

"Suffocation."

"Oh. So not accidental or medical." Having seen the event, I doubted it would be either of those, but I had hoped against hope.

"No."

"None of his neighbors saw or heard anything?" I persisted in asking.

"No." Jacob's eyes narrowed at me.

Catherine's gaze flicked between us again, probably trying to identify why Jacob was suddenly treating me like a suspect. I kind of wanted to know that too. Or maybe he just didn't want civilians acting like armchair detectives. I supposed it didn't really matter. As long as the killer was found.

"I'll let you get back to it, then," I spoke into the silence. As I turned, Jacob touched my shoulder.

"What's your phone number?"

My eyes widened, and he finally smiled.

"In case I have any additional questions," he clarified and a blush burned across my alabaster skin. His smile broadened, and I broke eye contact.

"Of course." I spelled my name for him and provided the requested number. I risked eye contact again before leaving and there was something unreadable in his eyes. He removed a card from his wallet, scribbled on it, and handed it to me.

"My cell is on there too. Text me if you have any additional information." Catherine tilted her head inquisitively at this statement but said nothing. Maybe Jacob didn't usually give out his cellphone number?

"It was nice meeting you," I stated by rote. "I wish it had been under better circumstances."

"It was nice meeting you too," he replied.

I hugged Catherine goodbye, we promised to talk soon, and I walked away. I felt Jacob's eyes on me until I passed into the darkness beyond the streetlights and reached my car. Once inside, a whoosh of air escaped. What on earth was happening to me? It must be the emotions of the evening, I decided, and headed home to replenish my energy.

CHAPTER THREE

Ten minutes later, I was through the gated entrance to my subdivision in The Lakes and pulling into my garage. When people thought of Las Vegas, naturally they thought of the desert, but I needed to live near water and so I did. It was a manmade series of lakes smack in the middle of the Valley. My oasis in the desert. Kinda looked like California, but more affordable.

I breathed deep once I'd entered my home and locked the door behind me. I was more drained than I thought. I fought dizziness and fatigue, stripped off my jeans and tank top, and crossed to the sliding glass doors that opened onto my backyard. I paused beside my pool, debating whether to dive in here, or slip into the lake. Some people made fun of its unnatural colors, but although manmade, it was an actual lake. With fish, turtles, and ducks even.

I walked down the stone stairs to my wooden dock, and slid into the cool water. I dropped below the surface and allowed the water to swaddle me. I could breathe underwater, so I sunk to the bottom.

Fish approached me and I reached out my hands, fingers touching their scaly sides. They knew I belonged, despite looking like the humans they saw through the top of the water. I closed my eyes, my energy store rising.

Air bubbles seeped out of my lungs as I laughed at two fish darting at each other, almost like they were playing a game for my benefit. Showing off. I added my own hand to the play, moving it between them, and soon I'd been accepted as part of it. They moved up to and around my hand, sometimes riding the waves my hand created when I fluttered my fingers. I needed this.

Oh, and I was not a mermaid, though sometimes mythology recorded my kind as such. I was a nixie or naiad, otherwise known as a water spirit. And, although I was long-lived, I was not immortal. Unfortunately. Because how cool would that be?

Once replenished, I floated to the surface. I peered through the prism at the top of the water, making sure nobody was watching. My neighbors have caught me skinny dipping in my pool, but I'd rather not draw attention coming out of the lake. One, we weren't allowed to swim in the water. And, two, it probably looked weird that I'd been underwater for over thirty minutes.

The houses on either side of mine remained dark. I stood motionless on my dock, the water evaporating off me. I resumed moving and my skin was dry by the time I reached the sliding glass door. I entered, staring with longing back where I came. How the water called to me. It might seem strange that a water spirit would live in a desert, but Vegas had its upside. Namely the Paranormal Talent Agency. I chuckled at the nickname for Catherine's office and headed upstairs to take a shower; my lake was not a natural body of water, I wasn't taking the risk of picking up any bacteria!

Later, back at my computer, I decided to look into the Los Angeles murder that Facebook user mentioned. I found one local article, and the few details provided were similar enough to what happened to Chad that my skin crawled. I made a few notes and noticing that it was now after midnight, decided to follow up on it in the morning.

Nightmares plagued my sleep. I watched Chad die over and over again. And even though I didn't see it, my mind created the image of Chad suffocating. I watched him struggle to find breath he never would, petechial hemorrhaging around his eyes, lips turning blue. The light left his eyes as his body, starved of oxygen, lost to the unseen force. The firecracker noise surrounded me in these dreams, taunting me with its familiarity.

The next morning, I woke completely unrested shortly after dawn. Ugh. I was an 8-or-9-hours-of-sleep per night being; getting under six would make for a miserable day. Then I reminded myself that a young man lost his life, sobering my thoughts. Time to see what I could learn. I briefly considered reaching out to Jacob, but after the way he looked at me like a suspect, I decided to try finding something to bring him. Like I was an armchair detective. Exactly what I imagined he would not appreciate, I admitted to myself.

I shrugged and turned on the television to the local news. There was a brief mention of Chad's murder, but nothing new in it. I answered business emails while I had coffee and banana bread; the death of the film's star would impact the release of my movie and there would be other fallout. Time to see what was going to happen.

A couple of hours later, I heard the start of my favorite local morning show, *Entertainment Daily*. Elizabeth Addison, the normally perky brunette co-host, sounded grim as she announced the show's top story. Usually they go for upbeat and, of course, I watched it because I was in the entertainment biz.

I craned my head around my computer to see the screen.

"Last night, a rising actor, on the cusp of stardom, was brutally murdered in his apartment," she began, voice breathy yet sincere. She recapped what I already knew, but then said, "This is the second death under these circumstances. Two weeks ago, an actor in Los Angeles was found dead in his apartment, also following a social media live video. Police there are as stumped as our local Metro PD. Could these two be connected?"

The image cut to Jacob Dawson, glaring into the camera as he growled "No comment" at Elizabeth.

"That video was taken last night outside Chad's apartment complex. Police are being tight-lipped about any information they may or may not have thus far in both of these cases. We'll keep you updated."

I sat back in my wicker chair. Damn. Elizabeth was going hard-core. She seemed pretty interested in these cases. I wondered what else she might know that she wasn't revealing.

*****

An hour later, I stood in the lobby of the station waiting for the receptionist on the other side of the glass to let Elizabeth Addison know that Mia Fynn would like to see her. "Please tell her I'm the producer on the movie Chad Johnson shot right before his untimely death." I could tell the newscaster was hungry for information on that story. If anything would get her to see me, I was certain that was it.

Sure enough, the receptionist smiled at me and said, "Ms. Addison will be out shortly."

"Thank you," I responded and sat on the uncomfortable blue plastic chairs in the lobby, leaning my laptop bag against my leg. I glanced around at the headshots of the on-air talent while I waited. Not five minutes later, toothy smile wide, short curly brown hair perfectly coifed, Elizabeth Addison opened the locked door and strode toward me, hand outstretched. If she was taken aback by my green hair, she masked it.

"I'm Liz Addison," she said without preamble. "You must be Mia Fynn?"

I nodded and shook her hand. Strong grip.

"Let's head back to my office."

I nodded again and followed her back through the door, hearing it automatically lock behind us. We walked down a narrow hallway, into and through a wide cubicle-filled noisy main floor, and back to a corner office. Floor-to-ceiling windows separated the office from the cubicle area. I was impressed by the soundproofing when utter silence remained after she closed her door.

Liz indicated a chair opposite her utilitarian desk. "Please, have a seat." She waited a nanosecond after my butt hit the chair before talking. "So, you're the producer of Chad Johnson's movie?" I nodded and she continued. "What can I do for you?" There was an odd glint to her eyes, flashed so briefly I wondered if I imagined it, and then she was back to her folksy open newscaster persona. I tilted my head for a moment, considering, before letting it go and focusing on my reason for approaching her.

"I caught your story this morning on Chad," I started, my voice catching on his name. I cleared my throat. "I also am aware of the LA murder and was curious what else you knew, that maybe you held back in the broadcast."

Liz frowned. "No, unfortunately, I don't know any more information," she acknowledged. "I was hoping you might, and that's why you wanted to see me."

I heard the disappointment in her voice. "Right," I responded, mainly as a delay tactic, while I thought about where to go with my questioning.

Liz's brown eyes sparkled. "Although…"

I resisted the temptation to roll my eyes at her theatrics. "Yes…," I played along.

"I do have a source in LA," she said with a small coy smile.

"That's awesome," I reacted with more enthusiasm than warranted, because I sensed that was what she wanted.

"But…"

Oh, good grief. This woman would drive me batty if she kept this up. "Liz, do you or do you not have access to additional information?" I asked this sternly and it had the desired effect.

Liz dropped the act. "Yeah, I do. She's a detective in LA. She says she'll give me copies of what she has on the first murder."

"That's great. There must be something that will help us figure out what happened to Chad."

"It's not that easy," she warned. "She'll only give it to me in person."

"Hmm," I muttered. "Go to LA?"

"Yep."

It was a likely four-hour drive there and back, and that was *if* traffic cooperated getting in and out of Vegas. Not to mention the nightmare that was LA traffic. Or we could fly, but then we'd have the hassle at the airport, plus needing to rent a car. My brain screamed at me about needing more sleep, but if it could help solve Chad's murder, it'd be worth it.

"Oh, and I need to be back in time for tomorrow morning's broadcast," Liz added with a wicked smile.

I couldn't help it but I laughed. "You're enjoying this, aren't you?"

She sobered briefly. "I wish it was under different circumstances. But, yeah. This is what I went into journalism to do."

"You didn't do it to cover the latest It Girl's movie?"

Liz rolled her eyes then shrugged. "Nah, but that's kind of fun too," she admitted.

I calculated in my head. "We have about sixteen hours to drive to LA, meet with your source, possibly do any follow up, and drive back."

"Sounds about right." She smiled the first genuine smile I'd seen that morning. "What do you say?"

"Road trip." I mirrored her smile.

CHAPTER FOUR

Liz and I left straight from the studio, although I insisted on a quick stop first. "I need an energy boost," I explained.

Since Liz knew I was up late last night at the crime scene, she understood. She maneuvered her white Audi R8 Coupe (clearly being a media personality in Vegas paid better than I thought!) out of the station's parking lot and eased into traffic. We headed for the 215, watching for a Starbucks. Liz shot across three lanes of traffic when she spotted one and pulled into the drive thru. Thankfully, there were only two cars in front of us. It was amazing how often the line stretched into the street.

"What do you want?" Liz asked this as we pulled forward to order.

"Espresso macchiato, with an extra shot of espresso."

I heard the smile in her voice when she placed my order, getting a small house brew for herself. "I don't do fancy drinks," she tossed over her shoulder at me.

I laughed. "Your loss." In a few minutes, I sipped at my beverage of the gods. Appropriately caffeinated, we hit the road.

We drove the 215 to the 15 and followed the signs to Los Angeles. We were both pleasantly surprised that the traffic was light. Soon we left Sin City behind, heading toward the City of Angels. There was a joke in there somewhere, but I was still too tired to find it.

Our ride was uneventful as we passed through Primm, Barstow, and Victorville on our four-hour drive. Well, four-and-a-half hours. We did have to make a bathroom stop. Signs for San Bernardino informed us we were close, so Liz sent a quick text message to her contact, requesting an exact site for meeting.

"That seems a bit cloak-and-dagger," I commented. "Not to give us the meeting location ahead of time."

"She's a cop. They're paranoid by nature. Plus, she's violating her department's rules," she reminded me with a side glance.

I lifted my hands in a mea culpa. "That's true."

Liz watched for the exit off the 210 for Highland Park, our apparent meeting place. We exited Figueroa and within another ten minutes found ourselves near the neighborhood.

"Where are we meeting your contact?"

Liz laughed as she turned onto York. "Starbucks."

Hmm. Maybe I'd have a second coffee. I pointed to the building across from a 99cent store.

Easing the car into a space, we exited and stretched after the long drive. Liz opened the door to the squat building and a wiry Latina seated just inside lifted her chin at Liz in greeting. I followed her over to the table and we sat across from the officer.

"I'm Selina," she introduced herself, and I didn't miss that she only offered her first name.

"Mia."

"Do you have the files?" Liz drummed her fingers on the table in anticipation.

Selina placed her hand flat on the table and slid it toward us. When she removed her hand, a small thumb drive remained there. Liz quickly disappeared it into her pocket. "Be careful."

"Of course," Liz replied dismissively.

Selina's eyes darkened. "Seriously. Roger Miller was suffocated in a manner we can't identify. If what you're saying in Vegas is true, his killer has struck again."

"Thank you for the warning," I said, cutting my eyes at Liz. She really could be more appreciative and less cavalier. "And I know it's probably in the files. But, any suspects?" Selina shook her head. "Anything that stood out as unusual?"

"Other than the locked room?" she asked sarcastically.

"Yeah, other than that."

"There was one thing," she began, her eyes clouding over. "It didn't seem connected."

Liz and I waited for her to continue.

"Mr. Miller had a generally clean record with one notable exception."

My goodness, this was like pulling teeth.

Liz was a good deal less patient. "C'mon Selina, spit it out. We've got to get back to Vegas." They stared at each other for a beat and I wondered what their relationship really was. And then Selina dropped the bombshell.

"A year prior to his death, Roger Miller was investigated for the disappearance and possible murder of his girlfriend."

I sat back in the plastic chair in shock. Maybe Roger was a killer and his murder was revenge? "Wait, you said it didn't seem connected," I challenged.

"Yep. We investigated that angle and nothing really seemed to come of it." Selina unexpectedly chuckled at the matching expectant looks on our faces.

"Okay, okay. I'll tell you what we learned. 9-1-1 received a call from a motorist who had pulled off to the side of the road. The couple saw a damaged guardrail and the wife thought she saw light reflecting off of something metallic over the side in the bushes. The husband went down the side and found the wrecked car. Roger Miller was alone in the vehicle, unconscious and bleeding from several scrapes, but nothing that looked severe.

"We later learned at the hospital it was a combination of alcohol and head trauma that knocked him out. The passenger door was closed. There was no evidence that anybody else was or had been recently in the vehicle. Miller did not respond to the husband's attempts to rouse him, though it was confirmed he was breathing.

"The husband noted a piece of the guardrail had flipped up and pierced the windshield into the front passenger seat. First responders arrived and transported Miller to the hospital. When he awoke, he kept asking for his girlfriend, Juni. He insisted she was in the car with him. If," she stressed the word, "someone had been in that seat, he or she would have been impaled and would not have walked away from the accident."

My eyes widened slightly before I recovered. Vampire? That could explain a passenger who was there and then not there following an impaling. I made a mental note to check with my one and only vampire friend, Evie, when we returned to Vegas. She was an actress I met through the Paranormal Talent Agency, of course. I focused on Selina's voice.

"Here's where it gets weird."

"You mean it wasn't weird yet?" Liz asked with a chuckle and Selina smiled.

"Weirder," she amended. "Here's where it gets weirder. The easiest way to show that the girlfriend, Juni, wasn't in the car would be to find her, happy and whole. Right?"

We nodded and she continued.

"This kid, Miller, didn't have a last name for her, said he'd only known her a couple of months, and only had a partial picture. She had no other friends he knew of, nor where she worked, or even where she lived. We blasted what little we had over the local news and social media. We asked the public if they knew who this woman was. Nothing. No missing report was ever filed in LA that matched her picture. We entered her information into the national database and never got legitimate hits. It's like this girl popped into existence and then popped right back out." Frustration tinged every word of her statement.

Definitely vampire. The more Selina spoke, the more convinced I was.

"We charged Roger Miller with driving while intoxicated and reckless driving for his likely speed and no evidence of braking before the crash. But," she shrugged, "without a body, or any evidence this young lady even existed, there wasn't much else to do. He got court-ordered drug therapy and six-months' probation."

Liz and I sat quietly for a moment, processing all the information.

Selina looked at her watch. "If you don't have any other questions…" She waited half a second for Liz and me to shake our heads no and then she stood. "I've got to get back to work. I hope it helps," she said sincerely. "Don't be shy in sharing any of your information either."

We agreed to do so and remained seated as Selina left.

"What do you think?" I finally asked Liz.

"I think we need to review those files and then look into Roger Miller before we leave Los Angeles."

Her excitement was infectious and I smiled. "I was hoping you'd say that!"

After grabbing more coffees, we spent the next fifteen minutes staring at my laptop screen. Selina was nothing if not thorough. She provided us with copies of Roger Miller's autopsy report, the Facebook Live video of his murder, and scores of interviews with folks identified as his friends, family, or people of interest (although unfortunately, as Selina had stated, not as potential suspects). We reviewed the paperwork before watching the video. When we saw the side profile picture of Juni, we paused to take in the twenty-something raven-haired beauty. Oh, and vampires could have their picture taken, so this neither confirmed nor eliminated my hunch that she was a vampire.

"Witness protection program," I joked.

"Right? Who doesn't have a single social media account or even just a basic online footprint in this day and age?" Liz agreed.

"It is odd."

I brought up the Facebook Live video and made sure my sound was way down – didn't want to frighten anybody around us. The video was almost eerily identical to Chad's and I felt a lump in my throat at the fear both of these men had before being violently killed. We had to find something that would help solve these murders and prevent others.

Liz and I sat in silence for a few moments following the conclusion of the video. "Next step?" Liz asked.

"Let's talk to Roger Miller's mother before we head back to Vegas. Maybe her son told her something more or different than what he told the police following Juni's disappearance."

CHAPTER FIVE

Thirty minutes later we pulled behind a blue Honda Accord in the driveway of a modest Spanish Colonial home. I noted the well-kept lawn and bright flowers as we walked up the concrete path to the red front door. We did not call ahead, so I was hoping the car meant his mother was home. I glanced at my watch and cringed when I saw it was already 8 p.m. Liz knocked as I glanced up and down the street. Minimal traffic, no pedestrians. Definitely a suburban area. The door opened to reveal a middle-aged woman with bloodshot eyes holding a tissue.

"May I help you?"

Part of me wanted to back away from this clearly grieving woman – what were we thinking? – but Liz had already extended her hand. "Mrs. Miller?"

"Yes?"

"Roger Miller's mother?"

Her eyes clouded over and a single tear tracked down her cheek. She appeared resigned. "Are you with the press?"

I jumped in before Liz could answer in the affirmative. "Ma'am, we are so sorry for your loss. We heard about Roger's murder…" Mrs. Miller visibly paled at the word. "…while investigating the murder of my friend, Chad Johnson. You may have seen something about it on the news?"

Mrs. Miller thought for a moment. "I haven't seen or heard anything. But, then I've barely gotten out of bed," she directed this towards me, almost defiantly.

"I don't blame you," I simply said and the dam broke. Mrs. Miller audibly cried as she indicated we should follow her into the home.

Dark with all the blinds drawn and few lights turned on, I could tell even in the gloom that hers was a cared for home. My heart broke for the loss this mother had experienced.

"Please sit down," she directed us to a sectional couch in a pale blue abstract design. Liz and I sat on the edge of the sofa while Mrs. Miller moved to the loveseat facing us. Her hands lay limply in her lap.

"Mrs. Miller," I started, and she stopped me.

"Please call me Jacki," she said by rote.

I hesitated. Liz wisely remained quiet, to see how this played out. "Jacki, my friend and I are trying to gather information related to your son's death that might help us understand what happened to our friend, Chad, and prevent anyone else from being hurt. But, if this is too painful, we can leave."

Jacki raised her face and looked at us through watery eyes. "It's okay. Not talking about it won't bring him back. If I can help some other mother not go through this, then I will." She took a long, shuddering breath. "Ask your questions."

I brought Jacki through our understanding of the events that transpired on the night of the car accident and she confirmed that Roger told her the same story he provided the police, and that she had no reason to doubt what he said.

"Even though he'd been drinking?" I asked gently and Jacki looked away briefly before responding.

"Roger had only recently turned 21. He was still sowing his wild oats when it came to alcohol. He had made a couple of bad choices, but never anything like that. He'd never blacked out or hurt anyone."

Not that you know of, I thought to myself before refocusing on Jacki.

"I had no reason to doubt that he genuinely believed Juni had been in the car with him," she concluded.

"How do you explain the lack of evidence of anybody in the passenger seat?" Liz asked this.

"I don't."

That stumped us and for a moment nobody said anything. "We spoke to the police about Juni," I restarted the conversation. "It seems nobody really knew her well."

"I only met her once," Jacki stated. "Juni and Roger had only been dating a couple of months, but he was smitten with her." A genuine smile ghosted across her face then faded. "She never gave my son her last name."

"You didn't think that was odd?" Liz asked, doubt tinging her voice.

"At first, but Roger explained Juni said she had escaped an abusive relationship. She told him she didn't want to endanger him."

"Is that why there's only the one picture of her?" This made more sense to me now; although, not if she was a vampire. Hmm. Jacki was still explaining.

"She was worried about being found, so she didn't want any pictures. I snapped that one. She was very unhappy with me and asked me to delete the picture. I lied and told her I did." Jacki's face reddened at the remembrance of the deception. "I just wanted one picture," she finished defensively.

"I think it's okay," I assured her and she smiled gratefully before her mouth turned downward.

"After the accident, Roger spent weeks searching the area near the crash, first with the actual search parties and then on his own. He confided to me that he was having nightmares of her alone and scared in the woods."

My heart broke again for that grieving young man, trying to process the strange loss of his love.

"Once he finished his probation, he finally seemed ready to rejoin the world. I was so happy to have my son back," she said wistfully. "Then to have him taken again, forever." Her voice choked on the last word and she stared at her wringing fingers in her lap.

Liz and I shared a glance. We'd likely gotten all that we could from Roger's mom. I stood and Liz followed my cue. "Jacki, thank you so much for taking the time to speak with us."

She scrambled to her feet. "Was anything I said helpful?"

I smiled gently. "Yes. You've given us a few new angles to consider."

"I'm glad," she said. "You'll tell me if you find who did this to our boys?"

"Of course." I nodded and she clasped my hands in hers. On impulse I hugged her. She tensed but then relaxed.

"Thank you for listening."

Jacki watched us walk back to our car and we considered our next steps while we drove from her home.

"What do you think?" Sadness hung on me from Jacki and I needed to focus on something active.

"Let's head back to Vegas," Liz declared. "We can review what we have."

I concurred, though of course, directed Liz to the nearest coffee dispensing establishment, a Dunkin Donuts this time.

"Let's do some internet sleuthing and then review the information Selina provided," I suggested once we were back on the road for our four-and-a-half-hour drive home. Liz agreed and explained the Audi's awesome wifi hotspot capability.

I googled "Juni Los Angeles" and frowned at the screen.

"What?" Liz glanced over at me.

"Nothing, that's what. Absolutely nothing of use. The big goose egg. Nada." I was trying to think of another expression for nothing when Liz laughed.

"No more caffeine for you."

"Am I a little hyper?"

"Yeah, I'd say so." Liz paused. "It really is weird how there's nothing on Juni No-Last-Name. Even if she decided to drop off the grid, you can't erase your past like that. Unless she really was in the witness protection program."

Or she was a vampire, I silently added.

"What is it? You've got this weird expression on your face. I noticed it last time we talked about her having no history." Liz narrowed her eyes at me. "Spill it."

CHAPTER SIX

I widened my eyes in a parody of innocence. "I have no idea what you're talking about." I broke eye contact. I was not about to tell Liz I thought Juni was a vampire.

"Fine. Keep your little secret," Liz said, her tone light, but with an undercurrent of something darker.

"I agree it's weird that she truly seems to have popped in and out of existence," I repeated what Selina had said earlier. "An alternative explanation is that her first name is fake too."

"Hmm. That would make sense. And with no good pictures to run a google image search on, that would be an effective way for her to mask her history," Liz agreed. "Where does that leave us then?"

"Let's take a look at Roger Miller's social media accounts," I suggested and was already typing away on the laptop. A quick scroll through his Facebook, Twitter, and Instagram accounts confirmed the mother's reports. "He really was in love – and really depressed and guilty after the accident."

"Guess he shouldn't have been driving drunk," Liz snapped.

"Harsh, Liz. He was a dumb kid who made a mistake. You never made a mistake before?"

Liz lifted a single shoulder dismissively. "This isn't about me."

"That's true," I responded and closed the open browser tab. "Let's review what Selina gave us," I changed the subject.

The miles passed by in a blur (except for a single bathroom break, of course) as we reviewed each of the files. While watching Roger's Facebook Live video again, I had that same sense of déjà vu hearing the firecracker noise and made a slight grunt of irritation.

"What?"

"I don't know. There's something about that popping noise that I can't place and I know that I should be able to." Frustration was audible in my voice.

"You had the same reaction with Chad's video?"

"I did." I scrunched up my face trying to place the noise. I sighed loudly and slumped in the seat. "This is ridiculous."

Liz laughed. "Don't be so hard on yourself. Quit thinking about it and maybe it'll come to you."

"What do you think about Selina's conclusion that Juni's disappearance and the murder aren't related?"

"It could be a coincidence," Liz spoke slowly, thinking. "But. It seems like too big an event NOT to be connected. On the other hand, if it is connected, I'm having a hard time seeing how."

"Maybe Juni faked her death with the plan to come back and kill Roger when the heat had died down," I suggested my outlandish explanation with a giggle.

"Oh, I'm sure that's it," Liz agreed with a laugh. Soon we were both giggling at the ridiculousness of the idea. Clearly, she was right and I'd had too much caffeine!

After that, we sang along to the radio and made idle chitchat, letting our brains percolate with the information we'd gathered. Liz pulled into the television station parking lot and dropped me next to my car.

"I'll check in with you after my show."

"Give me a few more hours to get some sleep," I requested with a lopsided smile. "When I crash from the caffeine, it ain't gonna be pretty."

"Okay, get back to me when you're awake. We'll talk more about our next steps." She glanced at her watch. "I'm off to catch a few winks myself."

"Sounds good," I agreed and Liz drove off. I sat in my car for a moment. It wouldn't be dawn for a few hours, so I took a chance and texted Evie.

You home?

Sure. Isn't this a bit early for you?

I have some questions, best done in person.

Uh-oh. Everything okay?

With me, yes. I need your help with something.

Come on over.

I drove towards the Arts District and Evie's condo. A parking spot opened up directly in front of the building as I passed through the final light and I zipped the Miata into the space. The front desk attendant had apparently been alerted that I was coming. When I showed him my ID, he didn't call Evie to let her know I'd arrived and instead waved me through to the elevators.

The ping of the elevator door sounded loud in the early morning silence when it opened on Evie's floor. I saw her door was slightly propped open; I knocked as quietly as I could.

"I'm coming in, Evie."

"Welcome!" was her response from around the corner in the condo.

I closed the door behind me and had taken only a few steps when both my phone and Evie's dinged with incoming text messages. She was faster than me at checking and laughed. "It's Catherine. She wants to know if she can come over."

I confirmed that was the text I received and responded yes. A slight knock on the door followed almost immediately. I opened it to Catherine's wide smile.

"I heard the elevator and then your voice. I figured it must be something interesting."

"I know why Evie's up, but why are you?"

"I was up early for a production starting today. On-call in case of any problems," Catherine explained, long blond hair pulled up in a ponytail. She closed and locked the door behind her. As the only human in the room, security was more of an issue for her than us.

Soon we were seated on Evie's couch, me marveling as I always did about her fabulous view of the city. The women turned to me.

"What's going on?" Evie asked, blue eyes curious.

I brought them up to speed about the two murders and my trip to LA with Liz Addison. Evie was frowning before I could finish.

"I'm almost 100% certain there was no vampire in Vegas named Juni," she asserted. "Now, if you're right that she was using an entirely faked name, there's less certainty. Although I haven't heard anything about any vampires vanishing either. Of course, we don't check in and out of the city, so it would be possible for her to come and go if she's from here. I have no idea about LA. I can check with my people." She sent a quick text. "Show me her picture."

Evie and Catherine chatted while I turned on the laptop and brought up the half-profile image of our missing, presumed dead, woman, maybe vampire, Juni.

Evie frowned at the picture. "She doesn't look familiar at all." Her phone beeped with an incoming text and she glanced down. "Nobody fitting the description missing in LA, either. Probably not a vampire. Most likely just a drunk guy who is misremembering his evening."

Disappointment surged through me. I didn't know why I wanted Juni to be a vampire so badly. Maybe because then there might be some motive for Roger's murder? Although that wouldn't explain Chad's murder.

"Earth to Mia," Catherine said with a laugh, waving her hand in front of my face. I refocused on my friends.

"Sorry, guys. It just seemed important to me that Juni was a vampire. I really don't know why."

"Do you want to go through the rest of your material? Maybe Catherine and I will see something that you and Liz missed."

I thanked Evie for the offer and we methodically moved through each of the documents. The autopsy report confirmed suffocation, like we expected with Chad's forthcoming report, but no evidence on the body of how. No strangulation marks on the neck, for example.

The interviews of family and friends were the typical, *I can't believe this happened to him*, type of responses. We found it interesting how few people mentioned Juni.

Then we reached the last piece of evidence we had — the Facebook Live video. Between seeing Chad's in real time, and the multiple viewings of Roger's, I no longer wanted to watch. I faced my head away and tilted the screen more toward Catherine and Evie.

"Do you guys hear that popping noise? What is that?" Roger's words, so eerily similar to Chad's, pierced my heart. These poor young men, snuffed out before their lives had really even started.

I bolted upright just as Evie shouted.

"I know what that is!"

She and I faced each other and simultaneously exclaimed, "Djinn!"

Catherine looked back and forth between us, clearly not following. But, we'd figured it out. I sat back down and patted Catherine's knee, smiling at Evie.

"It's been bothering me since I first watched Chad's Facebook Live video. That popping noise, so much like firecrackers, sounded familiar. I just couldn't place it. And each time I watched Roger's, the same. Now I know."

"The murderer is a djinn," Evie added, which increased Catherine's confusion.

"A djinn is better known as a genie," I explained.

"How do you know that noise is from a genie?"

"If a djinn is angry enough, and this one must be to want to kill people, they create a popping noise that is a physical manifestation of that anger," Evie said.

"That means that even though I was wrong about her being a vampire, I was also probably right about Juni," I added. Catherine looked confused again.

"A djinn is an elemental being. When one dies, it reverts back to its element. If Juni was stabbed by the metal of the guardrail through the heart, that would certainly have killed her." I felt a moment of sadness at the death of the immortal, but not invincible, being.

"And since she would have reverted back to her elemental nature, there would be no evidence of her in the car."

The three of us considered the possibilities.

"How do you think that's connected to the murders?" Evie asked.

"I'm not sure," I answered as my mind worked through the logic. "I'm not aware of any djinn in Vegas…" Evie shook her head no, that she wasn't either.

"Since the first murder took place in LA, the djinn could be there. I don't know anyone to ask. We should operate on the assumption that the djinn could be in either city and travelled back and forth," I finished.

"Do you think this djinn will kill anyone else?" Catherine asked in a small voice.

"Since we don't know the motive behind the murders, I think we should assume it's likely," I answered grimly. "Even if the first murder is related to Juni's death, that doesn't explain Chad."

"He has zero connection to the paranormal as far as I know," Catherine added.

We pondered this inconsistency.

"There is a possibility," Evie said as she stood and walked toward the sliding glass doors leading to her balcony. She stopped and stared out into the dark. "I may be misremembering my elemental being knowledge, but aren't many djinn born as twins?"

I gasped. "Oh, my goodness. You might be on to something!" I stood as well and paced back and forth in front of the couch while I worked through this new angle. "If Juni had a twin, that djinn could be our killer. How do we find her? Or him?"

Evie frowned. "I think the twins are usually same-sex, but honestly, I don't really know. I think, either way, we'll have a heck of a time finding a djinn that probably doesn't want to be found."

"Why?" Catherine asked.

"Oh, djinn are fun," Evie answered with a laugh.

I explained further. "They can shape shift, fly, and become invisible."

"Ah, those *would* make it difficult," Catherine agreed and the three of us chuckled. "What do you want to do?"

"I want to talk to Detective Dawson," I blurted out.

Catherine arched an eyebrow. "Jacob?"

Evie looked confused. "Who?

"Detective Jacob Dawson is investigating Chad's murder," Catherine explained to Evie.

"Is he…like us?" Evie asked.

I shook my head no.

"Then why would we want to tell him anything? Would you tell him everything?"

"Of course not, Evie. But," I continued before she could interrupt, "if we give him the background, leaving out that Juni was probably a djinn, we can tell him to look for a sister. With the risk this sister poses to humanity, let alone exposing all of us with her actions, it's imperative we find her sooner rather than later. Maybe with their additional databases and stuff, Jacob'll have better luck."

"I guess that makes sense," Evie reluctantly agreed.

"And the LA cop too, right?" Catherine asked.

"I'll let Liz know and she can tell Selina. We just leave the paranormal stuff out of all of it," I concluded and the other women nodded in agreement.

A narrow band of light was surfacing over the mountain range outside the city. Evie gestured to it. "Sun is coming up, ladies, so I'll need to kick you out now. Time for my beauty sleep."

CHAPTER SEVEN

Sitting in my car, watching the light brighten around me as the sun came up, I considered my options. It was barely daytime. The detective was probably not even awake yet. Although Liz definitely was, she was likely prepping for her show in a couple of hours. The best thing, I decided, as I started my engine, was to go home and get my own beauty sleep for a few hours. I was truly running on fumes, after being up for ... how many hours? I started counting backwards to determine how long I'd been awake and then realized this was further proof of my exhaustion. Time to return to The Lakes.

Unfortunately, with the sun up, a skinny dip in the lake was not a good idea. I decided a quick swim in my pool would have to suffice. And I guessed I'd be neighborly and wear a swimsuit. Once inside my home, I padded silently across the natural stone floor while I stripped my clothes off. I grabbed the aquamarine one-piece off the back of the wicker chair in the breakfast nook (its permanent home when I wasn't wearing it) and slid the glass door open. Stepping out onto the concrete, I breathed in the crisp morning air. The mountains were visible in the distance.

Water caressed my skin as I dropped beneath the surface of the pool. No underwater life lived here so I swam a few laps, flipped a few somersaults for fun, and practiced what I liked to call, mermaid maneuvers. I realized I was smiling underwater and settled to the bottom. Colorful pebble-tec instead of boring plaster coated my pool and I delighted in the dolphin, turtle, and seal I had custom designed for the floor.

Despite the replenishing qualities of the water, the exhaustion from lack of actual sleep threatened to overwhelm me. I surfaced with reluctance. I felt someone's eyes on me and a quick glance to my left identified the source.

"Hi, Elliott," I called out to my neighbor and swam to the side closest to our shared wall. He had a dazed look on his face.

"How—?" he asked, and I groaned under my breath. I knew better than to stay underwater so long during the daytime.

I hoisted myself out of the pool and began the short walk to where he stood on the other side of the shared concrete wall. His eyes tracked the water dripping off my slender figure. I squeezed the extra water from my long green hair and flashed a bright smile at my befuddled neighbor.

"You aren't going to sing me to my death, Mia, are you?" He asked with a nervous laugh, probably his idea of flirtation. I managed not to roll my eyes at his not-so-subtle joke that I was a siren. This was why humanity couldn't know about us. They wouldn't even get it right!

"Of course not, Elliott," I responded, modulating my voice slightly and watching his eyes glaze in response. "You didn't see anything out of the ordinary, did you, Elliott?" I'd reached where he stood opposite and touched his arm resting atop the short wall.

"Like what, Mia?" he asked in a daze.

"Exactly, Elliott." I smiled and saw that he was completely mesmerized. My green eyes sparkled and I giggled, the sound of a tinkling bell. "You enjoy the rest of your day, Elliott." He nodded like an excited puppy and I turned before I broke the spell with a real laugh. I felt his eyes watching me walk away, back toward my sliding glass door. After opening it, I turned to give him a slight wave goodbye, and then closed the door tightly.

I really hated entrancing humans when it was my fault they saw something they shouldn't. The need for discretion was always present. I knew better. Sometimes, though, the water just called to me. I shrugged even though nobody was watching, peeled off the wet bathing suit, and returned it to the back of the wicker chair before trudging up the stairs to my bedroom for a well-deserved nap.

Hours later, I woke finally refreshed physically and emotionally. My phone showed a text from Liz letting me know she was free. Before I called, I sent a quick text to Jacob, asking if he had time to meet today and where.

"Hey, Mia," Liz answered the call. Apparently, I'd already made it onto her Contacts list. I smiled.

"Hey, Liz, how was the show?"

"Very good. How was your nap?"

"Excellent." Chit chat out of the way, I dove right in. "I may have some new info. I thought I'd swing by and pick you up, then we could go see Jacob."

"Ooo, what new info?" I could hear the reporter in her salivating at my words.

I laughed. "I'm gonna make you wait."

"Tease."

"Are you at the studio or home?"

"Studio."

"Be there in fifteen." Ending the call, I read the response from Jacob that he was at headquarters for training today and to let him know when we'd arrived.

*****

Liz still wore remnants of her show makeup, I saw, when she opened the passenger door and hopped in my car. She'd changed into a t-shirt and jeans, though, from whatever fancy dress she wore for the show this morning.

"What do you know?"

"A friend of mine who knows people," I started, deliberately vague because I wasn't sharing Evie's paranormal status – and I knew it would drive Liz crazy.

"What friend? Who does she know?" I flashed a smile and Liz shook her head. "Fine. Continue."

"My friend who knows people said that although we don't have a last name for Juni, my friend has reason to believe we should be looking for a sister."

Liz's mouth fell open. "What... where... how... I don't understand," she finally completed a statement. Her mouth twisted while she thought.

"Without a last name at all, and uncertainty whether the first name is even real, how on earth could your friend, no matter what she does or who she knows, possibly have deduced that there's a sister?" Liz stared at me, her look indecipherable.

I made a noncommittal noise. "She just does."

"How are we going to bring this to Selina and Jacob? They're police officers," she needlessly reminded me. "There's no way they're going to accept this information, without thinking we know more than we're sharing with them. Do we know more than we're sharing?" She asked this question, a shrewd look on her face as she tried to figure out where I was coming from.

"That's all I can say," I replied honestly. Even if I trusted Liz more, she was a newscaster. There was zero chance if I told her the paranormal angle that it wouldn't wind up all over her show in the morning. I wasn't dumb.

"Hmm." Liz removed her phone from her purse and sent a text. Less than a minute later, her phone dinged, several times in a row, announcing responses. "Shocker. Selina wants to know how I could know this, who told me, and what more do I know." She gave me the side eye. "What should I tell her?"

I knew her question was mostly rhetorical, but I ticked off the answers to Selina's questions anyway. "You have your sources, you don't disclose your sources, and that's all you're willing to share right now."

"Or, how about this?" she countered. "I have my source, her name is Mia, and she's hiding the rest of the information."

The clear irritation in her voice surprised me. She was a reporter, after all; she should understand protecting sources. I guess she just wasn't used to being denied. "We'll start with this," I said gently. "And see what happens."

She nodded her head, though the crossed arms and frown suggested less agreement. Before she could say anything else, we arrived at Metro headquarters.

CHAPTER EIGHT

I pulled into the parking lot off of MLK Blvd and headed to the building on the left. Once inside, I texted Jacob. Two volunteers in bright yellow shirts sat behind a glass partition with a small opening at the bottom.

"We're here to see Detective Jacob Dawson," I announced to the hole. "He's on his way to get us."

"ID please," came the response.

Liz and I slid our driver's licenses through the hole, the volunteer dutifully made a note of our information.

"Phone number?" We each rattled this off. The door to the left clicked then opened as the volunteer slid visitor badges on lanyards through the hole. "Wear these at all times in the building and return them on your way out."

"Thank you," I spoke into the hole, before turning to Jacob walking through the open door. "Perfect timing, Detective Dawson."

The detective's eyes took in my appearance again – occupational hazard, or should I take this personally? Sheesh. I almost wanted to strike a pose for his benefit, but it wouldn't be that impressive, with my hair in a high ponytail, green t-shirt, and jeans over green wedges. He, on the other hand, looked business casual nice, with a short-sleeved blue shirt over dark khakis and boots.

My eyes finished their exploration and he had a soft smile when I met his gaze. "Good afternoon, Ms. Fynn. And Ms. Addison," he added a beat later, his expression souring when he recognized the newscaster.

"Try not to be so happy to see me," she quipped.

"What can I do for you ladies?"

"Liz and I took a field trip to LA," I started, "to look into the other Facebook Live murder."

Jacob's eyes were unreadable in an impassive face. "Okay."

"We uncovered some information we think may be helpful," I continued with a big smile. See how helpful I could be? He didn't bite.

"How did you investigate that case in another city? Friends in high places?"

"Wouldn't you like to know?" Liz retorted coyly and Jacob stiffened.

"What did you find out?"

I quickly brought him up to speed, skipping over the part with Selina giving us copies of department documents, and instead focusing on the deceased's social media info and our talk with his mother.

"We have an unexpected new direction you can pursue," Liz finished with a sly smile. "We're hoping to make a deal."

"We are?" Liz shot me a look and I realized I said that out loud. Would have been nice if she had clued me in beforehand.

"We'll give you our information if you promise me an exclusive when you learn more."

"I don't have the authority to make a deal like that, Ms. Addison," Jacob said tonelessly.

"You're a detective, aren't you?"

"I'm on a team. It doesn't work like that."

"Yes, it does."

"No, it doesn't. And I'm not going to argue with you like we're children. If you don't wish to share your information without a quid pro quo...," he turned to head back to the locked door.

"Jacob, wait!" He turned back, more at my use of his first name than my request, I would guess. My face reddened. "I'll give you what we have."

"What?!"

"Liz, I get that you want the scoop, but solving the murder is more important," I explained to my indignant partner. She harrumphed and crossed her arms. Jacob was now smiling.

"Look, Ms. Addison, I can try. That's the best I can agree to," he offered.

"I'll accept that," she agreed, mollified at least a little by his concession.

"We believe the murders of Roger Miller in LA and Chad Johnson here were committed by the same person," I began.

Jacob nodded. "LAPD and I agree."

"We also believe that the murders may be related to Roger's girlfriend, Juni."

"We looked at that angle and dismissed it," Jacob disagreed.

"Why?" Liz asked.

Jacob paused before answering. "Juni had no connection to the victim here; and she was long-gone or long-dead by the time of either victim's murder."

"That's true," I agreed. "But, we have reason to believe that she may have a sister who is seeking revenge for Juni's death."

If Jacob's eyebrows could rise any higher at my comment, they'd launch off his head. "Where did you get information that Juni has a sister?" His eyes narrowed at us.

"We aren't in a position to share that right now," Liz responded primly, and I glanced down to hide the laughter in my eyes. Even *she* didn't know where my information came from!

"What is the connection between this alleged sister and the second victim? If you're assuming she killed Roger because she believes Roger killed Juni, both very big ifs, by the way," he over-enunciated to make his point, "what possible reason could she have to kill Chad?"

"We don't know," I admitted, and Liz smacked me in the arm. "We don't," I reminded her, rubbing my upper arm. She packed a wallop.

"Anything else?" Jacob pointedly checked his watch.

"Nope, that's it. We just thought you should know," I finished lamely.

Jacob sighed. "No. Thank you. I'll make a note of it and let the FBI know when they arrive." His eyes appeared stricken the moment the words left his mouth. Or, more accurately, the initials.

Liz's eyes, however, lit up like it was her birthday. "The FBI is getting involved? Really?"

Jacob closed his eyes for a moment, knowing he couldn't retract his words. "Yes. That isn't public knowledge. You didn't hear it from me."

"Of course," I assured him, already worried what Liz might do with that information.

Liz extended her hand and Jacob clasped it, rather reluctantly it seemed to me. When their hands separated, he moved his in my direction. I reached out to shake goodbye.

A visible spark popped between us and then his hand enveloped mine. "Damn, that static electricity," I mumbled.

"Are you okay?" he murmured. His thumb rubbed my skin.

My cheeks flushed as heat flared in his eyes. How could we have this much attraction? I didn't even think he liked me.

Our hands separated and I answered, "I'm fine." I glanced at Liz, my heart sinking when I saw the smirk on her face. "We hope the information is helpful." I yanked the visitor badge lanyard over my head, Liz following suit, and flung them both at one of the volunteers.

I grabbed Liz's arm and steered her toward the glass door. I felt his eyes on me and despite my better judgment, risked a glance over my shoulder while we opened the door to exit. He had tilted his head, regarding me with another unreadable expression. I gave a half wave and scooted through the door before he had a chance to respond.

Liz wisely stayed silent until we were safely back in my car. "You two should just get a room," she crowed.

My cheeks flushed again. "I don't know what you mean."

"The heck you don't." She laughed. "There was a visible dang spark when you touched. Visible," she repeated. "That doesn't happen every day."

"Sure, it does," I argued. "It's called static electricity. Just like I explained to Jacob."

"Don't you mean Detective Dawson," she teased.

I sighed. "Whatever. We're done."

"What do you mean, we're done," she demanded, all trace of laughter gone.

I exited the parking lot onto Alta Drive, considered whether or not to take the 15 or surface roads back to the television station, while I deliberately delayed answering. Of course, I was going to continue to look into the murders. But, now that I knew for certain there was a paranormal aspect, I really didn't want a reporter of any kind involved. Too risky. Liz waited me out.

"We've given them a name. And now the FBI will be involved," I finally stated, not meeting the eyes I felt staring at me.

"Are you kidding? This is our story!"

"No, it's a probable serial killer," I countered. "And we are not the best people to solve it."

Liz stewed in her seat while I drove in the silence. I began to rethink my stance. Not about telling her about the paranormal underworld; I was for sure not breathing a word about that.

No, I was thinking about the adage, keep your enemies closer than your friends. Not that I considered Liz an enemy, but if I wanted to stay on top of what she was learning, continuing to work with her was the best way. What would be our next step that didn't involve the paranormal? I decided to pitch the question, sans the paranormal.

"What would be our next step then?"

"You'll keep investigating with me," she said excitedly. A twinge of guilt surfaced at my deception.

"Of course," I answered with a smile.

"Let's think a minute." Liz tapped her finger against her lip as she considered our next move. She jolted up in the seat, straining the seat belt. She faced me. "I know a tech guy; maybe he can do more with the partial picture of Juni. Also, I'll see what he can find on the dark web."

"Sounds like a plan," I agreed. "Since both victims were actors, I'll check in with friends of mine who know most of what's going on in Vegas." Liz eagerly agreed to our plan.

My mind raced. Technically, I'd already spoken to Catherine and Evie, but maybe they'd heard something new. Because I was actually stumped. I was fairly confident the murderer was the dead djinn's twin sister, but I was at a complete loss about how to find her. It'd been two days since Chad's murder and two weeks since Roger's murder. If she killed again, we probably had about ten days.

CHAPTER NINE

I was wrong about the ten days. I learned that when I reached out to Catherine the next morning. I chose the wrong day to sleep in.

"Did you see the news?!"

"Good morning to you too, Catherine," I answered with a laugh. "No, what did I miss?"

"There's been another murder!"

My good cheer died with her statement. "What happened?"

"In LA again, another actor," she explained. "My phone started blowing up before dawn. I'll bet Liz covers it on her show. It starts in ten minutes."

"I'll text you after the segment," I stated.

"Sounds good."

I ended the call and clicked the television on to wait for *Entertainment Daily* to begin. They teased the story in the show's intro and then broke for one set of commercials before presenting the meat of the story.

Liz looked good, in a fire-engine red sleeveless shift that fell decorously to her knees. With her four-inch Jimmy Choo's, she was captivating. Her eyes sparkled despite her somber expression and tone when she spoke.

"Details are scarce, and police aren't talking, but it appears the Firecracker Killer has struck again."

"Firecracker Killer?" I asked the air. "When did we start calling her that?"

"Last night, around midnight, another actor was killed while doing a Facebook Live video," she intoned. A graphic appeared with The Firecracker Killer in neon over a recorded video. My heart sank as I realized it was *the* video.

"Hi, everyone, for those of you who don't know me, I'm Bradley Reese," he introduced himself, setting off a set of cute dimples in his baby face. He couldn't be much more than twenty, with that mop of brown curls and smooth skin. The video paused as Liz continued to speak.

"And just like in the first two videos, Bradley realizes something isn't right."

Back to the video graphic. I closed my eyes, not wanting to see this baby die. Soon that part arrived.

"Do you hear that? What's that noise?" Bradley asked as popping sounds filled the space. And then silence.

"Police discovered the body after several viewers called 9-1-1," Liz told her own viewers. "Police have not used the expression *serial killer* yet." Though you now had, Liz. I was sure they appreciated that. "But, a source tells me—" Don't do it Liz! "—that the FBI has been called in to assist with the investigation. Maybe because the killer is crossing state lines? As a reminder, the first murder occurred in LA, the second here in the Valley, and the third now back in LA. We'll update you as we learn more information." Wide, toothy smile for the audience and then cut to commercial.

I sat back on my couch, thinking. At least she didn't disclose we thought an unidentified twin of a dead woman was the killer. That placated me a little. Liz sure did give up everything else. I knew Evie was getting her vampire sleep, but I grabbed my phone off the coffee table and texted Catherine.

Ugh. Come over?

Be right there.

About thirty minutes later, a knock on my door. I opened it immediately. Catherine looked paler than normal. I gave her a hug before stepping aside for her to enter my house.

On the way to the breakfast table, I paused at the refrigerator. "I know it's morning, but do you want a drink?"

Catherine laughed. "Yes, but I'm going to pass."

I figured she would. I just wanted to make her laugh. Mission accomplished. We settled into the wicker chairs. *Entertainment Daily* still played on the screen in the living room, but muted. "What do you think?"

"Honestly, I don't know." She stared out my sliding glass doors for a moment before turning to me. "I've told all my clients no more social media videos until the killer is caught."

"That sounds wise," I responded. "Why offer a target? Just for a little publicity."

"Exactly. Some of the younger ones who still believe they're invincible," she half-smiled at that, "tried to argue with me, but I made it clear. I will drop anybody who doesn't follow this order. And yes, it most definitely was an order," she answered my unasked question.

I nodded, unsmiling. "Good for you. They need to take this seriously. Especially since we don't know what Juni's sister wants."

"You're that certain it's the djinn's twin?"

"Yes. I am. That popping noise sealed the deal for me. There's really no other explanation. I just wish I had a motive."

Obviously hearing the frustration in my voice, Catherine gave my shoulder a squeeze. "You'll come up with something. What's next?"

I checked the time on my phone. "As soon as the show is over, I'm calling Liz. She has a friend working the digital angle to see if we can get anything. After that, we'll probably check in with Jacob again."

Catherine wasn't fast enough to hide her smile.

"What?"

"I find it interesting."

"Find what interesting?"

"You using Jacob's first name."

"So? We're friendly," I explained defensively. Why was I defensive?

"You light up when you say his name," she casually added.

My mouth dropped open. "I do not!"

She laughed openly now. "Yes, you do."

"I do?"

She nodded.

I sighed. "He's good looking, that's for sure," I admitted.

"That he is."

"Maybe when this is all over..." I stopped myself. "I don't think he even likes me. He treats me like a suspect!"

"That's just his nature," she explained. "There was definitely a spark. Literally."

"You don't know the half of it," I muttered and at her expression, filled her in on our second meeting.

"Well, then, I'd say there's definitely a spark!" She cackled at her own wit. We filled the rest of the time with idle chitchat until the show finished. The instant the show ended, I texted Liz. I didn't mention the FBI disclosure. I didn't like it, and I guessed Jacob didn't like it, but she was what she was.

Any new info?

Tech guy messaged. He's got news!!!! Wanna come get me?

On my way.

Catherine had been reading this over my shoulder and stood up at my final text. "Let me know if you need anything from me," she offered.

I gave her a hug at the door, told her to take it easy, and headed out to pick up Liz at the television station. I chuckled as I wondered if I'd ever see her actual home.

Liz stood tapping her foot when I drove up to get her. She hopped in before I'd even come to a complete stop.

"Good morning to you," I greeted her.

"I've already entered Chris's info into Google Maps. Just follow her instructions," she responded. "He's in Aliante," she added and I groaned. "Yeah, I know, but if I know my guy, it'll be worth it."

Aliante was at least a thirty minute drive from the television station. I stifled a response and simply hoped she was right about him being worth it.

"You caught the show." A statement, not a question.

"I did. How did you get the video so quickly? The murder was just last night."

"I have my sources."

Rolling my eyes, I stayed quiet. She jumped in to fill the silence.

"Okay, okay. Since the second murder, people have started taping when actors do Facebook Live videos. Quite a few people emailed me the video after the murder."

It was creepy how she sounded so cheerful. Another man died. Good grief.

"But, we really need new information. Chris is a genius online, so if he says he's got something, it's going to be good. I promise."

Her excitement was infectious and I smiled at her enthusiasm. "He didn't give you even the tiniest hint?"

"Nope, but that's Chris. He loves his drama," she laughed. I joined her; that was probably why they got along so well.

She scrolled through her cellphone. I drove in the silence while she checked whatever it was she was checking and soon we were pulling up to a two-story beige stucco house. It was virtually indistinguishable from half the homes in Vegas but appeared well-kept.

*****

A young man with smooth dark skin and dreadlocks opened the door with a wide smile.

"Hello, Liz and friend." He gave Liz a quick hug.

"Mia," I offered as we shook hands.

"Chris." He winked at me. "I can see by your expression that I do not fit your stereotype."

I reddened but acknowledged the remark.

"Unless you happen to live in the basement and this is really your mother's house," I quipped back and he belly laughed.

"Ah, but Mia, you know there are no basements in Vegas."

"Guest room?"

He laughed again. "No on both counts." He stepped aside to grant us entry. "Welcome to my humble abode. Although I will admit that I had interior decorating assistance."

"It clearly paid off," I responded and looked around. His home was beautifully appointed with matching earth-toned neutrals everywhere, a splash of red on throw pillows, and abstract art pieces on the walls.

"Thank you very much. Please, please, have a seat at the dining table." We gathered around a laptop on the table, chairs already thoughtfully arranged in a semicircle.

"Okay, let me show you what I found." Chris was all business once we were seated. "I don't know your technical background, so I'll go through all the steps," he said to me.

"Here's the picture that Liz gave me to start with," and the familiar image of Juni filled the screen. "As you know, image-detecting software doesn't work very well on partial images." He closed the image and opened up a new one. I gasped. "I know, right? I took your image and worked my magic to fill in what the other two thirds of her face looked like. I can't guarantee it, but I suspect this is pretty close."

Looking at the image of a front-facing Juni, I had to agree with him. If I saw the partial and this whole image side-by-side, I would be certain they were the same woman. Long brown hair. Dark, almost black eyes.

As if reading my mind, Chris hit a few keys and the partial popped up beside the full image rendering. I could see Liz nodding beside me.

"Dang, Chris. You are a genius."

"Thank you, Liz, but if that's all I could do, that wouldn't be as helpful, no?"

"True," she agreed with a chuckle.

"Good thing I did more." He closed those images and brought up a video, clearly showing the inside of a casino. "I ran a search for my new image. Nothing popped in criminal databases."

I opened my mouth to ask how he had access to those and closed it quickly. Not really my business.

"When I ran it against general photos and videos posted on the internet, well, that's when things got interesting." Without another word, he clicked start for the video. A cute couple, clearly inebriated, were talking to each other and the person holding the phone. Since they were obviously not Juni, I correctly assumed what I was looking for was in the background.

"Wait for it," Chris intoned and I leaned forward.

There! He hit the pause for the video just as a woman walked into frame behind the happy couple. Holy cow, it was definitely Juni. Chris waited for our reactions.

"Where is this, Chris?" Liz asked, her eyes squinting as she tried to see details that would disclose the location.

I realized why Chris was waiting. "*When* is this?" I asked instead and Chris nodded his approval.

"Exactly, Mia. The where is important, Liz, and it's at the Golden Nugget at Fremont. But, Mia hit the nail on the head. When I checked the time stamp for this video, it's a week ago."

To her credit, Liz instantly understood. "This is right before the murder. Well after Juni died," she exclaimed.

Chris nodded. "Yep, which makes things interesting. Either your girl Juni isn't dead, or this is the twin sister you're looking for."

My head was spinning. If I was wrong about Juni being a djinn, then this very well could be Juni and she likely was our murderer. If I was right about Juni being a djinn, then this was likely her twin sister who was our murderer. But, if this was Juni, what was her motive for murder? Angry at Roger for some reason. But why kill the others? And if it was the twin sister, I was still back to my question of her motive for the murders of Chad and Bradley...too many ifs. I realized Liz and Chris were staring at me.

"What are you thinking?" Liz asked.

"Did you find her on any of the security footage at the Golden Nugget?"

"I may have access to certain private databases," he coyly answered, "but even I cannot access casino security footage. And I don't know anybody who would give me access. Do you?" This last directed at Liz.

She frowned while she thought. "Not at the Golden Nugget."

"No other videos popped with her image?" I asked Chris.

"I'm afraid not."

I winked at them both. "Then it looks like we're heading to Fremont!"

CHAPTER ELEVEN

Fremont used to have so much free parking, I lamented before I pulled over to my usual metered spot. Whenever I headed to Fremont, I kept it simple and grabbed a metered spot on Sixth Street. I was usually only a couple of blocks from anywhere I wanted to go in the area. I fed $4 to the meter. That should buy us enough time.

Liz and I walked to the Fremont Street Experience, which housed the Golden Nugget Hotel & Casino, among many other colorful attractions. Sometimes it was best to avert your gaze! I totally understood making a living, but I didn't really need to see a middle-aged man with a beer gut wearing an American flag bikini. Liz and I heard a thumping beat and saw a small crowd gathered around one of the street artists. Liz rolled her eyes when I pulled her closer.

"Really, Mia? How long have you lived in Vegas?"

"I like the dancing," I confessed. We peeked around the edge of the crowd. "Dang." No dancers. Just a guy doing a card trick. Probably a pretty good one, with the crowd he attracted, but still. I usually only stopped for the dancers. They reminded me of the movements of underwater creatures so close to my heart.

We continued past the card dealer. Past the man spray painted silver standing statue still. Past the woman sitting cross legged on the concrete playing a flute. Past the two women wearing showgirl outfits calling out to the men, "Take a picture with a showgirl!" I admired the elaborate red and blue headdresses of the women but carefully avoided eye contact. They usually tried for the guys, but making eye contact with any of the street artists increased the likelihood of engagement, and some of them could be pretty darn aggressive. And we had neither the time nor the interest in engaging. But I wished them lots of luck with the tourists.

Liz and I reached the Golden Nugget Hotel & Casino. We stared up at the entrance. It wasn't quite as impressive during the day as it was all lit up at night, but the gold-lined rounded cover over the entrance and the faux-gold plating on the exterior walls were still pretty sparkly. I was thankful that I didn't require breathing to survive when we entered the casino. It was midday so not quite as bad as it would be in the evening, but the smoke crawled over my skin. Liz coughed and grimaced.

"Ugh," was all she said but I understood.

We stepped off to the side just inside the door to get our bearings. It was a casino; lots of flashing lights and random jingles coming off the various slot machines. Casinos made most of their money off the slot machines; something I'd never really understood. You had zero control over the outcome. It was 100% luck if you won. At least with the table games, if you had skill, you could tilt the odds a little bit. I internally shrugged. I didn't gamble, so to each their own.

"Now we find a security guard," I stated, searching the floor for one.

"There!" Liz pointed over toward the far end of the space, where a man stood impassively like an endcap on the row of slots. We approached him, side stepping the tourists in their shorts and flip flops, holding either cameras or alcoholic beverages, rarely both.

"What's our story?" Liz asked.

"I'm not sure," I admitted. "But, I'm fairly certain this guy won't be able to help us. We need his boss."

"Good point. Let's just ask for him."

We'd reached the security guard. "How can I help you?" he asked, courteously, if clearly by rote.

Liz gave him her biggest smile. "We'd like to talk to the head of security, please." The guard's eyes narrowed and he looked closer at the two of us.

"Maybe I could help you…"

"We'd rather discuss it with him," she demurred.

The guard stared down at us for a beat and then understanding dawned in his eyes. "I know you," he said, almost but not quite accusatory.

"Well," Liz responded, looking down and fluttering her lashes. I just barely managed not to laugh at her fake-coy routine. Oh brother.

Now the guard was excited. "You're Elizabeth Addison! From that morning show."

Liz held up her hands. "You got me."

The guard lowered his voice. "Is this about a story?"

Leaning in to whisper, matching his tone, Liz answered, "I can't confirm or deny that." Then she winked.

"For you, Ms. Addison, I'll get Mr. Maliton. But, I'll be honest. He's probably not going to want to help," the guard warned us.

"That's okay," she assured him. "If you can get him, we'll take it from there."

We could definitely take it from there.

CHAPTER TWELVE

The guard spoke into a walkie talkie, requesting Mr. Maliton to the floor.

A few minutes later, a slim man in a gangster business suit approached. He looked like he got lost in the 1940s. If I'd been drinking anything, I might have shot it out my nose.

"Johnny, what can I help with?" Mr. Maliton directed the question at the guard, with a quick flick of a glance at the two of us.

"The ladies requested to see you, sir," Johnny responded, keeping it simple. Smart.

Mr. Maliton looked like he wanted to say something more to Johnny, probably about the complete lack of information contained in that statement. He thought better of it, and addressed us instead.

"What can I help you ladies with?"

He nodded at Johnny, who moved away discretely.

Liz smiled at the security head. "We'd like to take a look at your security cameras," she requested with complete confidence. Unfortunately, the bold approach failed.

"I'm afraid that's not possible," Mr. Maliton responded.

"Let's start over," she replied, sticking out her hand. "I'm Elizabeth Addison, with *Entertainment Daily.*" Although the security head accepted her offered hand, inwardly I cringed. I watched the screen drop over his eyes. She lost him and didn't even know it yet.

"It's a pleasure to meet you, Ms. Addison," he politely stated. "You still can't see the security footage. Company policy."

Liz tried to ply her feminine wiles on the man, since playing the media card didn't work. I tuned them both out. I needed a distraction for Liz so I could entrance Mr. Maliton. A glance around the casino floor found nothing that could help. Screw it.

"Mr. Maliton?" I directed the question squarely at the security head and watched as his eyes took on the familiar glazed expression.

"Yes?"

"We understand that it's company policy, and we certainly wouldn't want you to get in trouble," I explained, hoping Liz wasn't being impacted too much.

My voice entranced anyone within earshot, to some degree.

"Thank you, I appreciate that," he said in a monotone.

"But, we really need to see that security footage."

He frowned, his training fighting the sound of my voice. He'd lose, so I waited.

"Okay."

"Thank you." I touched his arm and he smiled at me. I risked a glance at Liz, confirmed by her eyes that unfortunately, she'd been entranced too.

"Can we see them now?"

"Of course," he agreed and walked away.

"Come on, Liz," I said, and she followed along too.

Our little train made its way through the casino floor to a room off a short hallway. It looked like a scene out of a movie. A man sat before a bank of television screens, each of which clearly showed sections of the casino floor. The man appeared surprised to see Mr. Maliton at all, let alone trailed by two women. He jumped to his feet.

"Good afternoon, Mr. Maliton," he spluttered.

"These ladies need to see some security footage, Rick."

Rick gaped at Mr. Maliton and then us. "Sir?" As if maybe he didn't hear him correctly.

"Please show them whatever they need."

"But, sir?"

"Is something about what I've said unclear?" Mr. Maliton's voice, despite still sounding soft and sleepy, registered with Rick.

"No, sir," he replied smartly.

"Thank you, Mr. Maliton," I said with a final touch of his arm. "We'll take it from here." Rick's eyes bugged out at this exchange, especially when his boss nodded at us and walked out of the room.

"Hi, Rick," I said with a little wave. Out of the corner of my eye, I saw Liz give a small shake of her head now that the entrancement was broken. I resolutely did not look at her and focused on our new best friend, Rick.

"Thank you in advance for all your help."

"Uh, sure. What do you need?" His thoughts were clearly telegraphed on his face: Who is this green-haired chick and why did my boss give her carte blanche? I managed not to laugh.

"We need to go back about a week," I explained, showing him the time stamp on the image Chris gave us. "The camera that shows this angle, looking for the woman in the background."

Rick stared back and forth between the image and his cameras, working out which one would show that view.

"Aha!" He pointed to a screen on his right. I compared the two and nodded my agreement. He spun in his chair to a computer behind him, began typing away.

"Give me a sec, and I'll find that spot," he called over his shoulder. I watched as images fast forwarded, rewound, while he looked for this exact moment. And then there she was. Our mystery woman. Rick saw her and hit pause.

"There's your image. Now what?"

Liz, who seemed to have fully shaken off the entrancement, chimed in. "Let's go backwards until she leaves frame, so we can see where she entered. We'll track her movements."

Rick nodded his understanding and we began what I thought would be a painstaking process of tracking the mystery woman throughout the casino. Except that it wasn't, because we couldn't.

"That's weird," Rick muttered. We re-watched.

The three of us could clearly see the woman in one frame, but she was absent on any frame prior. It was as if she had just popped into existence. And then she was in about twenty seconds of frame before she seemingly vanished again.

We watched this twenty second clip over and over; Rick even checked other cameras at that time, to see if she was in any other footage. She was not. We were baffled. The other two tried to figure out how she could appear and disappear like she seemed to.

"Camera failure," was Rick's explanation, though he didn't sound like he really believed. And he shouldn't. I knew he was wrong; this was enough additional confirmation for me that the mystery woman was a djinn.

The reason I was baffled right along with the other two was wanting to know why. Why was Juni/Twin Sister appearing at all?

"Oh my goodness!" I exclaimed when I finally saw it. The other two jumped at my exhalation.

"What?" Liz cried.

"Rick, back the video up ten seconds." He complied. "There! Do you see him?" Rick and Liz followed my finger. Rick didn't know who I was looking at, but Liz did.

"Is that Chad?"

"Yes," I confirmed, staring at the dead lead in my film, looking very much alive. Our mystery woman was staring at him, and although her face was expressionless, it was clear he was her target.

"Rick," I turned to our helpful security agent. "Can you make me a copy of this twenty seconds of coverage?"

"Of course," he readily agreed. He was still obviously confused, but Mr. Maliton had made it super clear that we were to get whatever we wanted. I hid a smile.

"Thank you."

I turned to Liz while he made the copy. "Now we have at least a visual connection between Chad and the mystery woman."

"Is this where she first meets him?"

"That's a good question. She doesn't interact with him at all that we see, but it seems evident that she's tracking him. Does that suggest to you that she was looking for him? Already knew him somehow?"

Liz followed my line of questions. "What if she already identified him somehow and now wanted to…what?"

"I don't know," I admitted. "Let's get a copy of this to Jacob. Maybe he and the FBI will know more." I saw Rick's ears perk up at those initials and I regretted stating that in front of him. Oh well, who was he gonna tell?

Rick handed me a flash drive. "Here's the video." I knew he was dying to ask questions, but he admirably restrained himself.

"Thank you very much, Rick," I said. "You've been a big help."

Liz and I left the security guard at his post, monitoring the camera feeds, and returned to my car.

CHAPTER THIRTEEN

Liz suggested going back to the station to download the clip to her work computer, where we could then more easily share it with Selina and Jacob. I bit my tongue at what I was sure was her real reason: making sure she had a copy for herself.

"You aren't going to air this yet, are you?" I finally just asked her.

"Not yet."

I guessed that'd have to do. While I drove to the station, Liz texted Selina to inform her the video would be coming. Once we arrived at the station, I texted Jacob asking to meet.

"You know, you could just email him the video," Liz teased after I told her who I was texting.

"I'd like the opportunity to talk to him," I responded casually but she wasn't buying.

"Just admit you like him and want to see him."

We were sitting in her office now, door firmly closed. I took this time to analyze my fingernails, saw that a manicure would be nice. Had I ever gotten a manicure before? Surely, though honestly, I didn't recall.

Liz laughed at my silence. "Fine, ignore me. That was pretty cool, what you did," she changed the subject.

"What are you talking about?" I knew what she was talking about.

"Convincing the head of security to show us the security footage. How did you do that exactly?" She was still going for light and easy, but I heard the undercurrent.

"I just explained that we needed it," I reminded her. "You were there. You heard me."

"Yeah, I did," she agreed, but when I glanced up from my nails, she was frowning. "It's kind of fuzzy though."

"Fuzzy? I don't get it," I stated the bold lie, but not really feeling guilty.

"Listening to your voice was quite musical. I never noticed that before."

"Hmm, thanks?"

"It's almost like—"

Our eyes met. "Like what?"

"I'm not sure." Big smile blossomed; totally fake, but I was okay with that. "Never mind," she finally stated, "at least we got what we needed."

I breathed a slight sigh of relief that she let it go. It wasn't good that her antennae were up and twitching, but it was worth the risk.

Liz focused on her screen, transferring the video from the flash drive to her computer. While she finished that and sent the email to Selina, my phone pinged an incoming text. "Jacob?" she asked and I nodded.

"He says he can meet in an hour. Did you want to come?"

The universe heard my unspoken request when Liz shook her head no. "I'm going to wrap a few things up here, including sending this video to Chris for his input; maybe we can meet up later at your place for drinks and catch up on our progress?"

"Sure," I agreed.

"I'll see you tonight," Liz commented with a quick glance at me.

Guess I'd been dismissed.

CHAPTER FOURTEEN

Jacob apparently convinced his higher ups that being in training while there was now a serial killer bouncing back and forth between LA and Las Vegas was not a good idea. He asked if we could meet at a fast-casual restaurant in Downtown Summerlin. They had a great pizza place there, so I readily agreed. Since I had an hour, I popped by my condo to transfer the video file to my laptop before heading to meet him.

I turned off of Sahara Ave onto a road that wrapped around the open-air shopping center behemoth. Luckily, my destination was a little off to the side, where there was usually ample close parking. I grabbed a spot and headed for the restaurant. Jacob was already sitting at a patio table. My heart skipped a beat. The sun reflected off his blond hair and I could see his broad shoulders straining the threads of his gray t-shirt.

Not to admit that Liz was right, but I really was glad that it was just me and Jacob at this meeting.

He looked up at the sound of my footsteps and smiled when he saw me.

"Hi, Ms. Fynn," he said as he stood.

"Didn't I ask you to call me Mia?"

"Hi, Mia."

"Hi, Jacob."

We stood staring at each other with matching grins. Like teenagers. I broke the moment first.

"You ready to head inside?"

He indicated I should go first, though he was careful to open the pizzeria door for me. I ducked under his arm and he followed me. We made idle chit chat about traffic and the weather as we placed our orders. He paid for my food, despite my stating it wasn't necessary. This wasn't a date, I reminded myself, though I didn't say that to Jacob.

We sat at an outside table for more privacy and to enjoy the beautiful sunny day. I handed him the flash drive with the video.

"I figured you might want the original copy," I said by way of explanation for not simply emailing it. Not terribly logical, since it was already a copy, but Jacob didn't challenge my statement.

"Thanks. Can you tell me more about what's on it?"

All I had texted was that I had a video showing the possible murderer. I skipped the background information involving Chris. "We saw a clip of a woman on an iPhone video from someone who had been on vacation here. We figured out where that video was taken and went there. We then found security footage—" Here Jacob lifted one eyebrow. I continued.

"Footage that showed that same location and time. And there she was. More importantly, there was Chad."

Jacob whistled low in appreciation. "You actually found a video showing this unidentified woman and the murder vic?"

I nodded, inordinately proud of myself. "Yes, it clearly shows her looking at him."

"Really? That's interesting. I'll watch the video in a second, but since you seem to have deliberately not mentioned it, where did you get this video?" He was smirking, so I knew he was teasing, but I tensed and he noticed.

"Hey, what's wrong?"

I shook my head. "Nothing, sorry. The video is from the Golden Nugget."

Now both of his eyebrows shot up. "You successfully got security footage from a casino? Without a search warrant? What did you do? Bribe them?" He was still joking, but there was definitely an edge.

"Of course not!" I exclaimed. "Although honestly, I wouldn't have had a problem doing that," I admitted. "I just asked nicely."

"Okay." He stared at me while I strove for a carefully neutral expression. He sighed. "I'll accept that."

"I thought maybe between the department's and the FBI's resources, you guys could do more with the video. The date and time on it correspond to shortly before the murder. It seems highly unlikely that it's not connected."

"Based on your description, I would tend to agree. Okay, let's fire it up."

Jacob remained silent while he watched the twenty second clip on my laptop. He hit play several more times. I was acutely aware of the heat of his body so close to mine as we leaned in toward the screen.

"Is this it?" he finally asked, confusion apparent in his voice.

"What do you mean? Yes, that's it." I pointed at the screen.

"Where does she come from and where does she go?" He asked this slowly.

I sighed. "Oh, that. Yeah, we don't know."

"You don't know? Did your source not check the other cameras?"

"Yes! He did. I was standing right there when he did. She's not on any of the other cameras."

"That's not possible."

Not if you're not human. "Security guy said there must have been a camera malfunction."

Jacob stared at me for a moment.

"More like a system malfunction."

"That's possible too," I conceded, hating lying to him. But what was I going to say? She was a djinn who popped in and out of our dimension. Not a chance.

"What are you thinking?"

"What?"

"Just now, I saw the wheels in your brain turning," he explained. "What were you thinking?"

Um. I tried for a version of the truth. "I'm trying to figure out why she was there."

"And you think this is Juni's sister, not Juni, even though no body was ever found?" He asked but really this was a dismissive statement.

"I do," I answered.

"Why?"

Now what did I say? "I just think that since the first murder victim was so adamant that Juni was in his car and nobody's seen her since that night—"

"Except possibly on this video," he interrupted.

"It seems more likely that it would be somebody connected to her," I continued as though he didn't speak.

"And somehow decided there must be a sister. Apparently, a twin sister," he amended with a gesture at the video paused on the mystery woman. "How did you come across this information?"

"Sources," I stated firmly. "Sources that I will not be providing to you, so please don't ask again."

Jacob looked taken aback by my tone but didn't push. "Since you provided the initial direction, I feel comfortable telling you that so far we have not been able to identify this woman further. Therefore, we have not been able to identify any family members, twin or otherwise." He paused to take in my reaction. "Therefore," he repeated, "it appears you have better sources than Metro or the FBI."

I heard the exasperation in his voice and wished I could help him. "I'm sorry I can't help more," I said instead.

We stared at each other. He started to say something several times but didn't. I waited. I didn't know what else to tell him that didn't put my kind at risk. I was however disappointed to hear his report. Liz and I were going to have to solve this ourselves. Without Liz learning the real truth. I sighed before I could stop myself.

Jacob misinterpreted the sigh. "No, I'm sorry. I don't mean to pressure you. I understand protecting sources. I just want to solve this before anyone else gets hurt." The naked worry I saw in his eyes threatened my resolve, but I held steady.

I reached out to cover his hand with my own. The familiar zap of electricity brought smiles to both our faces. "I guess that's going to keep happening." I chuckled but didn't move my hand, nor did he withdraw his.

"It's okay, Jacob," I assured him. "I know you're just trying to do your job. I'm sorry I can't help more," I repeated.

Jacob squeezed my hand, sending pleasurable shock waves through my body. "I appreciate everything you're trying to do. Even if you're hanging out with the press."

We both laughed and the moment was broken. Our hands separated and we gathered up the trash from our lunch. Jacob walked me to my car.

This was not a date, I kept reminding myself.

His look of uncertainty when we reached my car had me wondering if he was experiencing the same indecision. He brushed his fingers across my cheek, surprising us both with the action and the small spark.

"I guess I'll need to be more careful when I touch you," he said softly. My lips ached for him to kiss me, but he took a step back and shook his head. "Apologies, this is neither the time nor the place."

"No apologies necessary," I responded.

He smiled and turned to walk away. I focused on the words he spoke. If this wasn't the time or place, that suggested some other time or place would be right. I was disconcerted by how happy the thought made me.

CHAPTER FIFTEEN

I texted Catherine and Evie to meet me when the sun set; Catherine texted back immediately confirming, and I knew Evie would respond when she awoke. It was only mid-afternoon, so I had several hours to kill. I decided to conduct more of my own research to see what I could find. With a glass of Riesling in one hand and my laptop in the other, I made myself comfortable on the bleached wood Adirondack chair on my patio and dove in.

A knock at my door startled me. I realized it must be my ladies arriving. I couldn't believe I completely lost track of time.

"Coming!" I called out, though it was uncertain I could be heard through the door. I closed the sliding glass door behind me, set down my laptop and empty glass on my dining table, and headed to see which of my expected visitors had arrived.

"Did you forget I was coming?"

"Liz! Of course not. What time is it?" I made a show of checking my watch. "Did you text me you were on your way?"

She appeared genuinely contrite and I felt guilty for being rude. After all, we did have plans; it wasn't her fault I forgot. I just knew that her presence would alter how the evening went. Catherine appeared behind Liz.

"Hey, Mia," Catherine said to me but looking at Liz.

"Hi, I'm Liz," she introduced herself, hand outstretched.

"Catherine," she responded to Liz.

"Right. Where are my manners? Please, come in. We have one more coming." I moved to allow them entrance.

"I didn't know it was a party," Liz called over her shoulder.

Catherine stared at me and I shrugged. We would keep it brief and then have our paranormal conversation after Liz left.

As I was closing the door, three sharp knocks sounded. I pulled it back open to see Evie's smiling face.

"Hey, Mia," she said and we hugged.

"We have another guest," I said in a low voice and felt her shift to see around me. We released the hug and she followed me in.

Liz and Catherine were already seated at the dining table. I introduced Evie to Liz and she joined the ladies.

"Drinks?"

"None for me," Evie declined my offer with a smirk that piqued the interest of Liz. I inwardly rolled my eyes. Thanks, Evie.

"I'll take whatever wine was previously in this glass," Liz accepted my offer.

"Same," Catherine chimed in.

Although Catherine and Evie recognized Liz, she briefly explained who she was and they reciprocated with the basics. I joined them at the table with the wine.

"I brought another bottle."

"Excellent," Catherine responded.

"Okay, now that we're all here," I began. "Let's talk about the murders."

Liz glanced between Evie and Catherine.

"They both knew Chad," I offered as explanation for their presence. "They helped me figure out that Juni has a twin sister."

"The more the merrier," Liz responded blithely, but I saw her immediate interest when I disclosed them as the source of our biggest piece of information. I was probably going to regret telling her that.

I brought Evie and Catherine up to speed regarding the security footage and then summarized my quick lunch with Jacob. I blatantly ignored Evie's and Catherine's reactions to learning that I had lunch with Jacob, but Liz didn't.

"She totally likes him, am I right?"

Evie guffawed and Catherine actually snort-laughed. "Oh yeah," they agreed.

"Thanks ladies, but who I may or may not like is not the focus of this meeting," I reminded them, which just sent them into hysterics. "Why is this so funny?"

"Because you both clearly like each other and it's funny watching you dance around that," Liz said bluntly. I was undecided whether I liked this personality trait.

"Anyway," I said to bring them back on track. "What do we think?"

The three women were quiet. Frankly, we were all at a bit of a loss.

"If only we knew where she was going to be," Catherine said offhand with a small chuckle.

"That's it!"

"What's it, Liz?" I asked.

"We need to know where she's going to be," she explained, and we stared at her. "We need to bait her."

"This isn't a movie," Catherine responded.

"I think it has merit," Evie disagreed. "What do you think, Mia?"

I slowly nodded my head. "Catherine's right that it's not a movie. On the other hand, Evie has a point too."

"Do you like the idea or not?" Liz asked.

I laughed. "Like? I don't know about that! But, I think it's probably our best bet."

Catherine frowned and I hurried to continue.

"Look at it this way. Based on her pattern, she's likely going to kill again within a day or two. Even with the additional information we've given law enforcement, I doubt they'll find her before another murder occurs." I didn't add that as a djinn, law enforcement almost certainly would be unable to capture her; and unless they surprised her and shot her through the heart, they weren't going to kill her either.

"Okay, what do you guys have in mind?" Catherine asked.

"What do we know about her pattern?" Evie answered a question with a question.

"She's picked actors all three times," I began. "And she's alternated between here and LA. Our best bet is an actor here in town, since the third murder was in LA."

The women nodded.

"I wouldn't feel right about putting an actor at risk," Evie objected.

"We could bring the police in on our plan; maybe they could use an undercover officer as a fake actor?"

"I have a better idea, Catherine," Liz said.

We looked at her expectantly.

"I'm going to do it."

"What? What are you talking about? You're not an actor. Or male," I argued, pointing out the gender preference of our killer.

"Look at it logically. Even if we have an undercover officer, how are we going to get Juni or her twin sister to pick him as the next victim? We have to bring her to us."

"True, but whatever you're going to do, an undercover officer could probably do," Catherine argued.

Liz was shaking her head. "No, he can't. Our hypothetical undercover officer doesn't have a television show."

"That's good," Catherine reluctantly admitted.

"Even if she doesn't watch the show, if I say I want to interview her, that's gonna go viral on social media within thirty minutes. I can practically guarantee it," she crowed.

"I think she's right," I agreed.

"And we can still have the police involved for additional protection," Catherine mused.

Believe it or not, as much as the ladies were right about me wanting to see Jacob, I didn't think bringing the police in for our plan made sense since they couldn't do anything to the djinn. Except I couldn't explain that right now without telling Liz everything about the paranormal underworld. Instead, I nodded at her.

"I'll call Jacob."

CHAPTER SIXTEEN

"Are you women insane?" As predicted, Jacob didn't like our plan. He sat at my dining table, staring at me, Liz, Catherine, and Evie like we'd all sprouted second heads. "This is a terrible idea and there's no way Metro will support it."

"Technically, Detective, as a free citizen, you can't stop me from going on my own show and asking her for an interview," Liz countered sweetly. "We've informed you of the plan and you can either participate or not."

If the tension radiating off of him were physical, it would knock Liz on her bottom. He looked at each of us in turn. "Surely you realize this won't work," he tried another tack.

"Why not?" Evie asked.

"Once you announce on air and all over social media what you're doing, every Tom, Dick, and Harry is going to camp out in front of your house. She's never going to show with the circus in town."

Liz frowned. That had obviously not occurred to her. She brightened. "I disagree. What is it that law enforcement says about so many serial killers? They want to brag about what they've done. They want people to recognize their brilliance. They want to tell their stories. Right?"

"True. But how is she supposed to get to your home, if it's surrounded by the press and the curious?"

"Well, Detective, I live in a gated community, so that'll cut down some."

Jacob snorted. "Please. Those gates won't hold anybody out. Besides, won't that keep her out too?"

"Look, maybe you're right. But this is a woman who has been able to get in and out of locked homes without breaking anything or leaving any forensic evidence behind. I have no doubt that with the proper motivation, she'll figure her way around the gate, press, and the lookie loos." She shrugged. "I'm not worried."

"There's nothing I can say that will talk you out of this." We shook our heads no. He sighed. "Fine. I'll talk to my superiors. I doubt they'll spare more than an officer or two for what they'll consider a farce. I'll be there, of course." Our eyes briefly met and I smiled.

We reviewed the details and decided to put our plan into motion the next morning. After the group departed,

I moved to my couch with my third glass of wine. I hoped we were doing the right thing.

*****

"Good morning in the Valley!" Liz welcomed viewers to *Entertainment Daily* with a toothy smile and a fabulous form-fitting red dress and stiletto heels. Her smile dimmed.

"As viewers of this show know, the so-called Firecracker Killer has murdered three actors in as many weeks – Bradley Reese, Roger Miller, and Chad Johnson. These murders in Las Vegas and Los Angeles have set the West Coast entertainment world on edge, with promoters warning their clients not to use social media for streaming, and both local law enforcement and the FBI coming up empty."

Liz breathed deeply. Genuine nerves or for show? I honestly didn't know.

"Today, I'd like to formally invite the Firecracker Killer to come to my home, tonight, for me to interview during a Facebook Live video." She stared into the camera. "I know you have a story to tell. Let me help you tell it."

She turned to another camera, smiled. "What big charity event is in the works for the Valley? We'll tell you after the break."

The show cut to commercial and I sat back in awe. She did it. She actually asked a serial killer into her home.

*****

Time crawled while I waited for it to be time to watch Liz interview a serial killer. Just as I made up my mind to take a quick swim in the pool to burn off some nervous energy, someone knocked on my front door. I hadn't ordered anything online, and I lived in a gated community. I debated ignoring the knock but curiosity got the better of me. My jaw dropped when I saw the woman standing before me.

"Councilwoman Knollman? What an unexpected surprise," I squeaked out.

"Good afternoon, Ms. Fynn," Barbara Knollman, Las Vegas's resident demon councilwoman, addressed me formally.

"May I come in?"

I hesitated and irritation flashed in her eyes. "Of course," I agreed, stepping aside to allow her entry. Rumor said Barbara was a fairly laidback demon, but still. A demon. In my home. I shuddered as I closed the door behind her.

Barbara took several steps inside before turning to face me. "This is fine. I won't be here long."

"Why are you here?"

"I saw Ms. Addison's show this morning."

"Ah, yes. It was something," I hedged, wondering at her interest in the murders. Did she know something about the djinn?

"Something, indeed," Barbara agreed. "I understand you're working with her."

A statement, not a question. I didn't bother to wonder how she knew. She had moles everywhere. "Yes."

"What else does she know?"

"I don't understand the question."

"It wasn't complex. What else does she know besides what she reported in the broadcast?"

It hit me what she was asking. "Nothing about us," I assured the demon. If Barbara decided Liz was a threat, well, that wouldn't do much for Liz's lifespan. The brief look of disappointment on Barbara's face surprised me. Did she want Liz to know about us? Frankly, this was why I stayed out of paranormal politics.

"Did you know that I have precognitive abilities?"

Now my jaw really did drop open. "Um, I did not," I answered, my mind swirling.

"I share this because I want you to understand the importance of what I'm about to tell you," she explained. "You are on the right track."

"I am?"

"You are. Do not be swayed from it."

"Okay. Wait," I paused, thinking furiously, "which part? Helping Liz, keeping things from her, pursuing the killer?"

"I've said what I came to say," she responded, ignoring my questions.

Before I could try asking another way, she turned. "I'll see myself out."

And with that, she was gone.

CHAPTER SEVENTEEN

"How do I look?" Liz asked me this, spinning in a circle. "I'm going for upscale casual." She smoothed out nonexistent wrinkles on her violet nylon shift.

"You look great," I told her, amazed that she was concerned about her appearance at all. I finally got to see her house. It was a cute two-story in a gated country club neighborhood. On a tiny lot, however, so set-up was a challenge. Liz and I were the only ones in her home; we were currently in her home office.

She stood in front of a mid-size dark wood desk. Certificates and framed photos with famous folks dotted the walls. Unfortunately, the office was on the street-facing side of the home. Despite the gate, as Jacob had predicted, cars lined the street. People sat waiting in most of them. I idly wondered how many were press versus the curious.

Jacob and two officers commandeered the house next door, their cars safely hidden in the garage, the owners' vehicles relegated to the street. Catherine and Evie were with them. We'd been texting fast and furious while the time passed. I'd already updated them on the way weird visit from the demon councilwoman. They were as much at a loss as I was.

All three of the times of death were after the standard dinner hour and before midnight. The sun set about an hour ago, so it was almost time. The energy in the air crackled. I both wanted and didn't want Juni's twin sister to make an appearance. I hadn't told the others my actual plan.

A text notification vibrated my phone. Jacob.

"It's go time," I relayed to Liz, who moved behind the desk. I vacated the room. She logged on to Facebook and prepared to start streaming.

I watched the start of the Facebook Live video on my cellphone in a darkened room at the back of the house. There had been some concern that my presence in the home might keep the murderer from showing. Nobody really wanted Liz to be alone, though, so hiding in the back seemed the best option. My phone was on silent. I could hear the faintest hint of what she was saying from the other room.

Nothing happened and Liz started to repeat herself. "I'm here in my home, waiting on the appearance of the

Firecracker Killer. So far, he or she has not appeared." I was glad she decided not to use the feminine pronoun. I didn't think the police would want us to inform the world that we suspected the killer was female.

The random chatter on the video continued; I watched the comments scrolling by. They alternated between people calling Liz crazy for trying this or an idiot because the killer wouldn't show with such a contrived scene.

It looked like the latter were right.

Time stretched on and the comments slacked off. Ninety minutes into the now terminally boring video, Jacob texted me.

I'm calling it. She's not coming.

I'll let Liz know.

She was going to be disappointed. She'd been so excited about this plan. Standing in the doorway of the office, I made the universal slicing motion across my throat. *Kill it.* Liz subtly shook her head and continued speaking.

I texted this response to Jacob. I remained standing in the doorway for another five minutes before Liz accepted reality.

"Well, folks, it looks like the Firecracker Killer doesn't want to tell his or her story tonight. I'm signing off. Until next time." She gave a half-hearted smile and finally killed the stream.

"Dammit!" She pounded her fist on the desk, rattling pens in a yellow plastic cup with the MnM logo on the side. She ran a hand through her brunette curls. "That sucks."

I walked to the window and, peering through the blinds, watched the few remaining cars peel away. We heard the front door open.

"Ms. Addison, it's Detective Dawson."

"In the office."

Jacob, Catherine, and Evie entered the room a moment later and we stood silently.

"Guess you were right."

"I wish I wasn't," Jacob countered Liz's statement. She looked past the trio to the empty doorway.

"Where are the officers?"

"I sent them home."

"I see."

I watched this awkward exchange like a tennis match. Now what?

"I'm going to head back to the station to write up a quick report of the evening's activities."

"Or lack thereof," Liz added. "It's okay, you can say it."

"I'll be in touch." He turned to me at the window. "Mia, can I talk to you a minute?" My heart fluttered. I followed him from the room, resolutely ignoring the knowing expressions on the ladies' faces.

"Now that you're out of the investigation," Jacob started, and I didn't bother to correct his incorrect assumption, "I was wondering." He stalled.

"Wondering what, Jacob?"

He stared at the ground. "Would you like to have dinner with me?" he asked in a rush.

"A date?"

His cheeks reddened at my question. "Yes, a date."

"I would love to," I answered and our dopey smiles mirrored each other.

"Okay, I'll call you tomorrow."

"Sounds good." I reached my hand out, then withdrew it, wondering if I should hug him. But he was out the door before I'd made a decision. Guess neither one of us dated much!

Giggling greeted me as I reentered the office. There was no need to ask if they overheard.

"Mia and Jacob, sitting in a tree, K-I-S-S-I-N-G," Liz sang. The other two practically fell over laughing.

"Very mature, guys," I responded, but my ear-to-ear grin betrayed me. "Anyway, we'll get out of your hair. Come on, ladies."

Liz closed the door behind us.

Catherine and Evie took but a step before they stopped and faced me.

"What do you think?" Evie asked.

"I'm not sure."

"Do you think she didn't come because of the crowd?" Catherine asked.

"I don't think so. Since she can appear and disappear at will, the crowd wouldn't really have been a factor, I don't think."

"You think she just didn't want to be interviewed?" Evie asked.

"That's more likely," I acknowledged. "She's an immortal being. Whatever her reason for killing men like this, she's been around long enough to see technology as the blip that it is. Plus," I paused.

"What?" Catherine asked.

"It's unusual for a djinn to act this way – it's not unknown for them to kill, of course, but so publicly?" I shrugged.

Evie nodded in agreement. "You think maybe she's not thinking straight, that something's really wrong?"

"Yeah. I had hoped that she'd come tonight, so we could end this," I said vaguely. "But if she's not thinking clearly or logically, then all bets are off."

CHAPTER EIGHTEEN

The next morning dawned with a sense of foreboding and I wasn't sure why. A couple of scrambled eggs and a cup of coffee later, I turned on the television to see how Liz handled what happened last night. She seemed to shake off the disappointment well enough by the time we left.

"Good morning in the Valley!" Liz began with her normal greeting, again looking chic in a pink halter dress ending just above her knees.

"Thank you to those who tuned in last night to my Facebook Live attempt to interview the Firecracker Killer. If you watched, then you know that unfortunately, he or she did not show up for the interview." Fake laugh. Guess she hadn't let it go yet.

"Here's the thing, everybody. This is too important to let go. So, I'm not." Her eyes glittered. "Let's go again, Firecracker. I'm calling you out. You heard me. I think you didn't show up because you're afraid to tell your story. Maybe you don't have a story?" Her face looked ugly in that moment.

"I'll be back on Facebook Live tonight, waiting for you. If you don't come, I'll know you're scared. Oh," she added like it just occurred to her. "I have a picture of you now. I'd hate to share that all over social media before you have a chance to tell your side." She finished her not-so-subtle threat and smiled. I was flabbergasted that she told the world we had the murderer's image.

"And, of course, for those of you watching, please share this all over social media, just in case the Firecracker Killer simply didn't know about my invitation last time. We'll be right back."

The show cut to commercial and I waited for it. My phone started dinging as texts poured in from Catherine and Jacob. As if I had any idea she would throw down the gauntlet like this. I'd give the woman credit, she was tenacious!

*****

It was Capture the Murderer, take two, that night at Liz's home. Light from streetlamps glinted off of what I imagined were camera lenses in a couple of cars. That was about it. The circus mostly stayed away tonight; I guess they decided it wasn't worth the time. Jacob came again, but he wasn't here in an official capacity and he had no additional officers. Metro was chronically understaffed and his supervisors didn't believe Liz's "publicity stunt" warranted allocation of officers again.

Catherine and Evie were also present, mainly because, like me, they were worried that Liz might have truly pissed the djinn off.

Due to the lack of official support, no homes had been commandeered and the three of them camped out in an SUV across the street. They planned to watch the Facebook Live streaming on Jacob's laptop.

I, however, was back in the office with Liz. She sat at her desk, gnawing on her lower lip. Worried about a repeat no-show performance? Or worried that the murderer *would* show up?

"Do you think she'll show up tonight?"

"I don't know," I answered. "She clearly didn't take the bait the first night, but the way you goaded her—"

Liz hung her head. "Yeah. I hope that wasn't a mistake."

"Do you actually want her to show up or not?"

"Yes," she answered, that hungry look back in her eyes. "Are you ever going to tell me how you figured out the murderer is Juni's sister?"

The question was asked offhand but I heard the real question. "Probably not," I admitted. "What makes you ask about it now?"

"I think there's stuff you're not telling me."

"Everybody has secrets."

"Indeed."

We stared at each other, both trying to read what the other was hiding. Did she know something? I walked back through our conversations; I didn't believe I'd let anything slip.

You guys ready? Five minutes until go time.

"You ready?" I asked Liz. "That was Jacob checking in."

"As ready as I'll ever be," she answered. I gave her a thumbs-up and walked back to the guest room where I stayed last time.

Liz's image glowed from my cellphone screen. I was seated in a bean bag chair, legs akimbo, the light from the screen all that was on in this part of her home. Again, I kept the sound off, but could hear her voice from the other room as the Liz on screen moved her lips.

"Welcome back to everyone who chose to join me again tonight."

There were some comments but it was definitely not flying fast and furious like before. I guessed much of the audience also stayed away.

"A few people have questioned whether it was smart of me to challenge a murderer the way that I did." I winced in the dark. Liz smiled.

"Probably not. But, when you want to get the story." She shrugged with this admission. The comments below were a mixture of admiration for her gutsy move and chiding her for being an idiot. I was undecided at this juncture. I still believed what I told the ladies the other night. Our best bet was to bring Juni's sister to us.

Liz continued to talk but I was no longer listening. Something changed. The air felt heavier. I'd actually never met a djinn before. I didn't know if this meant her essence had arrived. Liz still chatted as though nothing had changed. I wondered if it was my overactive imagination.

POP POP POP POP POP

Guess not. I bolted from the chair at the firecracker sounds, a hair after I noticed Liz's smile slip. The murderer was in the house.

"Hello? Is that you? Firecracker Killer?" Liz's voice wavered only a bit when she called out.

I crept to the edge of the bedroom door, peeked around the corner. The house remained dark. Popping sounds filled the air.

"Hello? For those watching from home, you can hear the familiar sounds that have preceded the Firecracker Killer's entrance on the prior three videos," Liz continued in her newscaster voice.

I entered the hallway and made my way toward the front office.

"I hear the popping but I still have no visual on who exactly is present," Liz told her audience. "Hello? Please identify yourself," Liz instructed the apparent presence.

I almost laughed but didn't want to give away my location.

No verbal response but, if anything, the popping sounded louder. It felt like a jackhammer in my skull. Something must be about to happen. I reached the final corner before the office. I rounded the corner, saw the office entrance five feet before me.

The air at the office door shimmered.

"Something is happening!" Liz told her audience.

I took a few tentative steps forward.

"A shape is forming in the doorway," Liz reported.

An outline of a figure appeared.

"There's someone—" She stopped speaking.

A feminine form had fully materialized.

CHAPTER NINETEEN

"There's a woman. She has long brown hair, black eyes." She stuttered on this descriptor. "Tan, maybe bronze skin." She paused as the popping stopped. Silence filled the house.

"Are you Juni's sister?" I broke the silence and the woman turned. I recoiled from the anger on her face.

"Mia, what are you doing?"

"Who are you?"

The woman did not speak but *Jena* floated in my mind. I stepped closer, could see into the office now.

"Jena?" I asked.

"Jena? Who's Jena? Is she Jena? What are you doing, Mia?" Liz spun her laptop in our direction and stepped around the far side of the desk, intent on regaining control of her interview. I only had a few minutes.

The woman, Jena, took a single step toward me.

"You don't have to do this," I told her. I lowered my voice. "We're like you; let us help you." Jena's face remained impassive. Liz's did not.

"What are you saying? Mia, what's going on?" Liz stepped within touching distance of Jena and a blinding light engulfed the room.

I waited for my eyes to readjust when the light vanished. Jena was gone. Liz lay on the floor. I moved toward her as the front door opened.

"Mia?! Liz?" I heard Jacob's voice and then hurried footsteps. I was cradling Liz's head in my lap when Jacob, Catherine, and Evie rushed into the room.

Relief flashed across their faces, presumably that I was okay, and then worry replaced it as they saw Liz.

"She's unconscious," I explained.

Jacob pulled his cellphone from his pocket to call for an ambulance. Catherine and Evie hung back.

"What happened?" Jacob resumed the detective role, and I gave a modified version of events. He quirked an eyebrow when I stated that I came around the corner and saw a woman standing in the doorway of the office.

"You didn't see or hear anything prior to that?"

"Just the popping noises."

"She just appeared?" Disbelief dripped from his words.

"I can only tell you I came around the corner and she was there," I insisted, which was a version of the truth.

"Stay here," he ordered and left to check all the windows and doors of the house.

Evie and Catherine moved in closer.

"What really happened?" Evie whispered.

I shook my head. "Wait until we're alone."

Flashing red and blue lights penetrated the window blinds. A few seconds later, emergency responders entered the home, followed closely by backup law enforcement. The EMS folks checked Liz's vitals – strong, it appeared – and lifted her onto a stretcher to carry to the ambulance. Catherine, Evie, and I watched in silence as they headed toward the door.

"Do any of you wish to accompany her?"

Catherine looked at me and Evie before answering the EMS woman in the affirmative.

"Thanks." I gave her a quick hug and she left with the ambulance. Evie and I remained in the office, leaning back against the desk, waiting. I imagined Jacob was not done with me yet.

Sure enough, after speaking with the backup officers briefly, he asked us to follow him outside. The officers were securing the scene. It was not clear a crime had been committed, or if the reported woman was the killer, but they weren't taking any chances.

Jacob indicated I should sit in the passenger seat of the SUV, while he got behind the wheel and Evie clambered into the backseat.

"What did you see during the streaming?" I asked.

Jacob gave me an inscrutable look then opened his laptop. "I recorded the video. This is what we saw." He pressed play. I watched the familiar opening, as Liz chattered. Popping sounds. Liz asking the murderer to show herself. Her look of surprise followed by a description of the woman. Then a muffled voice in the background. I was thankful you couldn't distinctly hear what I said. Liz questioning me, standing, spinning the laptop. I sighed in relief when the laptop stopped halfway around and faced the window. Jacob glanced at me sharply. Liz asked her final question, "Mia, what's going on?", the bright light flashed and the video stopped. It all happened much faster than I had thought.

"Mia, what *was* going on?"

I stared at Jacob, considering my response. "I've already told you what I saw."

"Why did Liz ask you that?"

I faltered this time. "I don't know." Weak. I knew it and Jacob knew it.

"Who is Jena?" Jacob stared at me through narrowed eyes.

I tried to think of a good explanation.

"It's not a trick question," he said drily.

"She's Juni's sister," I finally answered.

"The one you mentioned before," he confirmed.

"Yes."

"Are you ready yet to tell me how you found out about her?"

I swallowed audibly around the lump in my throat. "No."

"What else aren't you telling me?"

"I can't tell you anything else."

"Can't? Or won't?"

I remained silent.

A knock on the window broke the uncomfortable silence. Jacob started the car and rolled the window down.

"Sir. We were able to restart her computer." The officer handed Liz's laptop through the window. Jacob thanked him and rolled the window back up. The laptop actually appeared slightly singed; it was a miracle they were able to restart it.

Jacob opened the laptop, woke it from sleep mode, and clicked on Documents. His eyes scanned the rows and columns of icons. I couldn't see the details from here. Was he looking for something specific? He clicked on an icon and instead of a document, a video opened. Liz staring at the screen. Jacob hit play.

"Hello, this is Elizabeth Addison, coming to you from Las Vegas. As many of you know, I have been hot on the trail of the Firecracker Killer. This unknown person, recently identified as a woman, is possibly the sister of a woman murdered by the Firecracker Killer's first victim." Liz paused in the video and Jacob's eyes burned on me.

"If that sounds confusing, just wait. Today this case took on dimensions I never imagined." My mind raced to figure out what she was about to say. Liz's eyes practically glowed from her excitement, so I knew it must be big. On screen, Liz gulped a big breath. "I recently learned that there are supernatural beings living in Las Vegas."

My sharp intake of breath matched Evie's as Jacob muttered, "What the—"

Liz continued. "I have reason to believe that the murderer is not actually a woman after all, but a djinn, otherwise known as a genie. This previously believed-to-be mythical being—" Liz continued to talk but her voice had been replaced by a high-pitched whine in my ears.

How did she find out? And then I remembered my conversation with Catherine and Evie on the doorstep to Liz's house. Could she have overheard us somehow? I tilted my head back as a vague recollection of a security camera at her door floated to the surface of my memory. Did it have audio? Could she have turned it on to eavesdrop on us?

I tuned back in to Liz talking to the camera. "I also have reason to believe there is at least one supernatural being in the Valley capable of bewitching. This woman – whatever she is – can bend you to her will. And there's nothing you can do about it." On screen, Liz gave a final smile. "That's all I have for now, but I'll be back when I have more to report."

"Did she post this anywhere?"

"That's your reaction to the video?"

"What reaction did you want to see?" I asked softly.

"Maybe one more of surprise," he answered. "Like those of us who don't already know about the existence of these beings."

"You believe her crazy ramblings?" I asked with an arch of an eyebrow.

He didn't buy my nonchalance. "I heard your reaction when she said the killer is a genie. Don't insult me by trying to pretend otherwise." Hurt shined in his eyes as he looked at me; I dropped my gaze to my lap.

"I don't know what to say," I admitted.

"Evie, can you give us a minute?"

Without a word, Evie scrambled from the car.

"What did you say to the genie? To Jena?"

"I don't remember."

"You're lying. Are you involved with her?"

"What?!"

"Are you working with her?"

"No, of course not."

"You say that as though I can trust you." His voice was low with controlled anger. "If not for the supernatural stuff, I'd bring you in as a person of interest."

I closed my eyes against tears threatening to spill. "You'd arrest me?"

His voice softened. "I don't want to. But, you're not giving me anything. Help me out here," he begged.

Our eyes met. I reached out a hand to touch his cheek. The familiar snap of static electricity sounded and his cheek was rough against my fingers. We smiled before his slipped and his expression hardened. He jerked away from me.

"Are you the being Liz mentioned? Have you bewitched me? Does that explain this?" He gestured back and forth between us.

"No! Of course not!"

"No, you're not the being? Or, no, you haven't bewitched me? Can you bewitch people?"

I didn't answer.

"What are you?"

"I'm Mia."

"That's not an answer."

"That's the only answer I can give you."

CHAPTER TWENTY

Thank goodness it was midnight. I drove home from Liz's house in tears following my conversation with Jacob.

How could he possibly think I was working with a killer and I bewitched him?

Now I floated in the lake, recharging my energy. Tonight was way more emotional than I had anticipated. My fingers glided through the water, rubbed against curious fish, and my tension started to drain away.

Despite my efforts to keep my mind empty, thoughts of my failure returned. I wanted to understand why Jena was doing this. I wanted to reason with her to stop the killing. She seemed to be listening to me, until Liz interrupted. I sighed underwater, then laughed that there was still air in my lungs to push out.

What did I do now?

My thoughts turned to Liz. I had known she was up to something; I could tell by the sly glances and her reticence when she normally would bulldoze. It never occurred to me that she would have figured out about the paranormal. My role in her discovery saddened me. The paranormal underworld wanted to keep it that way. I hoped I hadn't put her at risk by exposing us – if she *outed* us. I couldn't imagine the fallout. The vampires in particular didn't take kindly to humans threatening their existence and they wouldn't hesitate to kill her.

I needed to talk to Evie. Actually, all of us needed to talk to Liz. Me, Evie, and Catherine. We had to explain the danger Liz could put herself in.

Hoisting myself out of the lake, I made my way into my home. Before I hopped in the shower, I texted the ladies. First Evie, who I knew was up; hopefully she was free.

Are you available? Meet me at the hospital. We need to talk to Liz.

And then Catherine, who might still be at the hospital. She hadn't texted an update.

You still at the hospital? Evie and I are coming. We need to talk to Liz.

Their affirmative responses arrived as I lathered. I texted them again before I backed out of the garage; I estimated fifteen minutes to the hospital and said I'd meet them in the lobby.

"How is she doing?" I greeted Catherine with the question and a hug.

"She's sleeping. I overheard the doctor telling Jacob that she's not in a coma and could wake up anytime."

"Jacob was here? How did he seem?"

"Seem?"

Oh right, Catherine wasn't there for any of our disagreement. "When Evie gets here, I'll bring you up to speed."

"I'm here," came a voice behind me. Catherine and I hugged Evie.

I summarized my conversation with Jacob. They stared at me in silence. "Relax, nobody died." I tried for light-hearted and failed.

"What do we want to say to Liz?" Evie asked this, changing the subject, for which I was grateful.

"Follow my lead?"

Catherine and Evie agreed to do so and Catherine led the way to Liz's room. Since she was mainly here for observation, she was in a regular, though private, room, and not the ER or ICU. Beeping machinery greeted us. Liz didn't look bad; she really did look like she was just sleeping, if not for the few wires monitoring her status.

"Should we wake her?"

"No need, Evie," answered the woman in question. She opened her eyes and smiled weakly at us. "I'm awake. Thanks for staying with me Catherine."

"I didn't know you knew I was here."

"I did."

A moment passed. Liz knew we were not there just to check on her, but she'd clearly decided to let us direct the conversation.

"Jacob is going to want to talk to you," I started. She nodded. "He thinks I'm working with Jena." Her eyes widened at that. "I was hoping that when you speak with him, you can straighten that misperception out."

"How do I know you aren't working with Jena?"

I gaped at her. "I've been working with you the whole time!"

"You've kept secrets from me the whole time." One hospital gown clad shoulder lifted. "How do I know you weren't hiding that too?"

I turned to Catherine and Evie for help. They looked stunned. Catherine was the first to jump in to defend me. "Liz, you haven't known Mia that long, but I can personally assure you that she's not a killer. In any way, shape, or form," she emphasized.

Liz's lip curled. "That and a couple of bucks will get me a cup of coffee."

"How could you think she's a killer?" Evie asked. "Aren't you a better journalist than that to be taken in?"

Risky to insult the woman whose cooperation we wanted, but when Liz's cheeks reddened I realized Evie took the right approach.

Liz sighed. "I know she's not involved," she allowed. "I'm just pissed you guys didn't tell me about the paranormal world."

"You'll tell Jacob I wasn't involved?"

"Yes, Mia, I'll tell Jacob you weren't involved." She paused. "If you do something for me."

"You're going to extort Mia? For you to tell the truth?" Evie sounded pissed. I didn't blame her; I wasn't feeling too charitable.

I headed off the ensuing battle. "What do you want?"

"Information."

We didn't have to ask what kind of information; we all knew what she wanted to know. "I can't give you what you want," I said.

"Then I can't say what you want." She pointedly closed her eyes. "You can go."

"We're doing this to protect you," Catherine insisted.

Liz opened a single eye. "Go on."

"We can confirm the paranormal underworld exists, but most of us want to keep it that way," Evie explained.

"And?"

"If you threaten to out us, you'll be killed," Evie responded simply.

"Us?"

I was really hoping that Liz would have missed that pronoun, so of course she didn't.

"I'm a vampire."

Liz stared open-mouthed at Evie. "A what?"

"You heard me. And my people will kill you without hesitation if you try to tell the world about us."

"You're a vampire?" Liz repeated.

"Yes. Keep up," Evie snapped.

"Okay."

"That's it? Okay?"

"What more do you want, Mia? I'll inform Jacob that you were not involved in any of the murders. I will also not disclose the existence of a paranormal underworld."

I breathed a sigh of relief.

"For now," Liz continued.

"For now?" Catherine questioned.

"There's an echo in this room," Liz retorted.

"Don't be a bitch," Evie snapped.

"Evie!" Catherine exclaimed.

"Sorry," Evie said, not sounding sorry.

"What do you mean, for now?" I redirected.

"Well, Mia, I want the whole story. I want Jena and the paranormal underworld." She smiled shrewdly. "If I wait for Jena to be caught, then I can have both. So, I'll wait," she concluded.

The three of us goggled at her.

"What about the risk to your life?" I had to think that self-preservation would be high on Liz's list of importance.

"Once I actually out all of you," she said, and I sensed that Evie wanted to knock the smug look off of Liz's face, "nobody would dare kill me."

Evie snorted. "Like my people care. You'll just have an 'accident'," she explained, putting the last word in air quotes.

"I'll take that chance."

This was probably the best we were going to do tonight. At least Liz wasn't going to say anything more about us right now and she'd clear things up with Jacob. We'd have to be satisfied with that.

"Thank you," was all I said.

Liz gestured for us to leave. "I'm tired. We'll talk later."

"Actually, Liz, now that I know your full plan, I don't think it's in anybody's best interest for us to continue to work together on this story."

"So be it, Mia," she answered and closed her eyes.

We took that as our unsubtle cue to leave and did. We remained silent walking down the hallway away from her room. I noticed an empty darkened room to our left and ducked inside. Catherine and Evie followed.

"What do you guys think?" I asked.

"We probably should report her." Evie said this but I could tell her heart wasn't in it.

"If we do, she'll be dead within twenty-four hours." Vampires had Cleaners for exactly this sort of job.

"I know."

We considered our options. We were all uncomfortable with the idea of signing Liz's death warrant.

"What happens if you don't?" Catherine asked.

"If the Family finds out after the fact, and they believe we knew, we're probably dead for not saying anything."

I expected this answer but Catherine clearly didn't. "You're kidding."

Evie and I shook our heads no.

"Well, dang, what do we do?" Catherine asked.

"If I may give an opinion?"

We turned as one to face the woman who had entered the room.

"Robin?" Catherine asked in distaste.

"Hello, ladies," Robin Landon addressed us. "I couldn't help but overhear—"

"Because you were eavesdropping," Evie interrupted.

"—your quandary," Robin continued as though uninterrupted.

We stared at her for a beat.

"And you have an opinion?" I asked.

"I do. I wanted to let you know not to worry so much about this," she said easily.

"Really? What does the councilwoman have to do with this?"

"Tsk, tsk, Mia," Robin scolded. "You know I won't answer that question. The councilwoman simply wanted you to know that she would take care of it."

"Take care of it," Catherine gulped. "Is she going to kill Liz?"

Robin laughed. "Not at the present time." We stared at her when she didn't continue. She sighed. "You're still on the right path. Liz is playing her part."

And with that, the demon's minion exited the room. We stood in silence for a moment.

"Okay, what do you guys think?" Catherine finally asked.

"Not to give Robin or Barbara too much credit, but my vote is we don't say anything. The Councilwoman told me before that I was on the right track. And now Robin says not to worry about it. Regardless of their involvement, I won't be able to sleep knowing I had a hand in someone's death," I finished and the other two nodded.

"Besides," I added with a hopeful smile, "maybe Liz is right. Maybe they won't kill her if she goes public, since she is a celebrity of sorts, and not just a random fruit loop on the internet."

"That is optimistic," Evie said, sounding doubtful.

"Yeah, I know, but what else have we got?"

"Maybe Barbara really will keep her safe?" Catherine asked.

"If that's actually what Robin meant," I countered.

"Maybe we can talk Liz out of it," Catherine offered.

"Unlikely, but there's no harm in trying," I agreed.

CHAPTER TWENTY-ONE

Back home, I was debating whether or not to slip into the lake or the pool when my house and mind filled with all-too-familiar popping sounds. I froze in my living room, head swinging side to side to see where Jena would materialize.

Next to my glass topped wicker breakfast table, I saw the shimmer in the air that preceded Jena's arrival before. I braced myself, wondering inanely whether or not she was coming in peace. Like she was an alien or something.

Jena appeared before me, her black eyes flashing like obsidian glowing from within. She glared; I remained silent. Waiting.

"How did you find me?"

No small talk for the genie I gathered. "You were captured on a vacationer's video; from there we found you on security footage at a casino."

"Who are you?"

"My name is Mia. I'm a movie producer. You killed," I swallowed audibly, "one of my actors. Chad Johnson." No reaction. "I'm also a nixie."

"Why did you want to find me?"

Her monotone voice unsettled me. "I wanted to help you."

"Help me how?"

"You can stop doing this."

"Why would I stop?"

Unsure what to say, I shifted. "How did you start?"

She stared as if trying to determine whether or not to tell me. If she wanted to kill me, she probably could before I could react.

"A year ago, my sister Juni Jawahir was killed by the human, Roger Miller."

"It was an accident."

She glared at me for the interruption. "I waited for the human system to bring him to justice, but they let him go." Her body hummed with hatred.

"I knew I had to have patience. I waited for a sufficient amount of time to pass. Even though I wanted revenge, I did not want to unduly bring attention to our kind," she anticipated my question.

"After a year, I decided enough time had passed and I exacted my revenge." She stopped like that was the end of the story.

"What about Chad? And Bradley Reese?"

"People like Roger care only for themselves. They care only about what other people can do for them. The fewer of them that exist in the world, the better the world will be."

"That's why you targeted actors? Because you think they care only for themselves?"

"Yes."

I was silent and she continued. "Once I killed Roger, I searched online for an actor promoting an upcoming Facebook Live streaming video. After I found Chad, I searched for him in person, followed him off and on. I decided he was the one. I waited for my moment."

Nausea bubbled up and Jena must have seen something in my face.

"Roger, Chad, Bradley. They're all the same. They wanted internet fame. I gave it to them."

Her complete lack of remorse unnerved me, but I pressed forward. "Not all actors are like that. Chad was a young man doing what he loved. Wanting to share that with the world."

A flicker of uncertainty crossed her face. "No."

"Yes, Jena. Even Roger's involvement with Juni's death was a horrible, horrible accident. He was devastated by her loss. He loved her. Surely you saw his social media posts when you were—" I paused to find another word for *stalking* "—gathering information."

Jena didn't respond.

"Jena, you can stop. Your existence can go back to normal."

"I don't want to."

Stunned by her admission, I struggled to find anything else to say. My secret goal, once I knew that the killer was a supernatural being, was to find out why and possibly help him or her without resorting to killing the being. And once I knew she was a djinn, I immediately recognized either she stopped or she was killed. I still didn't see another possible outcome. She was too powerful. I had to convince her to stop killing men.

"Why?"

"Because it's fun. These men don't deserve the life they've been given. I'm solving that."

"I can't let you keep—"

Jena laughed, an unearthly sound. "Let? As if you could do anything to stop me."

"I'm going to try."

"Don't make me kill you too." She dematerialized.

I collapsed on the couch, my heart racing. I failed. Other men were going to die unless I found a way to kill her. Dawn was a few hours away. I curled up on the couch for some relaxation before making another move.

The next morning, my heart in my throat, I called Jacob. It went to voicemail and I wondered if he was there and choosing not to answer.

"Hey, Jacob," I started, after the beep. "If you have some time, I'd really like to talk to you. It's important. It'll answer a bunch of your questions."

I ended the call. I didn't say I'd answer *all* of his questions, but maybe it was time to tell him at least a little bit more. If Jena wasn't going to stop, then anybody chasing after her was in danger.

My phone trilled notification of an incoming call. Jacob.

"Hey, Jacob."

"Hi, Mia."

Silence.

"You left me a voicemail."

"I did. Um." I paused.

"Mia, I don't have time for this."

The coldness in his voice hurt. "Can we meet?"

"I'd rather you tell me over the phone."

My eyes filled with tears. "I'd rather tell you in person."

"Fine. Text me where and when and I'll be there." He ended the call.

I held the silent phone in my hand, in shock. He hung up on me. I decided my place gave us the privacy I wanted given the subject matter. Hands shaking, I texted him my address to meet in one hour. I didn't know where he was in the city right now and I didn't want to be difficult.

Wait a minute. He was the one freezing me out. He wanted to keep it professional, I could keep it professional. A wave of sadness crashed over me at the thought of not touching him again or seeing his smile.

Whatever. He made his choice.

CHAPTER TWENTY-TWO

Exactly an hour later, my doorbell chimed. I opened the door and our eyes met. His were hard marbles in a granite face. He followed me to my breakfast nook.

"Please sit," I said and gestured to the wicker chair opposite me.

We sat simultaneously. He removed a small notebook and pen from his sports jacket inner pocket. "What do you have for me?"

"Jena appeared in my home," I started without preamble and that got his attention. I saw the worry in his eyes for a moment before the shutter dropped again.

"Appeared?"

"Yes." I explained to Jacob exactly what a djinn was and Jena's connection to Juni, as well as her admitting to me that she was the killer. "I am not working with her," I added.

"I know. Ms. Addison confirmed that when I spoke with her this morning."

My breath whooshed out in relief. "Okay, good."

"Is that it?"

"No. You may be in danger." I explained Jena's threat to harm anyone who got in her way.

"Can she be stopped?"

That was the million-dollar question, right? "Probably not," I admitted. "Not without killing her."

"How do we kill her?"

"Just how Juni died; her heart has to be pierced."

"How do we get to her?"

I chuckled. "You don't."

"That's not helpful."

My voice rose. "Well, forgive me for not wanting to be so quick to kill her."

"She's a murderer. And you just said the only way to stop her is to kill her, Mia!" His voice had risen to match mine.

"She's hurt because Roger killed her sister," I tried to remind him. "She's acting out of a weird warped grief."

"Are you seriously making excuses for the monster serial killer?"

I recoiled as if slapped. "Monster?"

Guilt clouded his face. "That isn't what I meant."

"Sure, it is."

"Mia—"

"You see me as a monster," I whispered.

"I don't know what to see you as," he argued. "You won't tell me who you are!" He stood and strode from the table toward the kitchen. He gripped the countertop with both hands. I stood and took a few steps toward him but stopped.

"Why does it matter so much what category I am?"

He faced me, anguish warring with anger on his face. "Because I don't understand. Any of this." He raked his hand through his hair. "What if you become like her?"

"Now I'm not just a monster, but you think I could be a killer?!"

"You tried to justify her actions and you don't want her to be harmed!"

We were yelling at each other when we both heard a popping noise. I scanned the room and, over the kitchen passthrough, I saw the shimmer in the living room. Jacob drew his gun as Jena completed her materializing.

"Jacob, no!" I shouted, but I was too late.

The shot rang out. Jena jerked backward against the couch. The anger in her eyes scared me. The popping increased exponentially in volume. Jacob covered one ear while training his gun on her figure by the couch. A second shot rang out. She reappeared between me and Jacob.

"I won't let you hurt her," Jena told Jacob. She stepped toward him, arms outstretched.

"Jena, no! He's not trying to hurt me!"

Jacob raised his gun again. Jena had reached him, grabbed him around the throat. His face mottled as he failed to draw in air.

"Jena, no!" I screamed again. I took several steps toward her. She whipped her face around to glare daggers at me.

"It's better this way. He'll only hurt you in the end."

She turned back to face Jacob, whose eyes now showed only the whites. He stopped struggling.

Unthinking, I grabbed a large knife from the wooden block on the counter. Jena's head turned toward me when the tip of the knife entered flesh.

The hurt I saw in her eyes wounded me. She tried to dematerialize but it was too late. Her eyes widened a final time before she turned to water and drenched me and Jacob, who had slumped to the floor.

I killed her.

To save him.

The conflicting statements spun around in my mind.

I wanted to go to him, but instead I sat at the table, lay my head on the top. Tears fell while I waited for him to regain consciousness. As he did, he leapt to his feet, surprised by his unsteadiness, gun in his outstretched arm. He spun, looking for Jena. Did not react when all he saw was me.

"Where is she? Where is Jena?"

I lifted my head, the tears still falling. "She's gone, Jacob."

"Gone? Where did she go?"

"Dead," I whispered.

That got his attention. He lowered his gun, really saw me. "Dead?"

My watery eyes met his. "I killed her."

"To save me."

I jolted at the words in my mind spoken aloud. "Yes."

He sat across from me again. "You did the right thing."

"Did I?"

"Yes, she was going to kill more people. You said so yourself."

"She was only trying to protect me."

"What?"

"Just now. She thought you were going to hurt me. She was confused. She was only trying to protect me." The tears fell faster and hotter now. I had never killed anyone before, let alone a fellow paranormal being. It felt horrible.

Jacob appeared shocked. "I would never hurt you."

I gave him a crooked smile. "I know that. She didn't. She thought she was protecting me," I repeated.

Jacob reached for me and I jerked backwards, up and out of the seat.

The pain consumed me and I needed to be away from this. From him. From where I killed her. I shook my head to knock the thoughts loose, but it didn't work.

"I have to go," I told Jacob. A strange white noise filled my mind. A low hum that was probably Jacob's voice tried to filter through but was unable.

"I have to go," I repeated, as I opened the sliding glass door. Even though it was the middle of a bright, sunny day, I needed my refuge. I needed my water. I needed to recharge.

I walked, fully clothed, down the stairs of my pool and settled at the bottom. That white noise continued with the low hum beneath. I ignored both and focused on the feeling of the water. A dark shadow appeared on the concrete of the other side of the pool.

I saw Jacob pacing, yelling at me in the water. I ignored him. He jumped into the water, grabbed me, and pulled me to the surface. He was spluttering as we broke through the water. I was weightless in his arms, not fighting or helping him. He brushed my hair off of my face.

"Mia, what are you doing?! This isn't the answer."

I stared into his face and then laughed morosely. "You think I'm trying to kill myself?"

He looked confused. "Aren't you?"

"No."

"Then why weren't you resurfacing?"

I was acutely aware of his arms around me now and the heat suffused my body. "I don't need to resurface," I explained without thinking. I cuddled in closer. He tensed but held me. Then the guilt returned. I killed someone. I struggled against him and he released me.

We stood before each other in my pool. His eyes a torrent of confusion, desire, and fear.

"You should go," I told him before sinking back to the bottom of the pool. He remained standing there for several long minutes, watching me, waiting to see what happened. I closed my eyes to leave him to it. I guessed he must have seen whatever it was he needed, because underwater waves jostled me as he exited the pool.

CHAPTER TWENTY-THREE

The next morning probably dawned sunny and warm, but I didn't know, because I never left my bed. Shades drawn kept my bedroom in relative darkness, tiny slivers of light peeking around the edges of the wood blinds.

My phone remained on silent. I imagined people were trying to reach me, but I didn't care. My thoughts were a maelstrom. This was what it had come to.

I killed someone. A paranormal being driven mad by grief, true. But still. With more time, maybe I could have helped her. I killed her to protect a man who thought I was a freak. At least nobody else would die. This was cold comfort as I curled into a ball under my comforter.

Other than a banana and bathroom breaks, I stayed in bed watching the sun through the blinds march across the sky and become dusk. I started to feel weirdly self-indulgent spending the day in bed. I sat up and stretched, grabbed my phone off the nightstand. Dang, my phone blew up while I was sleeping. Notifications of texts, phone calls, and voicemails filled the screen. Catherine and Evie, of course. Jacob. That one surprised me. He made his feelings pretty clear before he left yesterday. Well, before I fled and hid from him under the water, I supposed was the more accurate description. I sighed and began checking each of the texts and calls.

My doorbell chimed as I reached the final of the increasingly frantic messages from my friends. I had a feeling I knew who was there, once I confirmed with a glance at the blinds that night had fallen. I also had a feeling I knew who wasn't at the door. Jacob called twice but didn't leave a message either time. I left the warm comfort of the bed and threw on a satin robe before heading downstairs.

The doorbell chimed a second time. I opened the door. "You ladies are impatient."

Catherine and Evie threw themselves at me in a group hug.

"We were so worried!"

"I gave you until Evie woke up, but when you didn't respond, we decided an intervention was in order."

"You can't ignore us," Evie added. "We're your friends."

Catherine held up a bottle of wine. "We brought liquid libations."

Evie held up a gallon of chocolate chip cookie dough ice cream. "And comfort food."

I smiled at their enthusiasm. "Not that you can have either."

Evie pointed to her bag. "Not to worry. I brought a bottle of my sustenance too."

The three of us laughed as the women entered my home behind me. We paused in the kitchen to pour the drinks and scoop the ice cream. Then we collapsed on the couch.

Concerned eyes stared at me. I broke eye contact and stared instead at my fidgeting fingers.

"What happened, Mia? Jacob called me several times, asking about you. He said Jena was gone."

My eyes filled with tears. I looked at Catherine. "He called you?"

"He did. He wouldn't tell me anything else."

"What happened?" Evie echoed Catherine.

I inhaled a deep breath and told the whole ugly story of my fight with Jacob, Jena's misguided intervention, and my killing her. Both women gasped when I got to that part and my tears flowed freely.

"Oh, Mia. I'm so sorry you had to go through that," Catherine said softly. She leaned in to give me a tight hug. I took strength from her embrace, smelled the subtle scent of lavender.

"Thank you."

"You know there was nothing else you could have done, right?" Evie asked this pointedly. I shook my head. "Seriously, Mia, misguided or not, Jena was a serial killer. She was unstable. You saved lives by taking hers."

"That sounds all well and good," I responded more sharply than I intended. "But the bottom line is that I killed her when she was trying to help me." I gasped for air when the tears came harder.

Evie rose. She paced back and forth in front of us. "Bullshit," she finally said and my mouth fell open.

"What—"

"Don't give me that bullshit. I know what it's like to take a life, remember." I saw the haunted look in her eyes, a reflection of her own experience only a few months ago.

"Sometimes it's necessary. Killing Jena was inevitable. I can't believe you thought you'd be able to talk her down." She shook her head.

Her words both hurt and comforted me. "I'll never know," I argued and she cut me off with a flick of her wrist.

"Yes. You do. You're hurting because you know this was always going to be the outcome and you were deluding yourself thinking otherwise. You agree, right, Catherine?"

We both looked at Catherine, who held her hands up in the universal sign of *don't drag me into the middle of this.*

"You both have legitimate points." We waited for her to continue but she didn't. "That's all." She smiled serenely.

And for some reason, that turned the tide for me. I laughed, a deep belly laugh that might have cracked a rib if I kept going too long. It felt good, though, that laugh.

Catherine and Evie looked at me askance for a moment, looked at each other with a smile, and then all three of us were on the couch, laughing and hugging each other. I accepted this release and comfort.

I wiped tears from my eyes, of laughter not pain this time. "Wiser words were never spoken, Catherine." I held each of their hands.

"Thank you both for coming here. You are absolutely right. I probably was delusional to think I could talk an irrational immortal being out of destruction. At least it's over now and nobody else will be hurt. I can't lay around feeling sorry for myself. What would that accomplish?"

"Exactly," Evie concurred.

"Thanks, Evie, for being so blunt. And thanks, Catherine, for being so ... accommodating." I smiled and then my mouth turned down.

"What?" Catherine squeezed my hand.

"Jacob?" Evie asked. I nodded.

"Yeah. I thought whatever spark," I chuckled at the memories of the actual sparks flying, "we had might have led to something. He thinks I'm a monster." My voice fell to a whisper on the last word.

"Maybe," Catherine said. "But, he called you—"

"Didn't leave messages," I interrupted.

"He called me. He asked how you were doing. I wouldn't be so quick to dismiss him. Remember when I found out about Alex?" Her hunky boyfriend, Alexander Moore, was a half-incubus. "I needed time to process." She shrugged. "My guess is that Jacob felt blindsided, like I did, and needed time."

"And Ryan?" Evie asked. Her human boyfriend hadn't exactly jumped with excitement when he learned she was a vampire.

Hope glowed within me. "Do you really think?"

Catherine and Evie nodded.

I steeled myself and released their hands. "I'm going to put everything out there." I felt their eyes on me. I texted Jacob one last time. It was longer than I usually text, and probably I should have just called, but this was easier, and I still felt raw from his rejection. I hit send after typing the final line and smiled at my friends.

The ball is in your court now, as they say.

CHAPTER TWENTY-FOUR

I was impressed with myself that I did not continually check my phone for missed texts and calls from Jacob all night. I knew my phone was working. The lack of a text or a call by the next morning told me everything I needed to know. Maybe he called yesterday because he was simply a good guy. He wanted to make sure I was okay, but like a police officer checked in on a crime victim. Just doing his job. Not interested in more.

I swallowed past the lump in my throat and headed downstairs to make coffee. It was almost time for *Entertainment Daily*. I was curious if Jacob updated Liz like he said he would once the murders were solved.

"Good morning in the Valley! Welcome to *Entertainment Daily*. I'm your host, Elizabeth Addison." The smile dropped from her airbrushed-to-perfection face. Faux concern replaced it.

Stop it, I chided myself for my uncharitable thoughts. She was not a bad person, just career-driven.

"Many of you have been following the Firecracker Killer case for the past couple of weeks. I promised that I would inform all of you at the conclusion of the case. Well, that time has come. Citizens of the Valley, as well as Los Angeles, can breathe a sigh of relief that the Firecracker Killer is no more. But, let me warn you, this next part may sound outrageous, like a pathetic attempt to boost ratings. Most of you will want to dismiss what I say as pure nonsense. I understand. I felt the same way when I first heard about it." She paused dramatically and my heart was in my throat because I knew what she was about to say.

"How many of you have watched television and movies about vampires and genies? How many of you have laughed instead of been afraid because you knew it was fake?"

I put my hands over my mouth. She wasn't going to out us. She couldn't out us. Then I reminded myself that she said this was her goal. I closed my eyes for a moment, breathed deeply.

"I am here to tell you that it's real. I know, I know. It can't possibly be true. Let me tell you a story. You may remember when I exclusively reported I was in possession of a photo of the Firecracker Killer. Many of you tuned in to my Facebook Live where the killer failed to show; not very many of you tuned in for the second attempt. You missed a doozy if that's the case." An image of Jena appeared in the corner of the screen. Liz gestured to it. "This individual, Jena Jawahir, appeared. And I mean appeared. She shimmered into being in front of me, those popping sounds we all recognize now, preceding her. I tried to talk to her; I learned her name. And then she vanished just like that." Liz snapped her fingers; I couldn't believe she was telling the world, but at least it seemed she wasn't going to mention me. Yet, anyway.

"She later appeared in a private home, where she admitted, in the presence of law enforcement, that she was the Firecracker Killer. She attacked said law enforcement representative and then a brave citizen, at great risk to herself, killed the killer in self-defense." Liz paused again. She clearly relished the telling of this story.

"You may be wondering about this creature who could appear and disappear at will. I have come to learn that she is what's known as a djinn, genie to most of us. But she doesn't grant wishes." Liz provided a brief definition and explanation about genies. It seemed mostly taken from Wikipedia but was fairly accurate.

"So, who was Jena Jawahir?" There followed a timeline of Juni's death in Roger's car accident, the justice system releasing him, and then Jena's three murders.

"This genie would not have stopped – she said as much – had she not been killed." This conclusion seemed directed at me. Did Jacob tell her that I'd been feeling guilty?

"Now the big question. Was she alone? I'm here to inform you that she was not. She was alone in the killing, yes, but there is an entire paranormal underworld existing in Las Vegas. In addition to the genie, we have vampires and beings who can bewitch you with their voices. And that's just scratching the surface." Thank goodness for small favors, I guess, that she had not identified my species yet. I refocused as she continued.

"You know I don't usually track rumors." I arched an eyebrow. Really? "But, I've also heard that there's a whole agency providing representation for actors of the other-than-human persuasion." How did she find out about Catherine?!

"It seems as though we have become ground zero for the paranormal. If you've had any unexplainable things happen to you, I want to know about them. The paranormal exist – we need to know how far their reach goes!" With that and a self-satisfied smirk, she signed off. I fumed that she would sensationalize our existence, imply that we were somehow a threat. Sure, we had more abilities than humans, but except for the vampire Cleaners, we mostly left humanity alone. Sheesh.

I clicked off the television. A text notification pinged. Hope bloomed. Jacob?

CHAPTER TWENTY-FIVE

My hope dashed when I saw the text was from Catherine.

How did she find out about PTA???

I thought for a moment of possible ways.

I don't know. Could Evie have told her after she admitted being a vampire?

Yeah, maybe. I don't think she would have unless she thought she was protecting us in some way.

That makes sense.

I'll check in with her tonight. Maybe ask her what the Family thinks.

Sounds good.

I supposed it really didn't matter how Liz found out. Once the paranormal cat was out of the bag, nothing was going to stop Liz from digging until she found the answers she wanted. I sighed, wondering if she'd reach out to me again or not. And what my reaction would be if she did. More importantly, I wondered if the Family would eliminate her. I suspected Liz was right, though; she was too visible to be taken out now without drawing undue suspicion.

A knock disturbed my thoughts. I was thankful for the interruption and headed to open the door.

"Jacob!"

"Hi, Mia." He searched my face, for what I was uncertain.

I gestured inward. "Did you want to come in?"

A smile lit up his face. "Yes."

I followed him, confused thoughts swirling in my mind. Why was he here? I appreciated the view of his backside as we walked to my couch. We sat, our knees inches apart. The air between us charged.

"What can I do for you, Jacob?"

"I saw Liz's show."

"Ah."

"I wanted to, um, check on you."

"You did?"

Hurt shined in his eyes at my question. "You don't think I'd be worried about you?"

I shrugged. "I honestly don't know. We didn't leave things very…positive."

His cheeks reddened. "I didn't know what to say before. I don't like being lied to."

"I don't think I lied to you. Lie of omission, maybe."

He reached for my hands, the familiar spark making us both smile. "That's not what I meant. I'm screwing this up." His hands tightened around mine. "I'm not blaming you for anything. I missed you."

"It's only been a day."

"I still missed you."

"Me too."

We sat in silence, lost in each other's eyes. Then he frowned. "But, this—" He released me and stood. He walked to my sliding glass doors, stared out at the water, or maybe the mountains in the distance.

"Is what we feel real? Liz said you can bewitch people with your voice." He turned and I saw the fear and desire.

"Yes," I responded simply. "That's true. I can entrance people."

"Entrance," he repeated with a nod.

I approached him. When he stiffened, I stopped, tears pooling in my eyes. "I didn't do that to you. I promise." Some of the tension bled away, but I still felt a wall between us.

"Let me tell you who I am and then you can decide if that's something you want—" I coughed "—can live with." He nodded. "Although I am humanoid, I'm not human. I am a nixie." I chuckled at his confusion. "Most people have never heard of us. A nix, or a naiad, is a water spirit." Understanding dawned in his eyes.

"When you stayed underwater without breathing?"

"Exactly. A nixie can live on the land, obviously, but needs to return to the water regularly to stay alive."

"You live in a desert," he contradicted with a smile.

"I do. Hide in plain sight, right? Besides, why do you think I live in The Lakes? And have a pool?"

"Makes sense." His eyes clouded again. "What about—?"

I blew out my breath, knowing this was the make or break moment for us. "Nixie are sometimes called sirens. Are you familiar with them? You could say we're cousins. They're the more destructive members of our family." He reflected my smile.

"Yes, I can entrance people with my voice. I'm quite the spellbinding singer, in fact. But," I frowned, "I don't like doing it and so only do it when I feel that it's truly necessary. I've never done it to someone I … cared … about."

"You care about me?" Desire pooled in his eyes.

I caressed his cheek, feeling the bristly stubble. He must not have shaved this morning. "I do."

His hand captured mine against his face and he brought my palm to his lips for a delicate kiss. "I care about you too."

Tingles shot through me at his words and his touch. I leaned forward in anticipation but he leaned back, releasing my hands. "What?"

He looked so earnest I almost laughed but my stomach rumbled with worry. "I need to apologize," he started.

"That's not—" I interrupted to tell him it wasn't necessary but stopped.

Jacob smiled crookedly. "Yeah, it's necessary," he responded to my unspoken sentiment. "You frustrated me." I opened my mouth to object. "Please, let me say this." I closed my mouth and nodded.

"You frustrated me," he repeated. "Because of my insane attraction to you." We both smiled. "And also, because I knew you were keeping something from me. I never thought you were a killer. But, I knew it was something. Being another species is a pretty big *something*."

He stared at me and I could feel the electricity in the air between us. I wanted more than anything in this moment for him to take me in his arms.

"Then I had to worry that what I felt wasn't real."

I couldn't help it, I interrupted. "I never entranced you. You just legitimately find me sexy."

Jacob laughed a deep belly laugh. "I know. I believe you. And, I definitely find you sexy."

"The feeling is mutual."

"I'm glad."

Unable to wait for him to make his move, I wrapped my arms around him and rested my head against his shoulder. I listened to his heart beat and his breathing. "Oh, and I'm about 200-years-old." His arms tightened around me for a moment and then relaxed. He chuckled, low and sexy.

"Man, you are really robbing the cradle, aren't you?"

The last of my tension dissipated and I pulled back to gaze into his eyes. "Yes, I am," I said with a smirk. "There's a lot about me that you still don't know."

"I look forward to learning every single thing," he assured me.

The heat and electricity between us increased. "Kiss me."

Jacob did. A sigh escaped me. His lips, sweetly at first and then with more insistence, pressed against mine. I didn't know where we were headed, in this moment or as a couple. Right now, this was all I cared about. Being together. After our long lingering kiss, Jacob pulled away and I saw the light in his eyes.

"By the way, what are you going to do about Liz's big reveal?"

"I don't know. We're all out of the closet now. I guess that's a wrap!"

Or is it?

Here's a sneak peek at Episode 4…

EPISODE FOUR PREVIEW

As the founder and owner of Landon Talent Agency, could I ever have predicted I'd make a deal with the devil? Okay, technically, Barbara Knollman was a low-level demon. But still. I'd agreed to do the demon's bidding and, if I wasn't entirely sorry for having made that deal, I definitely had regrets.

Now I sat in the overstuffed leather chair opposite the Councilwoman, my hands clasped in my lap, eyes downcast, like I'd been called to the principal's office. Though, in a way, that was true.

"Robin, this has worked out perfectly," Barbara intoned. She stood at the window overlooking Main Street, immobile, her brown hair swept back in a tight bun. She returned to her chair behind the imposing solid wood desk and sat, her hands resting on its surface, talon-like fingernails displayed.

The effect worked.

I swallowed audibly and Barbara chuckled.

"You really wanted the paranormal underworld to be exposed like this?" I asked.

Barbara smiled, her small sharp teeth drawing attention. "Yes. I did. I foresaw the path to my success. It included the exposure," she explained, tapping her manicured talons against the fine wood-grain.

"I'm not sure I understand what this has been about," I admitted in a small voice.

Barbara looked condescendingly down on me, her minion. "I know. You will. Everyone will."

Don't miss the exciting concluding trilogy of the Paranormal Talent Agency!

THANK YOU!

Thank you so much for supporting my work and reading this collection. I truly hope you enjoyed reading it as much as I did writing it.

If you liked the book, please consider leaving a review wherever you purchased.

Just a few lines would be great. Reviews are not only the highest compliment you can pay to an author, they also help other readers discover and make more informed choices about purchasing books in a crowded online space. Thank you so much in advance.

If you didn't like the book or have concerns, please email me directly at
heather@heathersilvio.com

ABOUT THE AUTHOR

Heather has written fiction and nonfiction; she is also an actress and licensed psychologist. When she isn't working, she channels her inner flapper as a 1920s jazz and blues singer.

Visit https://www.heathersilvio.com for more information and to sign up for her weekly newsletter.